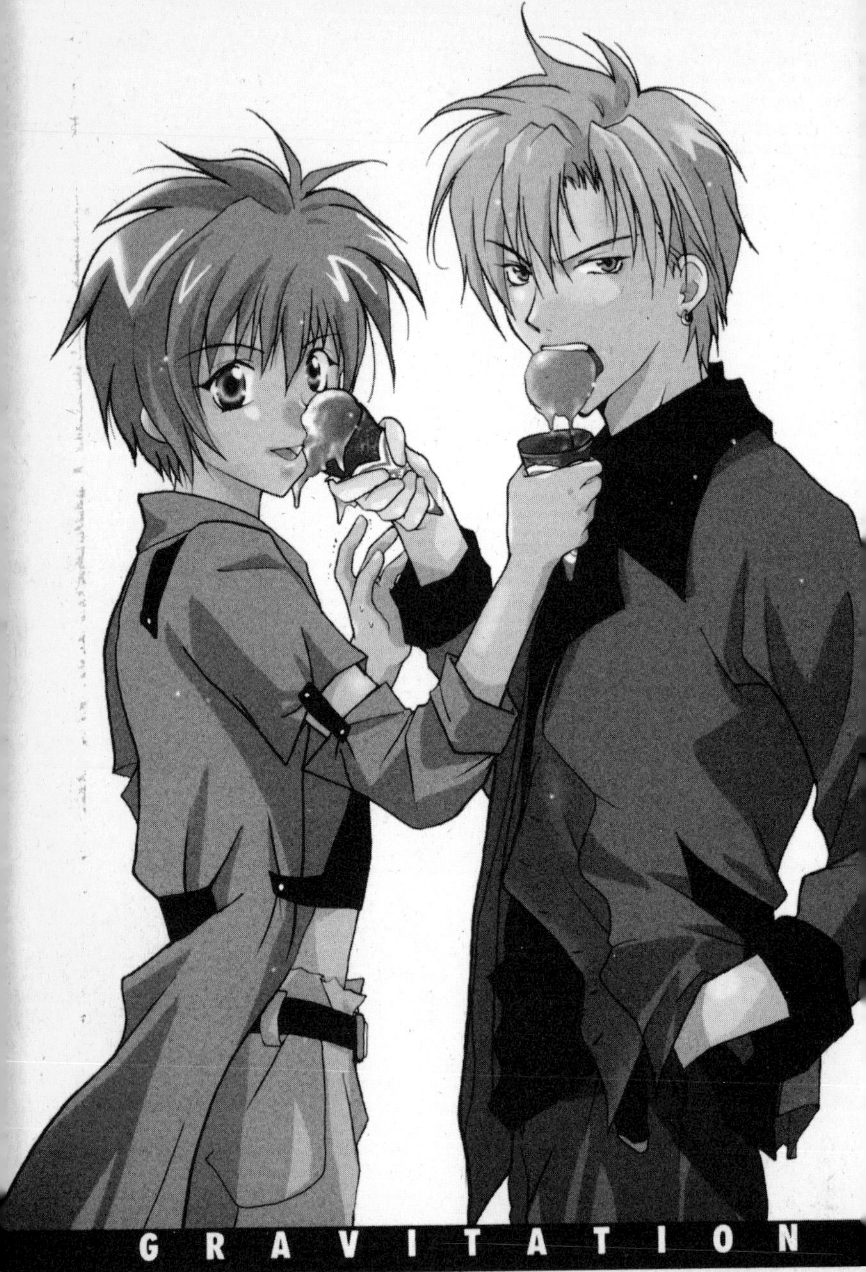

GRAVITATION

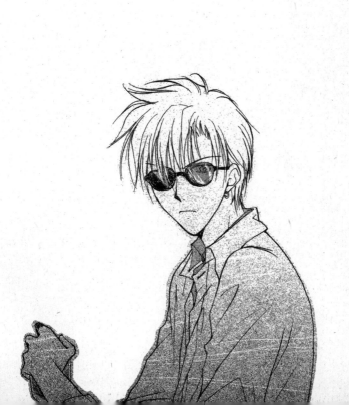

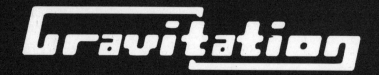

Volume 8

By
Maki Murakami

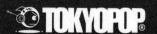

HAMBURG // LONDON // LOS ANGELES // TOKYO

Gravitation Vol. 8
Created by Maki Murakami

Translation - Ray Yoshimoto
English Adaptation - Jamie S. Rich
Copy Editor - Suzanne Waldman
Retouch and Lettering - Riho Sakai
Production Artists - Yoohae Yang
Cover Design - Raymond Makowski

Editor - Paul Morrissey
Digital Imaging Manager - Chris Buford
Pre-Press Manager - Antonio DePietro
Production Managers - Jennifer Miller and Mutsumi Miyazaki
Art Director - Matt Alford
Managing Editor - Jill Freshney
VP of Production - Ron Klamert
President and C.O.O. - John Parker
Publisher and C.E.O. - Stuart Levy

A 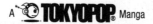 Manga

TOKYOPOP Inc.
5900 Wilshire Blvd. Suite 2000
Los Angeles, CA 90036

E-mail: info@TOKYOPOP.com
Come visit us online at www.TOKYOPOP.com

ISBN: 1-59182-340-4

First TOKYOPOP printing: October 2004
10 9 8 7 6 5
Printed in the USA

THE MEMBERS OF THE GRAVITATION BAND

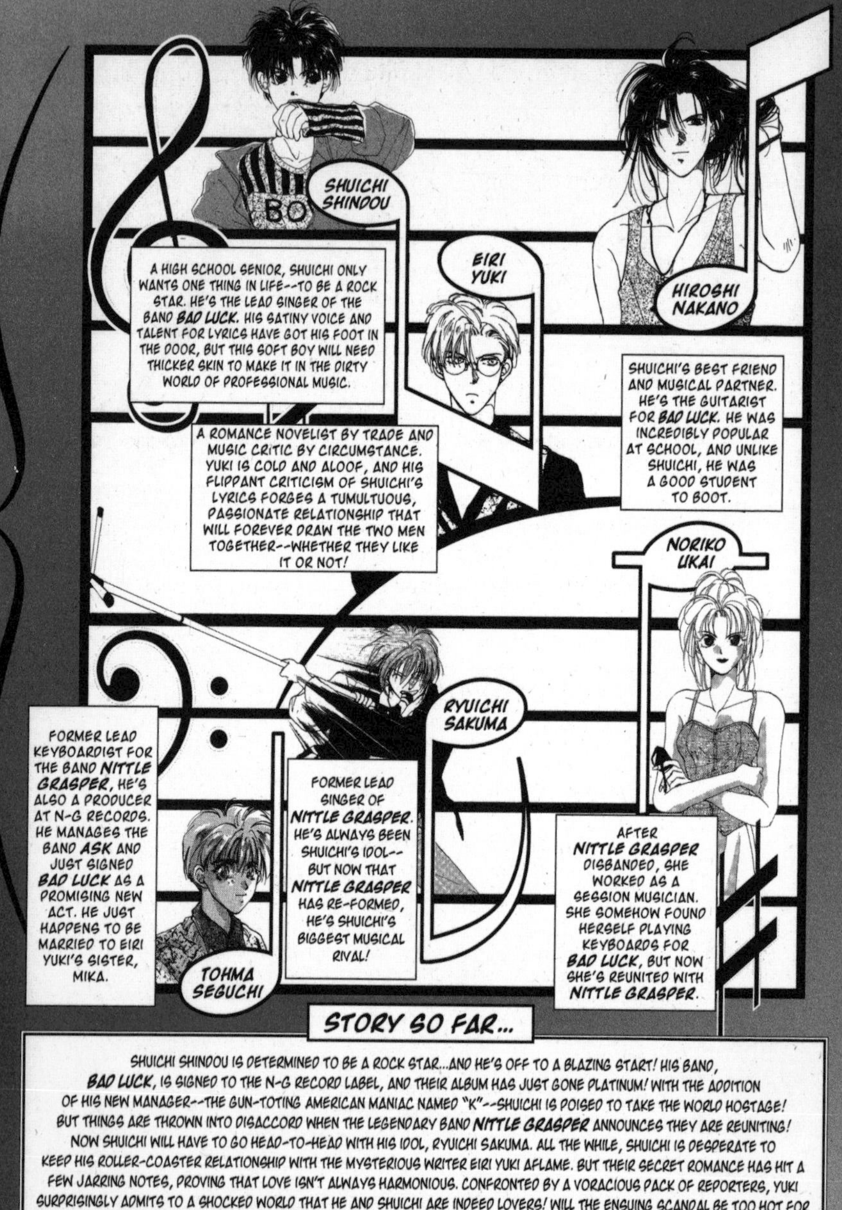
BO

SHUICHI SHINDOU

A HIGH SCHOOL SENIOR, SHUICHI ONLY WANTS ONE THING IN LIFE--TO BE A ROCK STAR. HE'S THE LEAD SINGER OF THE BAND ***BAD LUCK***. HIS SATINY VOICE AND TALENT FOR LYRICS HAVE GOT HIS FOOT IN THE DOOR, BUT THIS SOFT BOY WILL NEED THICKER SKIN TO MAKE IT IN THE DIRTY WORLD OF PROFESSIONAL MUSIC.

EIRI YUKI

A ROMANCE NOVELIST BY TRADE AND MUSIC CRITIC BY CIRCUMSTANCE. YUKI IS COLD AND ALOOF, AND HIS FLIPPANT CRITICISM OF SHUICHI'S LYRICS FORGES A TUMULTUOUS, PASSIONATE RELATIONSHIP THAT WILL FOREVER DRAW THE TWO MEN TOGETHER--WHETHER THEY LIKE IT OR NOT!

HIROSHI NAKANO

SHUICHI'S BEST FRIEND AND MUSICAL PARTNER. HE'S THE GUITARIST FOR ***BAD LUCK***. HE WAS INCREDIBLY POPULAR AT SCHOOL, AND UNLIKE SHUICHI, HE WAS A GOOD STUDENT TO BOOT.

NORIKO UKAI

AFTER ***NITTLE GRASPER*** DISBANDED, SHE WORKED AS A SESSION MUSICIAN. SHE SOMEHOW FOUND HERSELF PLAYING KEYBOARDS FOR ***BAD LUCK***, BUT NOW SHE'S REUNITED WITH ***NITTLE GRASPER***.

RYUICHI SAKUMA

FORMER LEAD SINGER OF ***NITTLE GRASPER***. HE'S ALWAYS BEEN SHUICHI'S IDOL--BUT NOW THAT ***NITTLE GRASPER*** HAS RE-FORMED, HE'S SHUICHI'S BIGGEST MUSICAL RIVAL!

TOHMA SEGUCHI

FORMER LEAD KEYBOARDIST FOR THE BAND ***NITTLE GRASPER***, HE'S ALSO A PRODUCER AT N-G RECORDS. HE MANAGES THE BAND ***ASK*** AND JUST SIGNED ***BAD LUCK*** AS A PROMISING NEW ACT. HE JUST HAPPENS TO BE MARRIED TO EIRI YUKI'S SISTER, MIKA.

STORY SO FAR...

SHUICHI SHINDOU IS DETERMINED TO BE A ROCK STAR...AND HE'S OFF TO A BLAZING START! HIS BAND, ***BAD LUCK***, IS SIGNED TO THE N-G RECORD LABEL, AND THEIR ALBUM HAS JUST GONE PLATINUM! WITH THE ADDITION OF HIS NEW MANAGER--THE GUN-TOTING AMERICAN MANIAC NAMED "K"--SHUICHI IS POISED TO TAKE THE WORLD HOSTAGE! BUT THINGS ARE THROWN INTO DISACCORD WHEN THE LEGENDARY BAND ***NITTLE GRASPER*** ANNOUNCES THEY ARE REUNITING! NOW SHUICHI WILL HAVE TO GO HEAD-TO-HEAD WITH HIS IDOL, RYUICHI SAKUMA. ALL THE WHILE, SHUICHI IS DESPERATE TO KEEP HIS ROLLER-COASTER RELATIONSHIP WITH THE MYSTERIOUS WRITER EIRI YUKI AFLAME. BUT THEIR SECRET ROMANCE HAS HIT A FEW JARRING NOTES, PROVING THAT LOVE ISN'T ALWAYS HARMONIOUS. CONFRONTED BY A VORACIOUS PACK OF REPORTERS, YUKI SURPRISINGLY ADMITS TO A SHOCKED WORLD THAT HE AND SHUICHI ARE INDEED LOVERS! WILL THE ENSUING SCANDAL BE TOO HOT FOR EVERYONE TO HANDLE? CAN SHUICHI PREVENT HIS CAREER FROM SPIRALING INTO A BLACK HOLE? ARE SHUICHI AND YUKI DESTINED TO DRIFT APART, OR WILL THEIR RELATIONSHIP BE STRENGTHENED AFTER THEIR LONG-AWAITED DATE TO DISNEYLAND? HOW LONG CAN THEY REMAIN INEXORABLY INTERTWINED, HELD TOGETHER BY A FORCE AS STRONG AS GRAVITY?

CONTENTS

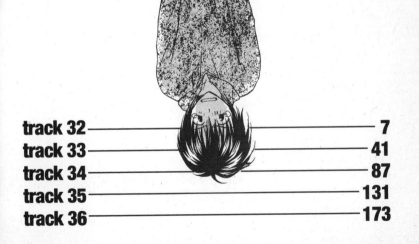

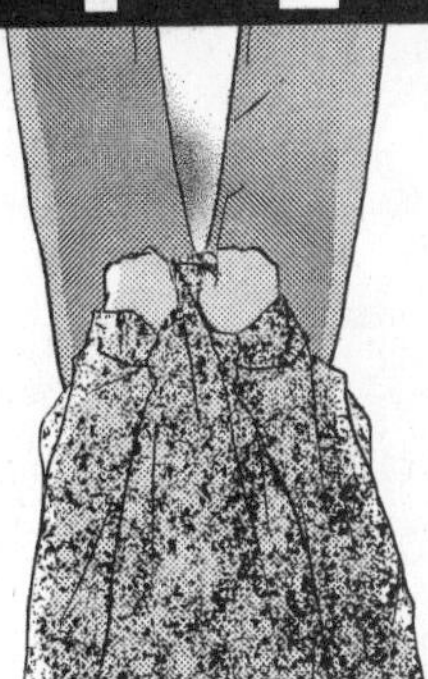

track 32 ———————————— 7
track 33 ———————————— 41
track 34 ———————————— 87
track 35 ———————————— 131
track 36 ———————————— 173

Gravitation

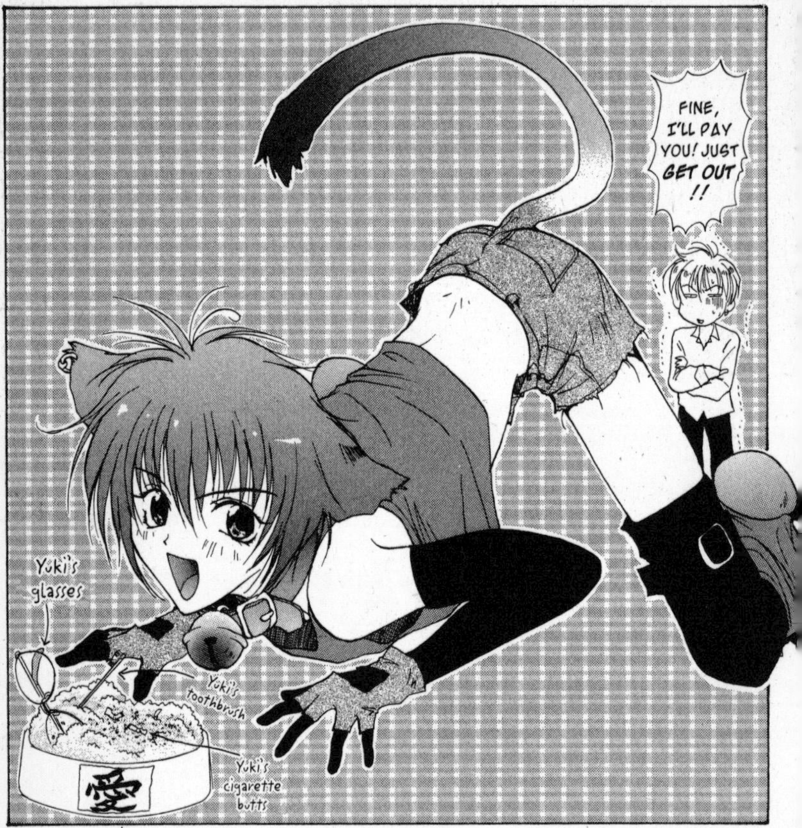
FINE, I'LL PAY YOU! JUST GET OUT !!
Yuki's glasses
Yuki's toothbrush
Yuki's cigarette butts
愛

Love

track32

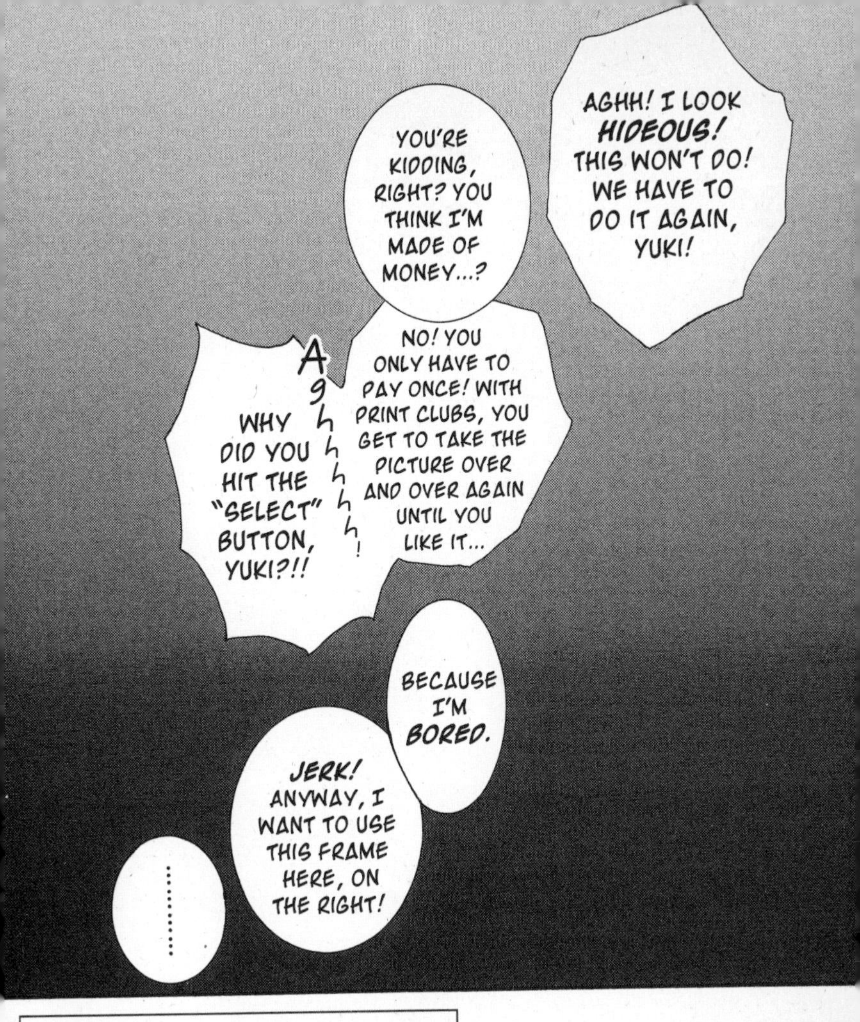
AGHH! I LOOK HIDEOUS! THIS WON'T DO! WE HAVE TO DO IT AGAIN, YUKI!
YOU'RE KIDDING, RIGHT? YOU THINK I'M MADE OF MONEY...?
NO! YOU ONLY HAVE TO PAY ONCE! WITH PRINT CLUBS, YOU GET TO TAKE THE PICTURE OVER AND OVER AGAIN UNTIL YOU LIKE IT...
Aghhhhh!
WHY DID YOU HIT THE "SELECT" BUTTON, YUKI?!!
BECAUSE I'M BORED.
JERK! ANYWAY, I WANT TO USE THIS FRAME HERE, ON THE RIGHT!
....

ABOUT GRAVITATION TRACK 32

Hello, everybody, it's been awhile!! It's me, scum of the earth Murakami!! I'm glad that we could meet here like this one more time! Somehow we've made it to *Gravitation* Volume 8! I'm doing my best--as always, my writing is sloppy, and the manga is really foolish, but Yuki always looks cool! How do you like it so far?! I'm always trying to come up with something better than the time before so that you'll like it even more!! I know there are plenty of parts that still aren't quite right, but maybe you can cut me some slack, okay? Pretty please?

But anyway, Tokyo is the picture of modern convenience, and here I am, the quintessential country bumpkin. But whattaya gonna do? See ya!

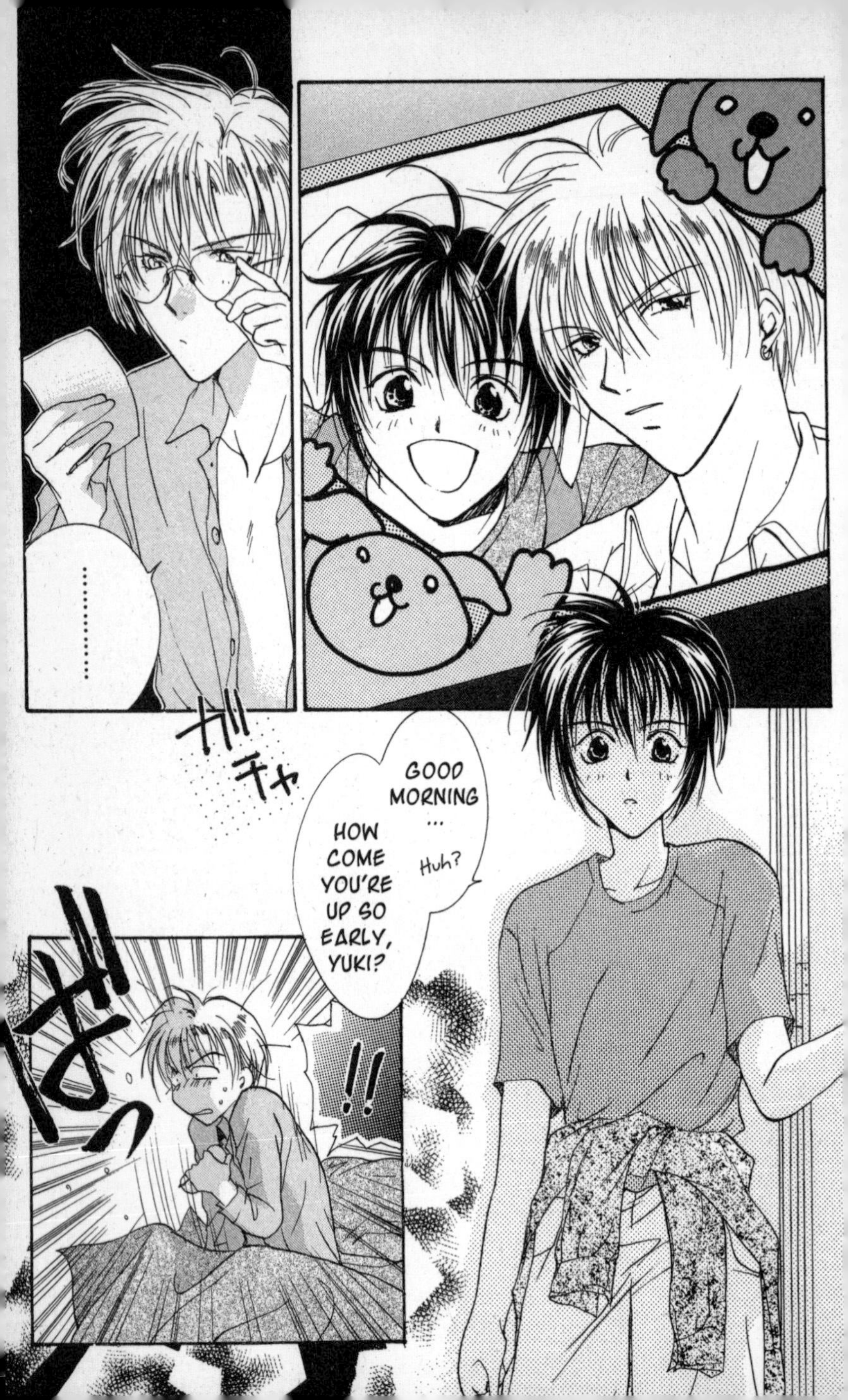
……
ガチャ
GOOD MORNING ...
Huh?
HOW COME YOU'RE UP SO EARLY, YUKI?
はっ
!!

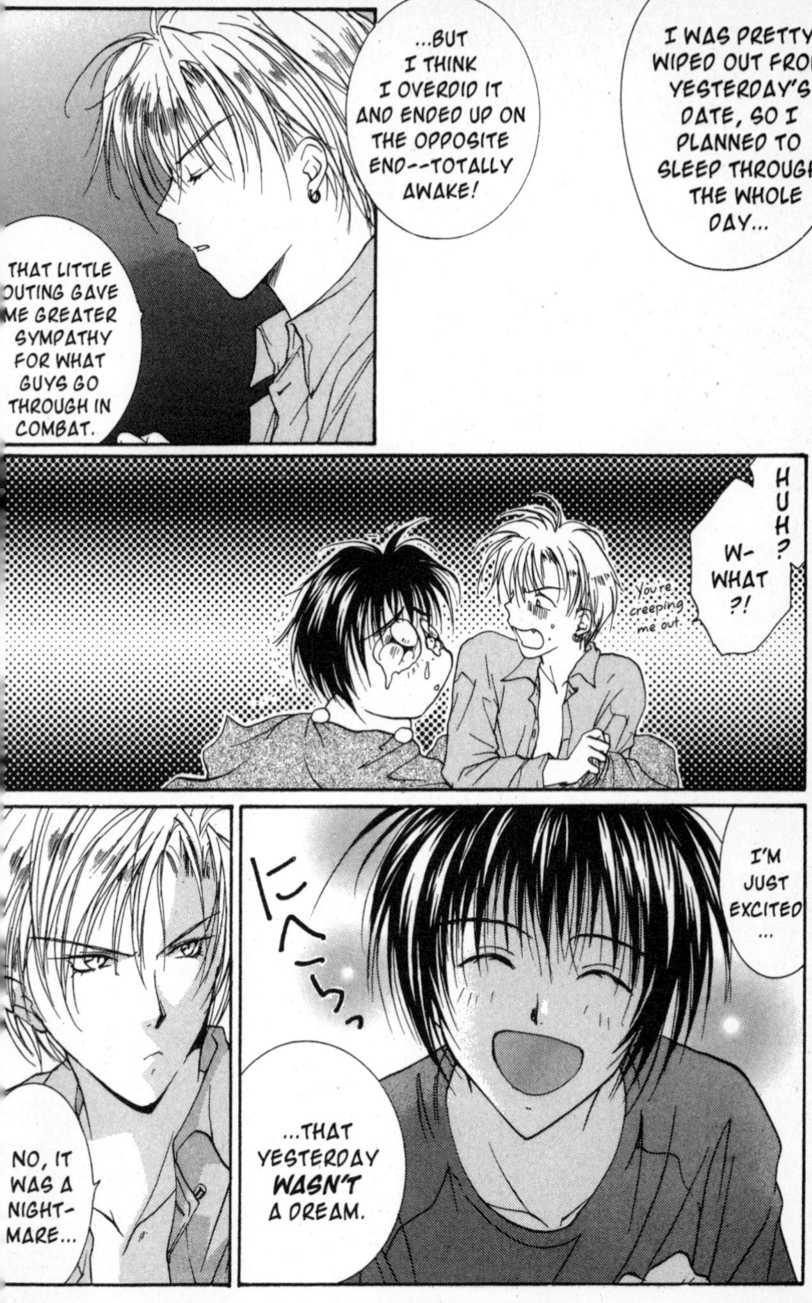
I WAS PRETTY WIPED OUT FROM YESTERDAY'S DATE, SO I PLANNED TO SLEEP THROUGH THE WHOLE DAY...
...BUT I THINK I OVERDID IT AND ENDED UP ON THE OPPOSITE END--TOTALLY AWAKE!
THAT LITTLE OUTING GAVE ME GREATER SYMPATHY FOR WHAT GUYS GO THROUGH IN COMBAT.
HUH?
W-WHAT?!
You're creeping me out.
I'M JUST EXCITED...
...THAT YESTERDAY **WASN'T** A DREAM.
NO, IT WAS A NIGHTMARE...

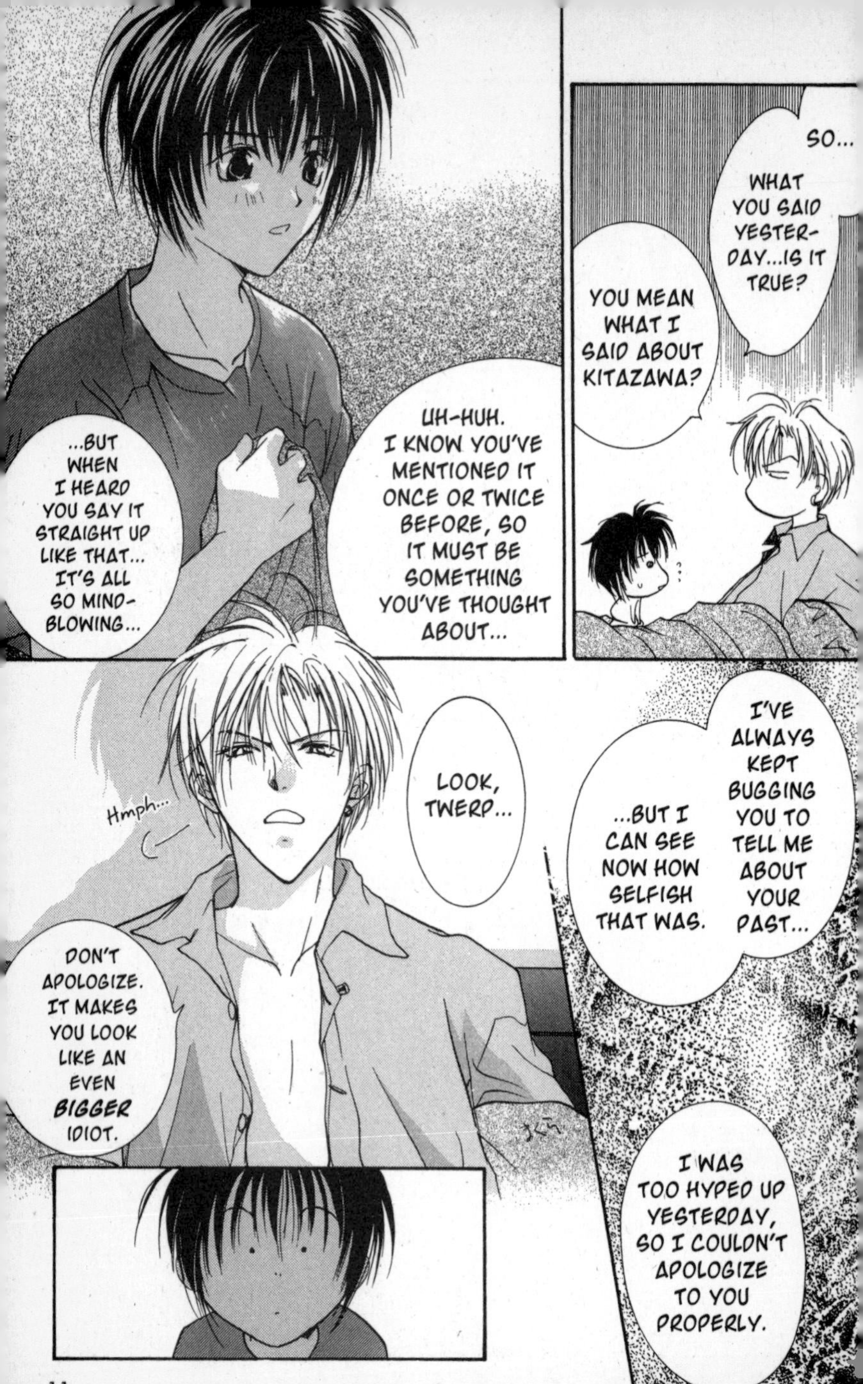
SO...
WHAT YOU SAID YESTER-DAY...IS IT TRUE?
YOU MEAN WHAT I SAID ABOUT KITAZAWA?
UH-HUH. I KNOW YOU'VE MENTIONED IT ONCE OR TWICE BEFORE, SO IT MUST BE SOMETHING YOU'VE THOUGHT ABOUT...
...BUT WHEN I HEARD YOU SAY IT STRAIGHT UP LIKE THAT... IT'S ALL SO MIND-BLOWING...
I'VE ALWAYS KEPT BUGGING YOU TO TELL ME ABOUT YOUR PAST...
...BUT I CAN SEE NOW HOW SELFISH THAT WAS.
I WAS TOO HYPED UP YESTERDAY, SO I COULDN'T APOLOGIZE TO YOU PROPERLY.
LOOK, TWERP...
Hmph...
DON'T APOLOGIZE. IT MAKES YOU LOOK LIKE AN EVEN BIGGER IDIOT.

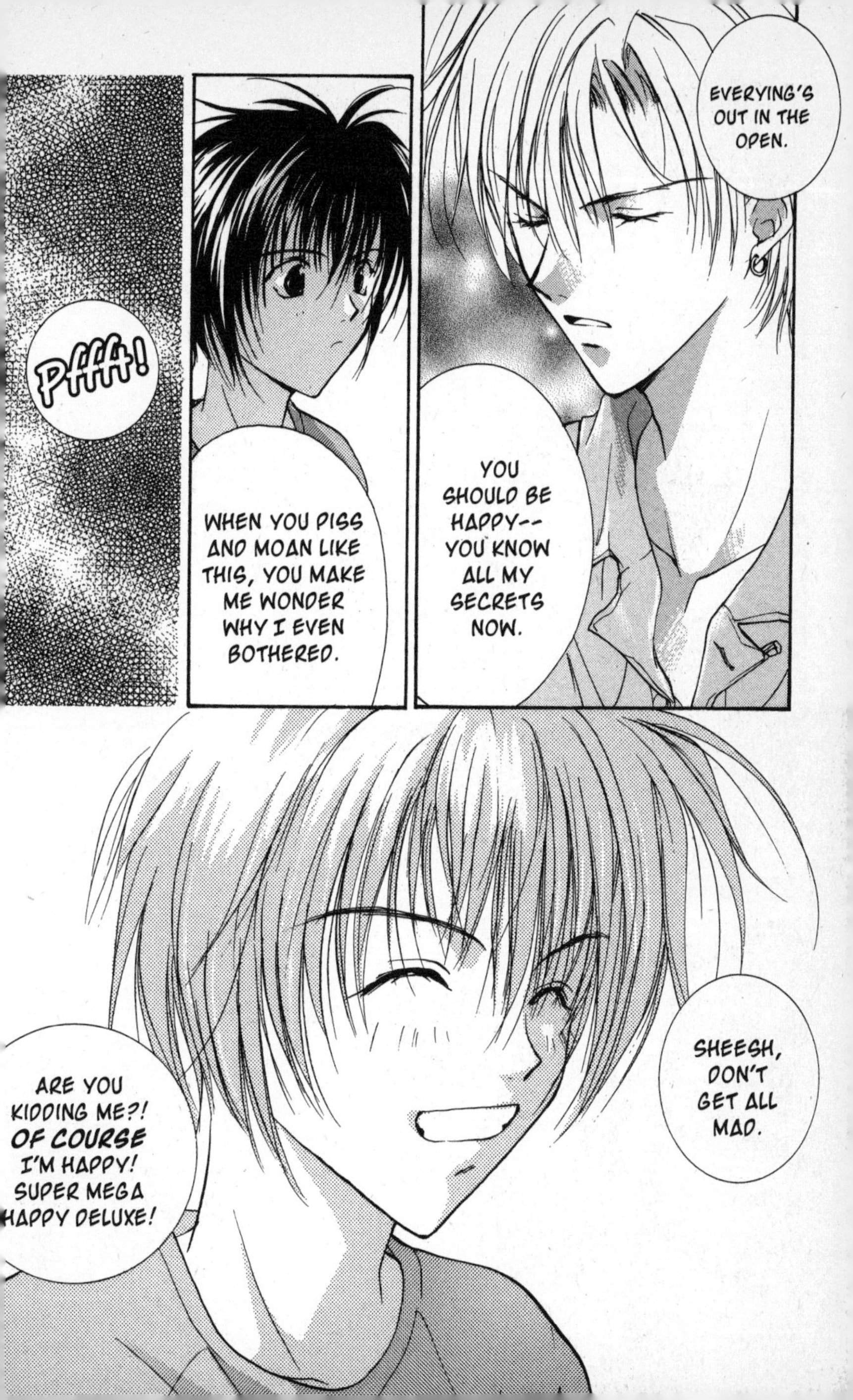
EVERYING'S OUT IN THE OPEN.
YOU SHOULD BE HAPPY--YOU KNOW ALL MY SECRETS NOW.
WHEN YOU PISS AND MOAN LIKE THIS, YOU MAKE ME WONDER WHY I EVEN BOTHERED.
Pffft!
SHEESH, DON'T GET ALL MAD.
ARE YOU KIDDING ME?! **OF COURSE** I'M HAPPY! SUPER MEGA HAPPY DELUXE!

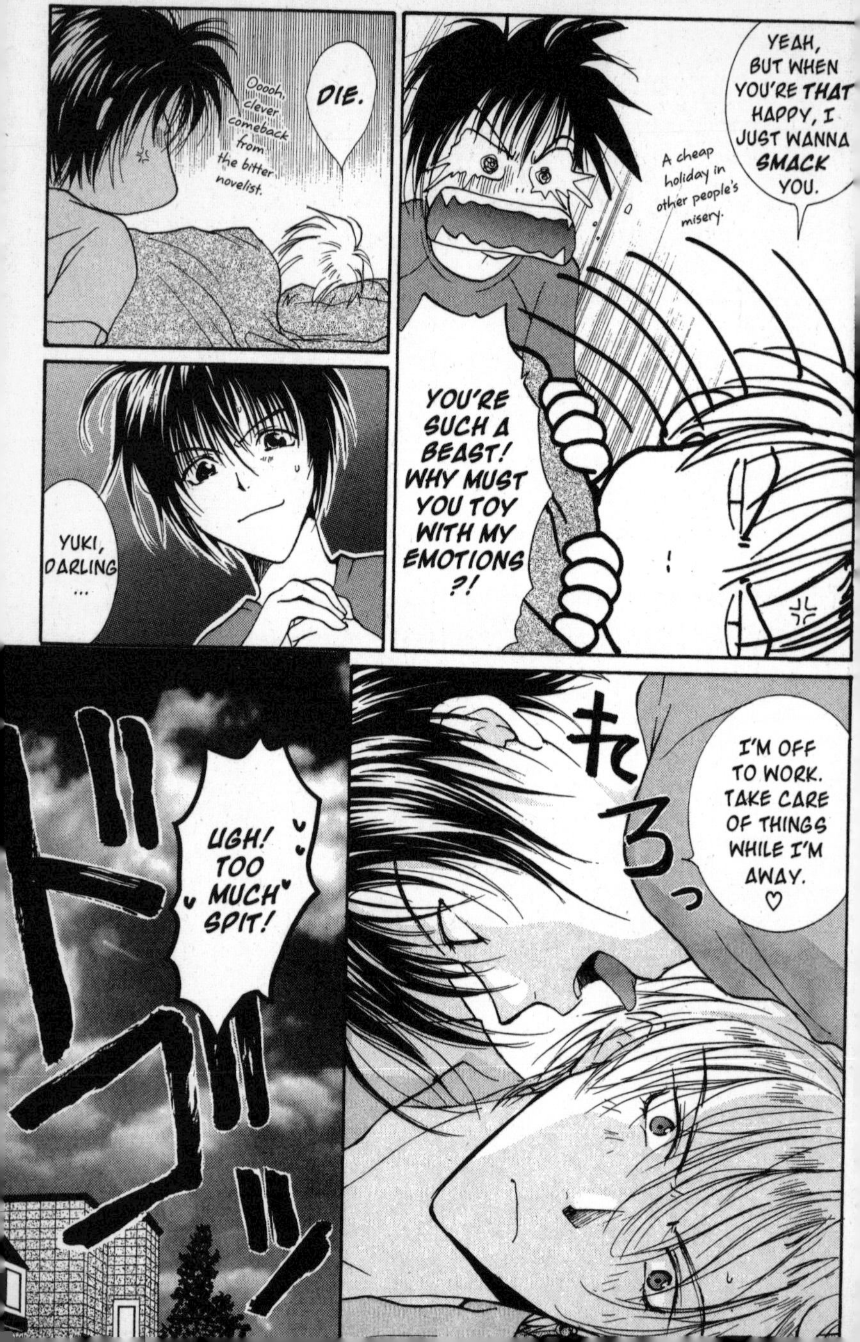
YEAH, BUT WHEN YOU'RE THAT HAPPY, I JUST WANNA SMACK YOU.
A cheap holiday in other people's misery.
YOU'RE SUCH A BEAST! WHY MUST YOU TOY WITH MY EMOTIONS?!
DIE.
Ooooh, clever comeback from the bitter novelist.
YUKI, DARLING ...
れろっ
I'M OFF TO WORK. TAKE CARE OF THINGS WHILE I'M AWAY. ♡
ドゴッ
UGH! TOO MUCH SPIT!

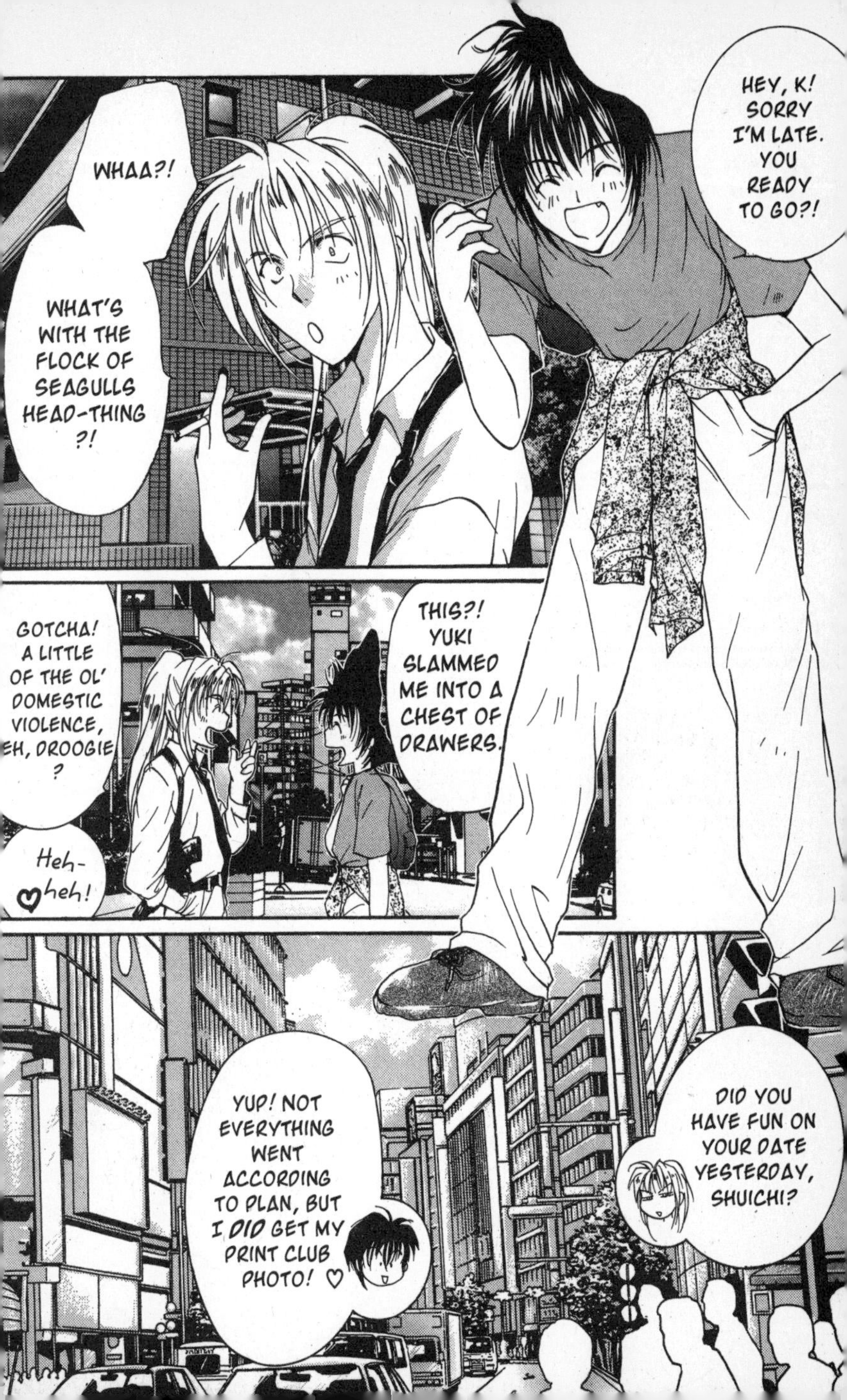
HEY, K! SORRY I'M LATE. YOU READY TO GO?!
WHAA?!
WHAT'S WITH THE FLOCK OF SEAGULLS HEAD-THING ?!
THIS?! YUKI SLAMMED ME INTO A CHEST OF DRAWERS.
GOTCHA! A LITTLE OF THE OL' DOMESTIC VIOLENCE, EH, DROOGIE ?
Heh-heh! ♡
DID YOU HAVE FUN ON YOUR DATE YESTERDAY, SHUICHI?
YUP! NOT EVERYTHING WENT ACCORDING TO PLAN, BUT I DID GET MY PRINT CLUB PHOTO! ♡

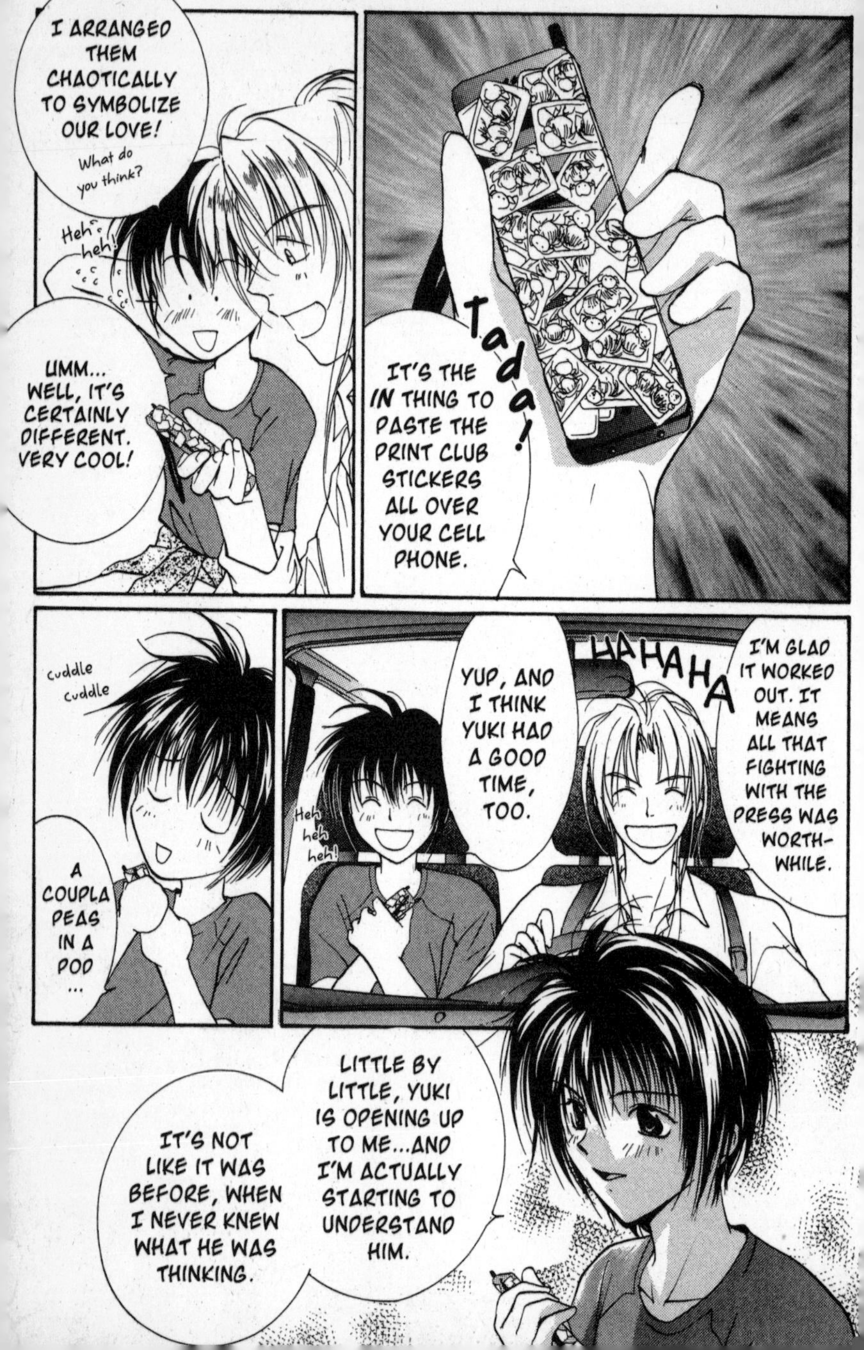
Tada!
IT'S THE IN THING TO PASTE THE PRINT CLUB STICKERS ALL OVER YOUR CELL PHONE.
I ARRANGED THEM CHAOTICALLY TO SYMBOLIZE OUR LOVE!
What do you think?
Heh heh!
UMM... WELL, IT'S CERTAINLY DIFFERENT. VERY COOL!
I'M GLAD IT WORKED OUT. IT MEANS ALL THAT FIGHTING WITH THE PRESS WAS WORTH-WHILE.
HAHAHA
YUP, AND I THINK YUKI HAD A GOOD TIME, TOO.
Heh heh heh!
cuddle cuddle
A COUPLA PEAS IN A POD ...
LITTLE BY LITTLE, YUKI IS OPENING UP TO ME...AND I'M ACTUALLY STARTING TO UNDERSTAND HIM.
IT'S NOT LIKE IT WAS BEFORE, WHEN I NEVER KNEW WHAT HE WAS THINKING.

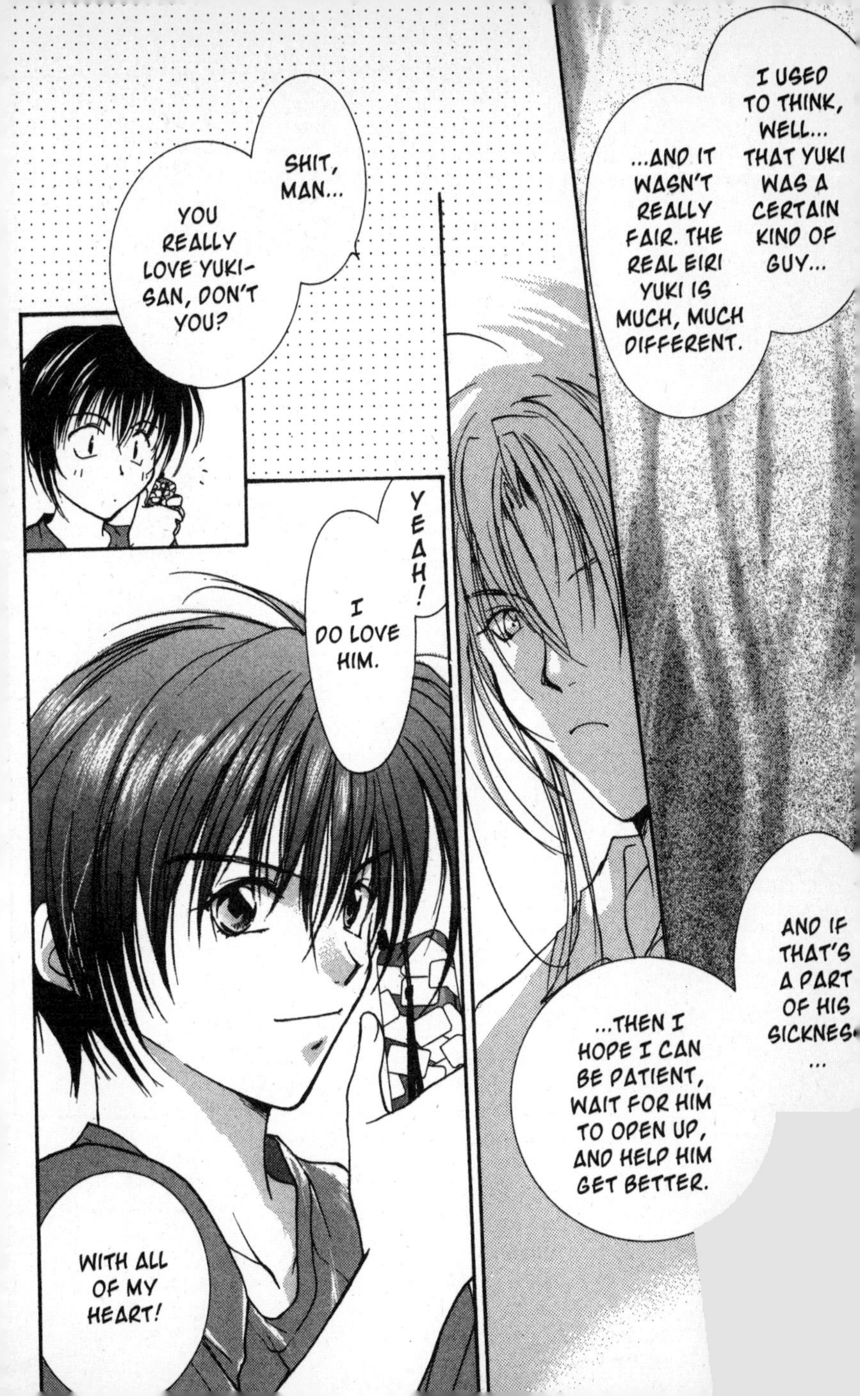
I USED TO THINK, WELL... THAT YUKI WAS A CERTAIN KIND OF GUY...
...AND IT WASN'T REALLY FAIR. THE REAL EIRI YUKI IS MUCH, MUCH DIFFERENT.
AND IF THAT'S A PART OF HIS SICKNES...
...THEN I HOPE I CAN BE PATIENT, WAIT FOR HIM TO OPEN UP, AND HELP HIM GET BETTER.
SHIT, MAN... YOU REALLY LOVE YUKI-SAN, DON'T YOU?
YEAH! I DO LOVE HIM.
WITH ALL OF MY HEART!

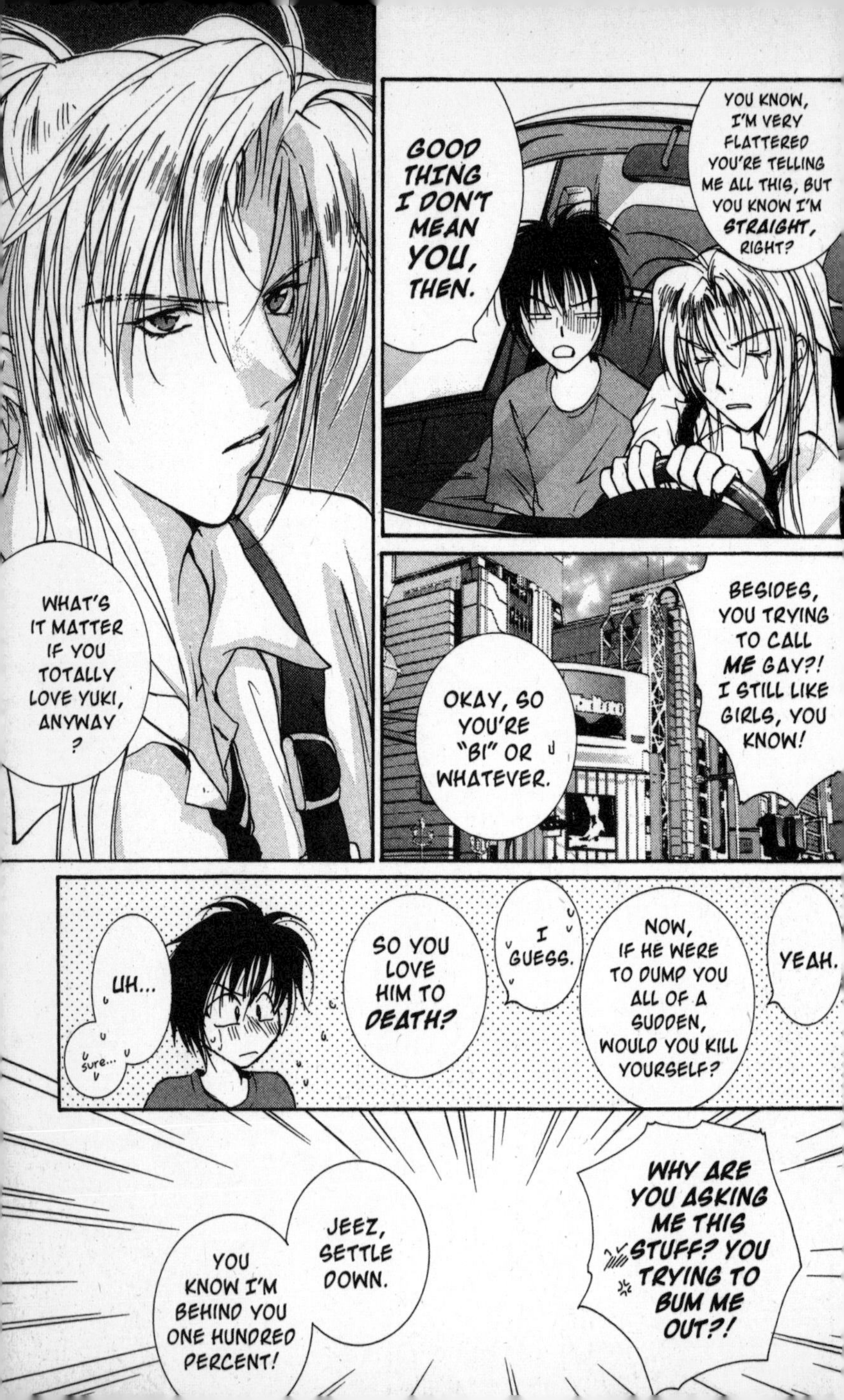
YOU KNOW, I'M VERY FLATTERED YOU'RE TELLING ME ALL THIS, BUT YOU KNOW I'M STRAIGHT, RIGHT?
GOOD THING I DON'T MEAN YOU, THEN.
BESIDES, YOU TRYING TO CALL ME GAY?! I STILL LIKE GIRLS, YOU KNOW!
OKAY, SO YOU'RE "BI" OR WHATEVER.
WHAT'S IT MATTER IF YOU TOTALLY LOVE YUKI, ANYWAY?
YEAH.
NOW, IF HE WERE TO DUMP YOU ALL OF A SUDDEN, WOULD YOU KILL YOURSELF?
I GUESS.
SO YOU LOVE HIM TO DEATH?
UH...
sure...
WHY ARE YOU ASKING ME THIS STUFF? YOU TRYING TO BUM ME OUT?!
JEEZ, SETTLE DOWN.
YOU KNOW I'M BEHIND YOU ONE HUNDRED PERCENT!

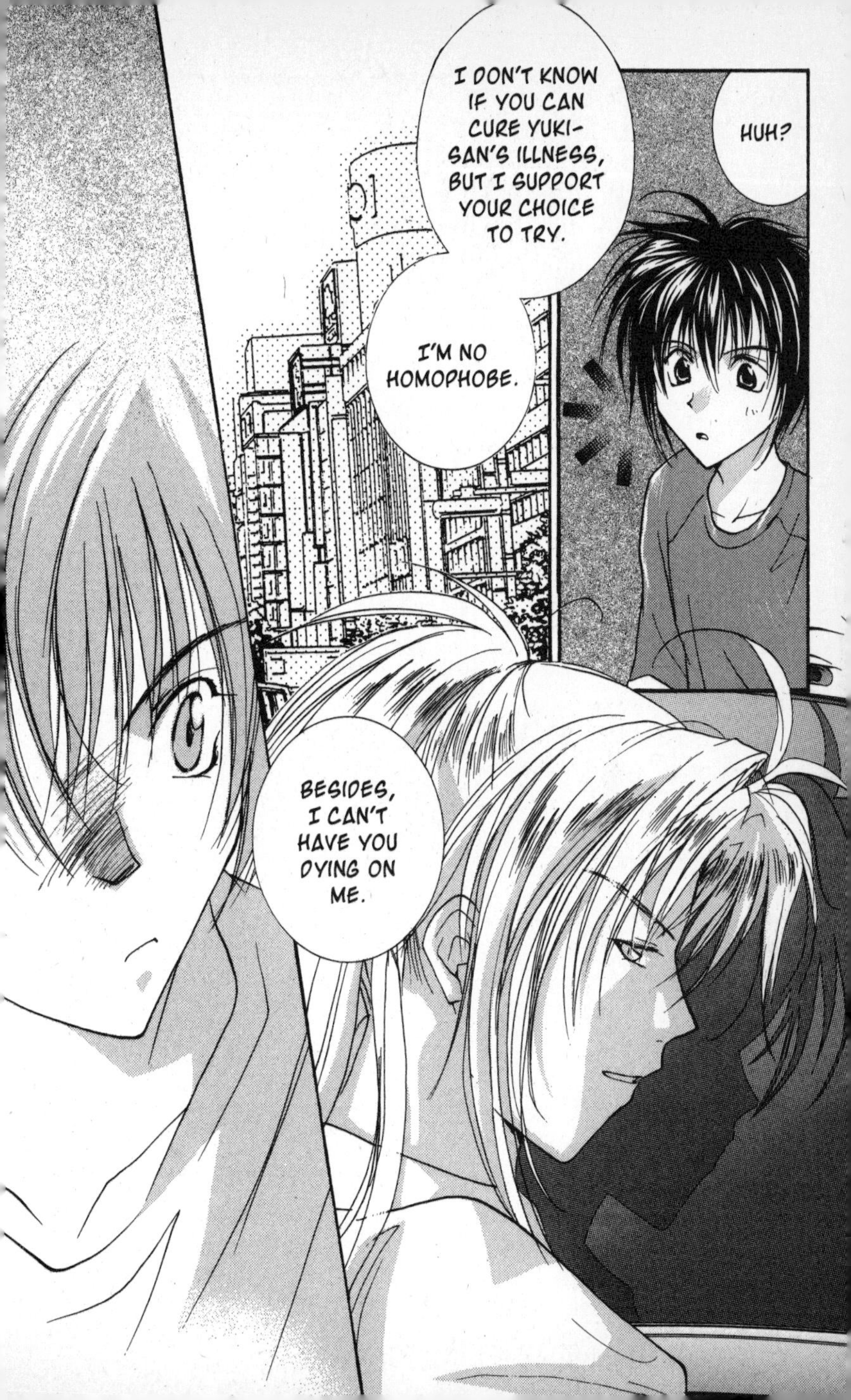
I DON'T KNOW IF YOU CAN CURE YUKI-SAN'S ILLNESS, BUT I SUPPORT YOUR CHOICE TO TRY.
HUH?
I'M NO HOMOPHOBE.
BESIDES, I CAN'T HAVE YOU DYING ON ME.

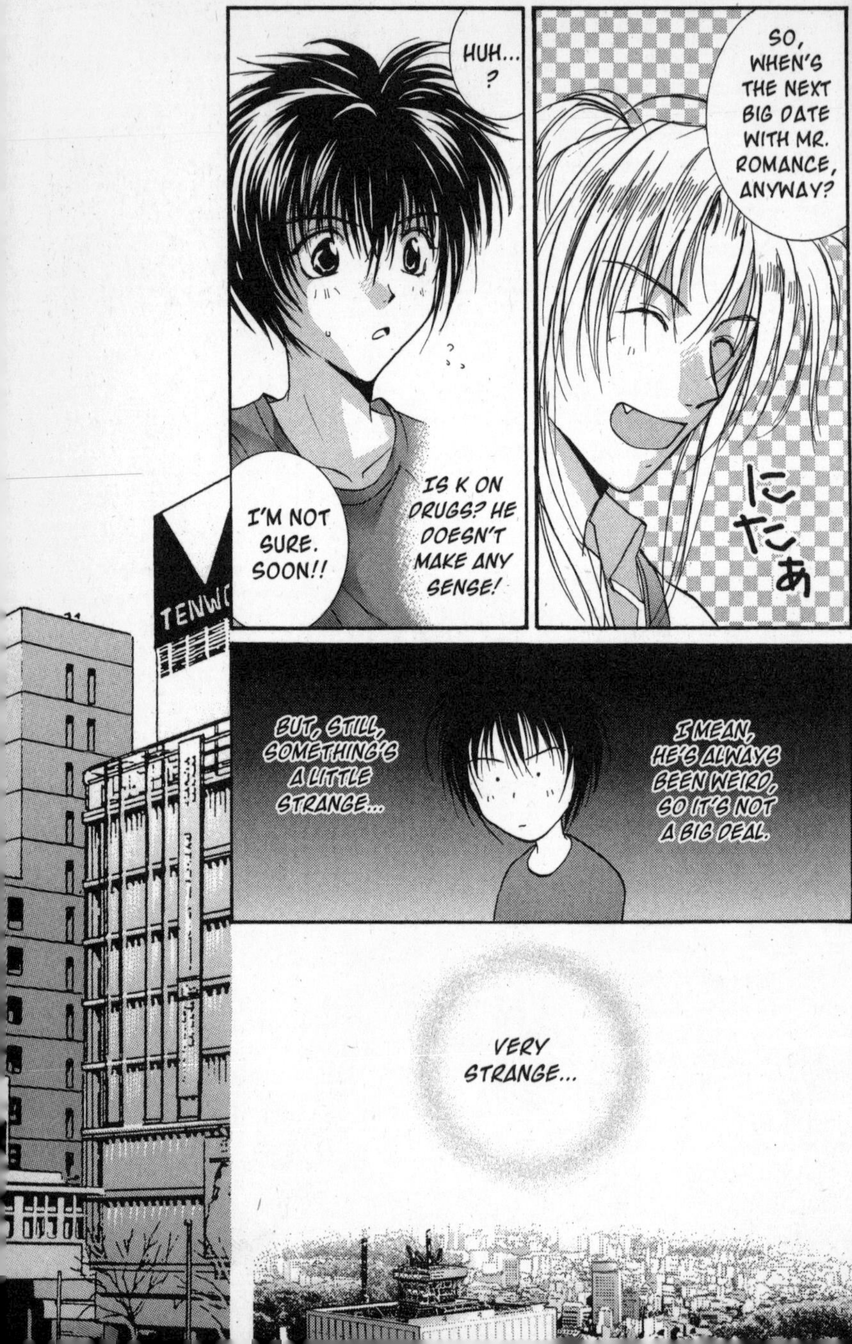
SO, WHEN'S THE NEXT BIG DATE WITH MR. ROMANCE, ANYWAY?
にやあ
HUH...?
IS K ON DRUGS? HE DOESN'T MAKE ANY SENSE!
I'M NOT SURE. SOON!!
I MEAN, HE'S ALWAYS BEEN WEIRD, SO IT'S NOT A BIG DEAL.
BUT, STILL, SOMETHING'S A LITTLE STRANGE...
VERY STRANGE...

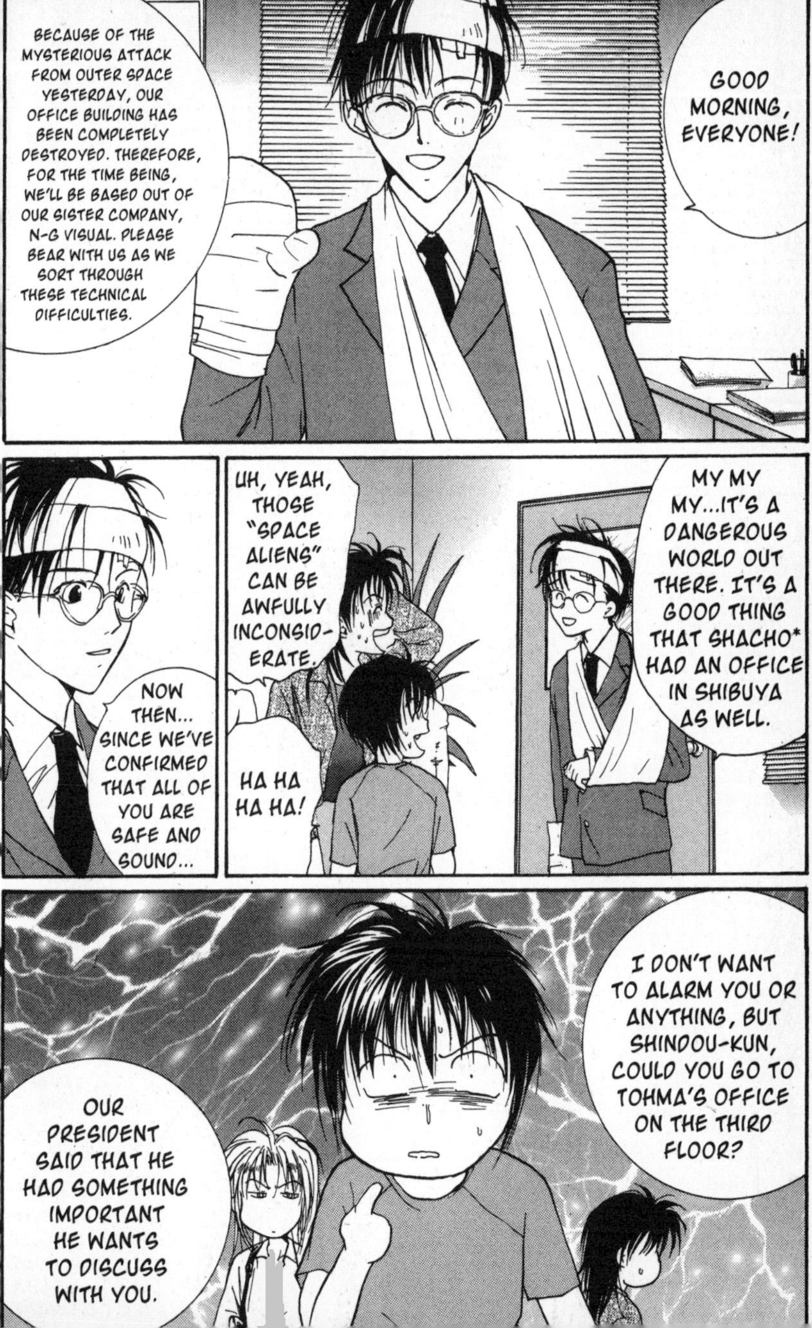
GOOD MORNING, EVERYONE!
BECAUSE OF THE MYSTERIOUS ATTACK FROM OUTER SPACE YESTERDAY, OUR OFFICE BUILDING HAS BEEN COMPLETELY DESTROYED. THEREFORE, FOR THE TIME BEING, WE'LL BE BASED OUT OF OUR SISTER COMPANY, N-G VISUAL. PLEASE BEAR WITH US AS WE SORT THROUGH THESE TECHNICAL DIFFICULTIES.
MY MY MY...IT'S A DANGEROUS WORLD OUT THERE. IT'S A GOOD THING THAT SHACHO* HAD AN OFFICE IN SHIBUYA AS WELL.
UH, YEAH, THOSE "SPACE ALIENS" CAN BE AWFULLY INCONSIDERATE.
HA HA HA HA!
NOW THEN... SINCE WE'VE CONFIRMED THAT ALL OF YOU ARE SAFE AND SOUND...
I DON'T WANT TO ALARM YOU OR ANYTHING, BUT SHINDOU-KUN, COULD YOU GO TO TOHMA'S OFFICE ON THE THIRD FLOOR?
OUR PRESIDENT SAID THAT HE HAD SOMETHING IMPORTANT HE WANTS TO DISCUSS WITH YOU.

* Editor's Note: Shacho is the Japanese term for a company's chief executive officer.

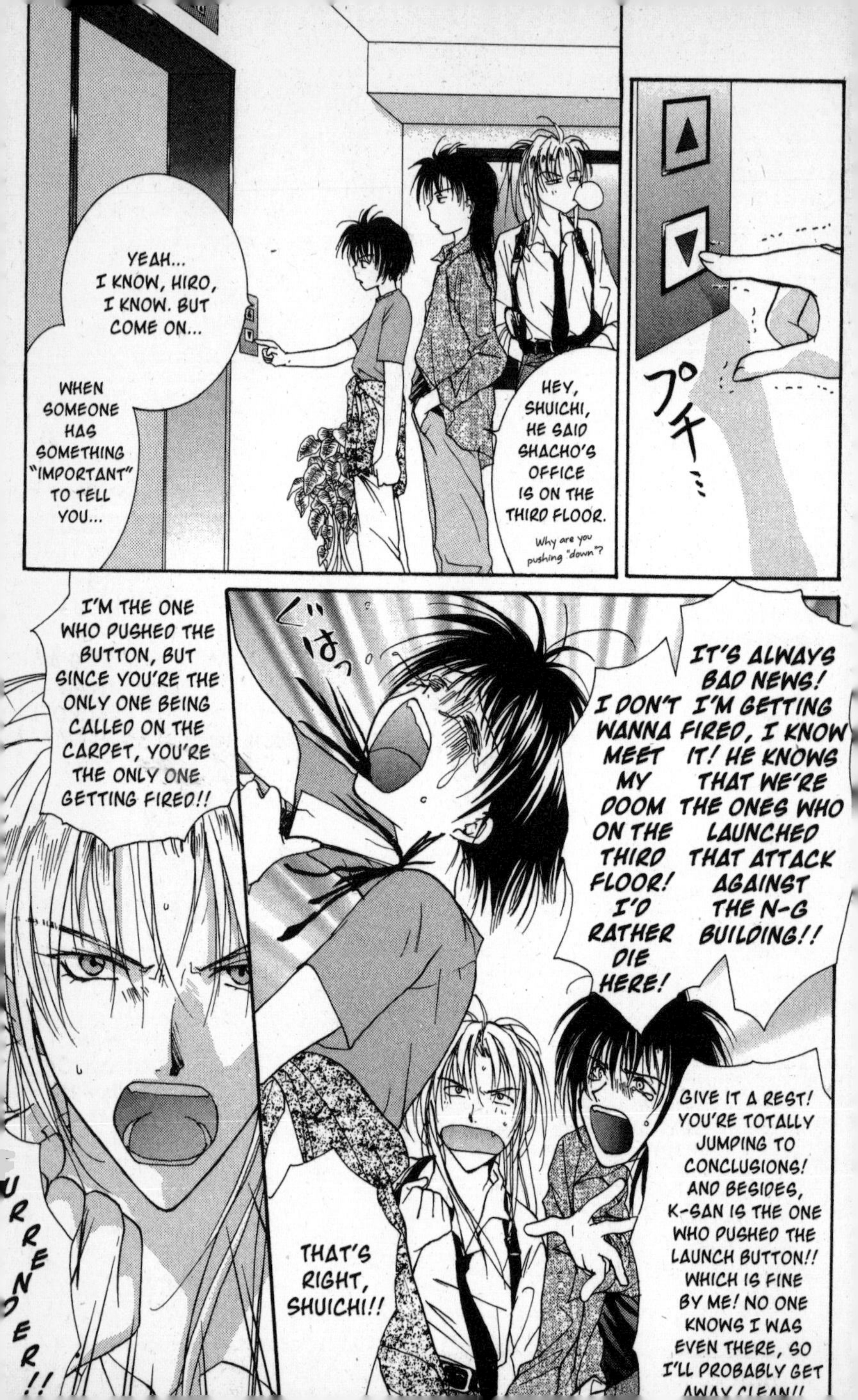
プチ
HEY, SHUICHI, HE SAID SHACHO'S OFFICE IS ON THE THIRD FLOOR.
Why are you pushing "down"?
YEAH... I KNOW, HIRO, I KNOW. BUT COME ON...
WHEN SOMEONE HAS SOMETHING "IMPORTANT" TO TELL YOU...
IT'S ALWAYS BAD NEWS! I'M GETTING FIRED, I KNOW IT! HE KNOWS THAT WE'RE THE ONES WHO LAUNCHED THAT ATTACK AGAINST THE N-G BUILDING!!
I DON'T WANNA MEET MY DOOM ON THE THIRD FLOOR! I'D RATHER DIE HERE!
ぐはっ
I'M THE ONE WHO PUSHED THE BUTTON, BUT SINCE YOU'RE THE ONLY ONE BEING CALLED ON THE CARPET, YOU'RE THE ONLY ONE GETTING FIRED!!
GIVE IT A REST! YOU'RE TOTALLY JUMPING TO CONCLUSIONS! AND BESIDES, K-SAN IS THE ONE WHO PUSHED THE LAUNCH BUTTON!! WHICH IS FINE BY ME! NO ONE KNOWS I WAS EVEN THERE, SO I'LL PROBABLY GET AWAY CLEAN!!
THAT'S RIGHT, SHUICHI!!
URRENDER!!

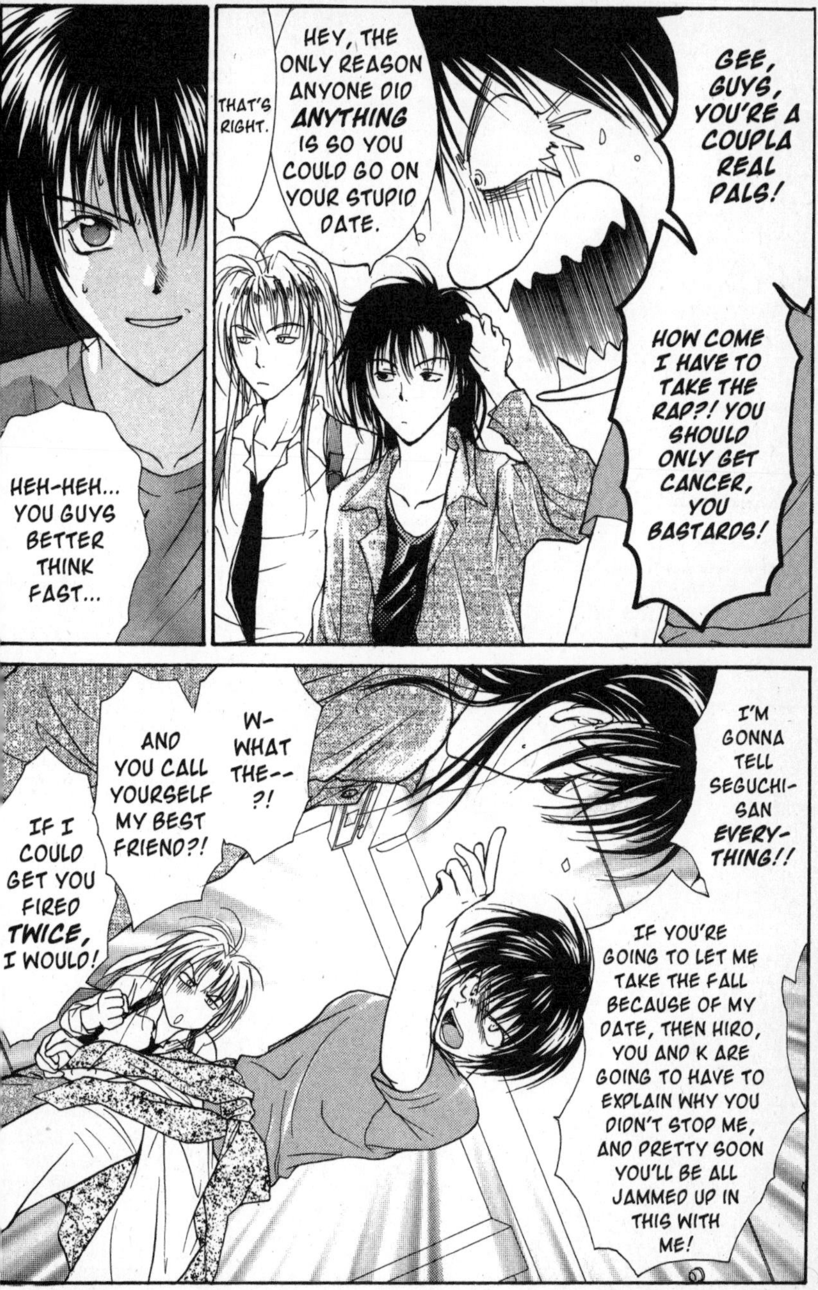
GEE, GUYS, YOU'RE A COUPLA REAL PALS!
HOW COME I HAVE TO TAKE THE RAP?! YOU SHOULD ONLY GET CANCER, YOU BASTARDS!
HEY, THE ONLY REASON ANYONE DID ANYTHING IS SO YOU COULD GO ON YOUR STUPID DATE.
THAT'S RIGHT.
HEH-HEH... YOU GUYS BETTER THINK FAST...
I'M GONNA TELL SEGUCHI-SAN EVERYTHING!!
IF YOU'RE GOING TO LET ME TAKE THE FALL BECAUSE OF MY DATE, THEN HIRO, YOU AND K ARE GOING TO HAVE TO EXPLAIN WHY YOU DIDN'T STOP ME, AND PRETTY SOON YOU'LL BE ALL JAMMED UP IN THIS WITH ME!
W-WHAT THE--?!
AND YOU CALL YOURSELF MY BEST FRIEND?!
IF I COULD GET YOU FIRED TWICE, I WOULD!

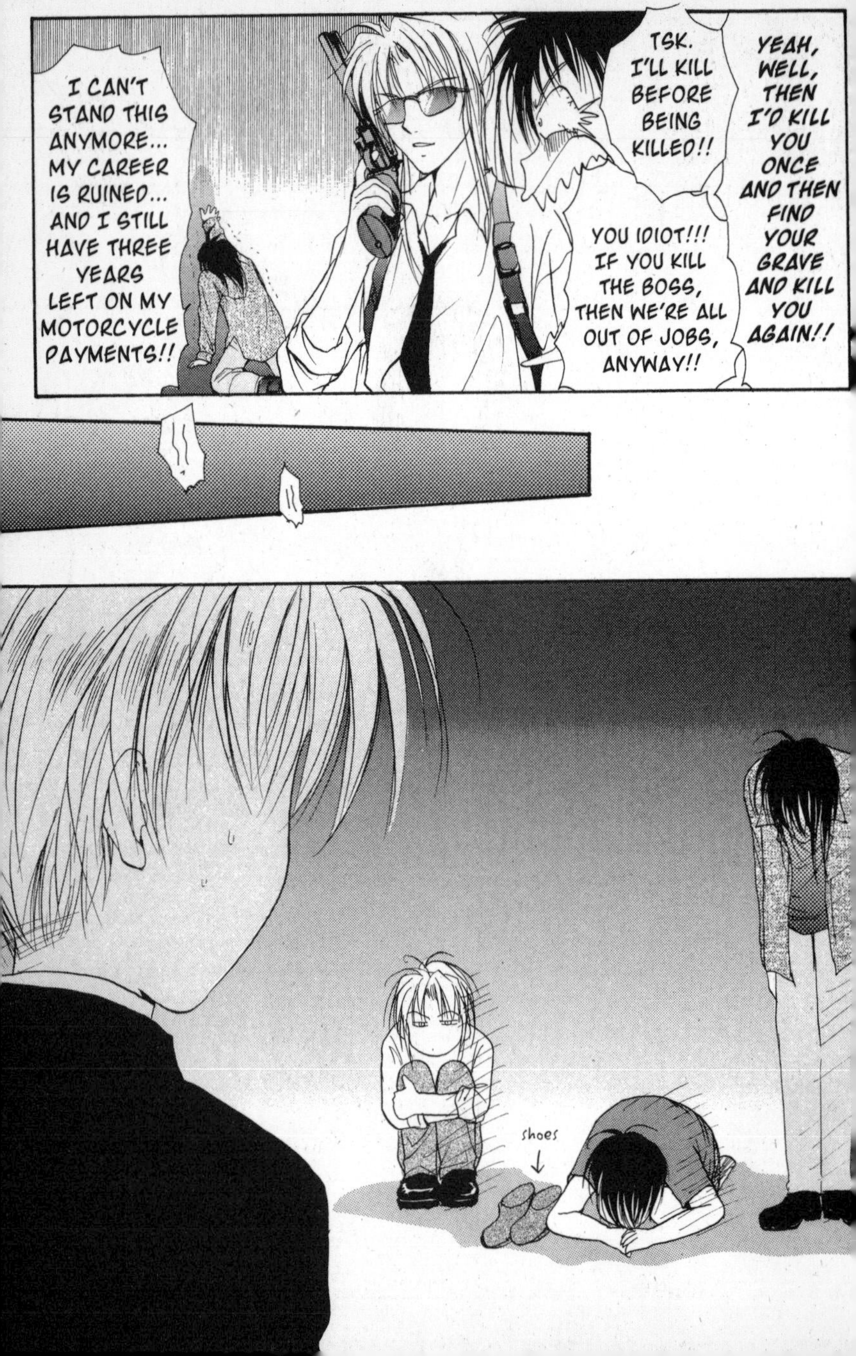

YEAH, WELL, THEN I'D KILL YOU ONCE AND THEN FIND YOUR GRAVE AND KILL YOU AGAIN!!
TSK. I'LL KILL BEFORE BEING KILLED!!
YOU IDIOT!!! IF YOU KILL THE BOSS, THEN WE'RE ALL OUT OF JOBS, ANYWAY!!
I CAN'T STAND THIS ANYMORE... MY CAREER IS RUINED... AND I STILL HAVE THREE YEARS LEFT ON MY MOTORCYCLE PAYMENTS!!
shoes

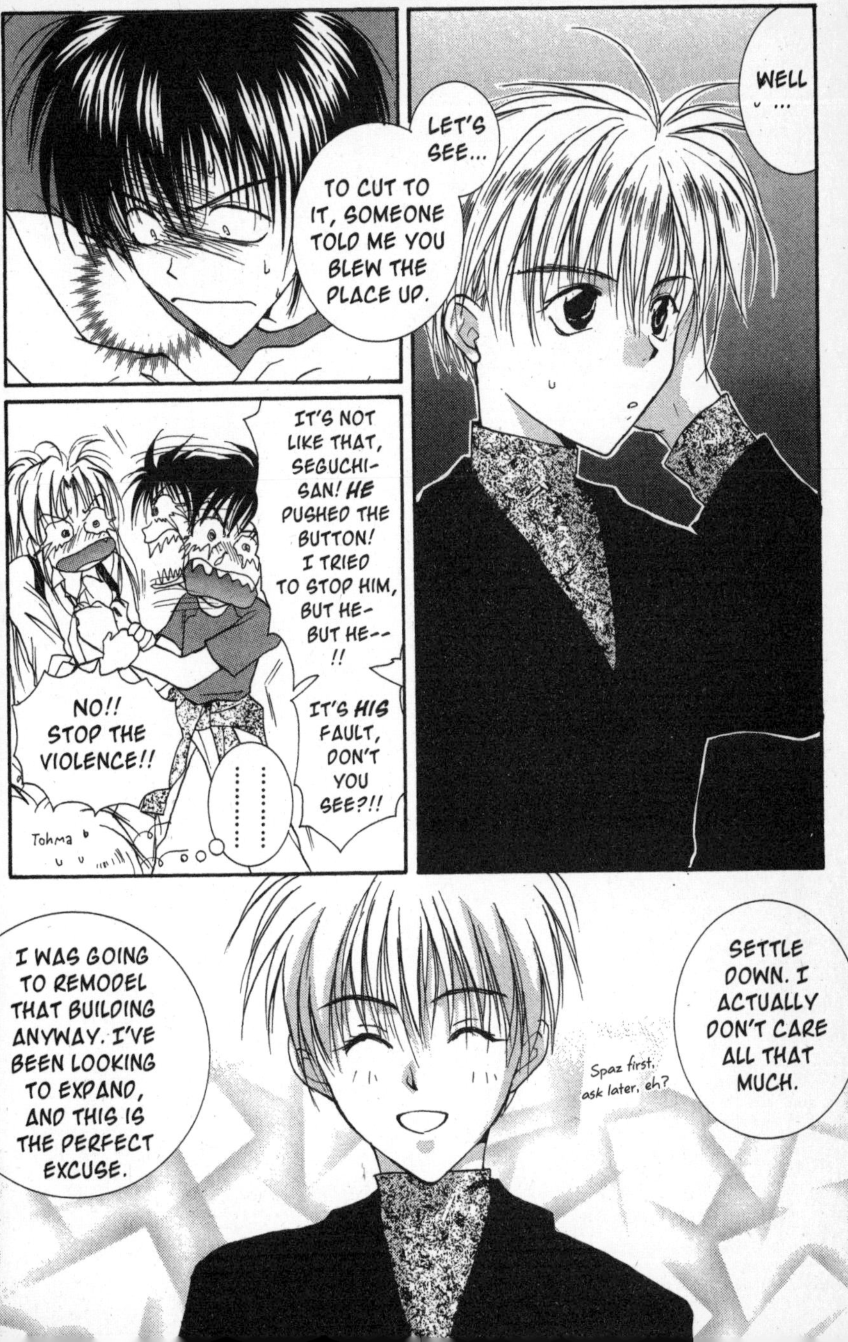
WELL ...
LET'S SEE...
TO CUT TO IT, SOMEONE TOLD ME YOU BLEW THE PLACE UP.
IT'S NOT LIKE THAT, SEGUCHI-SAN! HE PUSHED THE BUTTON! I TRIED TO STOP HIM, BUT HE- BUT HE-- !!
IT'S HIS FAULT, DON'T YOU SEE?!!
....
NO!! STOP THE VIOLENCE!!
Tohma
SETTLE DOWN. I ACTUALLY DON'T CARE ALL THAT MUCH.
Spaz first, ask later, eh?
I WAS GOING TO REMODEL THAT BUILDING ANYWAY. I'VE BEEN LOOKING TO EXPAND, AND THIS IS THE PERFECT EXCUSE.

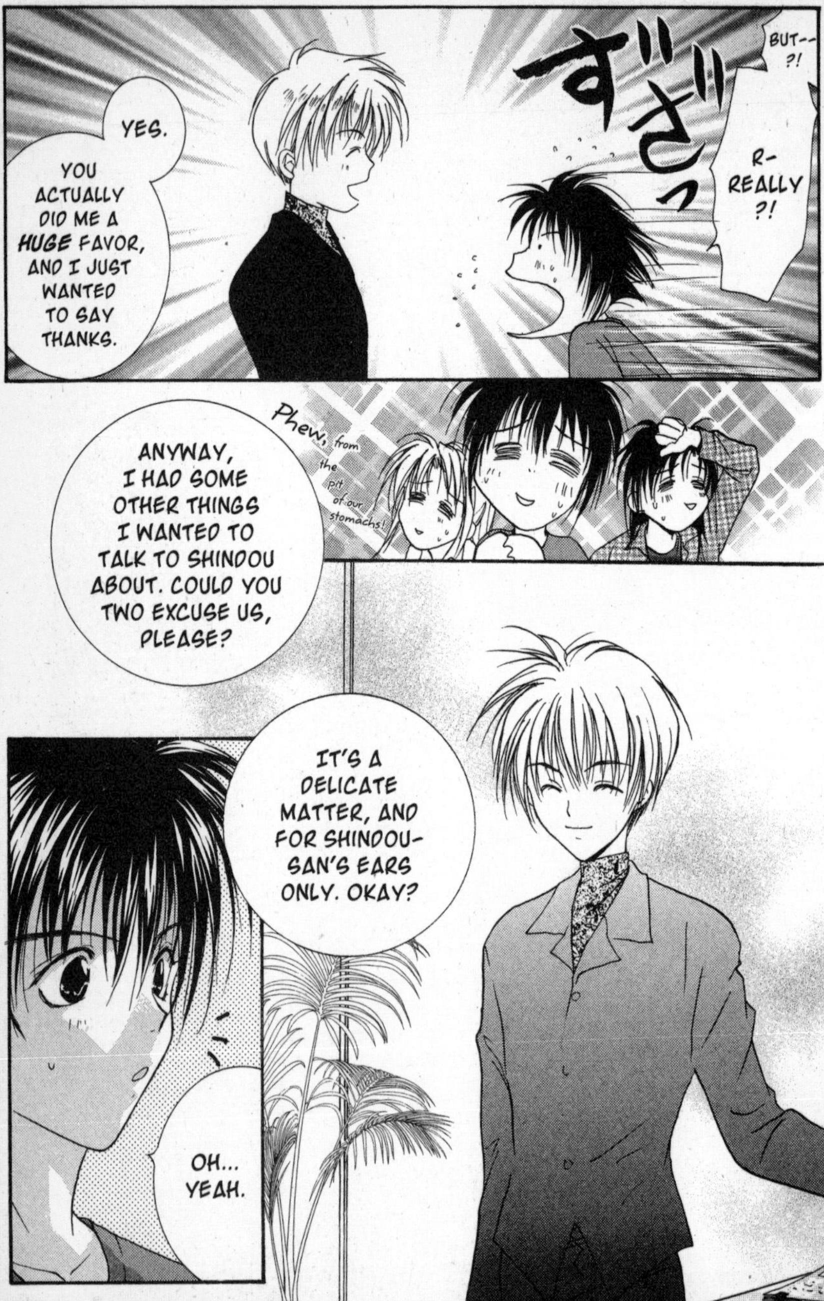
BUT-- ?!
R- REALLY ?!
ずざっ
YES.
YOU ACTUALLY DID ME A HUGE FAVOR, AND I JUST WANTED TO SAY THANKS.
Phew, from the pit of our stomachs!
ANYWAY, I HAD SOME OTHER THINGS I WANTED TO TALK TO SHINDOU ABOUT. COULD YOU TWO EXCUSE US, PLEASE?
IT'S A DELICATE MATTER, AND FOR SHINDOU-SAN'S EARS ONLY. OKAY?
OH... YEAH.

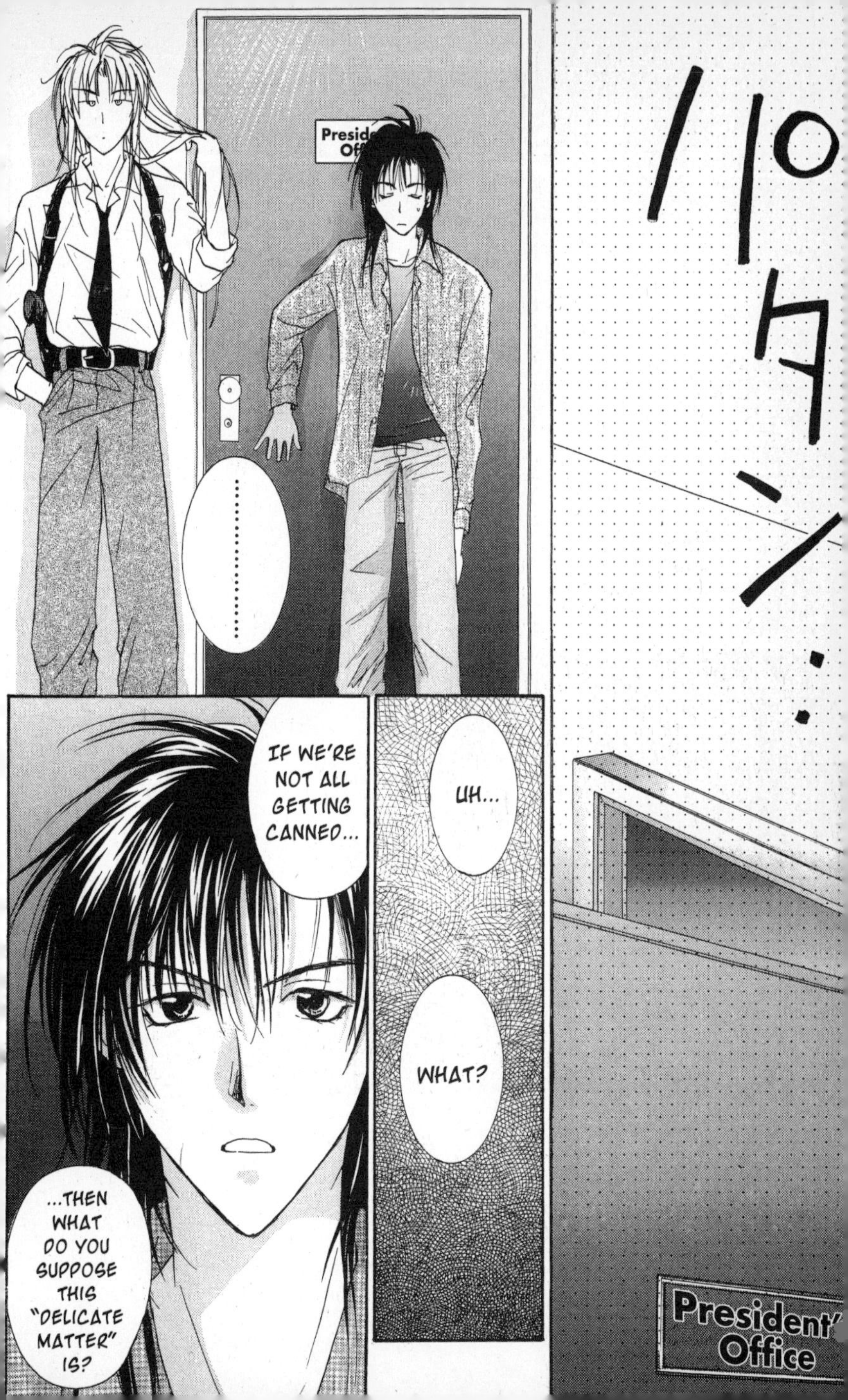
パタン‥
President'
Office
……
UH...
WHAT?
IF WE'RE NOT ALL GETTING CANNED...
...THEN WHAT DO YOU SUPPOSE THIS "DELICATE MATTER" IS?

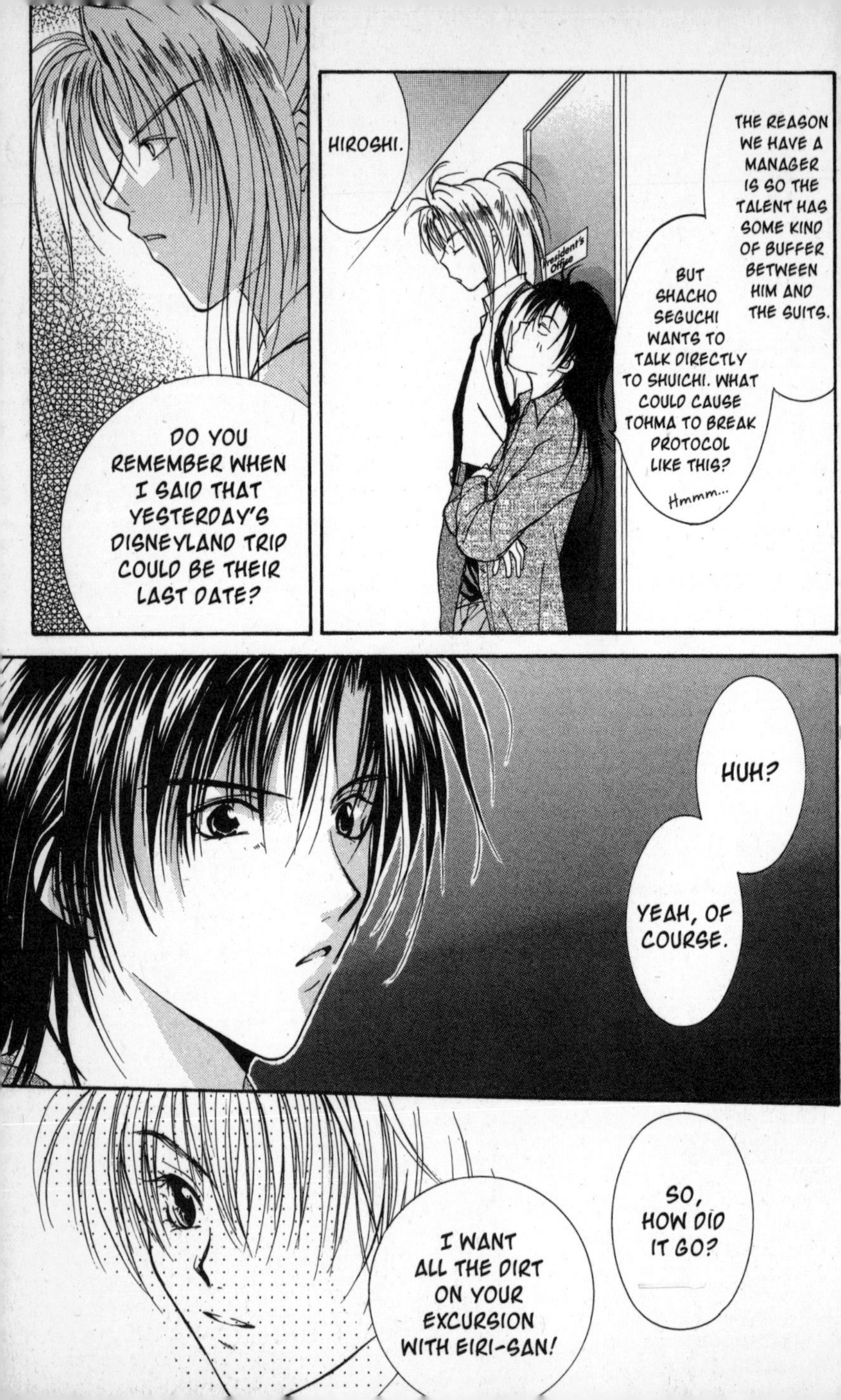
THE REASON WE HAVE A MANAGER IS SO THE TALENT HAS SOME KIND OF BUFFER BETWEEN HIM AND THE SUITS.
BUT SHACHO SEGUCHI WANTS TO TALK DIRECTLY TO SHUICHI. WHAT COULD CAUSE TOHMA TO BREAK PROTOCOL LIKE THIS?
Hmmm...
President's Office
HIROSHI.
DO YOU REMEMBER WHEN I SAID THAT YESTERDAY'S DISNEYLAND TRIP COULD BE THEIR LAST DATE?
HUH?
YEAH, OF COURSE.
SO, HOW DID IT GO?
I WANT ALL THE DIRT ON YOUR EXCURSION WITH EIRI-SAN!

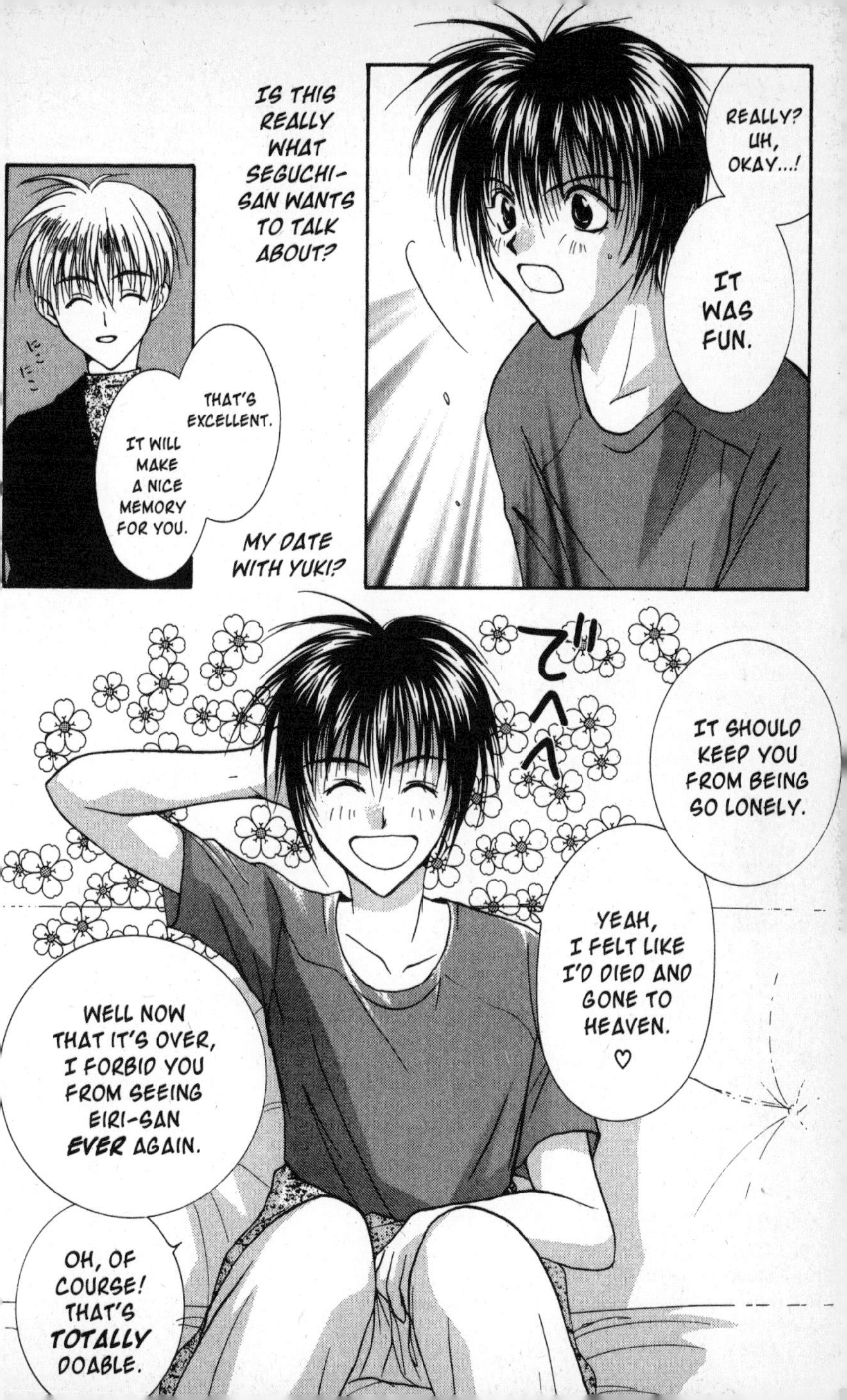
REALLY? UH, OKAY...!
IT WAS FUN.
IS THIS REALLY WHAT SEGUCHI-SAN WANTS TO TALK ABOUT?
MY DATE WITH YUKI?
にこにこ
THAT'S EXCELLENT.
IT WILL MAKE A NICE MEMORY FOR YOU.
でへへ
IT SHOULD KEEP YOU FROM BEING SO LONELY.
YEAH, I FELT LIKE I'D DIED AND GONE TO HEAVEN. ♡
WELL NOW THAT IT'S OVER, I FORBID YOU FROM SEEING EIRI-SAN **EVER** AGAIN.
OH, OF COURSE! THAT'S **TOTALLY** DOABLE.

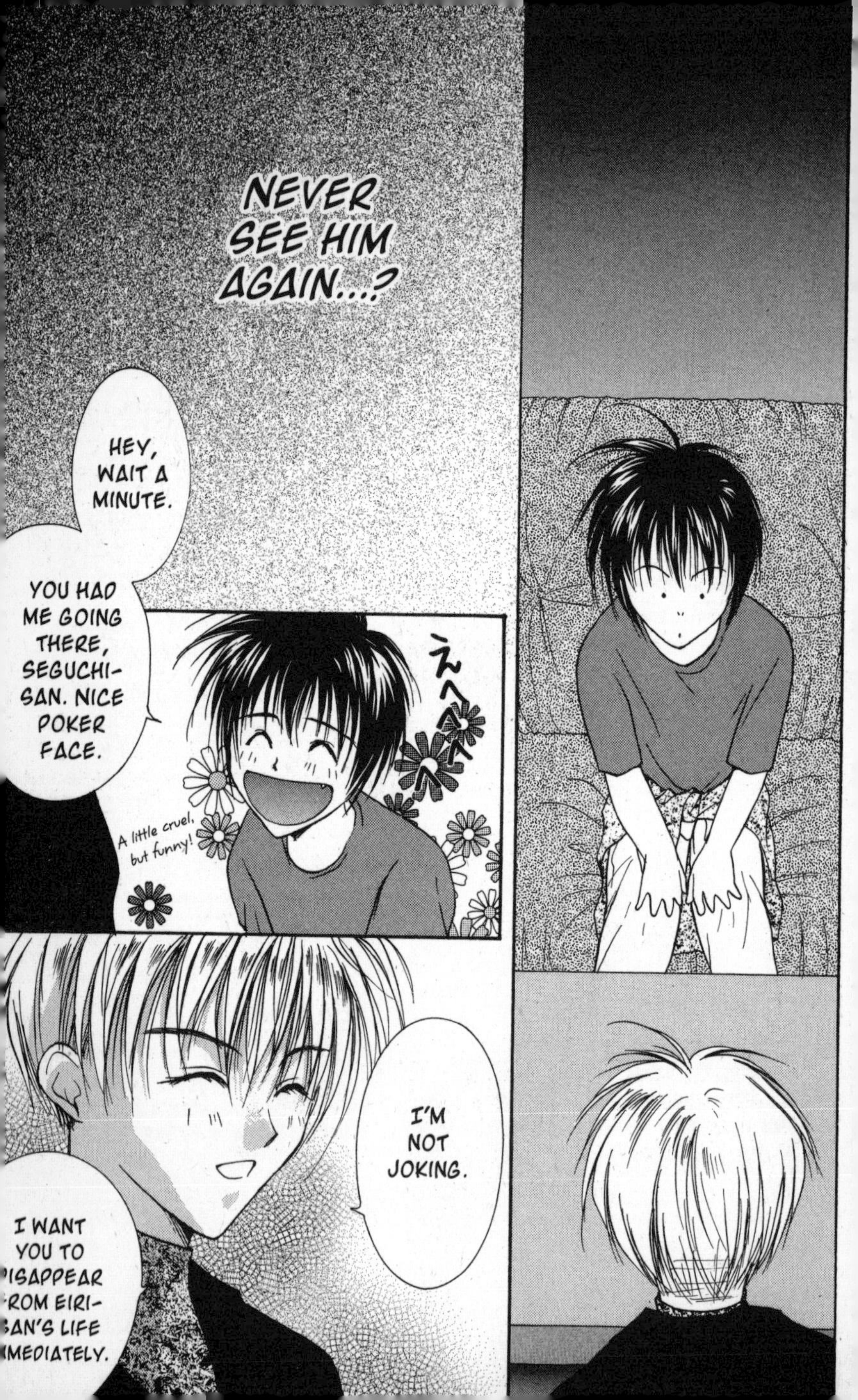
NEVER SEE HIM AGAIN...?
HEY, WAIT A MINUTE.
YOU HAD ME GOING THERE, SEGUCHI-SAN. NICE POKER FACE.
えへへへ
A little cruel, but funny!
I'M NOT JOKING.
I WANT YOU TO ISAPPEAR ROM EIRI-AN'S LIFE MEDIATELY.

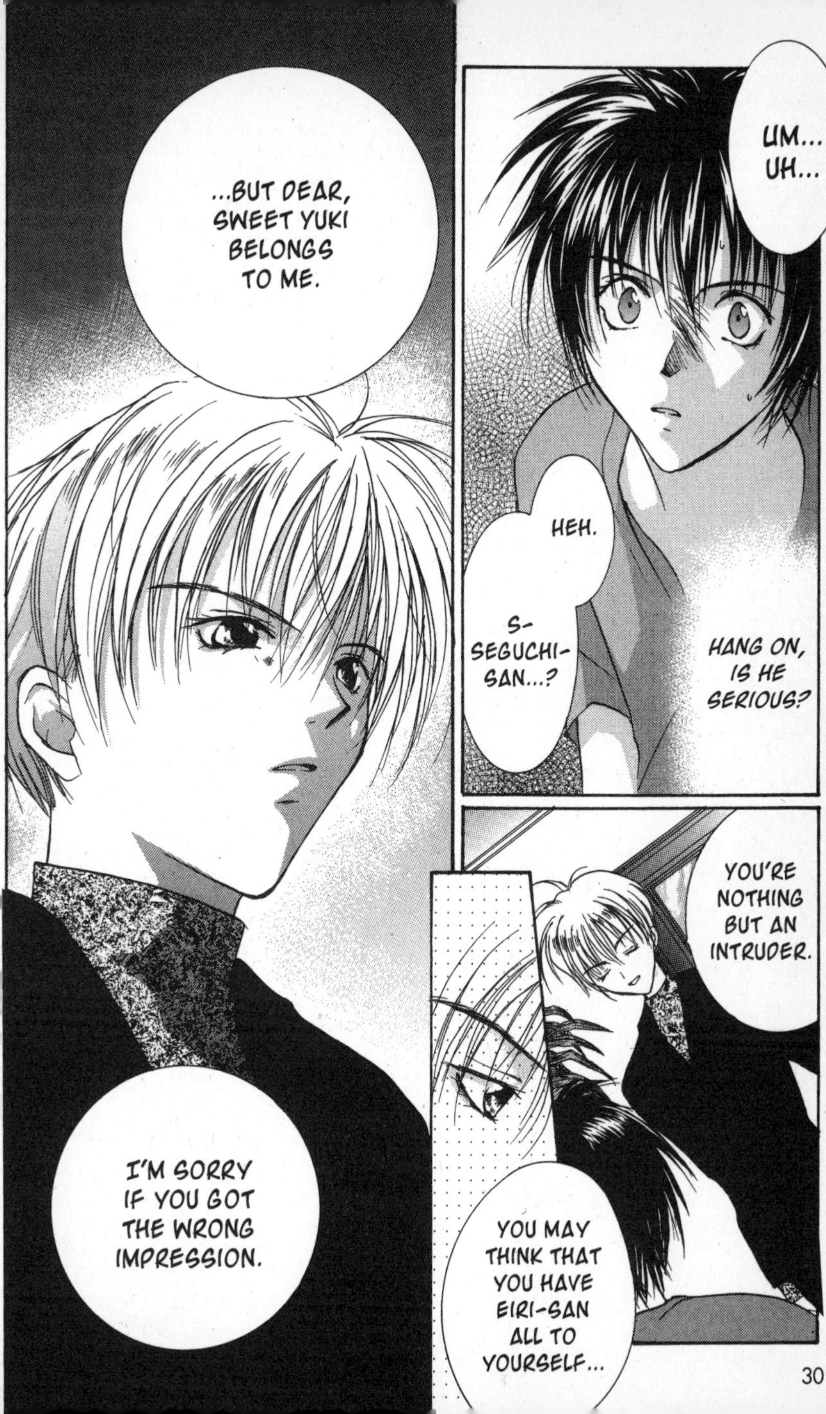
UM... UH...
HEH.
S-SEGUCHI-SAN...?
HANG ON, IS HE SERIOUS?
YOU'RE NOTHING BUT AN INTRUDER.
YOU MAY THINK THAT YOU HAVE EIRI-SAN ALL TO YOURSELF...
...BUT DEAR, SWEET YUKI BELONGS TO ME.
I'M SORRY IF YOU GOT THE WRONG IMPRESSION.

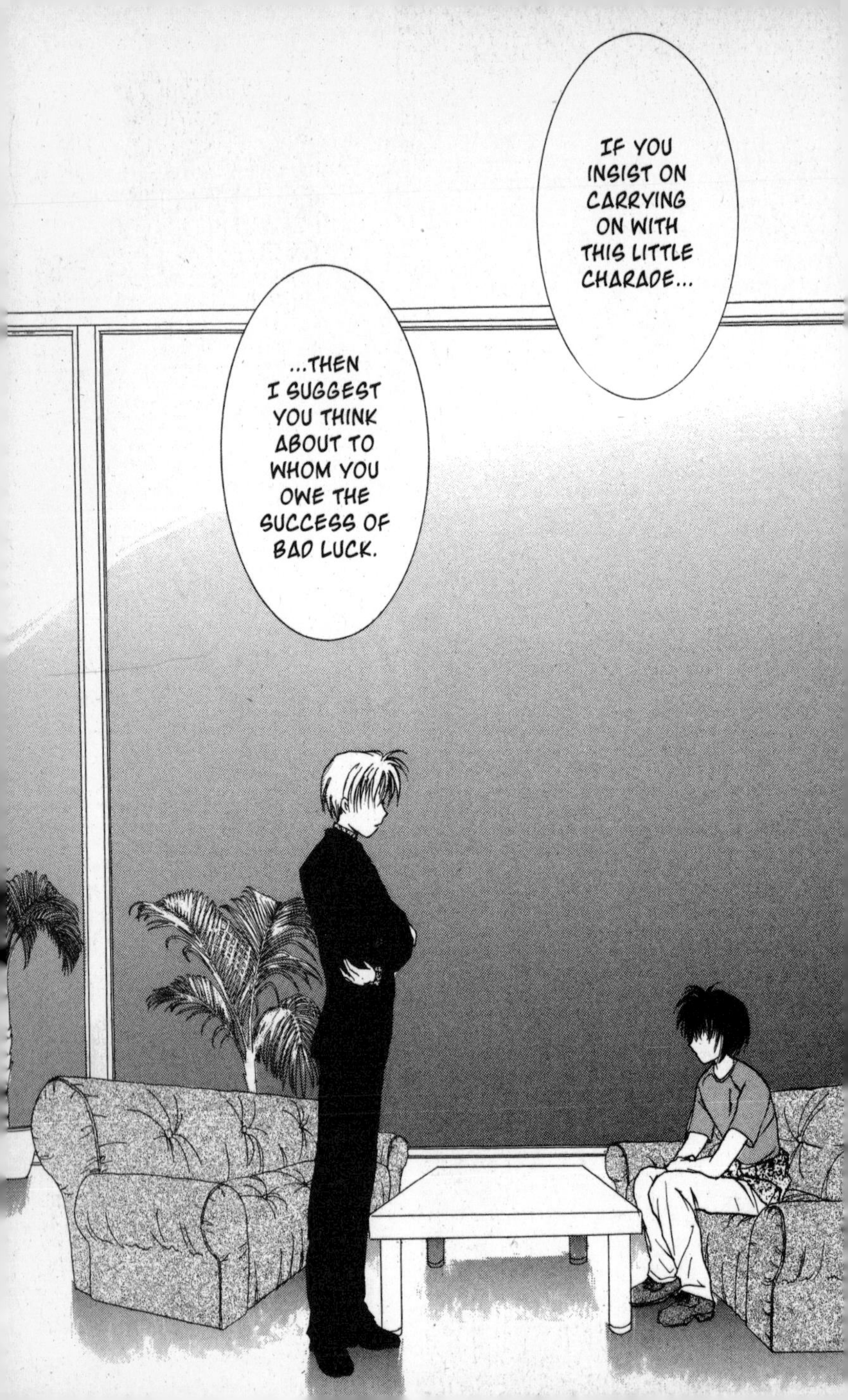
IF YOU INSIST ON CARRYING ON WITH THIS LITTLE CHARADE...
...THEN I SUGGEST YOU THINK ABOUT TO WHOM YOU OWE THE SUCCESS OF BAD LUCK.

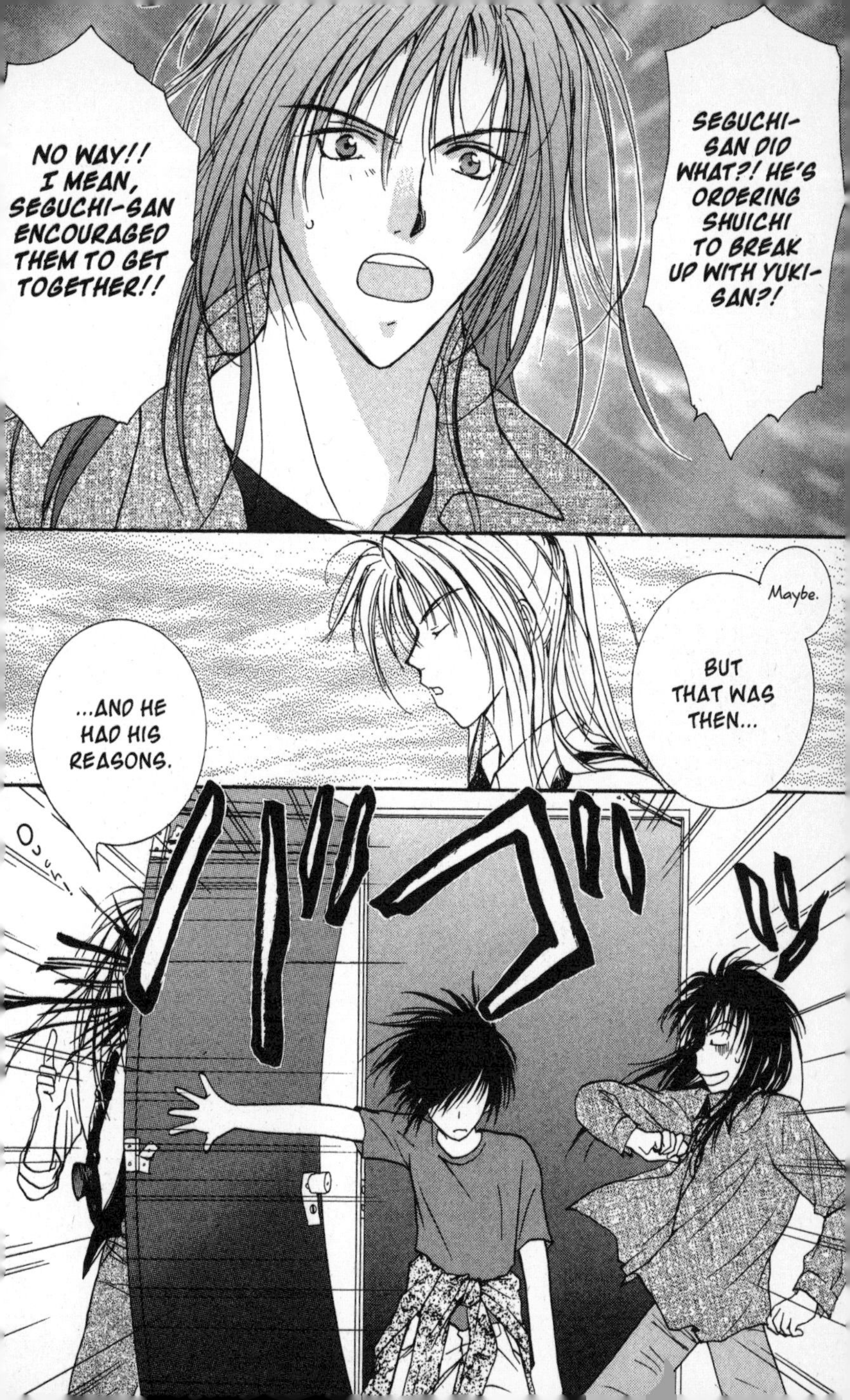
SEGUCHI-SAN DID WHAT?! HE'S ORDERING SHUICHI TO BREAK UP WITH YUKI-SAN?!
NO WAY!! I MEAN, SEGUCHI-SAN ENCOURAGED THEM TO GET TOGETHER!!
Maybe.
BUT THAT WAS THEN...
...AND HE HAD HIS REASONS.

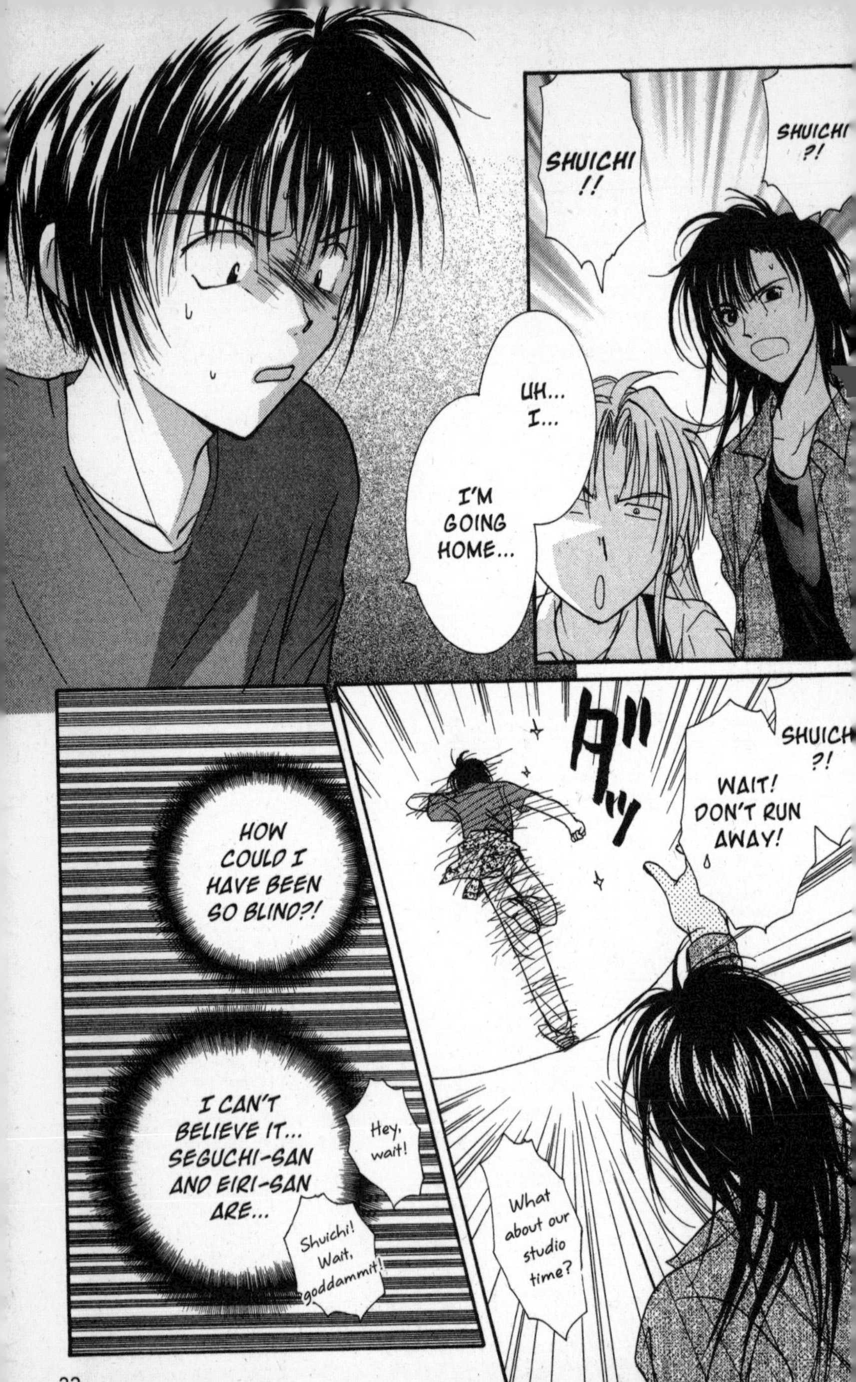
SHUICHI ?!
SHUICHI !!
UH... I...
I'M GOING HOME...
SHUICH ?!
ダッ
WAIT! DON'T RUN AWAY!
What about our studio time?
HOW COULD I HAVE BEEN SO BLIND?!
I CAN'T BELIEVE IT... SEGUCHI-SAN AND EIRI-SAN ARE...
Hey, wait!
Shuichi! Wait, goddammit!

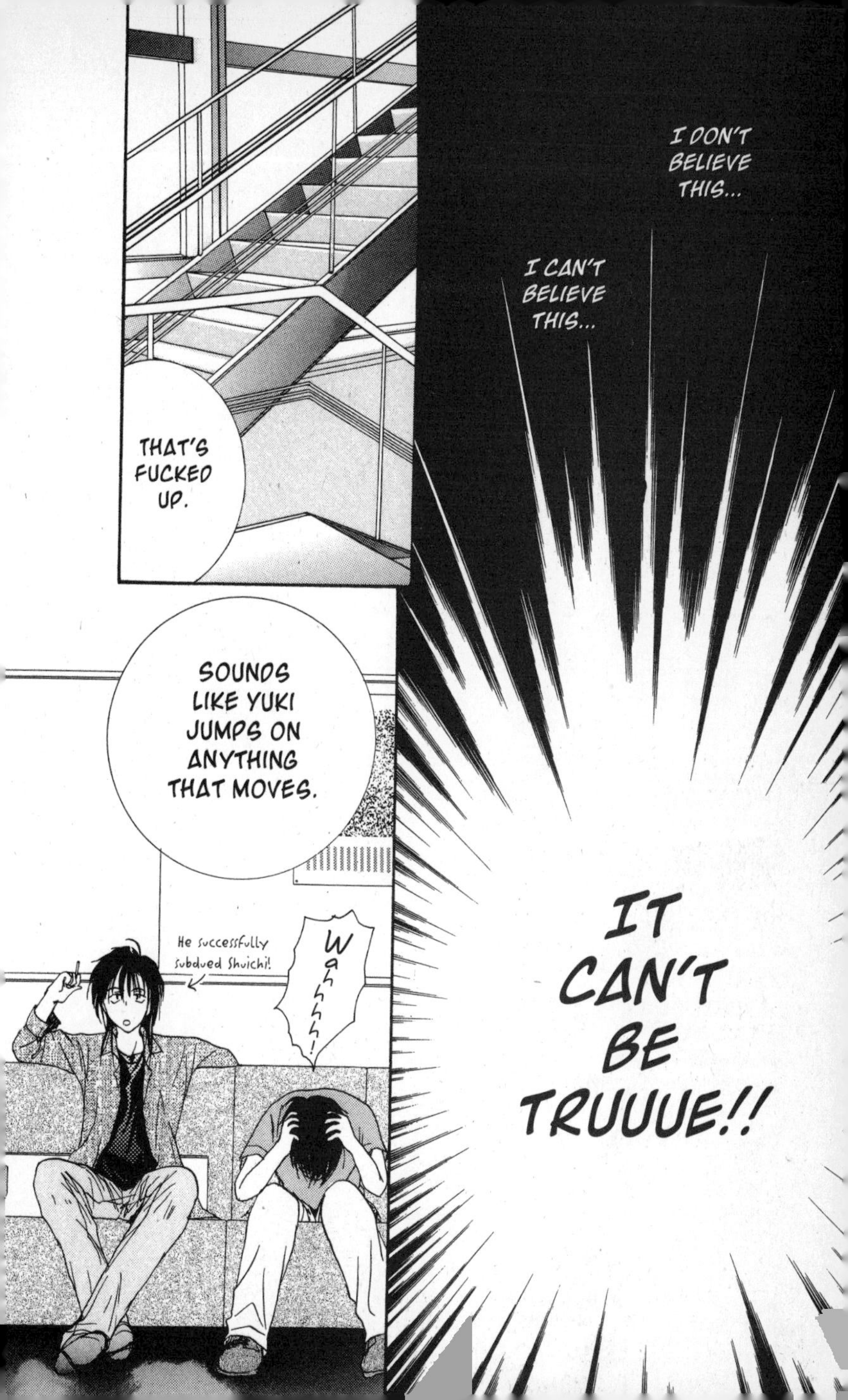
I DON'T BELIEVE THIS...
I CAN'T BELIEVE THIS...
IT CAN'T BE TRUUUE!!
THAT'S FUCKED UP.
SOUNDS LIKE YUKI JUMPS ON ANYTHING THAT MOVES.
Wahhhh!
He successfully subdued Shuichi!

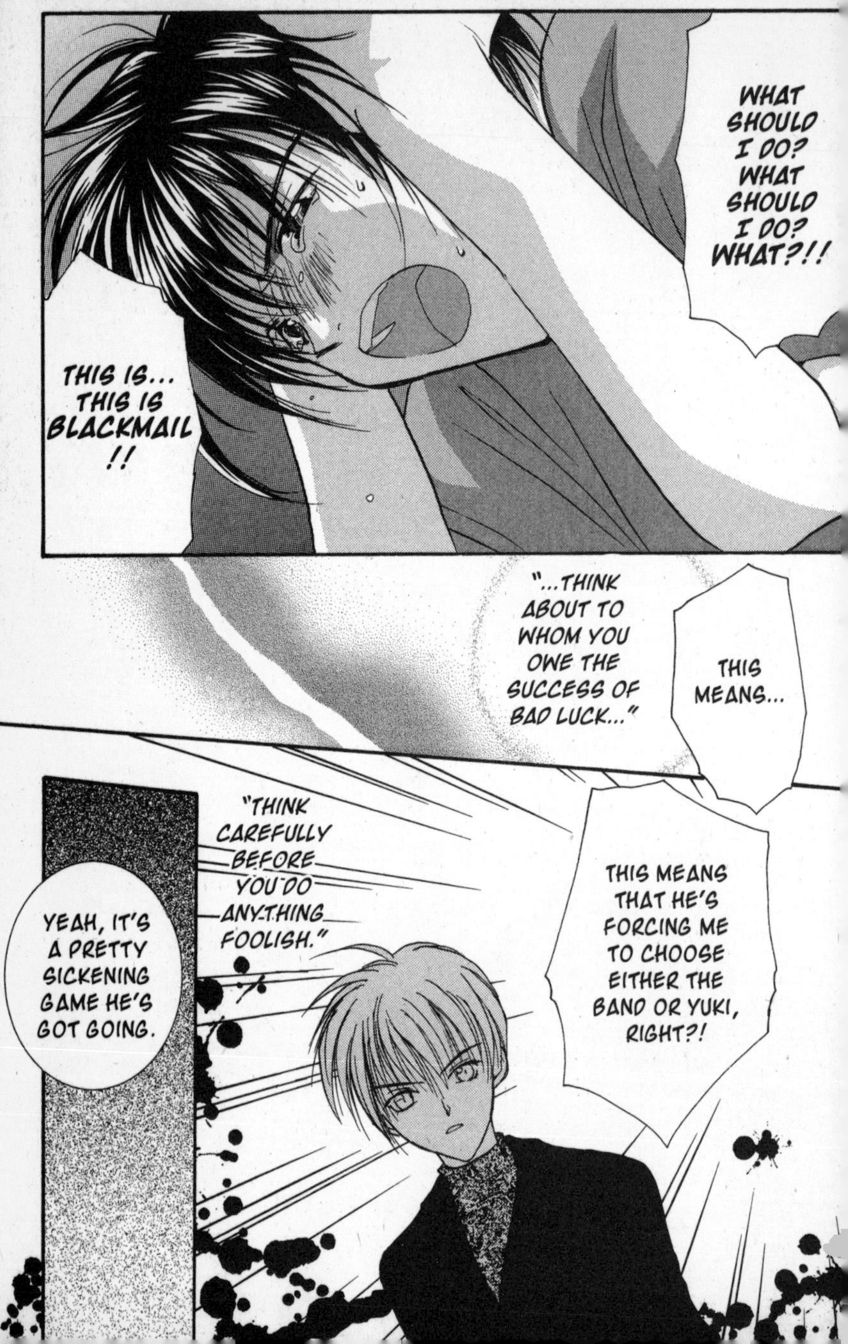
WHAT SHOULD I DO? WHAT SHOULD I DO? WHAT?!!
THIS IS... THIS IS BLACKMAIL!!
THIS MEANS...
"...THINK ABOUT TO WHOM YOU OWE THE SUCCESS OF BAD LUCK..."
THIS MEANS THAT HE'S FORCING ME TO CHOOSE EITHER THE BAND OR YUKI, RIGHT?!
"THINK CAREFULLY BEFORE YOU DO ANYTHING FOOLISH."
YEAH, IT'S A PRETTY SICKENING GAME HE'S GOT GOING.

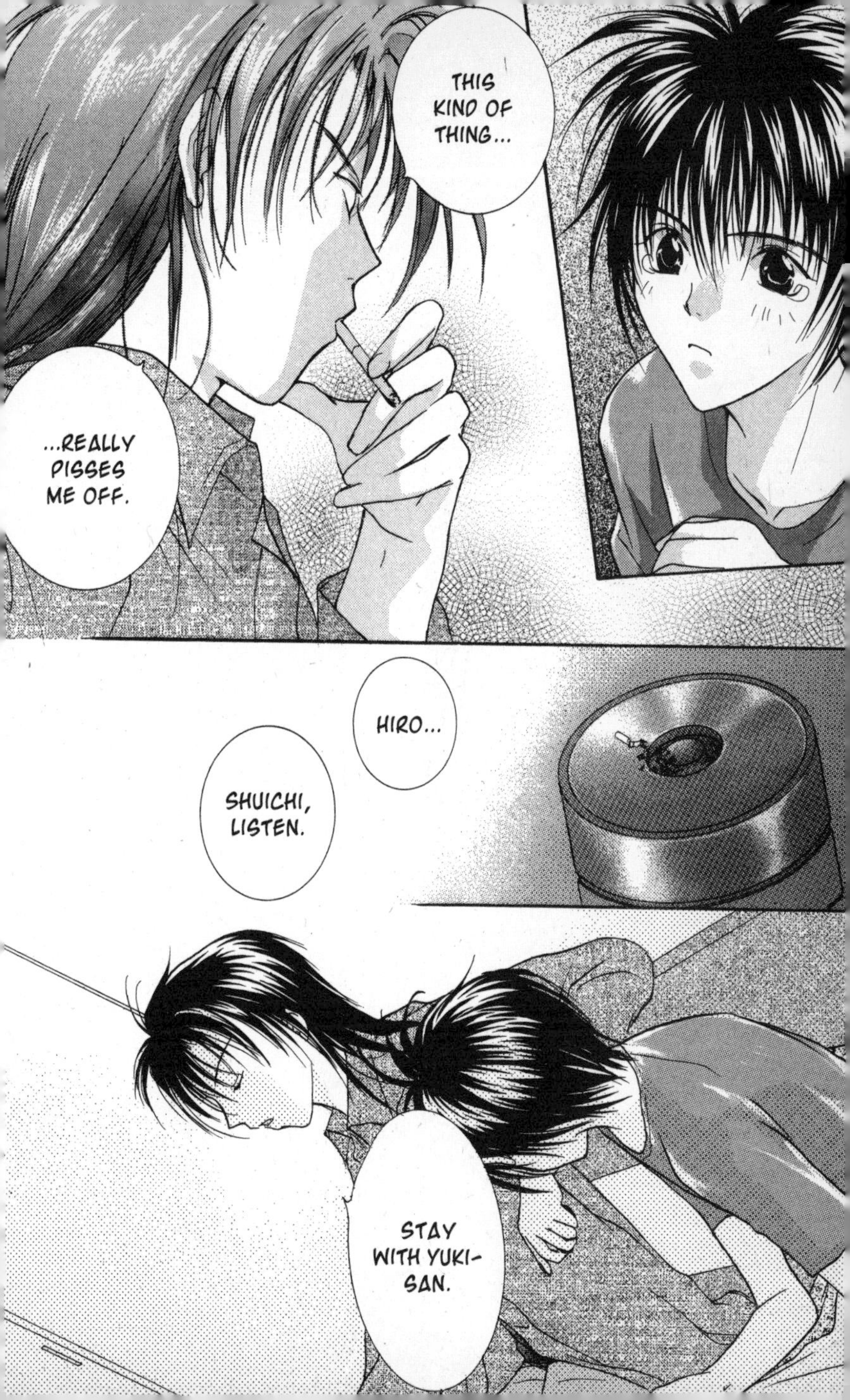
THIS KIND OF THING...
...REALLY PISSES ME OFF.
HIRO...
SHUICHI, LISTEN.
STAY WITH YUKI-SAN.

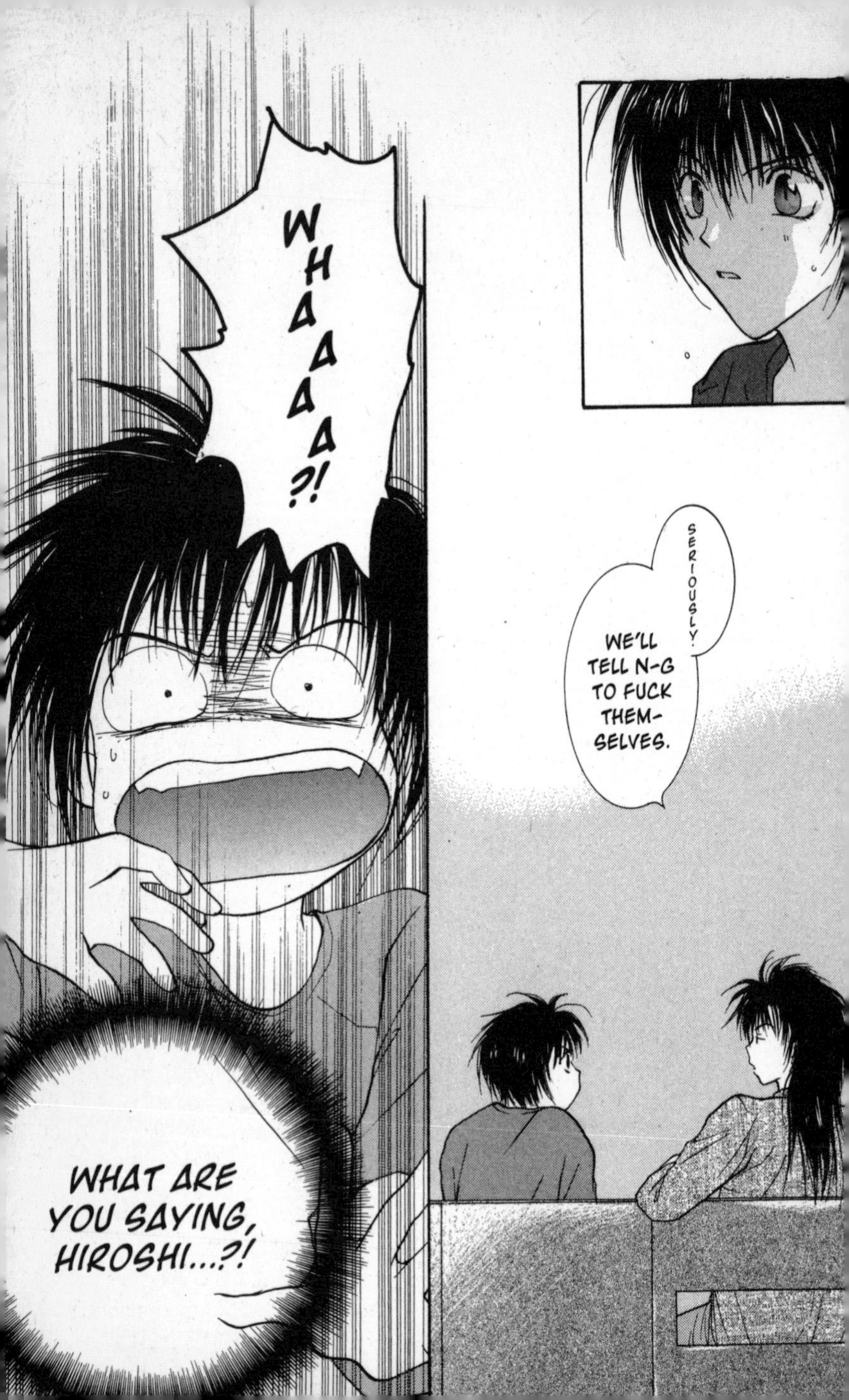
SERIOUSLY. WE'LL TELL N-G TO FUCK THEMSELVES.
WHAAAAA?!
WHAT ARE YOU SAYING, HIROSHI...?!

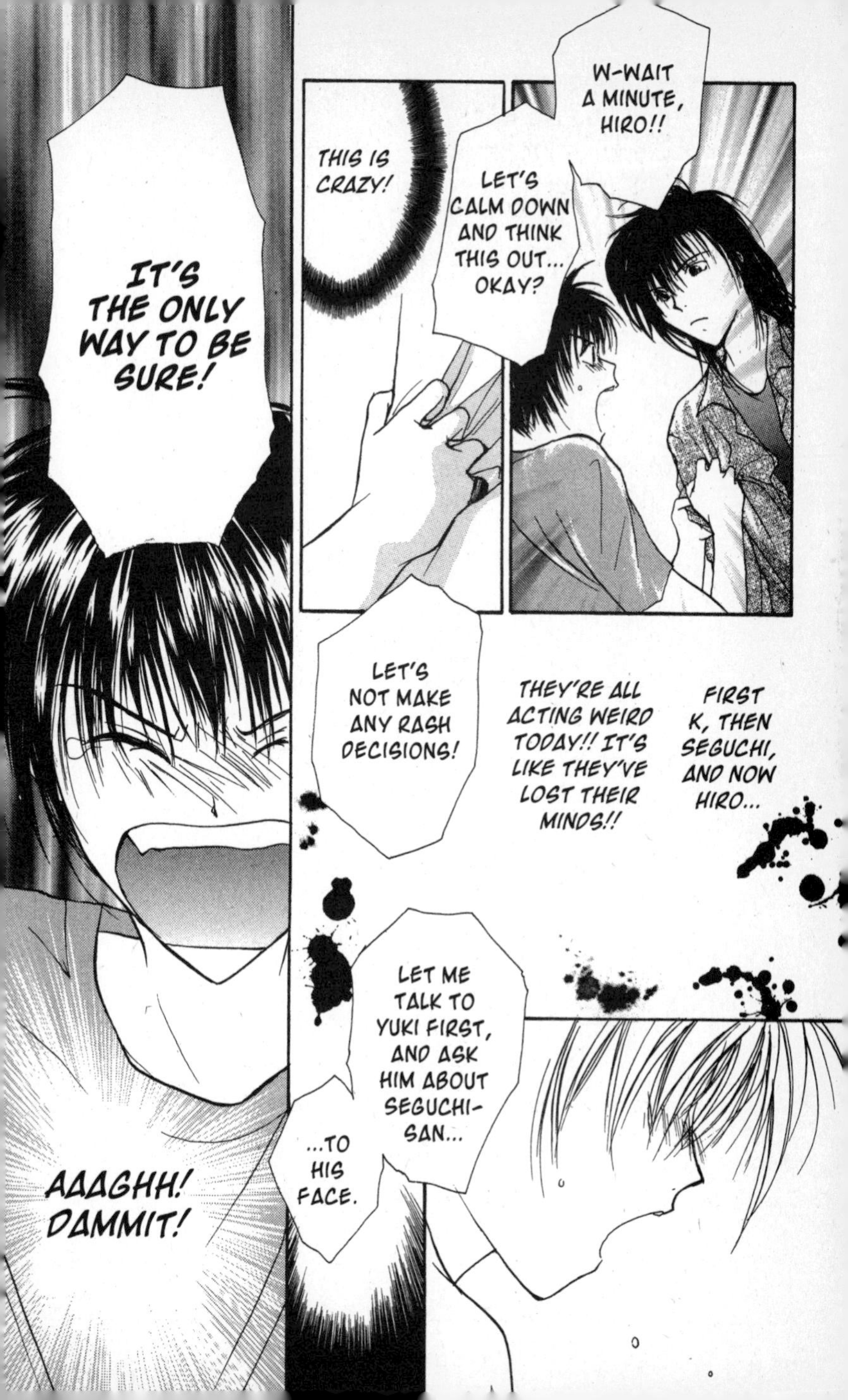
W-WAIT A MINUTE, HIRO!!
LET'S CALM DOWN AND THINK THIS OUT... OKAY?
THIS IS CRAZY!
FIRST K, THEN SEGUCHI, AND NOW HIRO...
THEY'RE ALL ACTING WEIRD TODAY!! IT'S LIKE THEY'VE LOST THEIR MINDS!!
LET'S NOT MAKE ANY RASH DECISIONS!
LET ME TALK TO YUKI FIRST, AND ASK HIM ABOUT SEGUCHI-SAN...
...TO HIS FACE.
IT'S THE ONLY WAY TO BE SURE!
AAAGHH! DAMMIT!

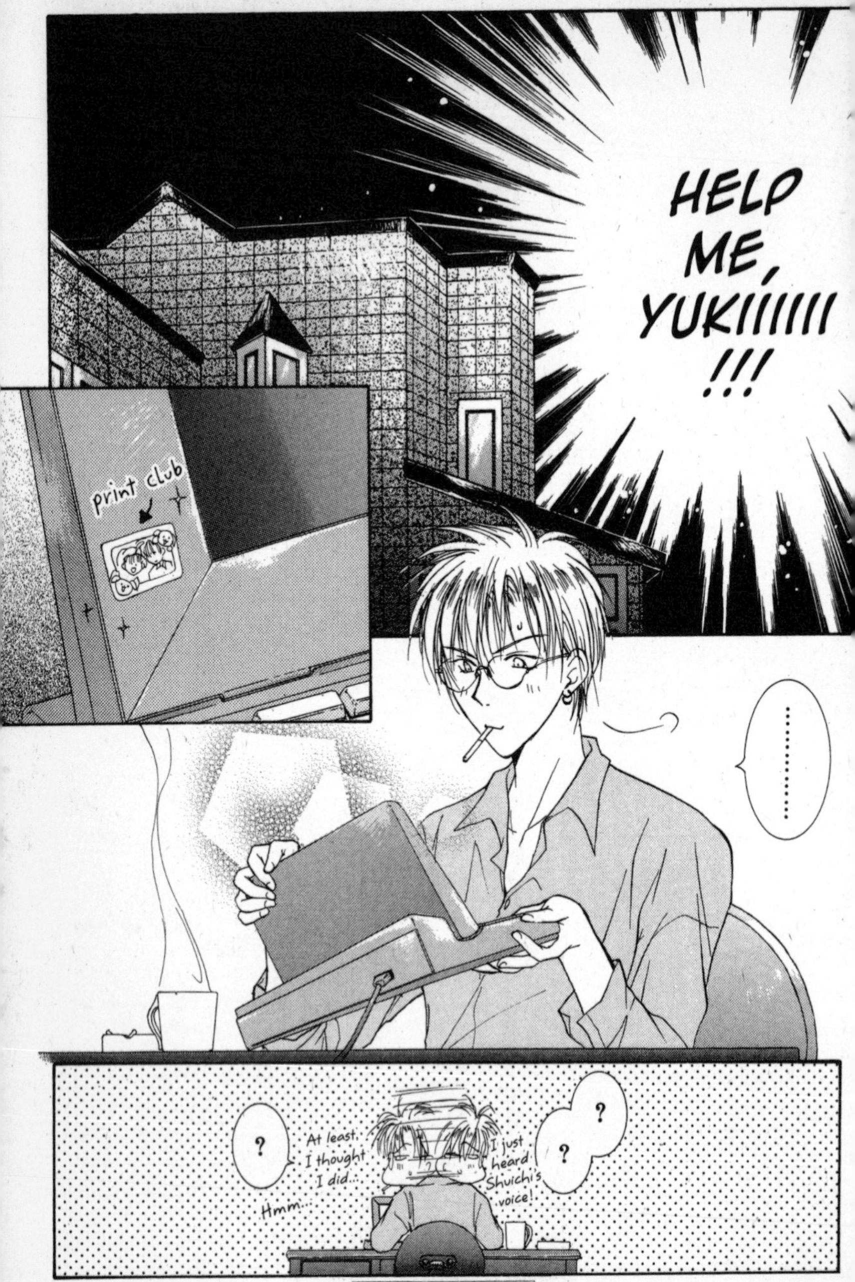
HELP ME, YUKIIIIIII!!!
print club
....
? ?
I just heard Shuichi's voice!
At least, I thought I did...
Hmm...
?

track32 ▶ END

As is our tradition (for the second time)!!
Piles upon piles of comments from
our readers (well, four at least)!
No, I mean five!

Okay, let's call it what it is. This is the secretly popular "monologues of why I love *Gravitation* by people who just happened to be standing nearby" page. Which means I was a most ungracious host and cruelly bugged the people who happened to be hanging out at my house. Thank you very much for putting up with me!

So, anyway, I'll start with the first person, and give her this whole page, with the others getting their own comments pages later on, complete with illustrations, SCATTERED throughout this manga volume. Please take the time to look for them. You might find a Want Ad or two, as well. I really need assistants. Well, ha-ha-ha!! Welcome back, my faithful readers!

By now you may have started to sense that the young lady below has more talent than I do without even trying!!

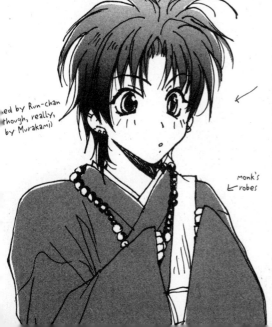

...ed by Run-chan though, really, by Murakami)

monk's
← robes

The person in this illustration is Tatsuha-kun, who isn't scheduled to appear in Volume 8 at all.

Murakami-san, you need to stop screaming strange noises and seducing your assistants when deadlines are close. It scares us. And also, you need to stop threatening to go back North whenever things get hairy. And please, stop singing "Gyan" whenever you hear the little kid running around upstairs. Someone's going to call the police one of these days. And please, don't say "shit" all the time. Otherwise, you're doing a swell job!

Gravitation

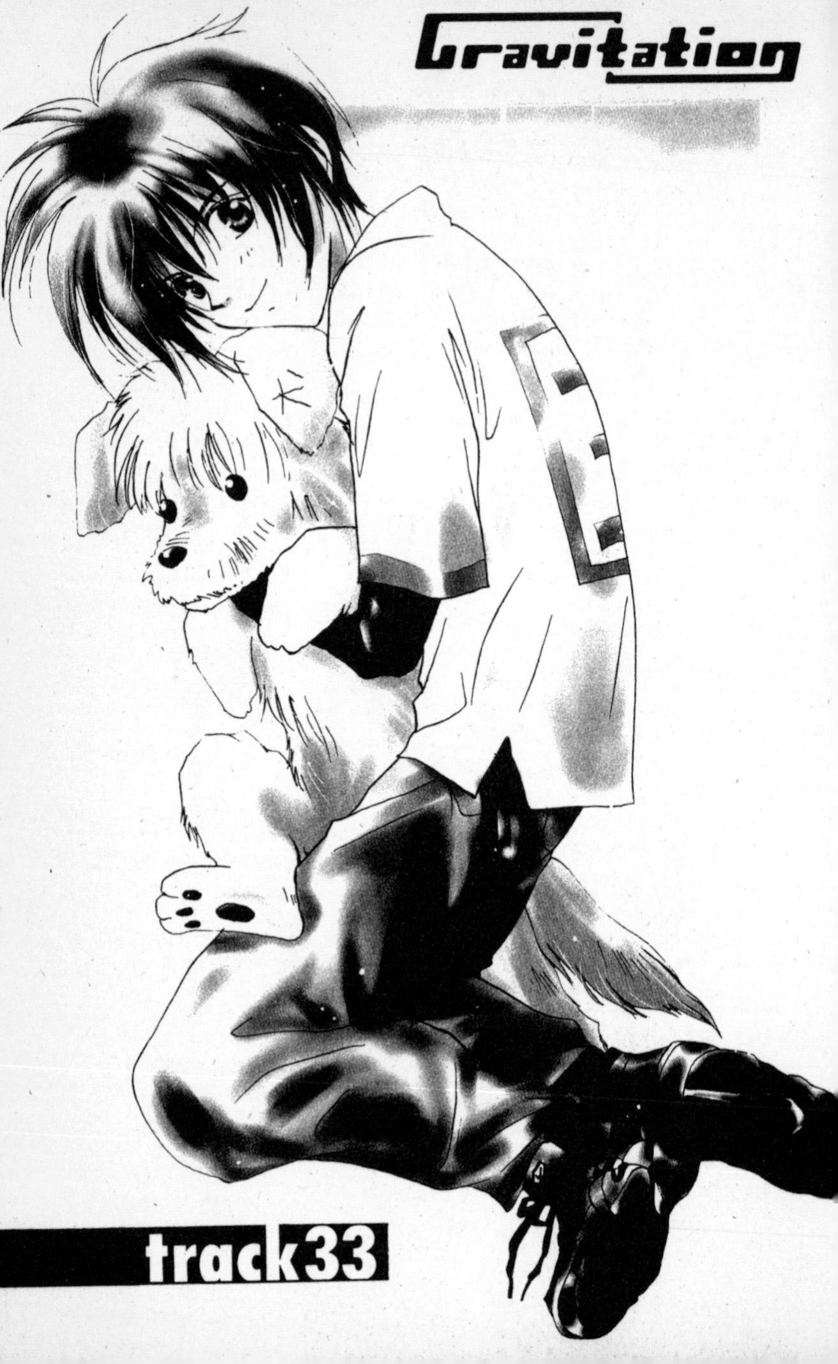

track 33

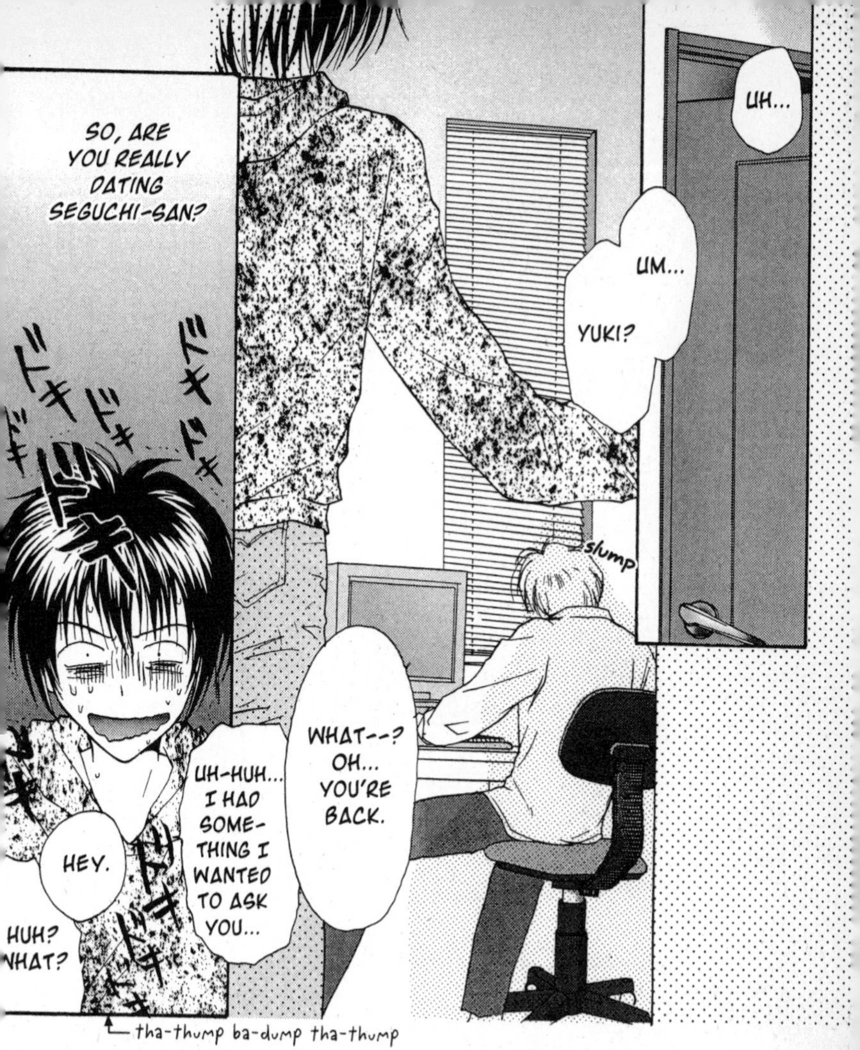
UH...
UM... YUKI?
slump
WHAT--? OH... YOU'RE BACK.
UH-HUH... I HAD SOMETHING I WANTED TO ASK YOU...
SO, ARE YOU REALLY DATING SEGUCHI-SAN?
HEY.
HUH? WHAT?
tha-thump ba-dump tha-thump

ABOUT GRAVITATION TRACK 33

During Track 32, I got sick and had to take time off twice. I'm very sorry for inconveniencing so many people. So, anyway, about Track 33, it's rather modest, and may not be all that intense, so some of you may find it boring. In the next chapters, I rev up the tension again, but to say it would be interesting just because I jacked up the tension--well, I don't know. Anyway, it doesn't really matter, but in the above panel, Shuichi sure does have a long head.

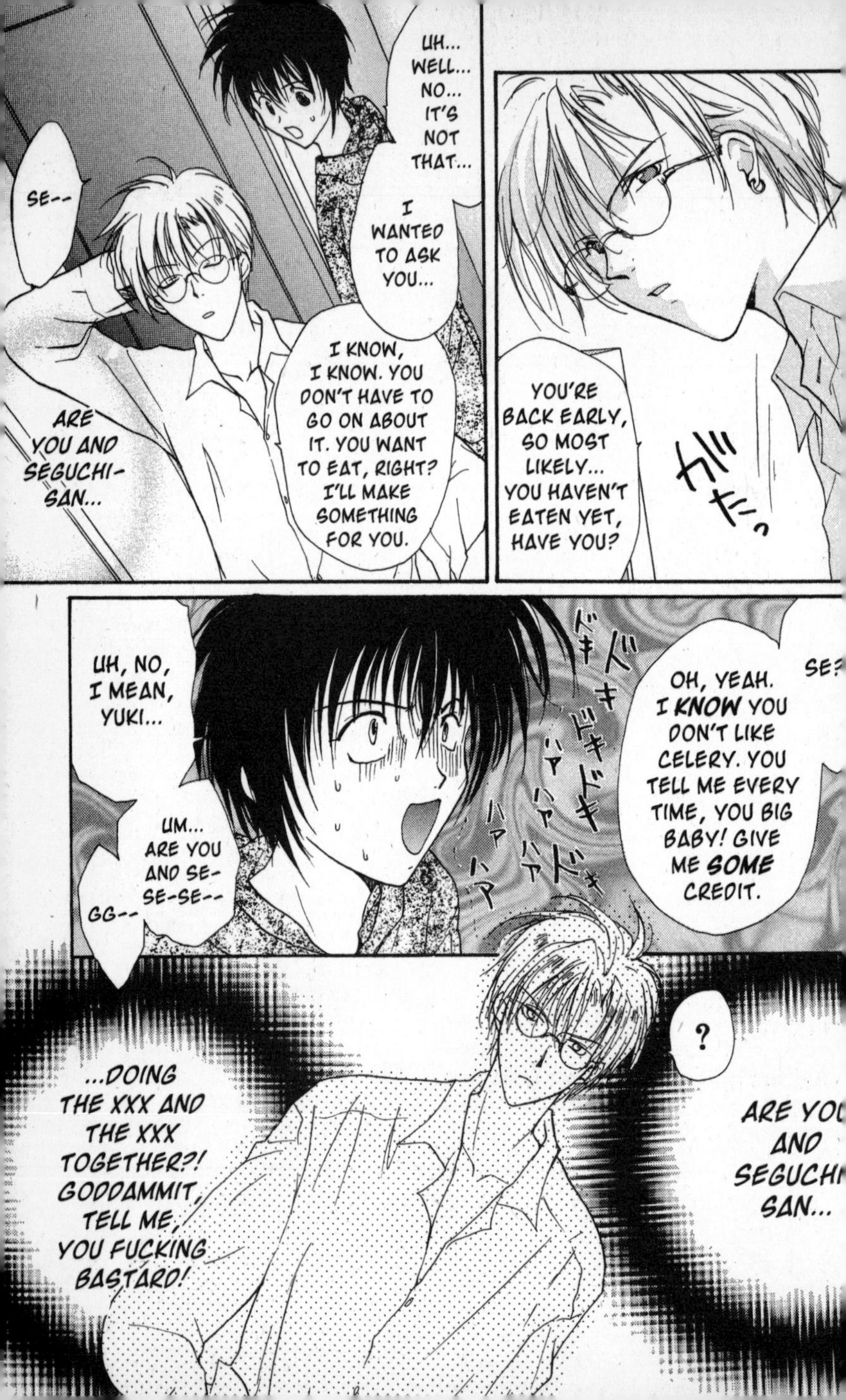
YOU'RE BACK EARLY, SO MOST LIKELY... YOU HAVEN'T EATEN YET, HAVE YOU?
UH... WELL... NO... IT'S NOT THAT...
I WANTED TO ASK YOU...
I KNOW, I KNOW. YOU DON'T HAVE TO GO ON ABOUT IT. YOU WANT TO EAT, RIGHT? I'LL MAKE SOMETHING FOR YOU.
SE--
ARE YOU AND SEGUCHI-SAN...
SE?!
OH, YEAH. I *KNOW* YOU DON'T LIKE CELERY. YOU TELL ME EVERY TIME, YOU BIG BABY! GIVE ME *SOME* CREDIT.
UH, NO, I MEAN, YUKI...
UM... ARE YOU AND SE-SE-SE-SE--GG--
?
ARE YOU AND SEGUCHI SAN...
...DOING THE XXX AND THE XXX TOGETHER?! GODDAMMIT, TELL ME, YOU FUCKING BASTARD!

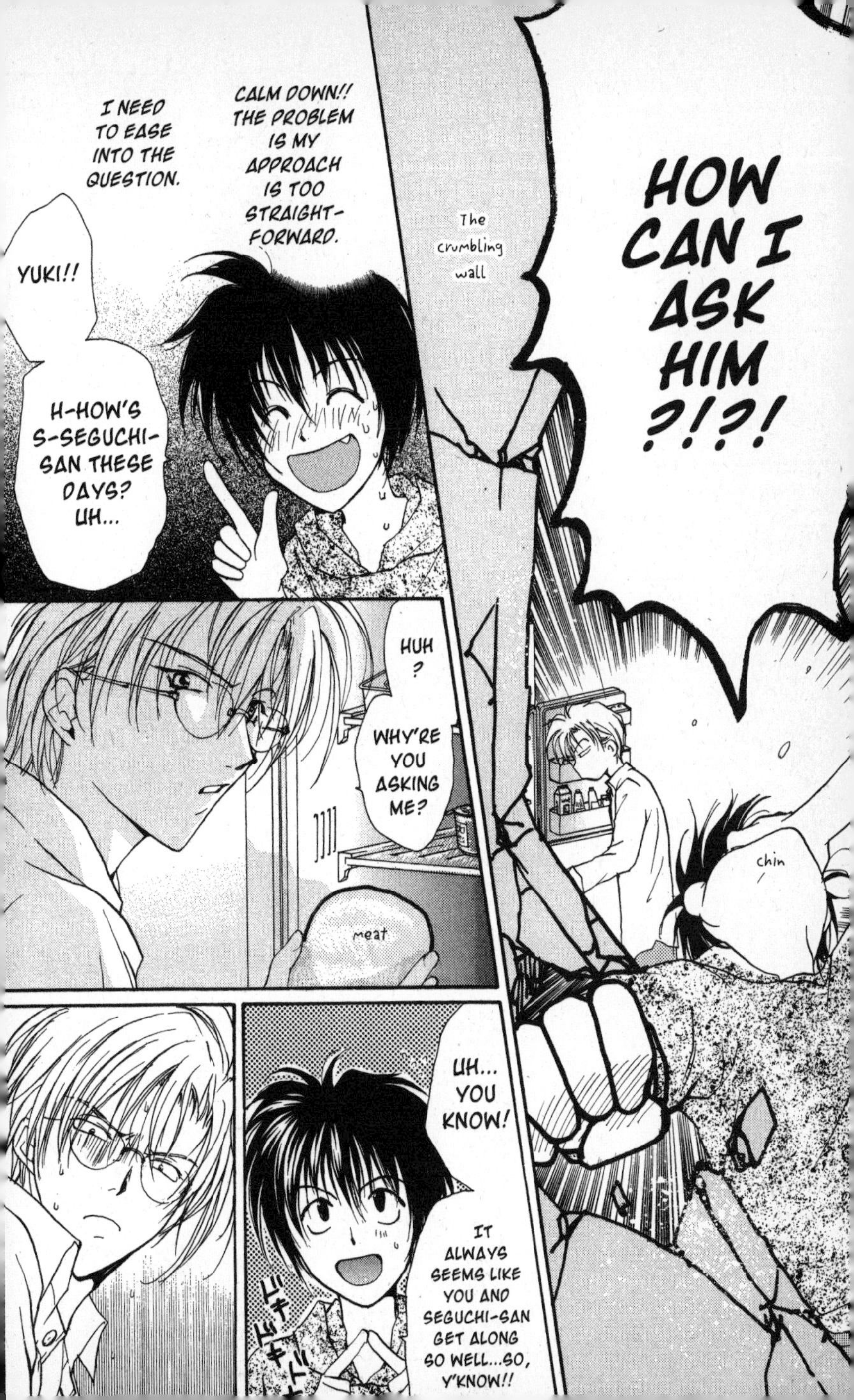
HOW CAN I ASK HIM?!?!
The crumbling wall
chin
CALM DOWN!! THE PROBLEM IS MY APPROACH IS TOO STRAIGHT-FORWARD.
I NEED TO EASE INTO THE QUESTION.
YUKI!!
H-HOW'S S-SEGUCHI-SAN THESE DAYS? UH...
HUH?
WHY'RE YOU ASKING ME?
meat
UH... YOU KNOW!
IT ALWAYS SEEMS LIKE YOU AND SEGUCHI-SAN GET ALONG SO WELL...SO, Y'KNOW!!

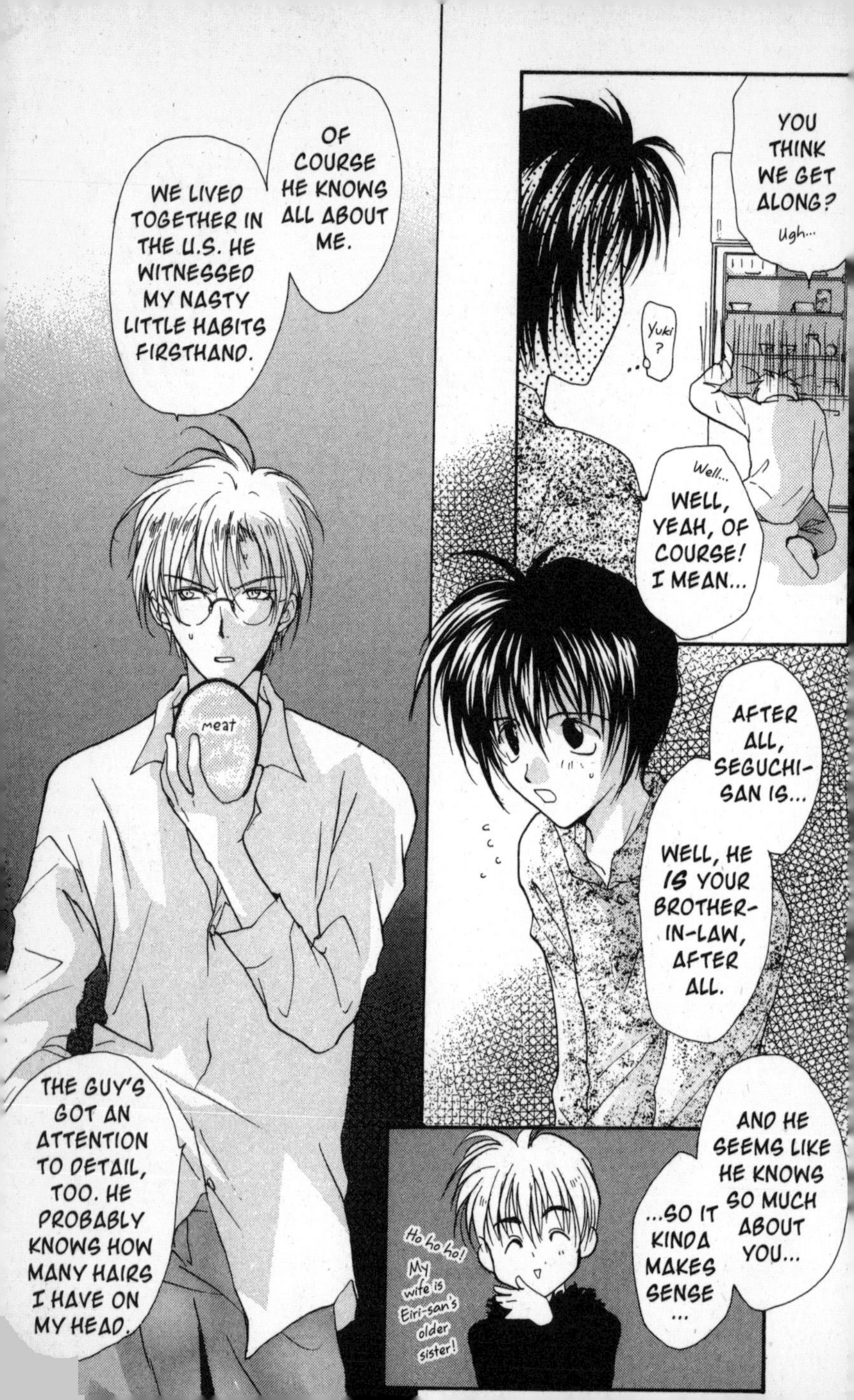
YOU THINK WE GET ALONG?
Ugh...
Yuki?
Well...
WELL, YEAH, OF COURSE! I MEAN...
AFTER ALL, SEGUCHI-SAN IS...
WELL, HE IS YOUR BROTHER-IN-LAW, AFTER ALL.
AND HE SEEMS LIKE HE KNOWS SO MUCH ABOUT YOU...
...SO IT KINDA MAKES SENSE...
Ho ho ho! My wife is Eiri-san's older sister!
OF COURSE HE KNOWS ALL ABOUT ME.
WE LIVED TOGETHER IN THE U.S. HE WITNESSED MY NASTY LITTLE HABITS FIRSTHAND.
meat
THE GUY'S GOT AN ATTENTION TO DETAIL, TOO. HE PROBABLY KNOWS HOW MANY HAIRS I HAVE ON MY HEAD.

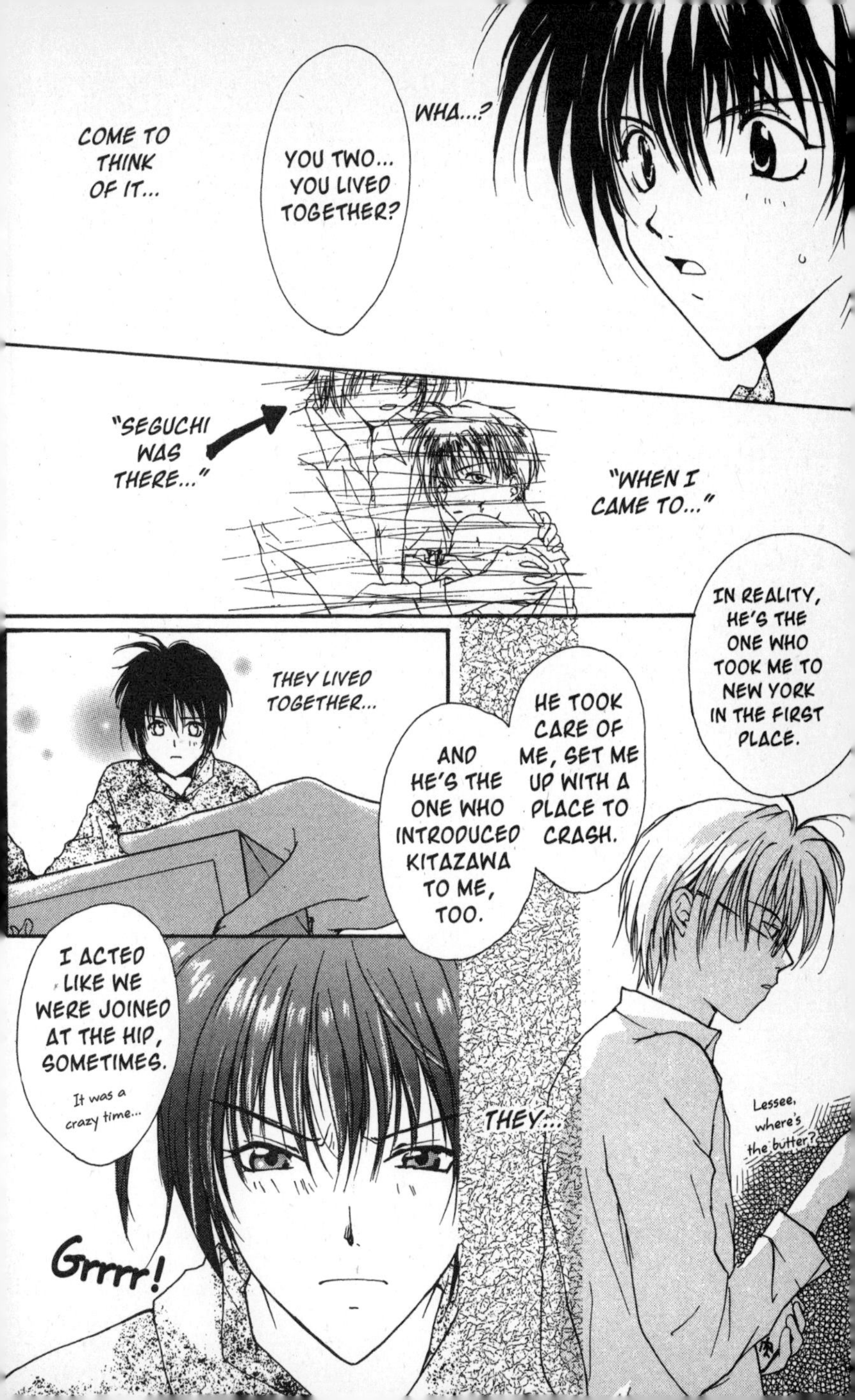
WHA...?
YOU TWO... YOU LIVED TOGETHER?
COME TO THINK OF IT...
"WHEN I CAME TO..."
"SEGUCHI WAS THERE..."
IN REALITY, HE'S THE ONE WHO TOOK ME TO NEW YORK IN THE FIRST PLACE.
HE TOOK CARE OF ME, SET ME UP WITH A PLACE TO CRASH.
AND HE'S THE ONE WHO INTRODUCED KITAZAWA TO ME, TOO.
Lessee, where's the butter?
THEY LIVED TOGETHER...
THEY...
I ACTED LIKE WE WERE JOINED AT THE HIP, SOMETIMES.
It was a crazy time...
Grrrr!

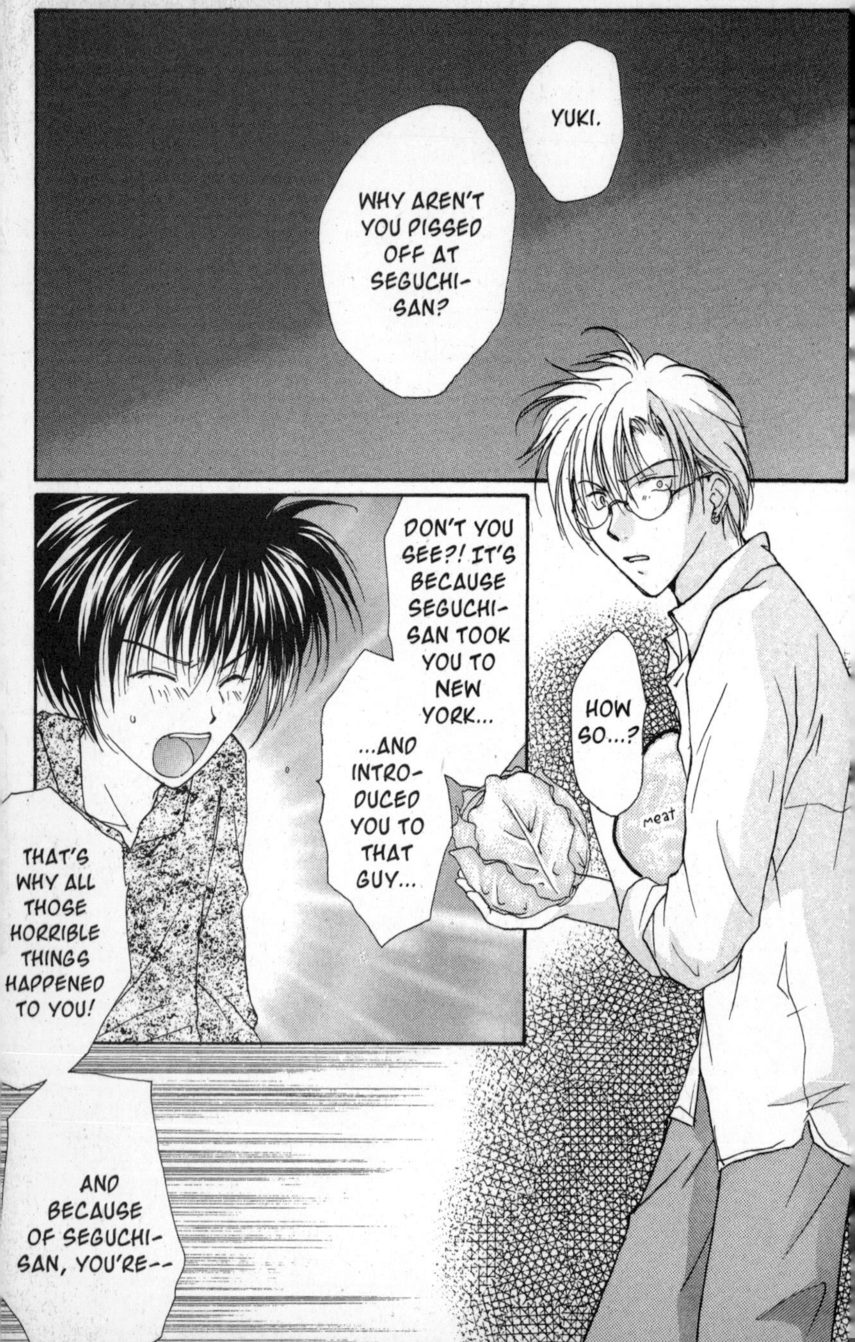
YUKI.
WHY AREN'T YOU PISSED OFF AT SEGUCHI-SAN?
HOW SO...?
meat
DON'T YOU SEE?! IT'S BECAUSE SEGUCHI-SAN TOOK YOU TO NEW YORK...
...AND INTRODUCED YOU TO THAT GUY...
THAT'S WHY ALL THOSE HORRIBLE THINGS HAPPENED TO YOU!
AND BECAUSE OF SEGUCHI-SAN, YOU'RE--

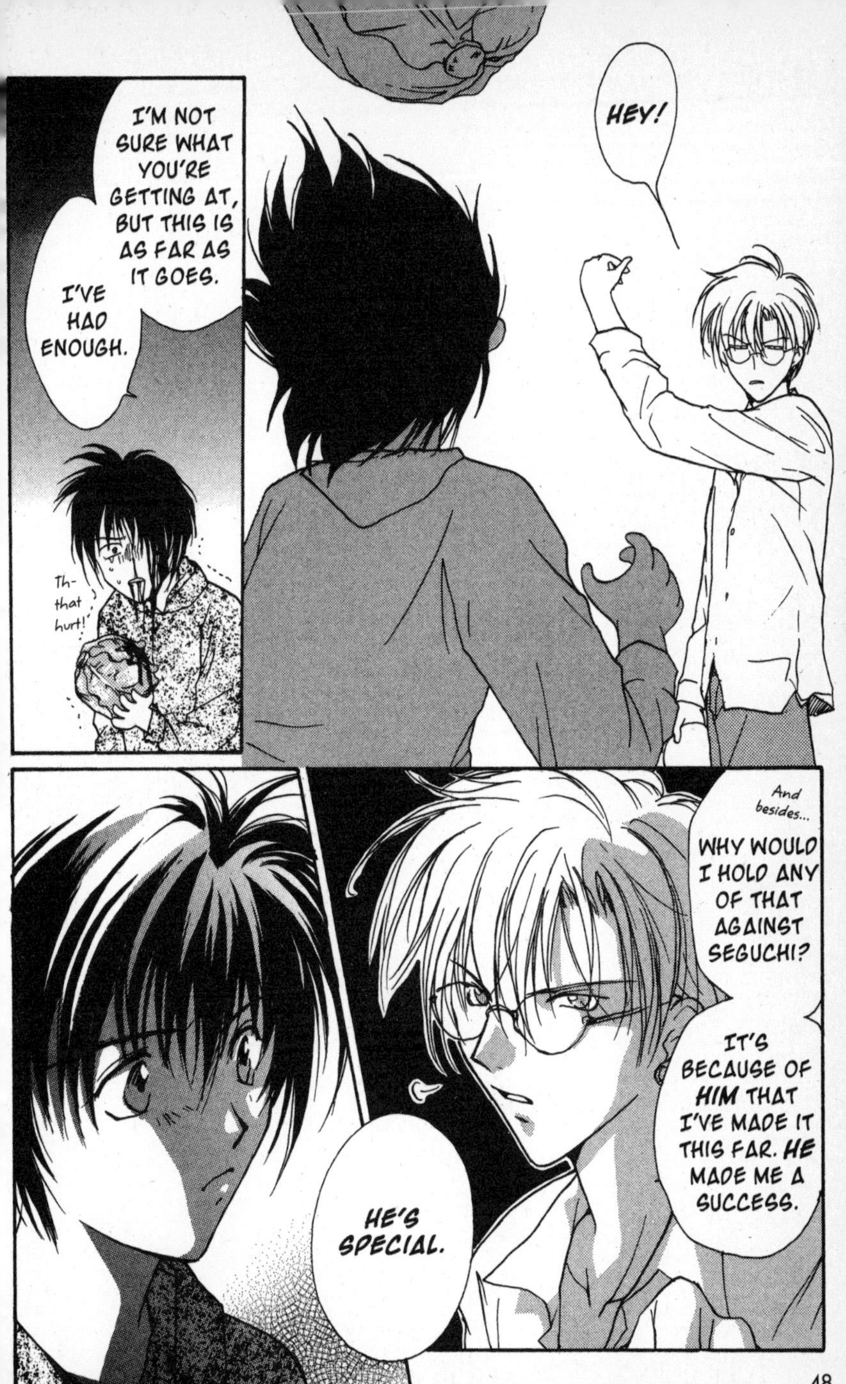
HEY!
I'M NOT SURE WHAT YOU'RE GETTING AT, BUT THIS IS AS FAR AS IT GOES.
I'VE HAD ENOUGH.
Th-that hurt!
And besides...
WHY WOULD I HOLD ANY OF THAT AGAINST SEGUCHI?
IT'S BECAUSE OF HIM THAT I'VE MADE IT THIS FAR. HE MADE ME A SUCCESS.
HE'S SPECIAL.

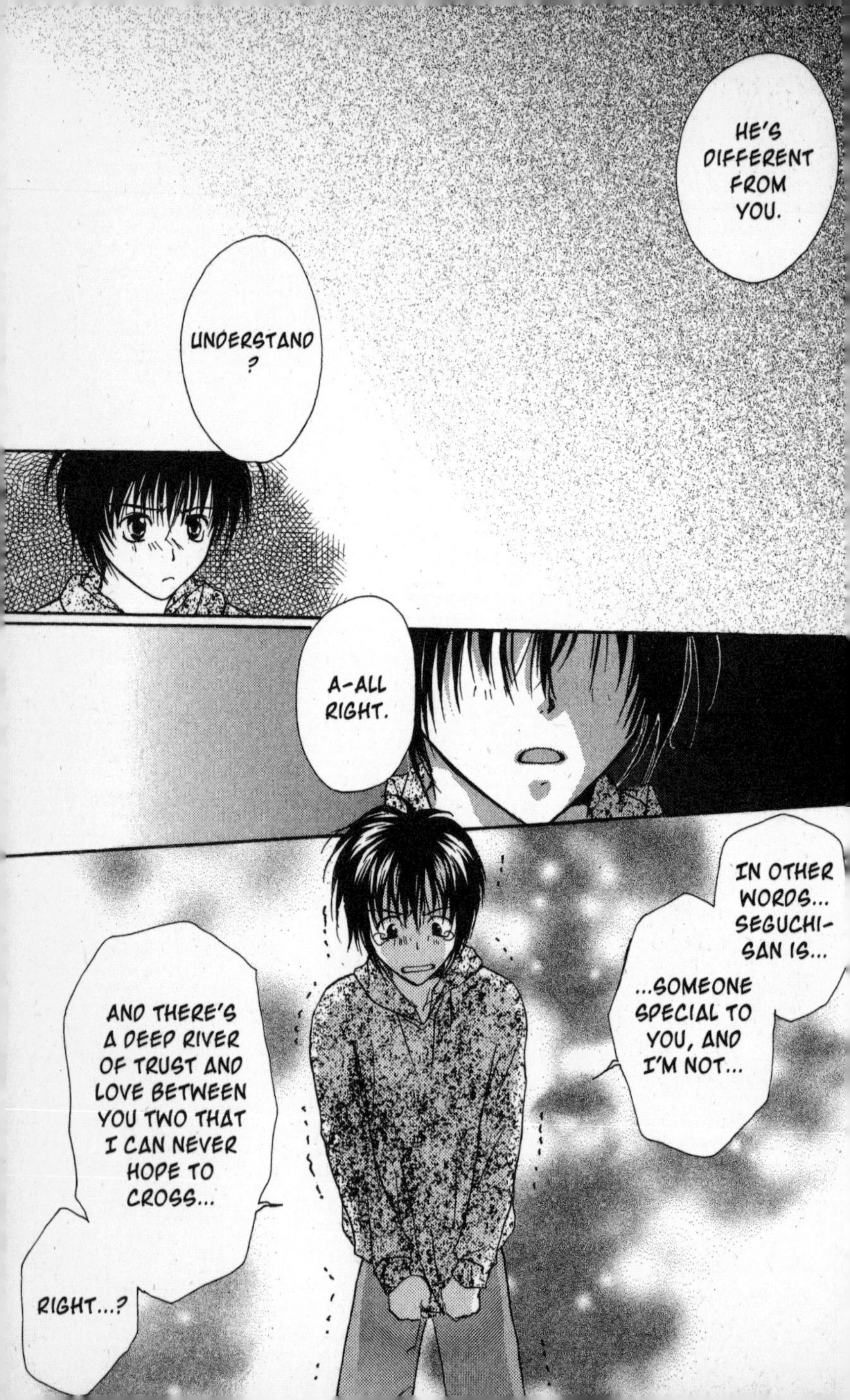
HE'S DIFFERENT FROM YOU.
UNDERSTAND ?
A-ALL RIGHT.
IN OTHER WORDS... SEGUCHI-SAN IS...
...SOMEONE SPECIAL TO YOU, AND I'M NOT...
AND THERE'S A DEEP RIVER OF TRUST AND LOVE BETWEEN YOU TWO THAT I CAN NEVER HOPE TO CROSS...
RIGHT...?

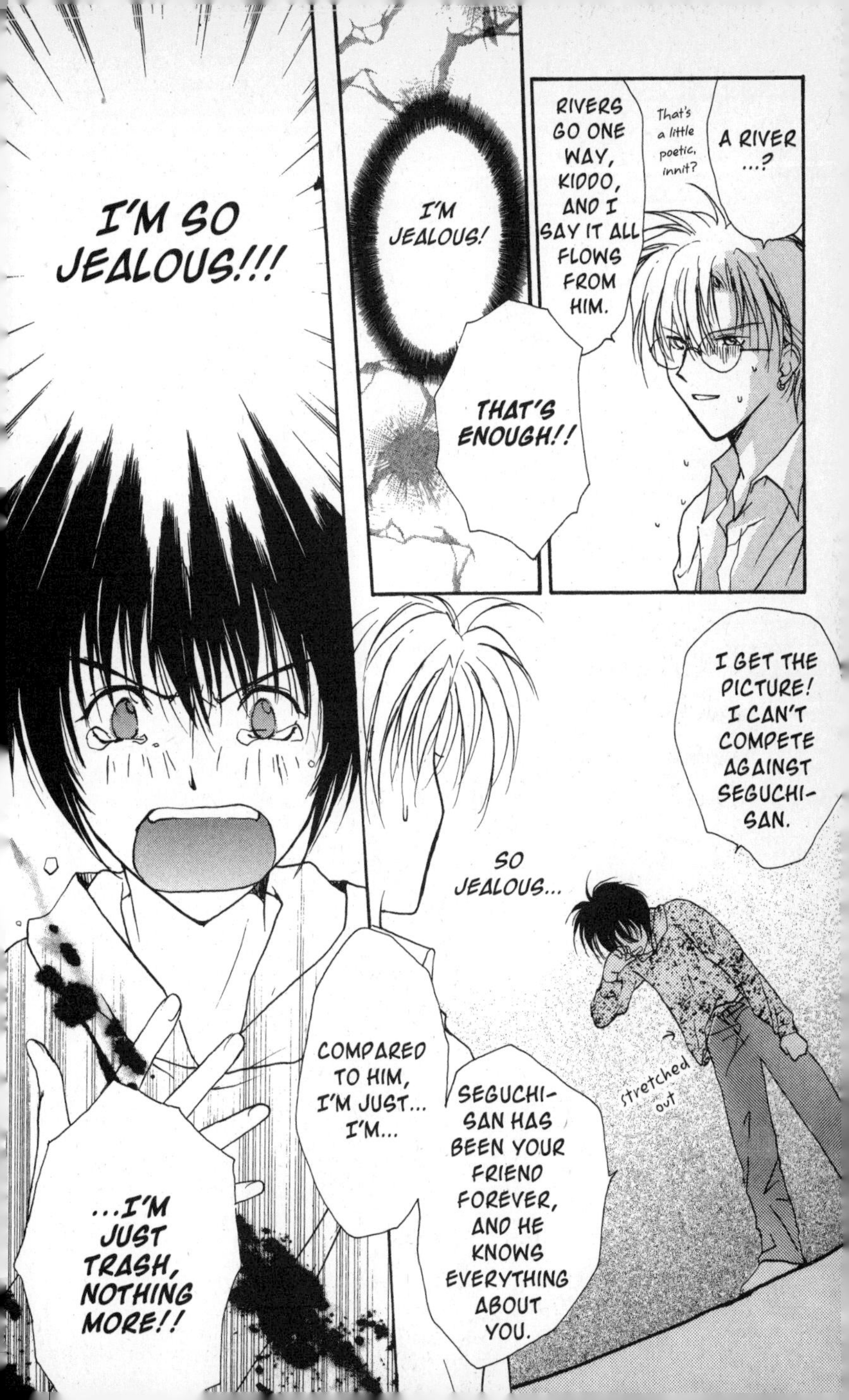
A RIVER ...?
That's a little poetic, innit?
RIVERS GO ONE WAY, KIDDO, AND I SAY IT ALL FLOWS FROM HIM.
I'M JEALOUS!
THAT'S ENOUGH!!
I GET THE PICTURE! I CAN'T COMPETE AGAINST SEGUCHI-SAN.
SO JEALOUS...
stretched out
SEGUCHI-SAN HAS BEEN YOUR FRIEND FOREVER, AND HE KNOWS EVERYTHING ABOUT YOU.
COMPARED TO HIM, I'M JUST... I'M...
I'M SO JEALOUS!!!
...I'M JUST TRASH, NOTHING MORE!!

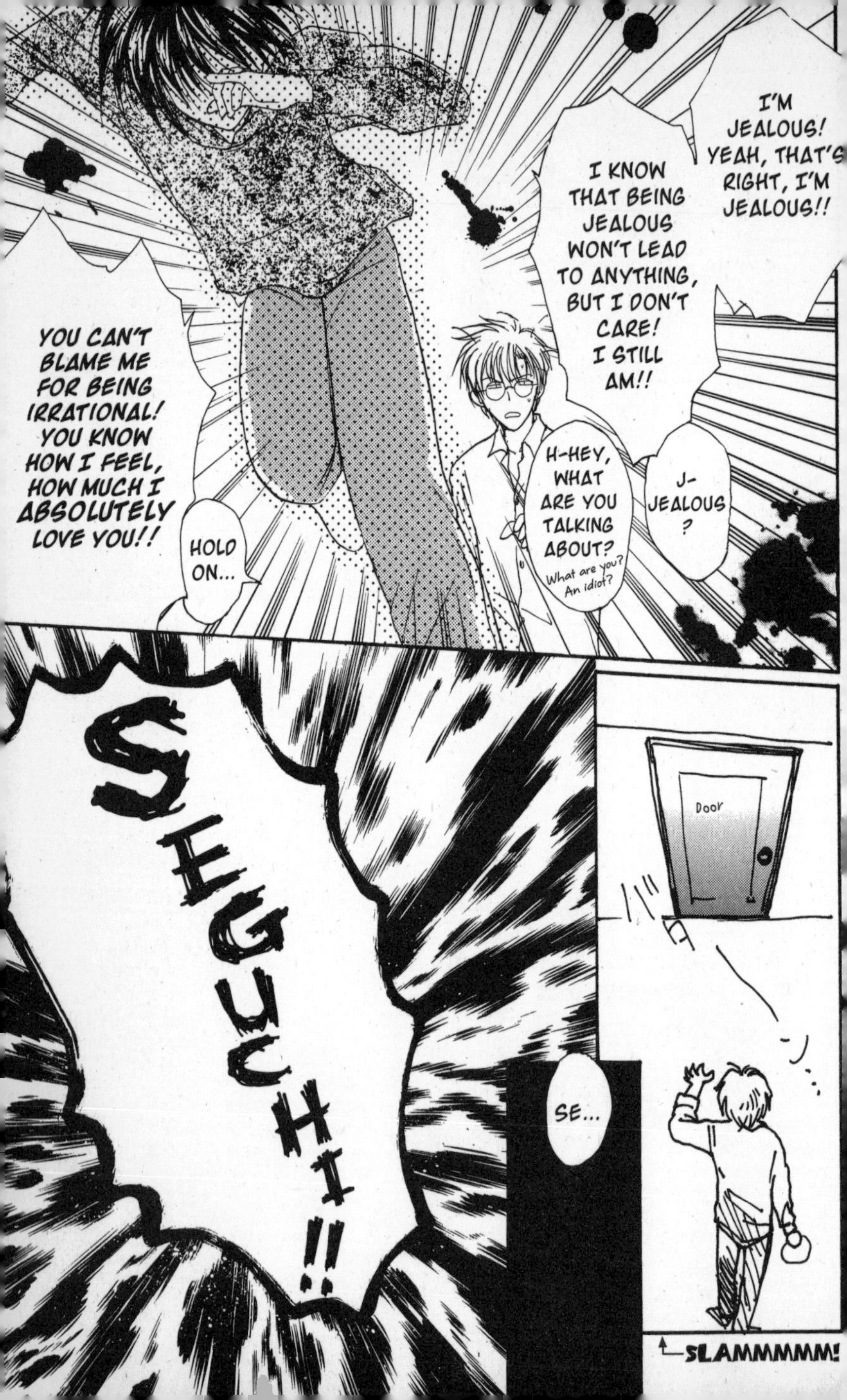
I'M JEALOUS! YEAH, THAT'S RIGHT, I'M JEALOUS!!
I KNOW THAT BEING JEALOUS WON'T LEAD TO ANYTHING, BUT I DON'T CARE! I STILL AM!!
J-JEALOUS?
H-HEY, WHAT ARE YOU TALKING ABOUT?
What are you? An idiot?
YOU CAN'T BLAME ME FOR BEING IRRATIONAL! YOU KNOW HOW I FEEL, HOW MUCH I ABSOLUTELY LOVE YOU!!
HOLD ON...
Door
SLAMMMMM!
SE...
SEGUCHI!!

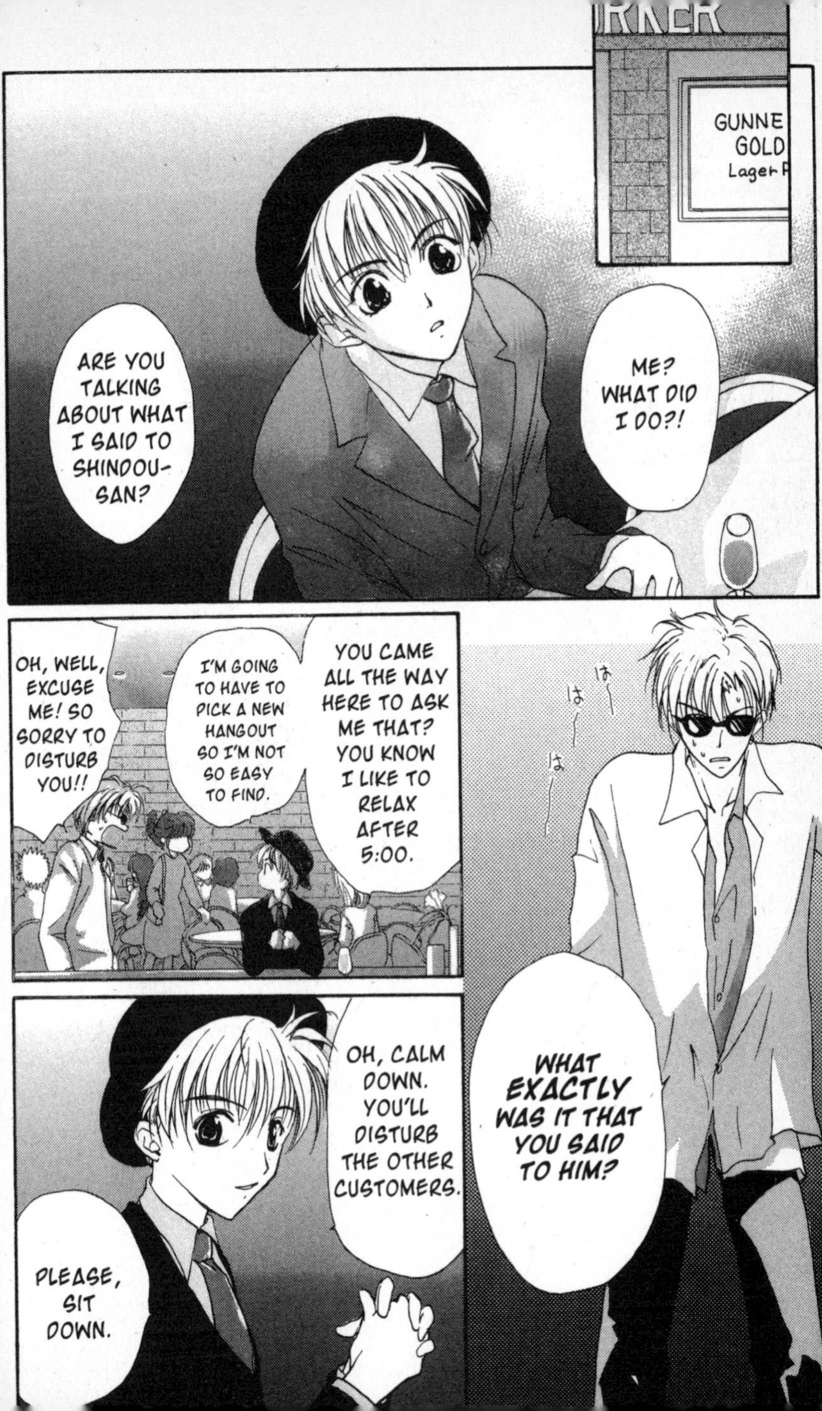
GUNNE
GOLD
Lager
ME? WHAT DID I DO?!
ARE YOU TALKING ABOUT WHAT I SAID TO SHINDOU-SAN?
は～は～は～
WHAT EXACTLY WAS IT THAT YOU SAID TO HIM?
YOU CAME ALL THE WAY HERE TO ASK ME THAT? YOU KNOW I LIKE TO RELAX AFTER 5:00.
I'M GOING TO HAVE TO PICK A NEW HANGOUT SO I'M NOT SO EASY TO FIND.
OH, WELL, EXCUSE ME! SO SORRY TO DISTURB YOU!!
OH, CALM DOWN. YOU'LL DISTURB THE OTHER CUSTOMERS.
PLEASE, SIT DOWN.

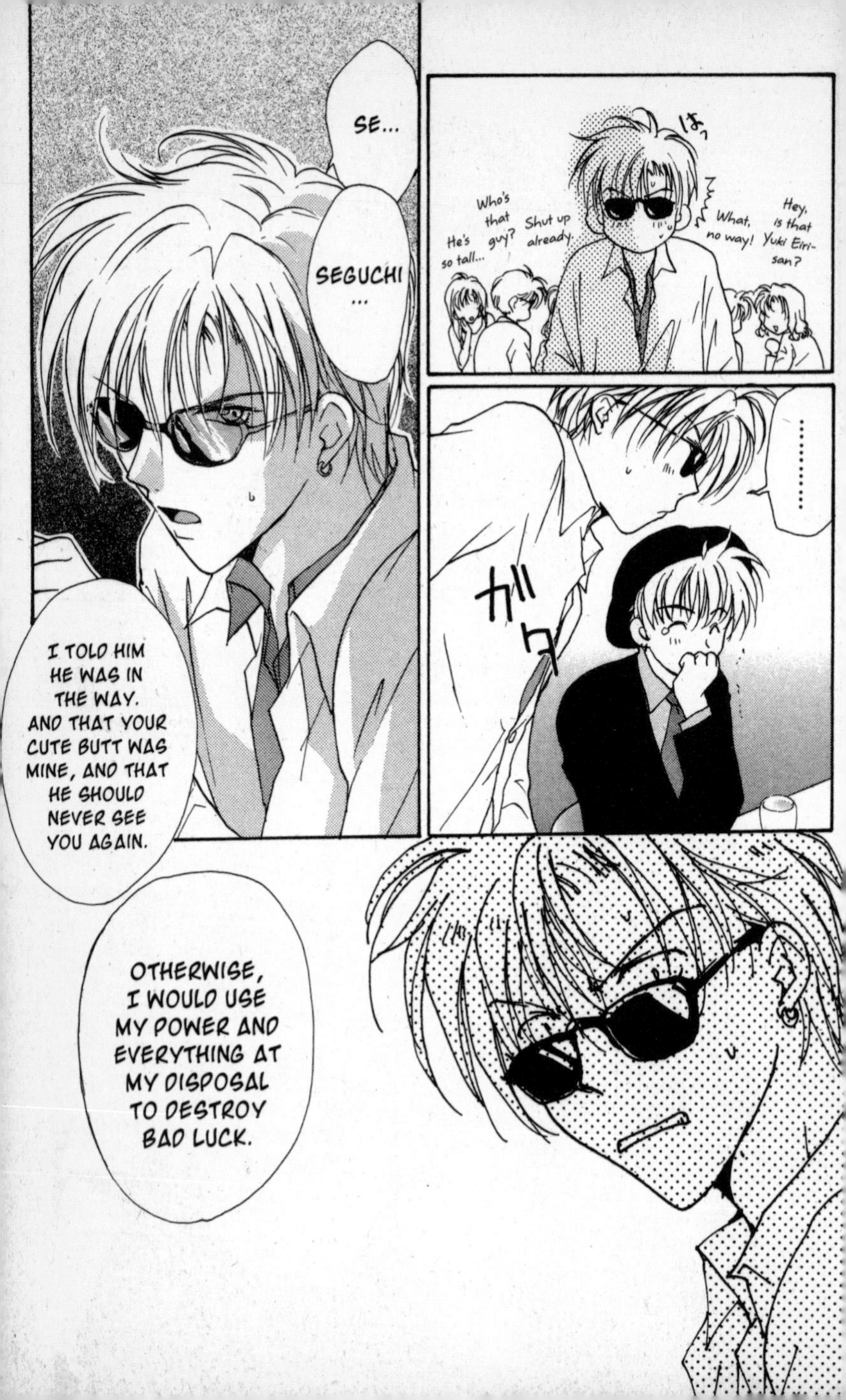
はっ
Hey, is that Yuki Eiri-san?
What, no way!
Shut up already.
Who's that guy?
He's so tall...
......
ガク
SE...
SEGUCHI...
I TOLD HIM HE WAS IN THE WAY. AND THAT YOUR CUTE BUTT WAS MINE, AND THAT HE SHOULD NEVER SEE YOU AGAIN.
OTHERWISE, I WOULD USE MY POWER AND EVERYTHING AT MY DISPOSAL TO DESTROY BAD LUCK.

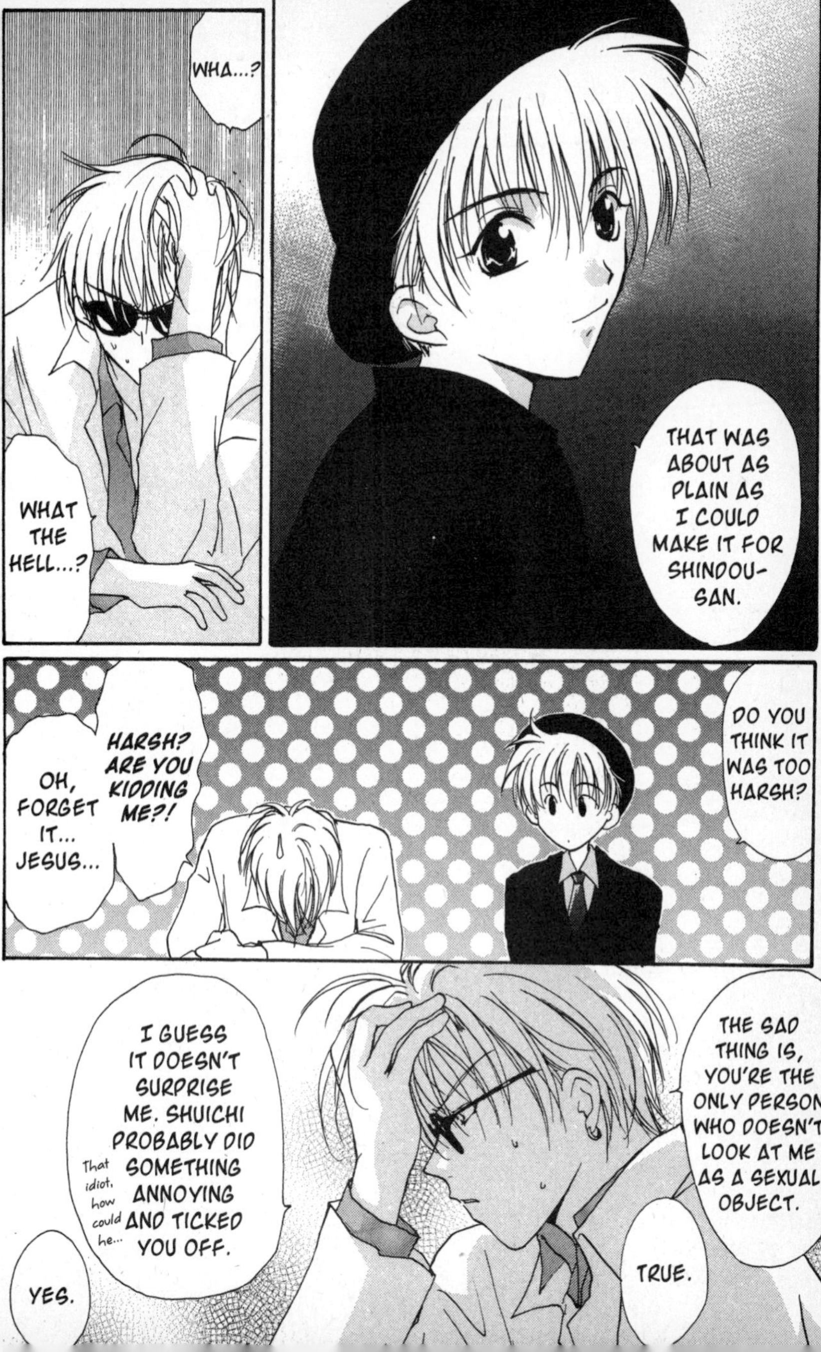
THAT WAS ABOUT AS PLAIN AS I COULD MAKE IT FOR SHINDOU-SAN.
WHA...?
WHAT THE HELL...?
DO YOU THINK IT WAS TOO HARSH?
HARSH? ARE YOU KIDDING ME?!
OH, FORGET IT... JESUS...
THE SAD THING IS, YOU'RE THE ONLY PERSON WHO DOESN'T LOOK AT ME AS A SEXUAL OBJECT.
TRUE.
I GUESS IT DOESN'T SURPRISE ME. SHUICHI PROBABLY DID SOMETHING ANNOYING AND TICKED YOU OFF.
That idiot, how could he...
YES.

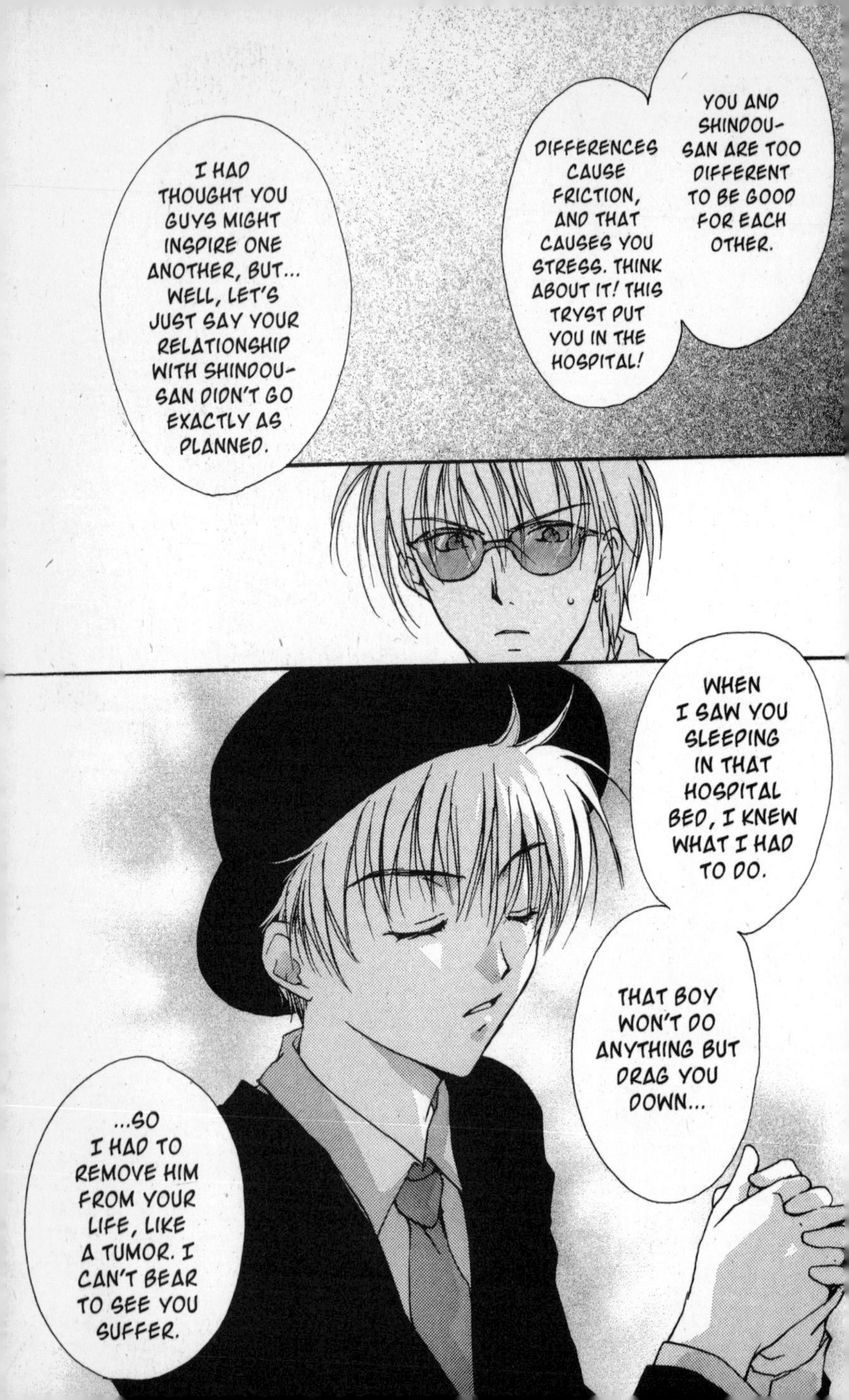
YOU AND SHINDOU-SAN ARE TOO DIFFERENT TO BE GOOD FOR EACH OTHER.
DIFFERENCES CAUSE FRICTION, AND THAT CAUSES YOU STRESS. THINK ABOUT IT! THIS TRYST PUT YOU IN THE HOSPITAL!
I HAD THOUGHT YOU GUYS MIGHT INSPIRE ONE ANOTHER, BUT... WELL, LET'S JUST SAY YOUR RELATIONSHIP WITH SHINDOU-SAN DIDN'T GO EXACTLY AS PLANNED.
WHEN I SAW YOU SLEEPING IN THAT HOSPITAL BED, I KNEW WHAT I HAD TO DO.
THAT BOY WON'T DO ANYTHING BUT DRAG YOU DOWN...
...SO I HAD TO REMOVE HIM FROM YOUR LIFE, LIKE A TUMOR. I CAN'T BEAR TO SEE YOU SUFFER.

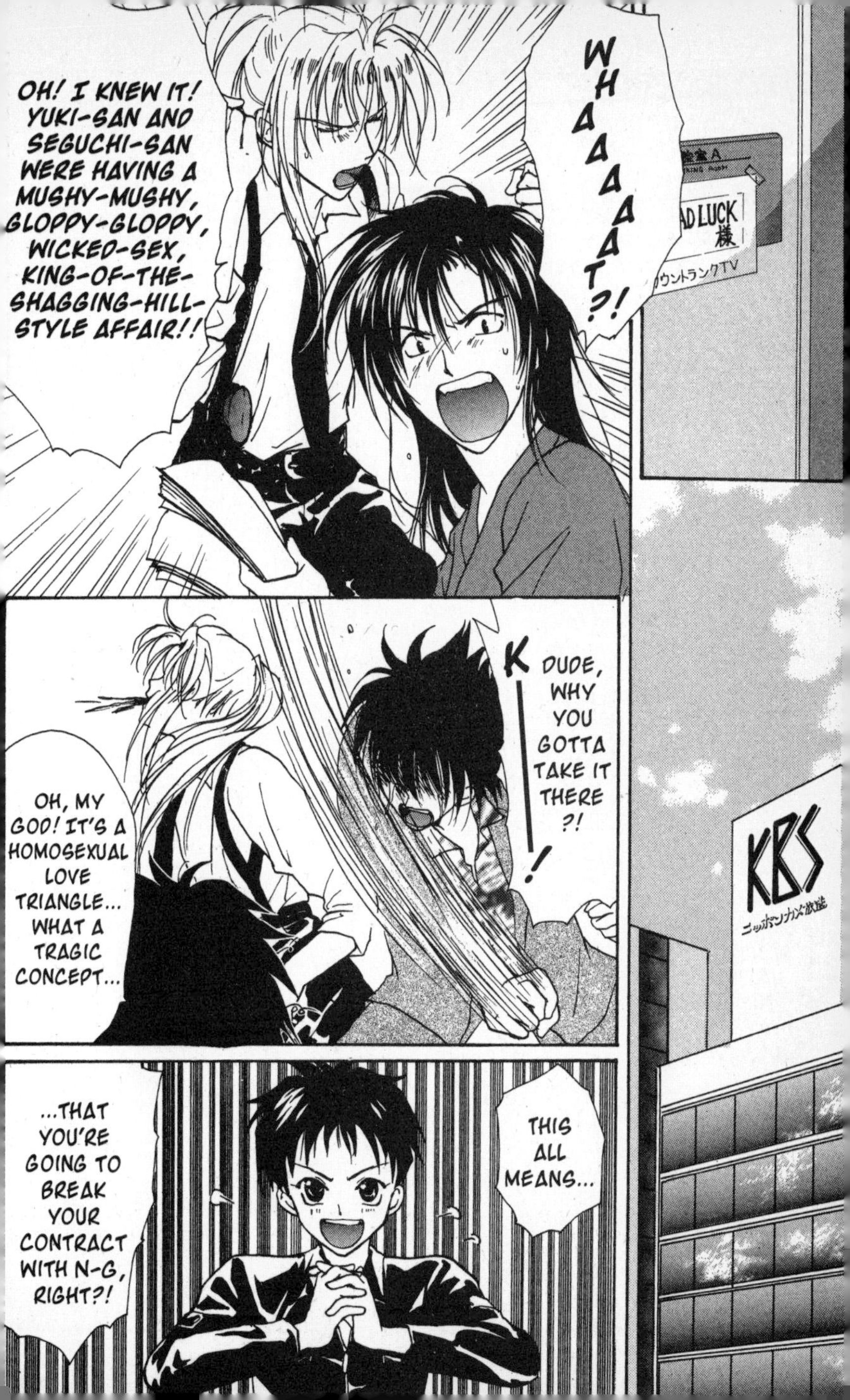
WHAAAAAAT?!
OH! I KNEW IT! YUKI-SAN AND SEGUCHI-SAN WERE HAVING A MUSHY-MUSHY, GLOPPY-GLOPPY, WICKED-SEX, KING-OF-THE-SHAGGING-HILL-STYLE AFFAIR!!
K—!
DUDE, WHY YOU GOTTA TAKE IT THERE?!
OH, MY GOD! IT'S A HOMOSEXUAL LOVE TRIANGLE... WHAT A TRAGIC CONCEPT...
KBS
THIS ALL MEANS...
...THAT YOU'RE GOING TO BREAK YOUR CONTRACT WITH N-G, RIGHT?!

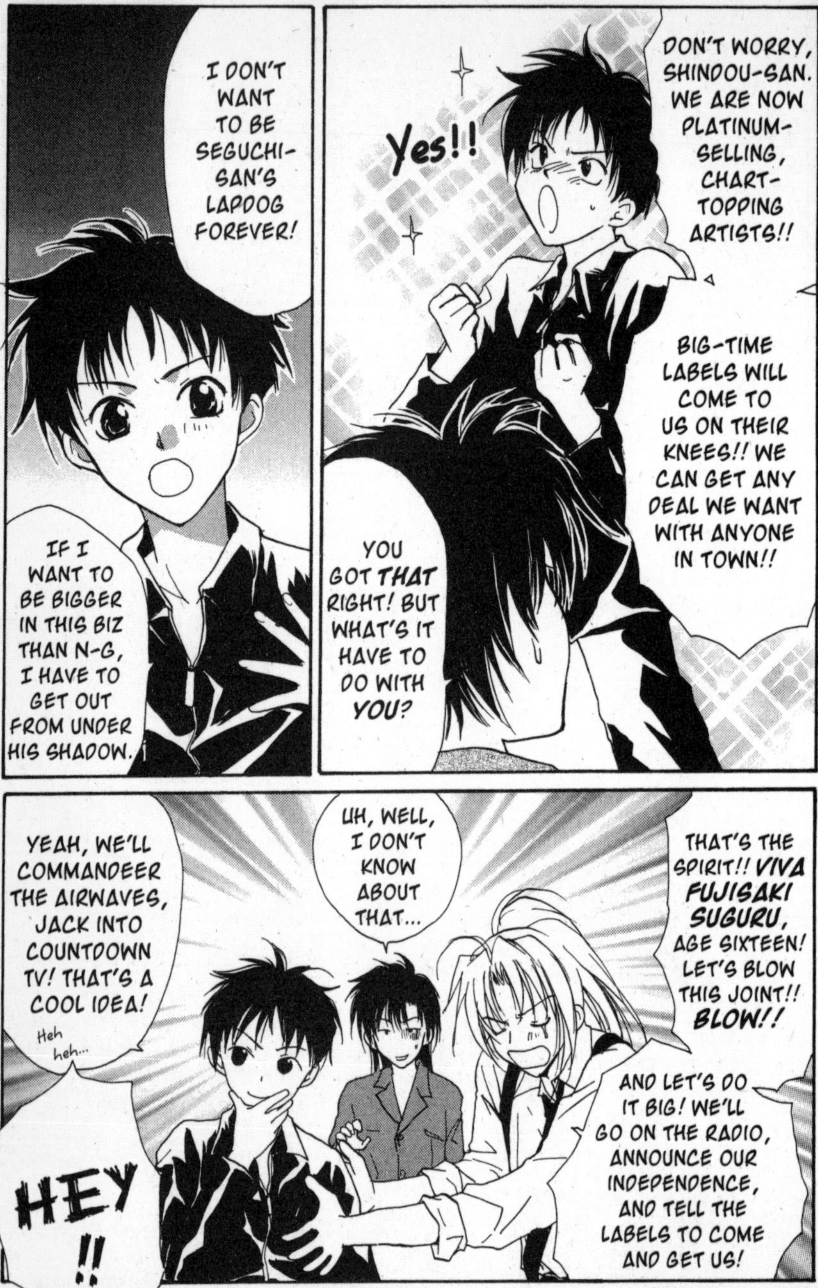
Yes!!
DON'T WORRY, SHINDOU-SAN. WE ARE NOW PLATINUM-SELLING, CHART-TOPPING ARTISTS!!
BIG-TIME LABELS WILL COME TO US ON THEIR KNEES!! WE CAN GET ANY DEAL WE WANT WITH ANYONE IN TOWN!!
YOU GOT THAT RIGHT! BUT WHAT'S IT HAVE TO DO WITH YOU?
I DON'T WANT TO BE SEGUCHI-SAN'S LAPDOG FOREVER!
IF I WANT TO BE BIGGER IN THIS BIZ THAN N-G, I HAVE TO GET OUT FROM UNDER HIS SHADOW.
THAT'S THE SPIRIT!! VIVA FUJISAKI SUGURU, AGE SIXTEEN! LET'S BLOW THIS JOINT!! BLOW!!
UH, WELL, I DON'T KNOW ABOUT THAT...
YEAH, WE'LL COMMANDEER THE AIRWAVES, JACK INTO COUNTDOWN TV! THAT'S A COOL IDEA!
Heh heh...
AND LET'S DO IT BIG! WE'LL GO ON THE RADIO, ANNOUNCE OUR INDEPENDENCE, AND TELL THE LABELS TO COME AND GET US!
HEY!!

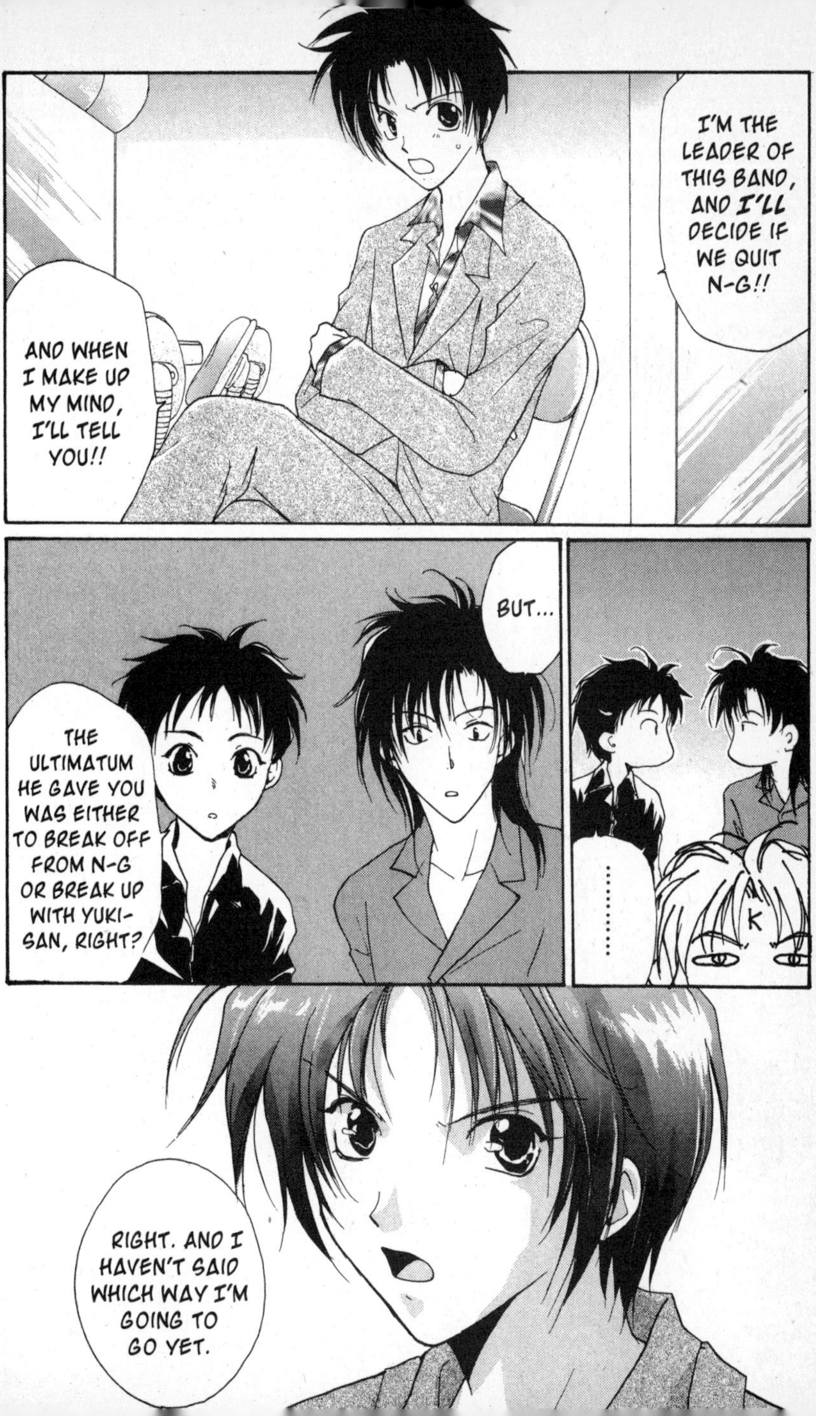
I'M THE LEADER OF THIS BAND, AND I'LL DECIDE IF WE QUIT N-G!!
AND WHEN I MAKE UP MY MIND, I'LL TELL YOU!!
......
K
BUT...
THE ULTIMATUM HE GAVE YOU WAS EITHER TO BREAK OFF FROM N-G OR BREAK UP WITH YUKI-SAN, RIGHT?
RIGHT. AND I HAVEN'T SAID WHICH WAY I'M GOING TO GO YET.

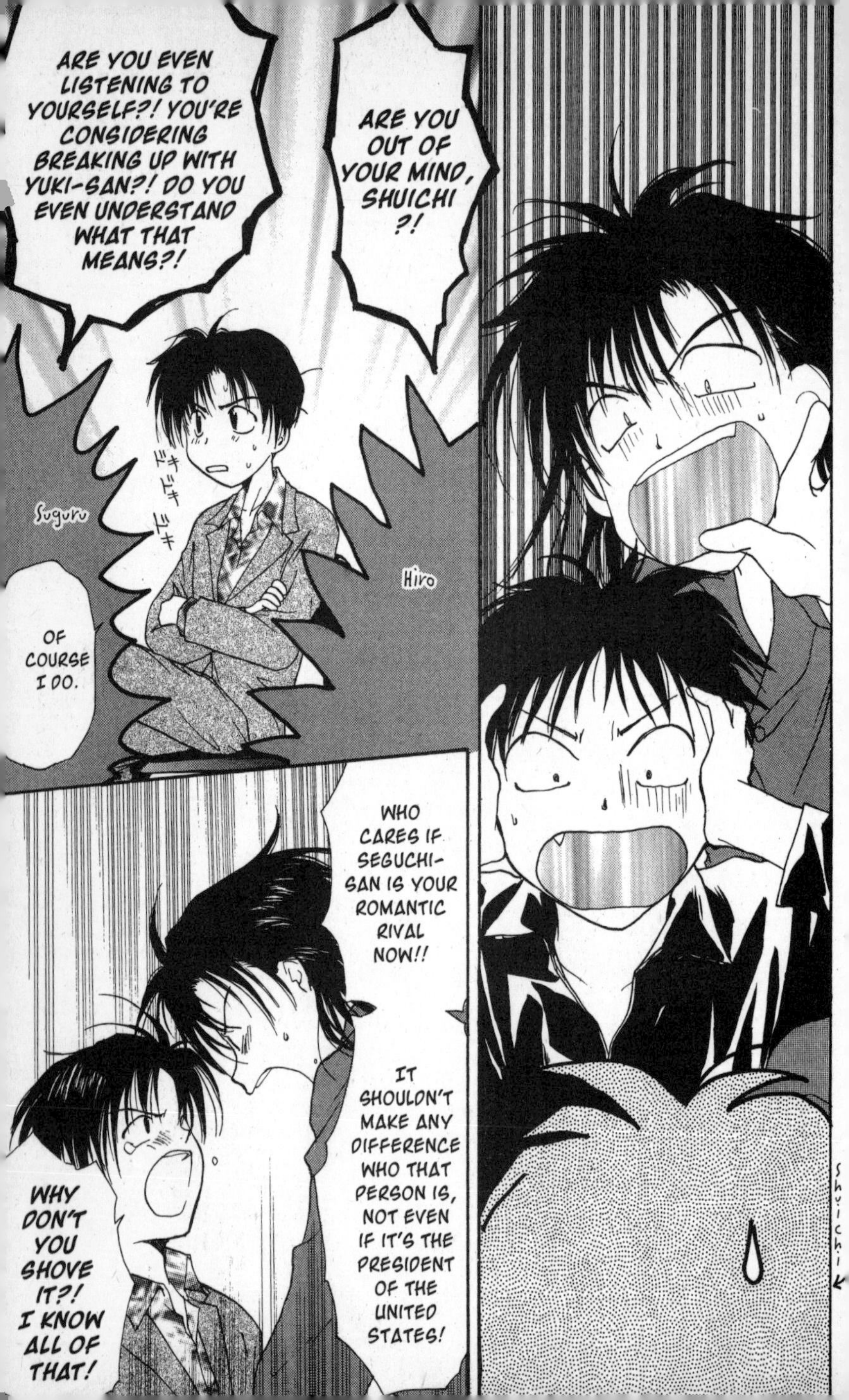
Shuichi
ARE YOU OUT OF YOUR MIND, SHUICHI?!
ARE YOU EVEN LISTENING TO YOURSELF?! YOU'RE CONSIDERING BREAKING UP WITH YUKI-SAN?! DO YOU EVEN UNDERSTAND WHAT THAT MEANS?!
ドキドキドキ
Hiro
Suguru
OF COURSE I DO.
WHO CARES IF SEGUCHI-SAN IS YOUR ROMANTIC RIVAL NOW!!
IT SHOULDN'T MAKE ANY DIFFERENCE WHO THAT PERSON IS, NOT EVEN IF IT'S THE PRESIDENT OF THE UNITED STATES!
WHY DON'T YOU SHOVE IT?! I KNOW ALL OF THAT!

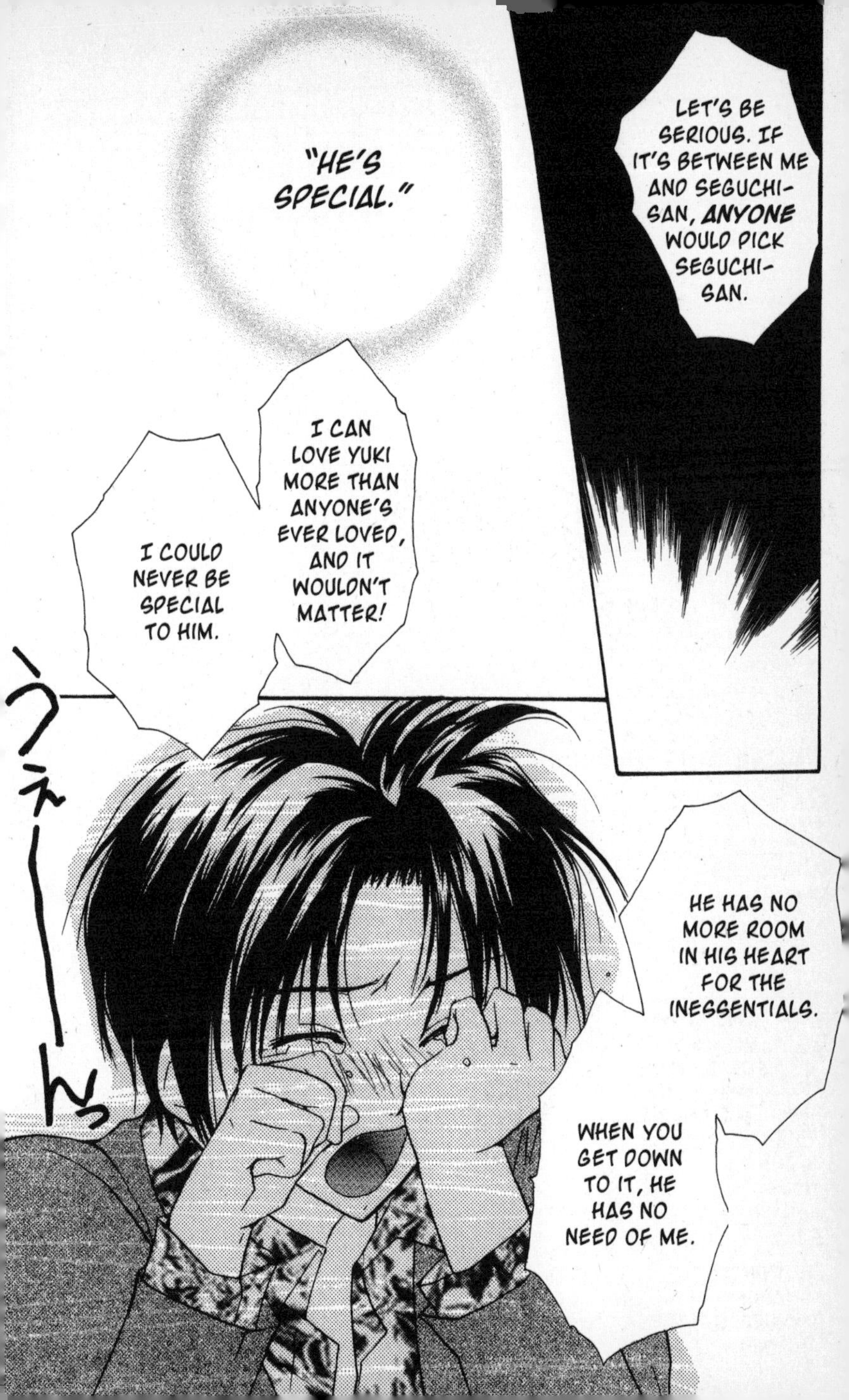
LET'S BE SERIOUS. IF IT'S BETWEEN ME AND SEGUCHI-SAN, ***ANYONE*** WOULD PICK SEGUCHI-SAN.
"HE'S SPECIAL."
I CAN LOVE YUKI MORE THAN ANYONE'S EVER LOVED, AND IT WOULDN'T MATTER!
I COULD NEVER BE SPECIAL TO HIM.
HE HAS NO MORE ROOM IN HIS HEART FOR THE INESSENTIALS.
うえーーんっ
WHEN YOU GET DOWN TO IT, HE HAS NO NEED OF ME.

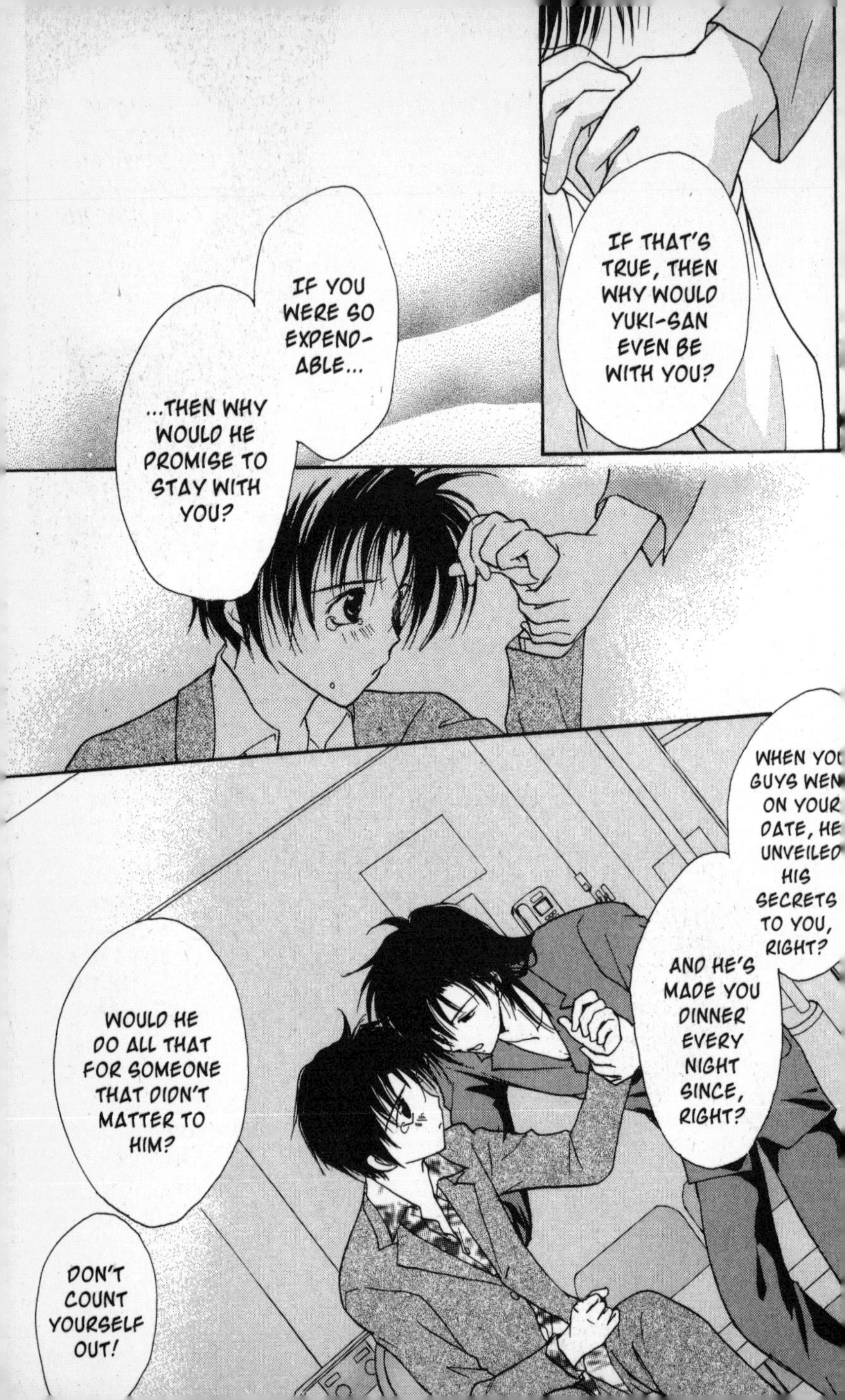
IF THAT'S TRUE, THEN WHY WOULD YUKI-SAN EVEN BE WITH YOU?
IF YOU WERE SO EXPEND-ABLE...
...THEN WHY WOULD HE PROMISE TO STAY WITH YOU?
WHEN YOU GUYS WENT ON YOUR DATE, HE UNVEILED HIS SECRETS TO YOU, RIGHT?
AND HE'S MADE YOU DINNER EVERY NIGHT SINCE, RIGHT?
WOULD HE DO ALL THAT FOR SOMEONE THAT DIDN'T MATTER TO HIM?
DON'T COUNT YOURSELF OUT!

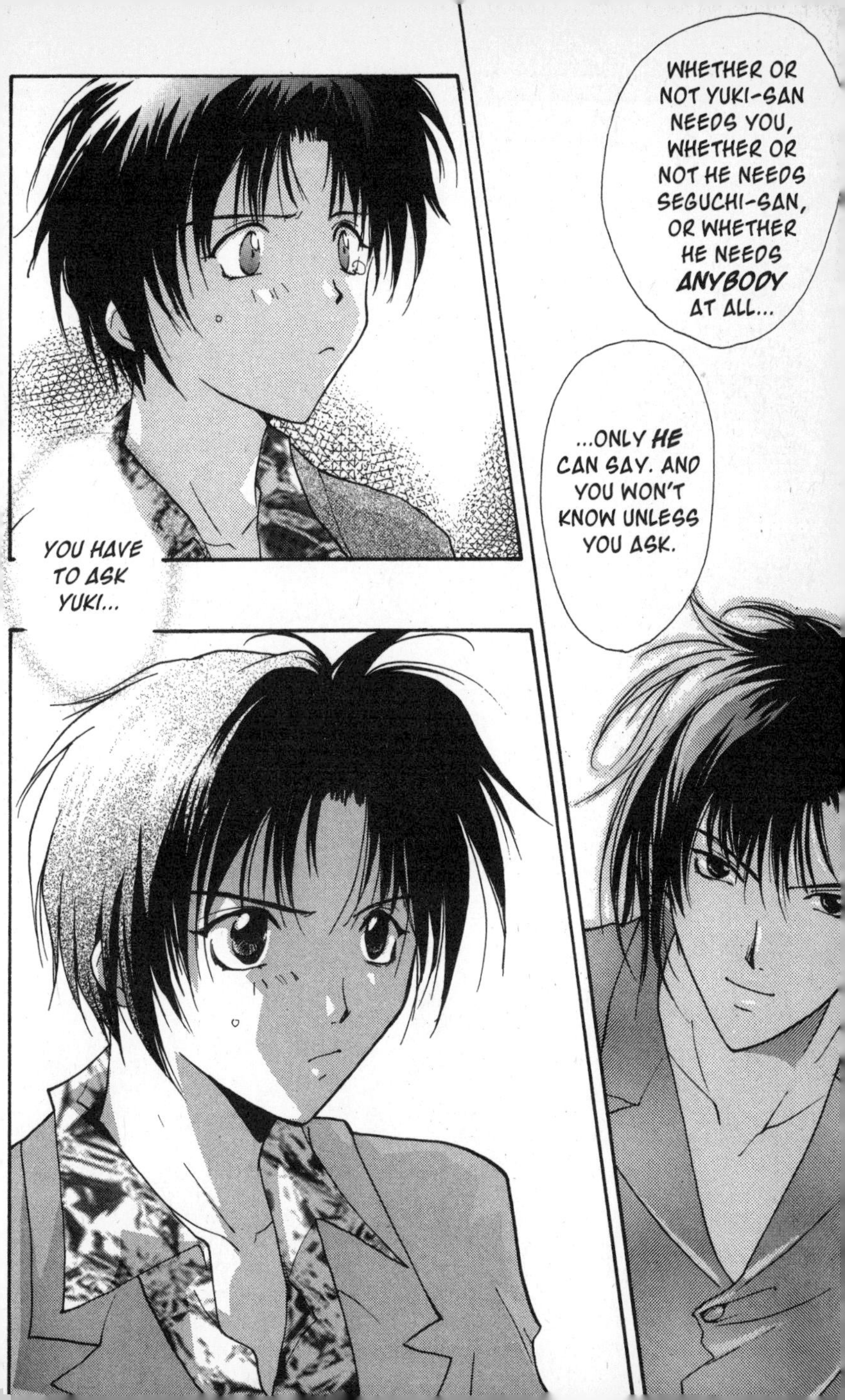
WHETHER OR NOT YUKI-SAN NEEDS YOU, WHETHER OR NOT HE NEEDS SEGUCHI-SAN, OR WHETHER HE NEEDS ANYBODY AT ALL...
...ONLY HE CAN SAY. AND YOU WON'T KNOW UNLESS YOU ASK.
YOU HAVE TO ASK YUKI...

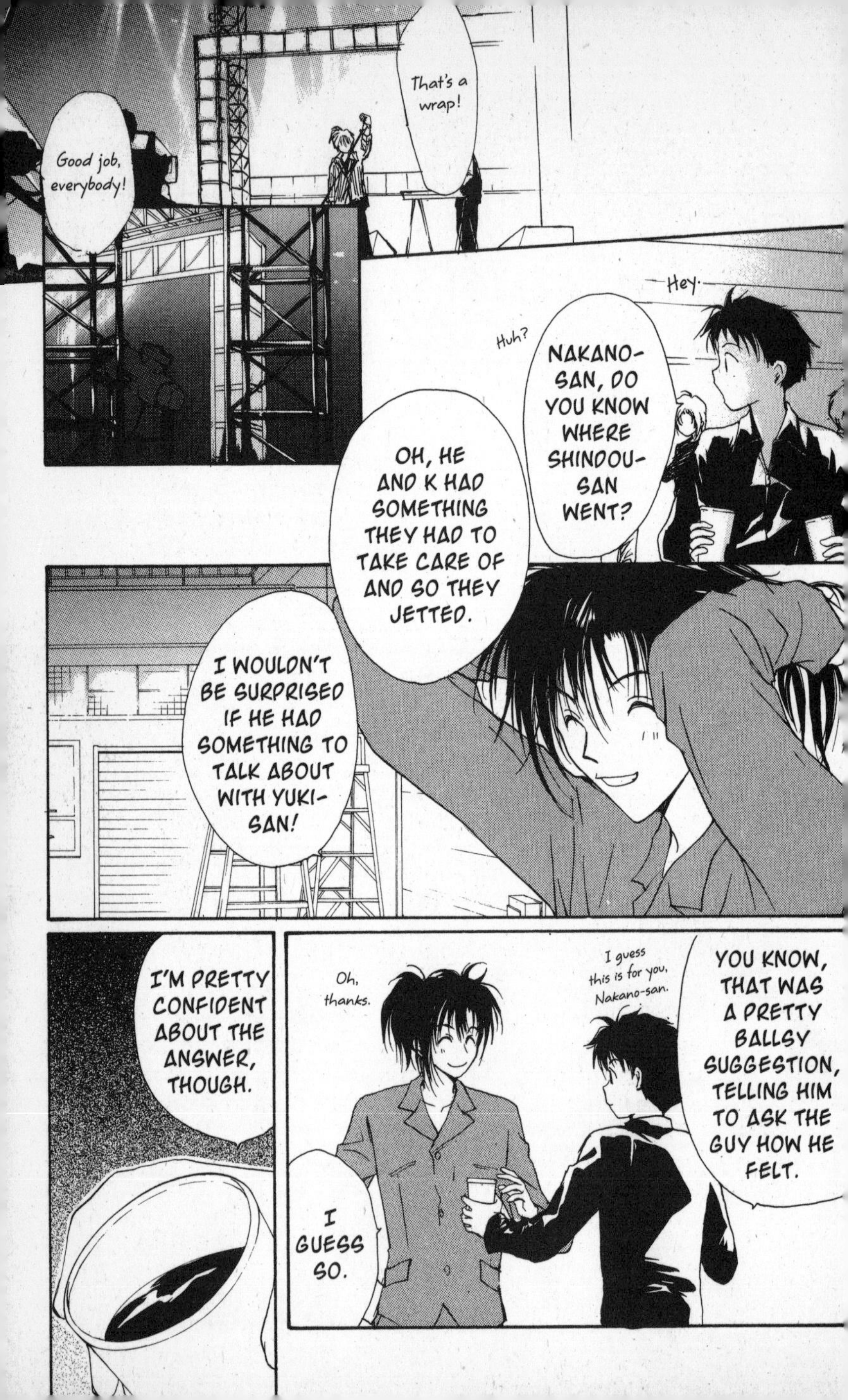
That's a wrap!
Good job, everybody!
Hey.
Huh?
NAKANO-SAN, DO YOU KNOW WHERE SHINDOU-SAN WENT?
OH, HE AND K HAD SOMETHING THEY HAD TO TAKE CARE OF AND SO THEY JETTED.
I WOULDN'T BE SURPRISED IF HE HAD SOMETHING TO TALK ABOUT WITH YUKI-SAN!
YOU KNOW, THAT WAS A PRETTY BALLSY SUGGESTION, TELLING HIM TO ASK THE GUY HOW HE FELT.
I guess this is for you, Nakano-san.
Oh, thanks.
I GUESS SO.
I'M PRETTY CONFIDENT ABOUT THE ANSWER, THOUGH.

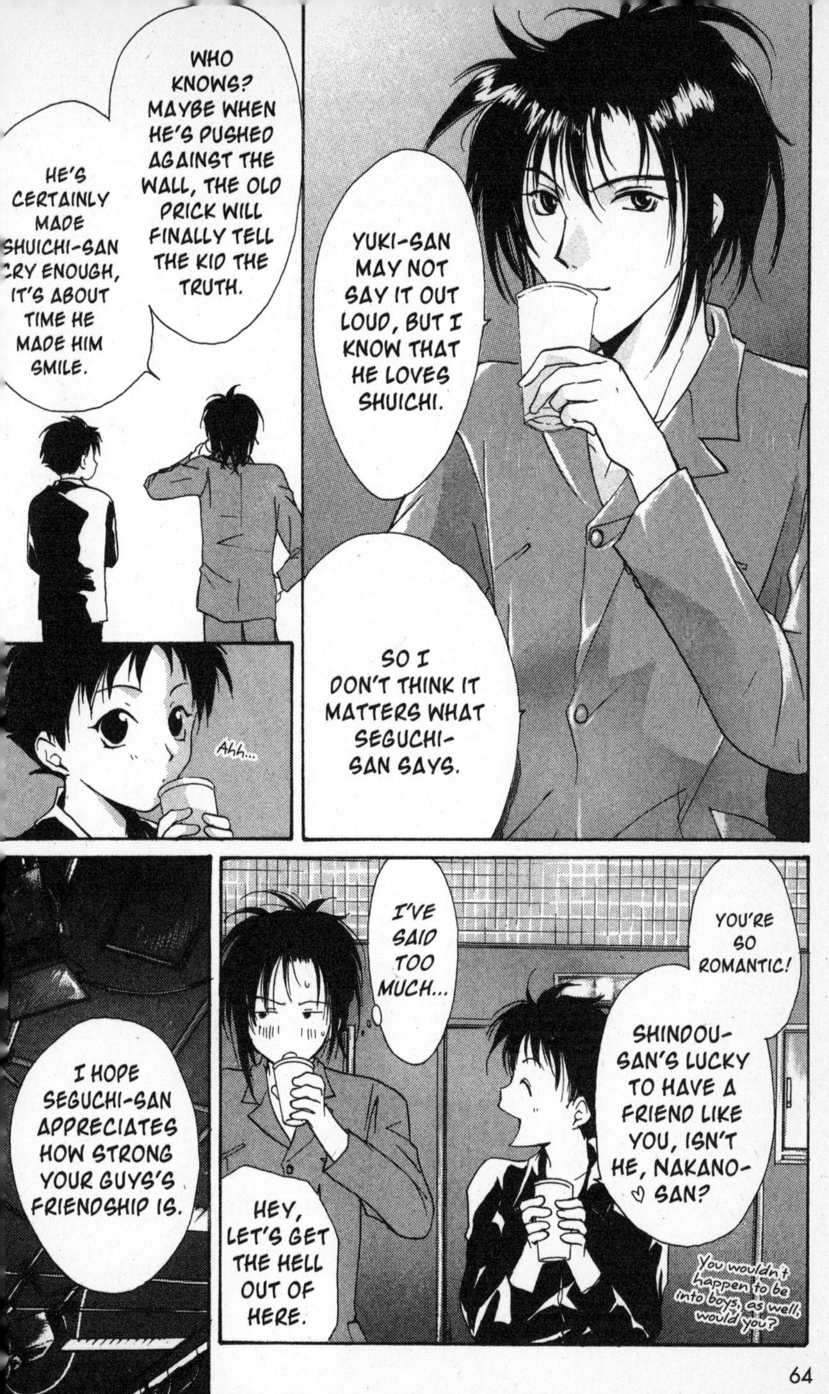
YUKI-SAN MAY NOT SAY IT OUT LOUD, BUT I KNOW THAT HE LOVES SHUICHI.
SO I DON'T THINK IT MATTERS WHAT SEGUCHI-SAN SAYS.
WHO KNOWS? MAYBE WHEN HE'S PUSHED AGAINST THE WALL, THE OLD PRICK WILL FINALLY TELL THE KID THE TRUTH.
HE'S CERTAINLY MADE SHUICHI-SAN CRY ENOUGH, IT'S ABOUT TIME HE MADE HIM SMILE.
Ahh...
YOU'RE SO ROMANTIC!
SHINDOU-SAN'S LUCKY TO HAVE A FRIEND LIKE YOU, ISN'T HE, NAKANO-♡ SAN?
I'VE SAID TOO MUCH...
HEY, LET'S GET THE HELL OUT OF HERE.
You wouldn't happen to be into boys, as well, would you?
I HOPE SEGUCHI-SAN APPRECIATES HOW STRONG YOUR GUYS'S FRIENDSHIP IS.

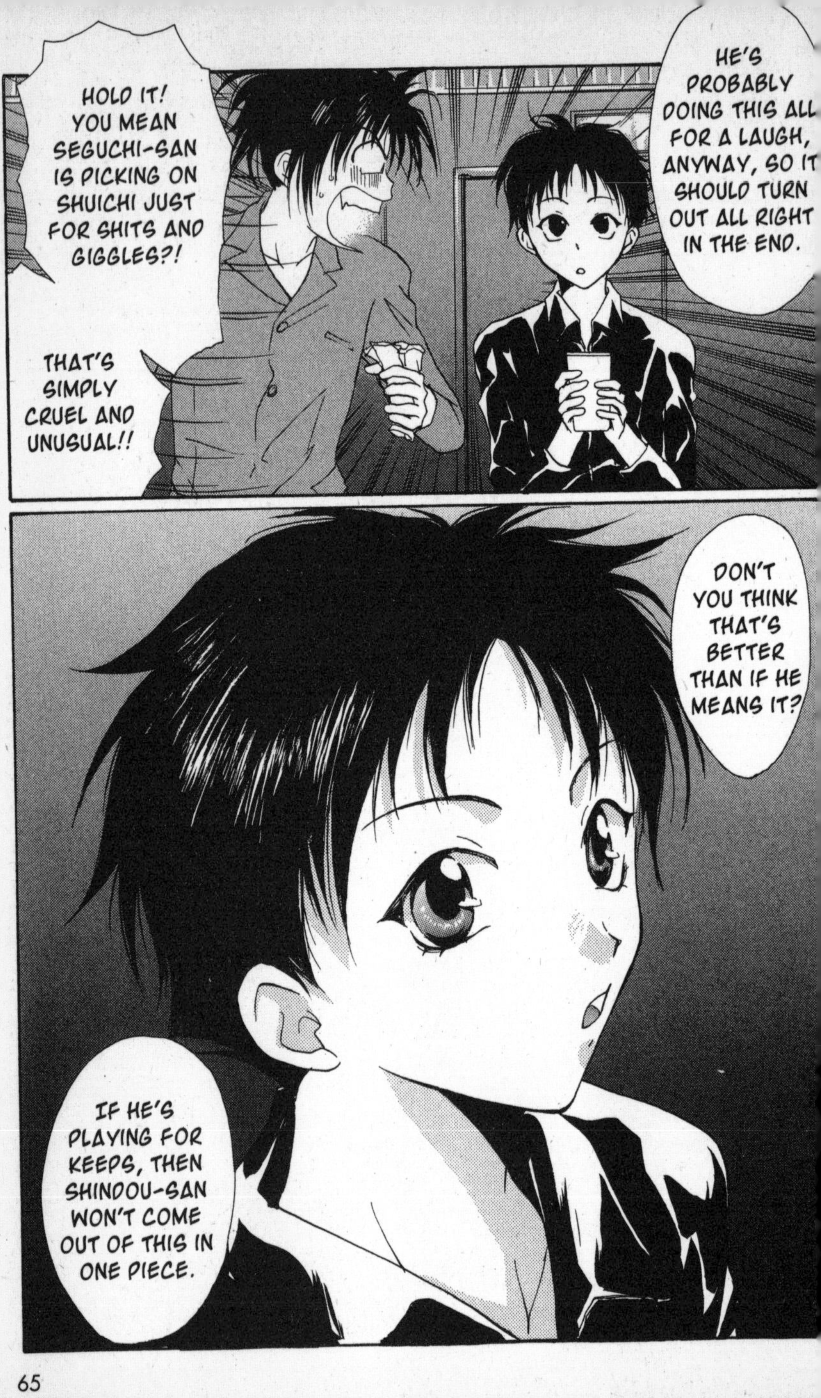
HE'S PROBABLY DOING THIS ALL FOR A LAUGH, ANYWAY, SO IT SHOULD TURN OUT ALL RIGHT IN THE END.
HOLD IT! YOU MEAN SEGUCHI-SAN IS PICKING ON SHUICHI JUST FOR SHITS AND GIGGLES?!
THAT'S SIMPLY CRUEL AND UNUSUAL!!
DON'T YOU THINK THAT'S BETTER THAN IF HE MEANS IT?
IF HE'S PLAYING FOR KEEPS, THEN SHINDOU-SAN WON'T COME OUT OF THIS IN ONE PIECE.

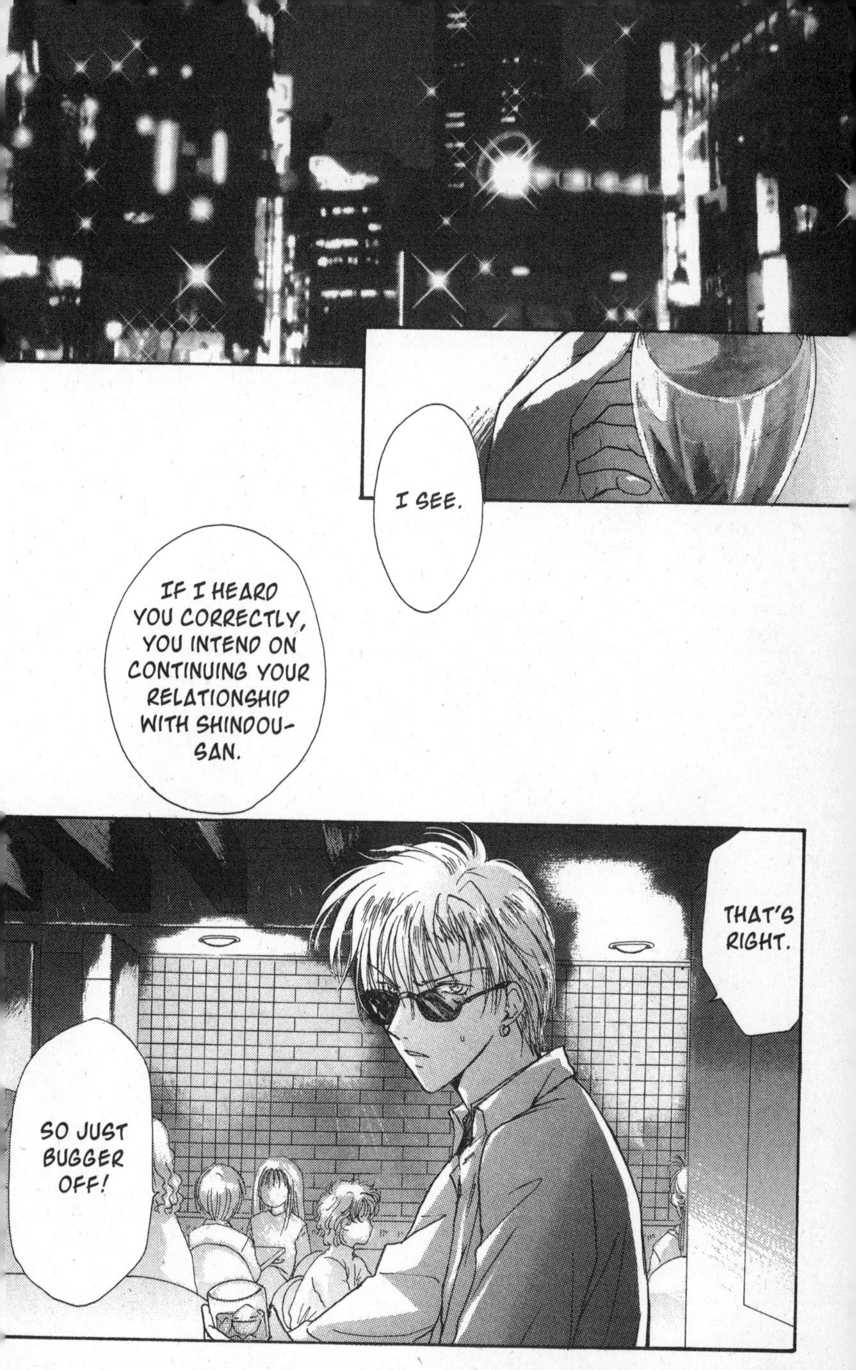
I SEE.
IF I HEARD YOU CORRECTLY, YOU INTEND ON CONTINUING YOUR RELATIONSHIP WITH SHINDOU-SAN.
THAT'S RIGHT.
SO JUST BUGGER OFF!

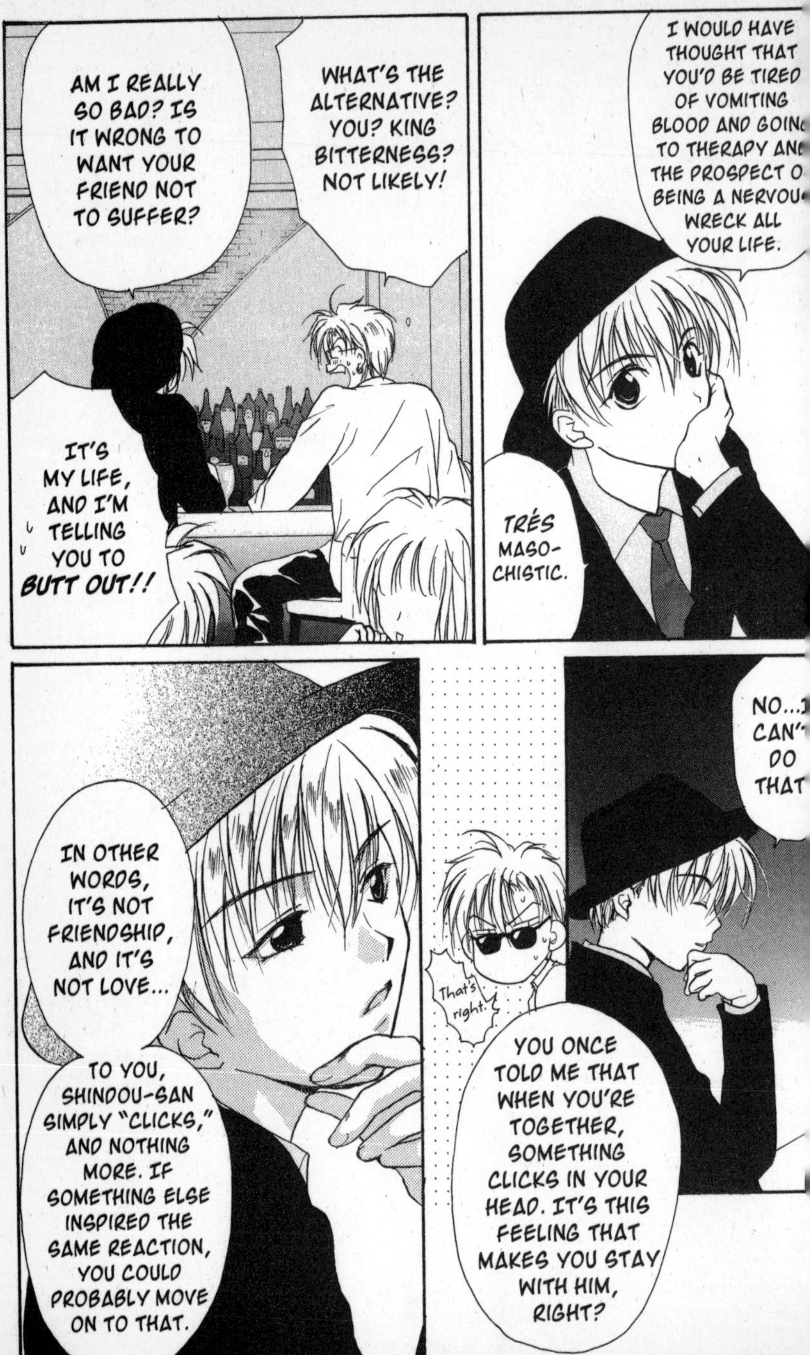
I WOULD HAVE THOUGHT THAT YOU'D BE TIRED OF VOMITING BLOOD AND GOING TO THERAPY AND THE PROSPECT OF BEING A NERVOUS WRECK ALL YOUR LIFE.
TRÉS MASO-CHISTIC.
WHAT'S THE ALTERNATIVE? YOU? KING BITTERNESS? NOT LIKELY!
AM I REALLY SO BAD? IS IT WRONG TO WANT YOUR FRIEND NOT TO SUFFER?
IT'S MY LIFE, AND I'M TELLING YOU TO BUTT OUT!!
NO...I CAN'T DO THAT
YOU ONCE TOLD ME THAT WHEN YOU'RE TOGETHER, SOMETHING CLICKS IN YOUR HEAD. IT'S THIS FEELING THAT MAKES YOU STAY WITH HIM, RIGHT?
That's right.
IN OTHER WORDS, IT'S NOT FRIENDSHIP, AND IT'S NOT LOVE...
TO YOU, SHINDOU-SAN SIMPLY "CLICKS," AND NOTHING MORE. IF SOMETHING ELSE INSPIRED THE SAME REACTION, YOU COULD PROBABLY MOVE ON TO THAT.

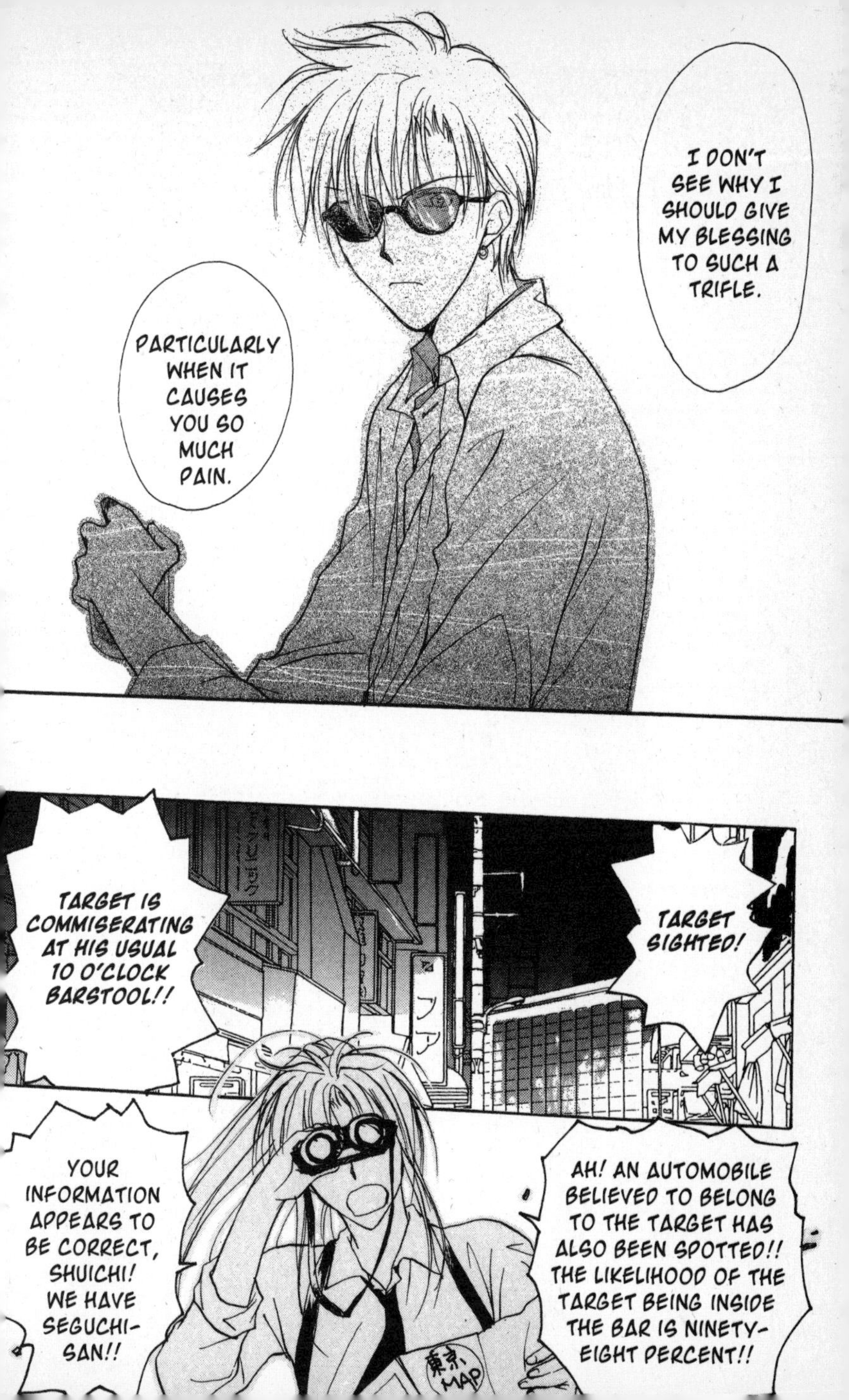
I DON'T SEE WHY I SHOULD GIVE MY BLESSING TO SUCH A TRIFLE.
PARTICULARLY WHEN IT CAUSES YOU SO MUCH PAIN.
TARGET SIGHTED!
TARGET IS COMMISERATING AT HIS USUAL 10 O'CLOCK BARSTOOL!!
AH! AN AUTOMOBILE BELIEVED TO BELONG TO THE TARGET HAS ALSO BEEN SPOTTED!! THE LIKELIHOOD OF THE TARGET BEING INSIDE THE BAR IS NINETY-EIGHT PERCENT!!
YOUR INFORMATION APPEARS TO BE CORRECT, SHUICHI! WE HAVE SEGUCHI-SAN!!
東京 MAP

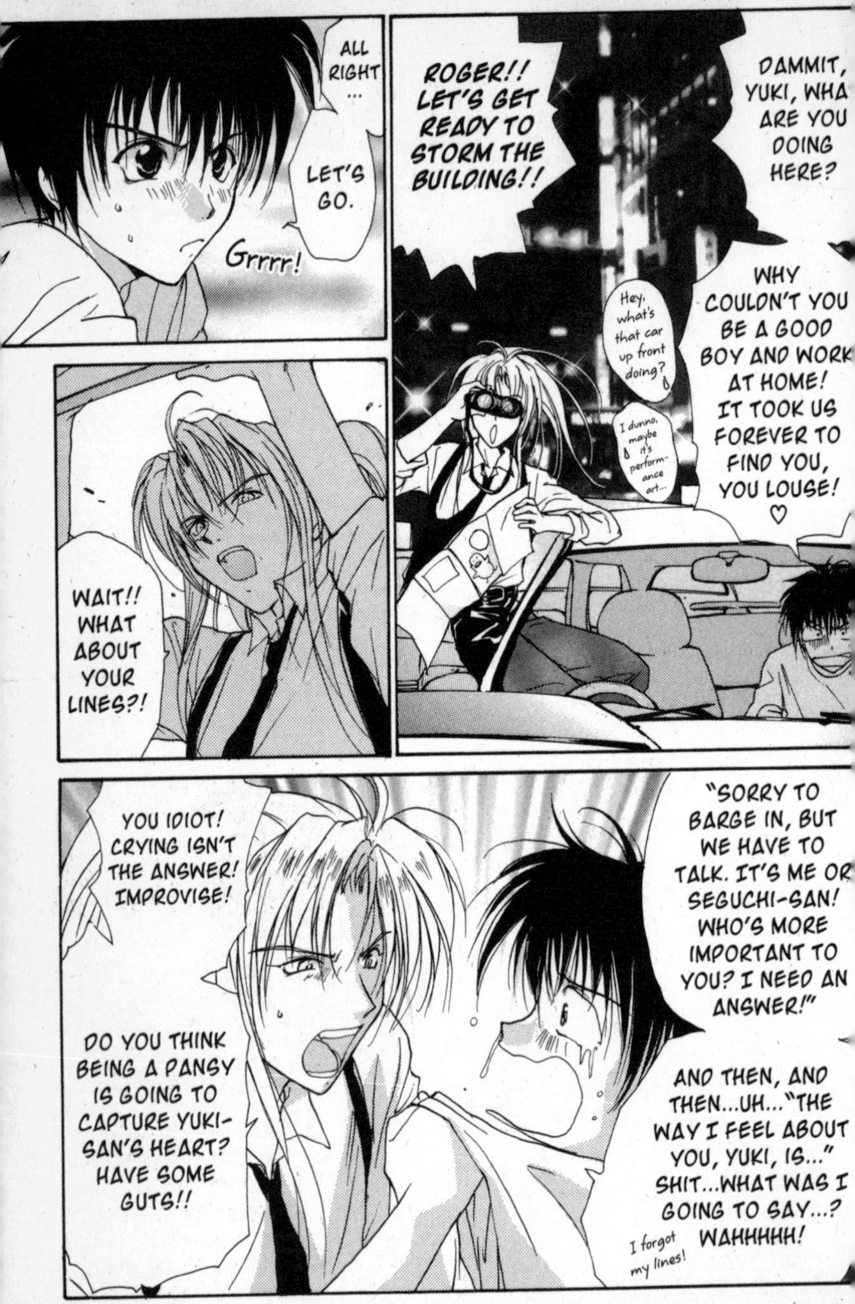
DAMMIT, YUKI, WHA ARE YOU DOING HERE?
ROGER!! LET'S GET READY TO STORM THE BUILDING!!
WHY COULDN'T YOU BE A GOOD BOY AND WORK AT HOME! IT TOOK US FOREVER TO FIND YOU, YOU LOUSE! ♡
Hey, what's that car up front doing?
I dunno, maybe it's performance art...
ALL RIGHT...
LET'S GO.
Grrrr!
WAIT!! WHAT ABOUT YOUR LINES?!
"SORRY TO BARGE IN, BUT WE HAVE TO TALK. IT'S ME OR SEGUCHI-SAN! WHO'S MORE IMPORTANT TO YOU? I NEED AN ANSWER!"
YOU IDIOT! CRYING ISN'T THE ANSWER! IMPROVISE!
AND THEN, AND THEN...UH..."THE WAY I FEEL ABOUT YOU, YUKI, IS..." SHIT...WHAT WAS I GOING TO SAY...? WAHHHHH!
I forgot my lines!
DO YOU THINK BEING A PANSY IS GOING TO CAPTURE YUKI-SAN'S HEART? HAVE SOME GUTS!!

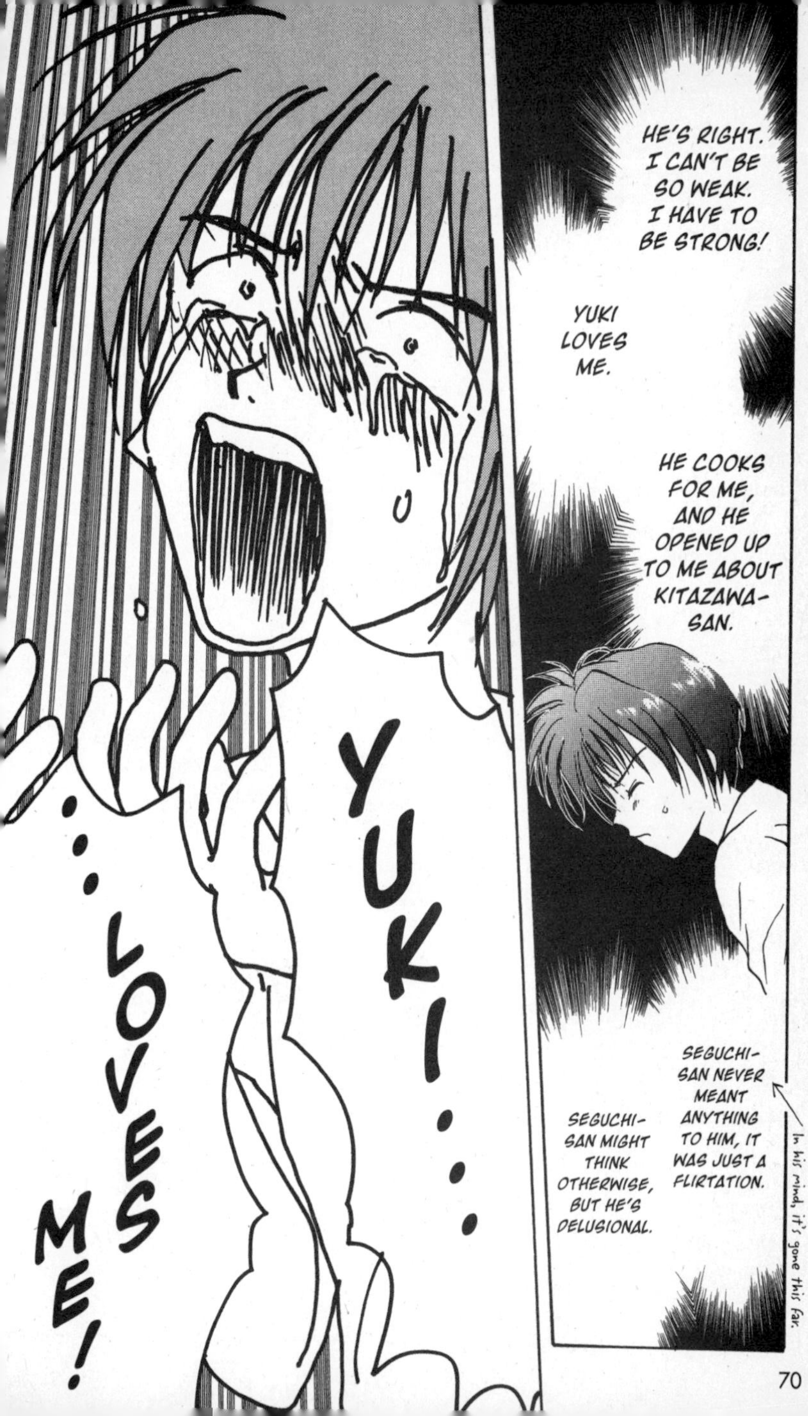
HE'S RIGHT. I CAN'T BE SO WEAK. I HAVE TO BE STRONG!
YUKI LOVES ME.
HE COOKS FOR ME, AND HE OPENED UP TO ME ABOUT KITAZAWA-SAN.
In his mind, it's gone this far.
SEGUCHI-SAN NEVER MEANT ANYTHING TO HIM, IT WAS JUST A FLIRTATION.
SEGUCHI-SAN MIGHT THINK OTHERWISE, BUT HE'S DELUSIONAL.
YUKI...
...LOVES ME!

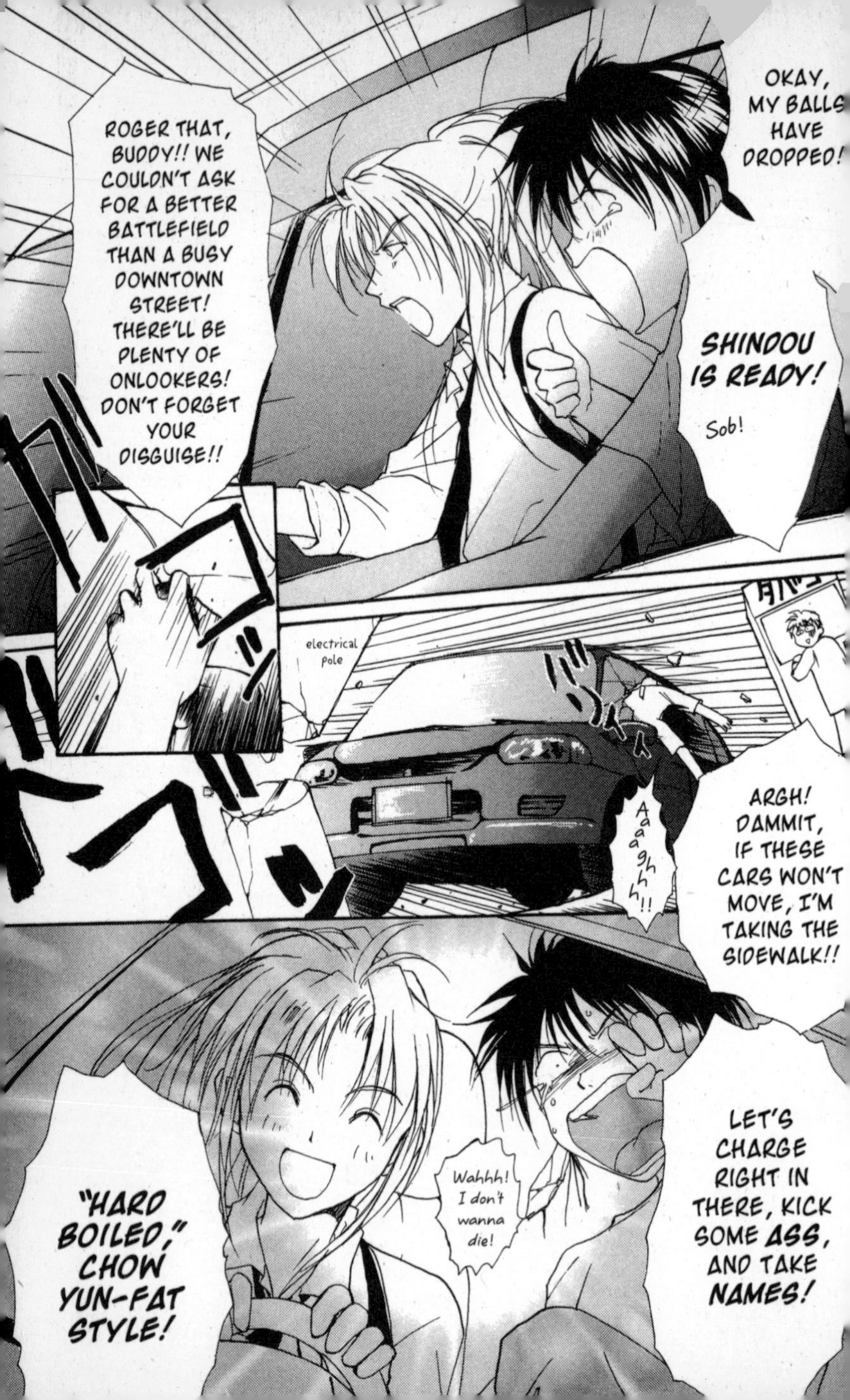
OKAY, MY BALLS HAVE DROPPED!
SHINDOU IS READY!
Sob!
ROGER THAT, BUDDY!! WE COULDN'T ASK FOR A BETTER BATTLEFIELD THAN A BUSY DOWNTOWN STREET! THERE'LL BE PLENTY OF ONLOOKERS! DON'T FORGET YOUR DISGUISE!!
electrical pole
Aaaaghhhh!!
ARGH! DAMMIT, IF THESE CARS WON'T MOVE, I'M TAKING THE SIDEWALK!!
LET'S CHARGE RIGHT IN THERE, KICK SOME ASS, AND TAKE NAMES!
Wahhh! I don't wanna die!
"HARD BOILED," CHOW YUN-FAT STYLE!

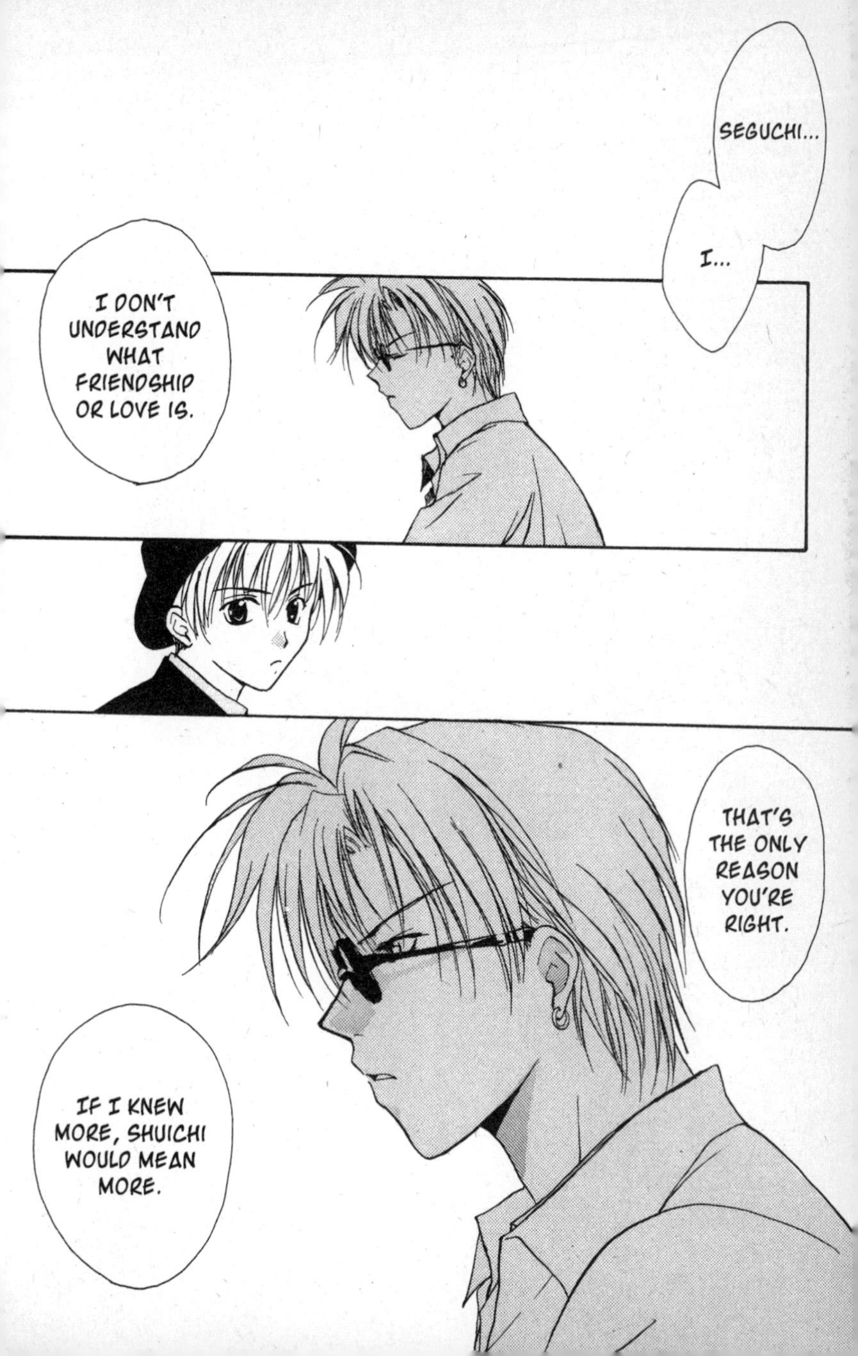
SEGUCHI...
I...
I DON'T UNDERSTAND WHAT FRIENDSHIP OR LOVE IS.
THAT'S THE ONLY REASON YOU'RE RIGHT.
IF I KNEW MORE, SHUICHI WOULD MEAN MORE.

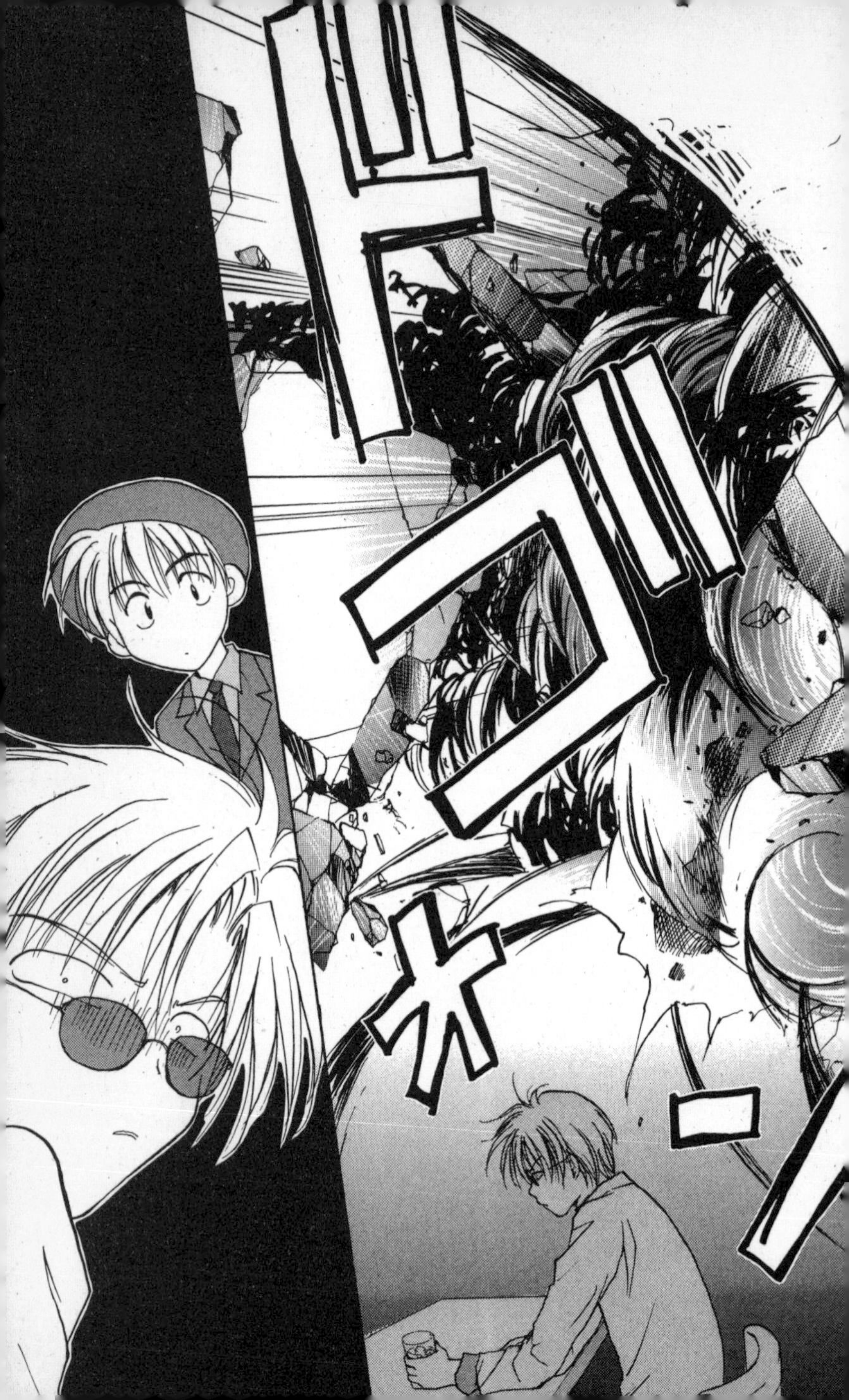
ドゴオーン

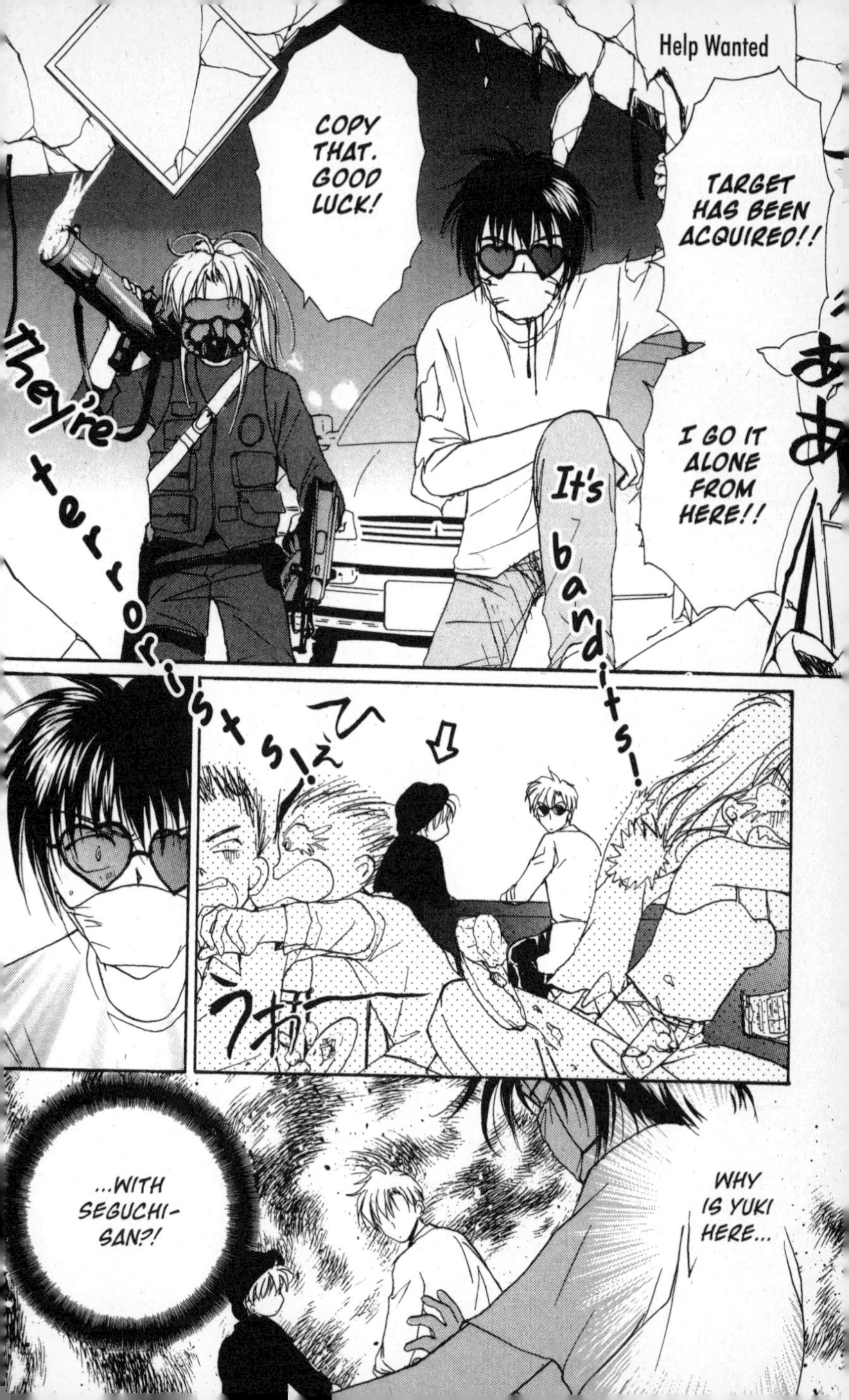
TARGET HAS BEEN ACQUIRED!!
I GO IT ALONE FROM HERE!!
COPY THAT. GOOD LUCK!
ああ
It's bandits!
They're terrorists!
ひえ
WHY IS YUKI HERE...
...WITH SEGUCHI-SAN?!

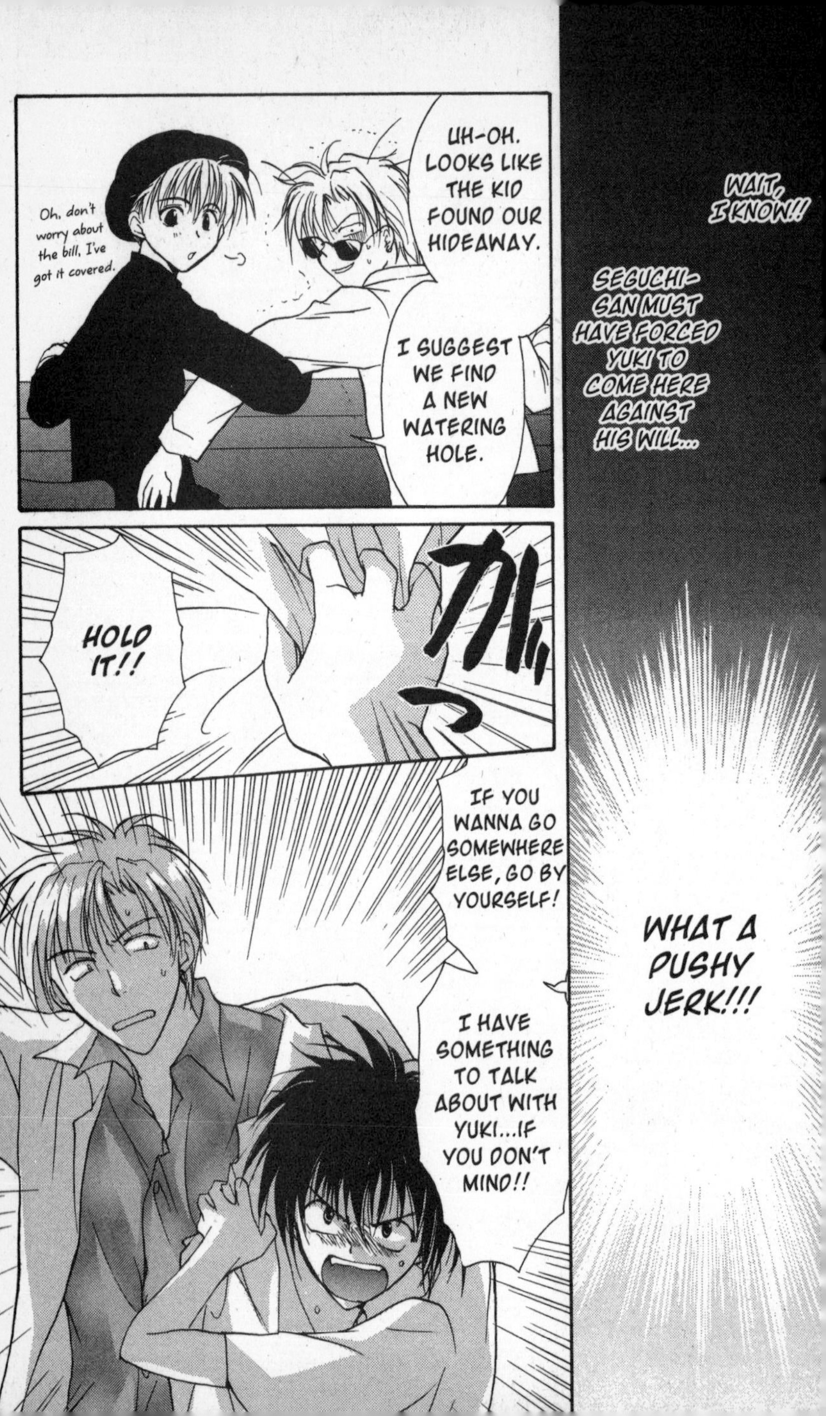
WAIT, I KNOW!!
SEGUCHI-SAN MUST HAVE FORCED YUKI TO COME HERE AGAINST HIS WILL...
WHAT A PUSHY JERK!!!
UH-OH. LOOKS LIKE THE KID FOUND OUR HIDEAWAY.
I SUGGEST WE FIND A NEW WATERING HOLE.
Oh, don't worry about the bill, I've got it covered.
カッ
HOLD IT!!
IF YOU WANNA GO SOMEWHERE ELSE, GO BY YOURSELF!
I HAVE SOMETHING TO TALK ABOUT WITH YUKI...IF YOU DON'T MIND!!

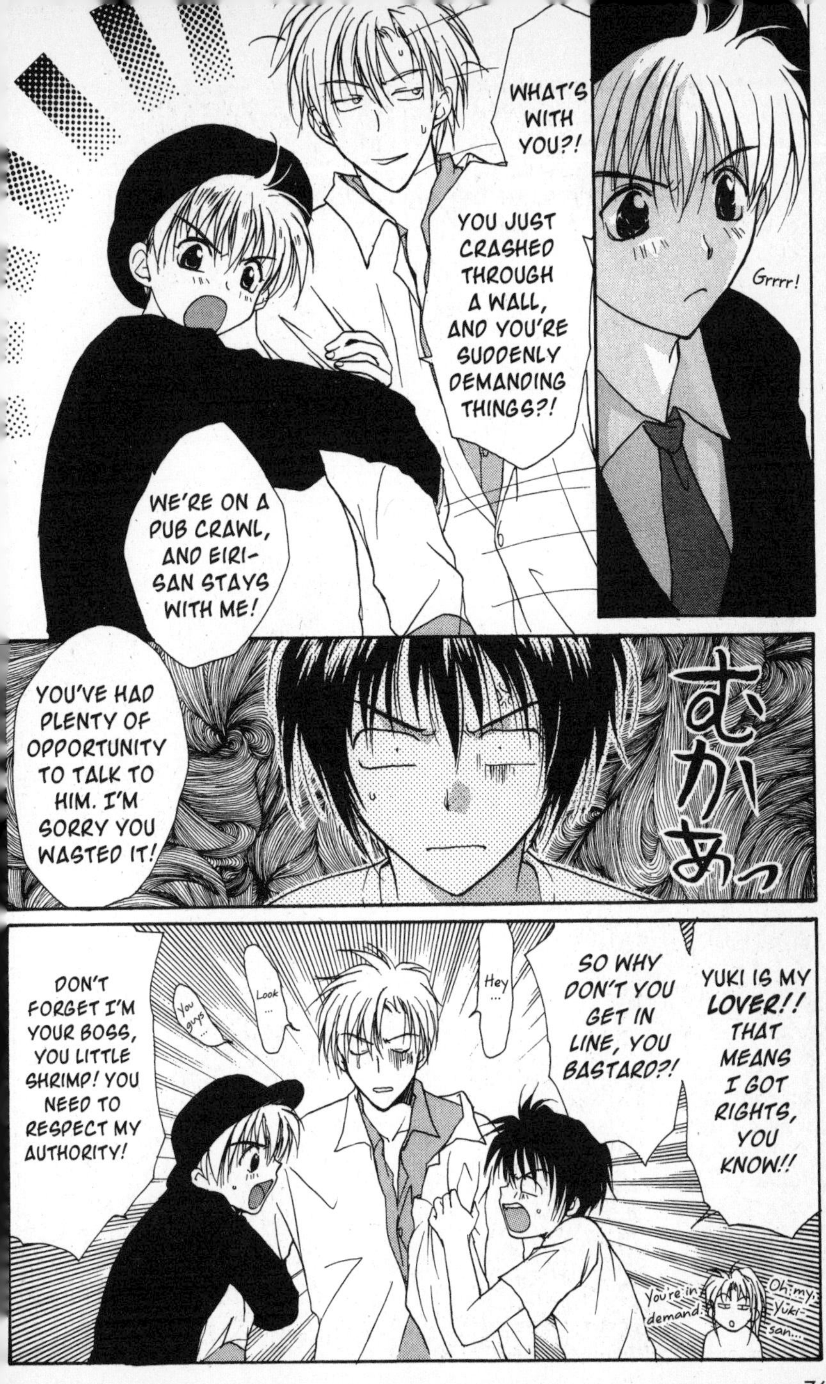
Grrrr!
WHAT'S WITH YOU?!
YOU JUST CRASHED THROUGH A WALL, AND YOU'RE SUDDENLY DEMANDING THINGS?!
WE'RE ON A PUB CRAWL, AND EIRI-SAN STAYS WITH ME!
むかぁっ
YOU'VE HAD PLENTY OF OPPORTUNITY TO TALK TO HIM. I'M SORRY YOU WASTED IT!
YUKI IS MY LOVER!! THAT MEANS I GOT RIGHTS, YOU KNOW!!
SO WHY DON'T YOU GET IN LINE, YOU BASTARD?!
Hey...
Look...
You guys...
DON'T FORGET I'M YOUR BOSS, YOU LITTLE SHRIMP! YOU NEED TO RESPECT MY AUTHORITY!
Oh my, Yuki-san...
You're in demand.

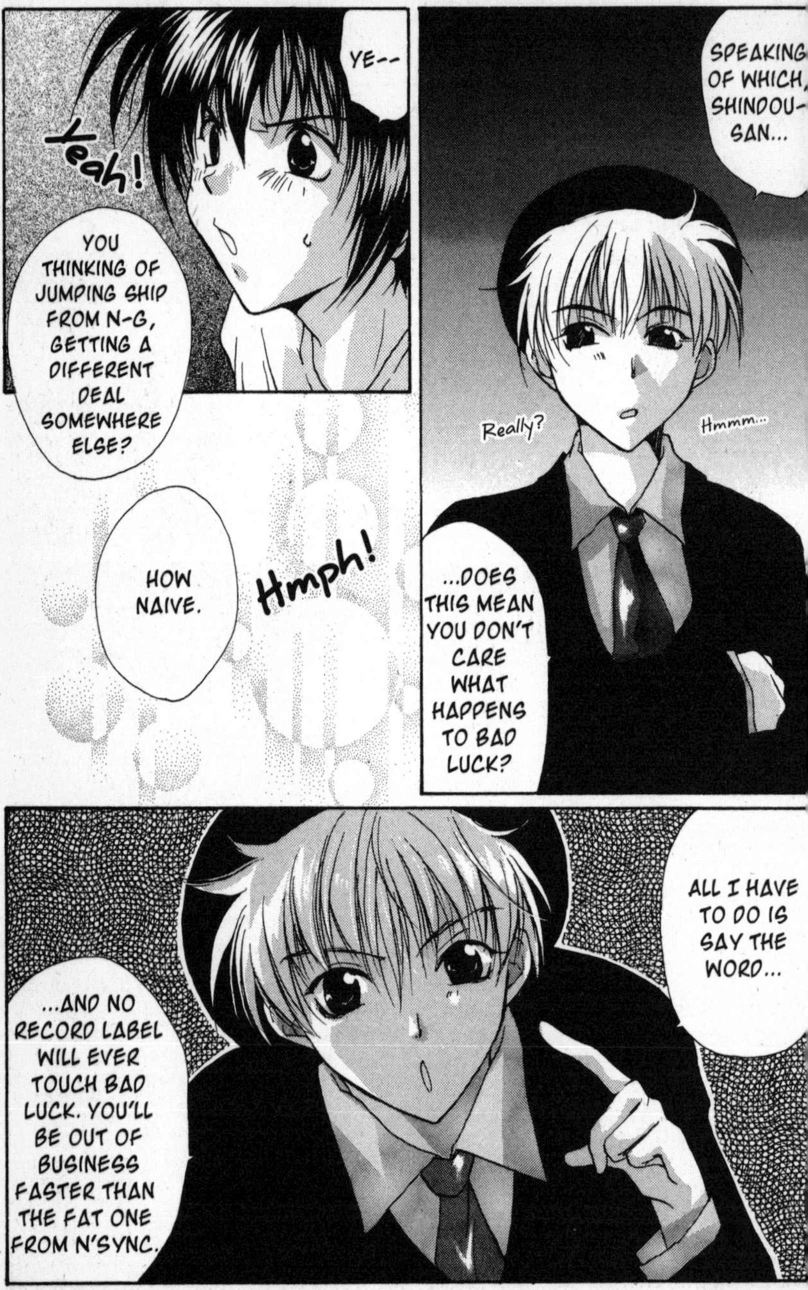
SPEAKING OF WHICH, SHINDOU-SAN...
Hmmm...
Really?
...DOES THIS MEAN YOU DON'T CARE WHAT HAPPENS TO BAD LUCK?
YE--
Yeah!
YOU THINKING OF JUMPING SHIP FROM N-G, GETTING A DIFFERENT DEAL SOMEWHERE ELSE?
Hmph!
HOW NAIVE.
ALL I HAVE TO DO IS SAY THE WORD...
...AND NO RECORD LABEL WILL EVER TOUCH BAD LUCK. YOU'LL BE OUT OF BUSINESS FASTER THAN THE FAT ONE FROM N'SYNC.

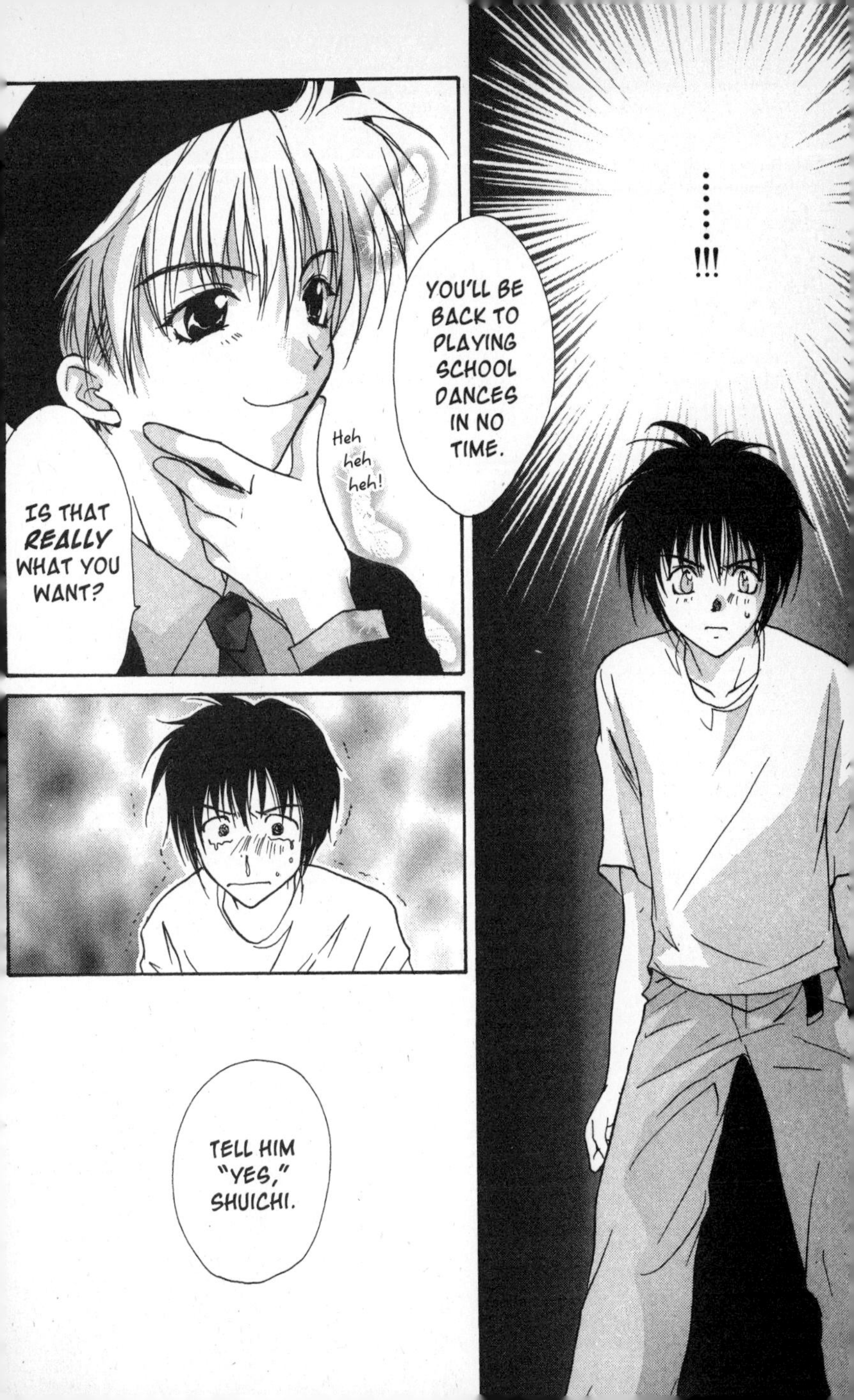
......!!!
YOU'LL BE BACK TO PLAYING SCHOOL DANCES IN NO TIME.
Heh heh heh!
IS THAT REALLY WHAT YOU WANT?
TELL HIM "YES," SHUICHI.

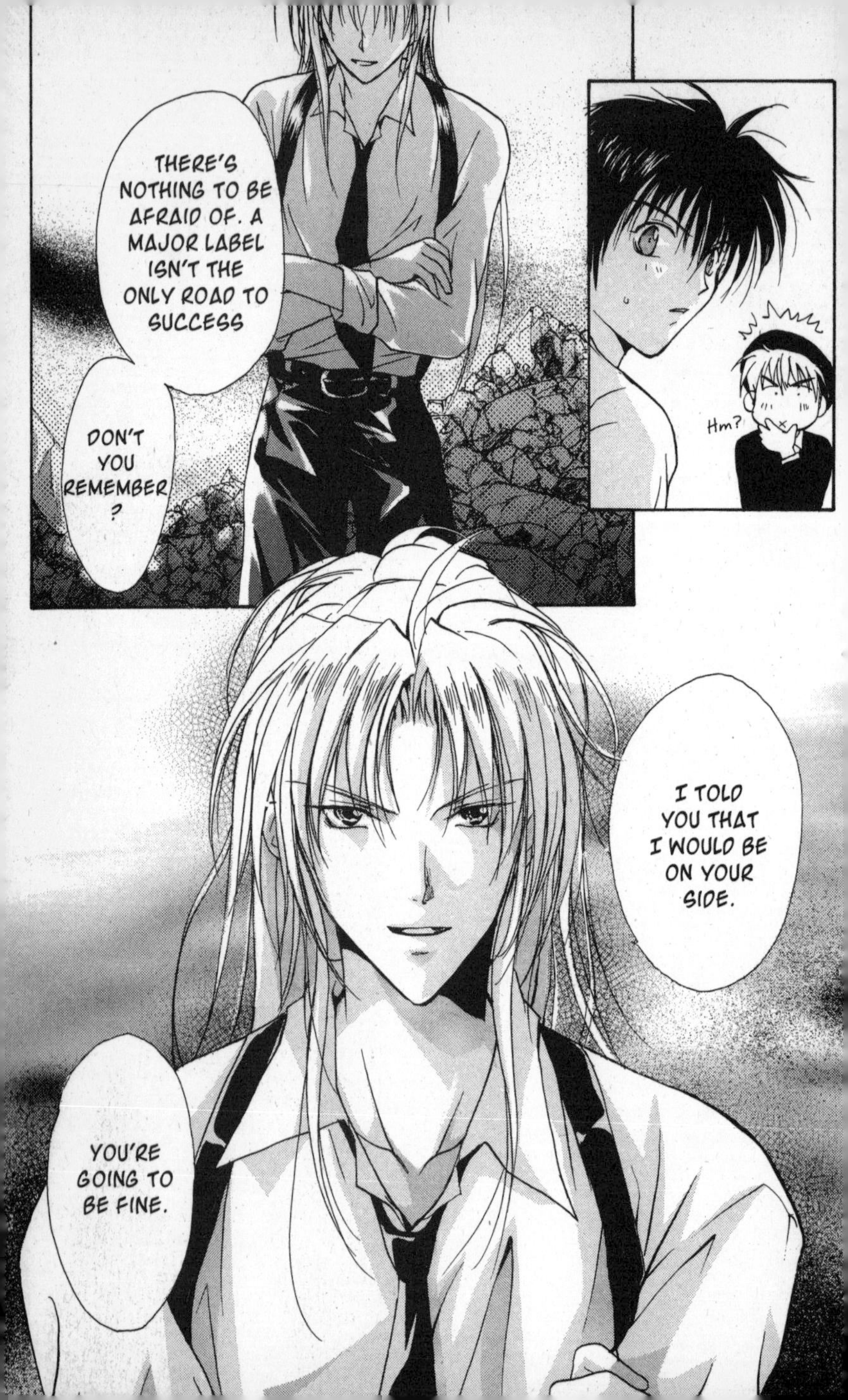
Hm?
THERE'S NOTHING TO BE AFRAID OF. A MAJOR LABEL ISN'T THE ONLY ROAD TO SUCCESS
DON'T YOU REMEMBER?
I TOLD YOU THAT I WOULD BE ON YOUR SIDE.
YOU'RE GOING TO BE FINE.

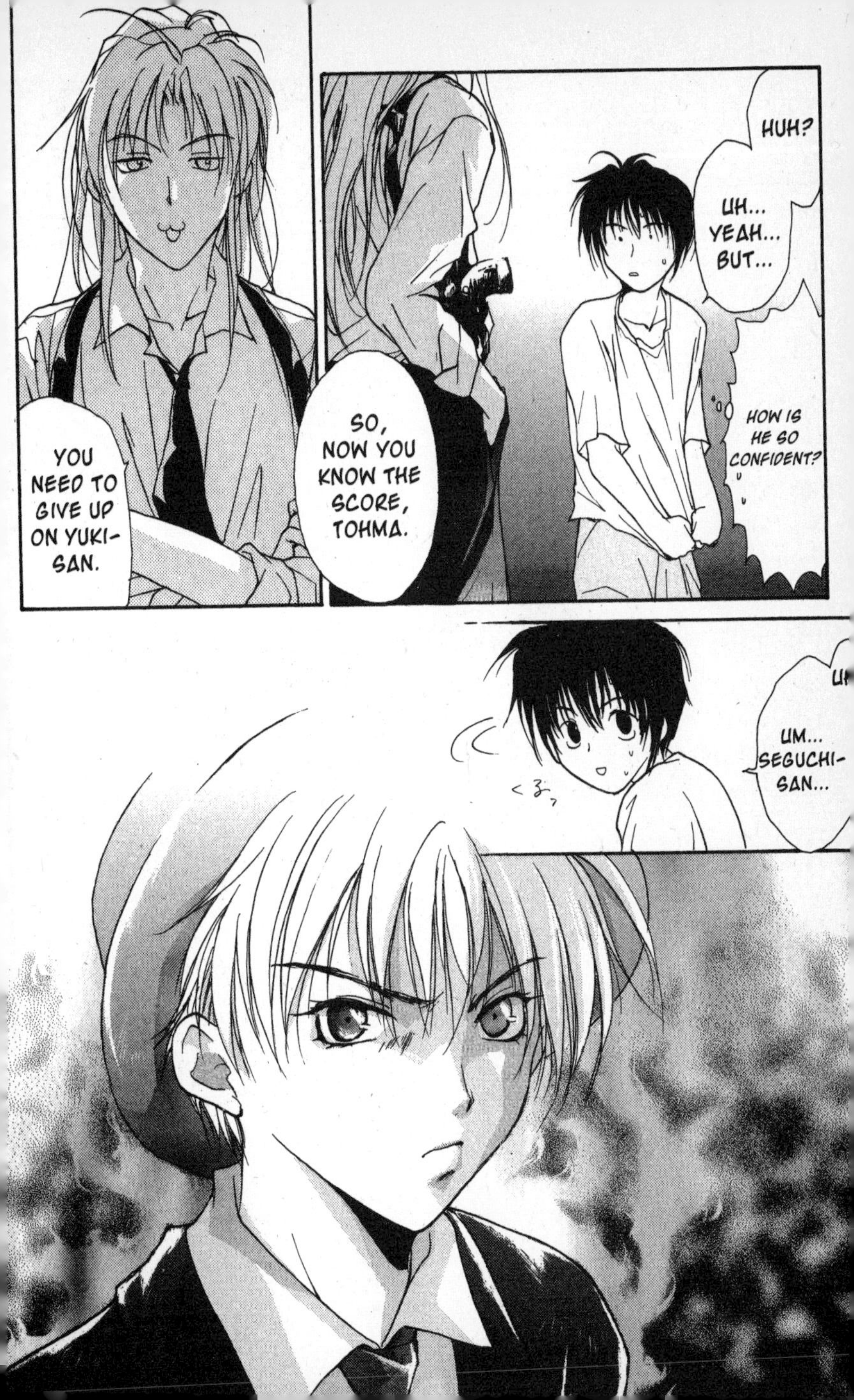
HUH?
UH... YEAH... BUT...
HOW IS HE SO CONFIDENT?
SO, NOW YOU KNOW THE SCORE, TOHMA.
YOU NEED TO GIVE UP ON YUKI-SAN.
UH
UM... SEGUCHI-SAN...

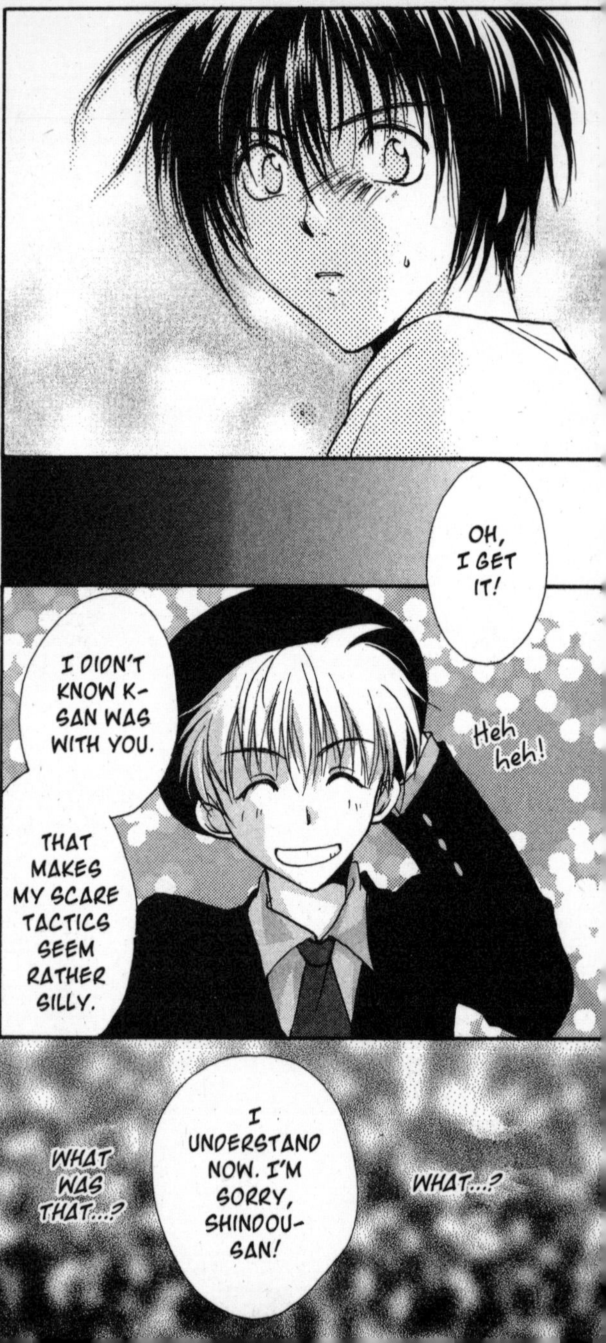
OH, I GET IT!
Heh heh!
I DIDN'T KNOW K-SAN WAS WITH YOU.
THAT MAKES MY SCARE TACTICS SEEM RATHER SILLY.
WHAT...?
I UNDERSTAND NOW. I'M SORRY, SHINDOU-SAN!
WHAT WAS THAT...?

Continued...

Tohma Seguchi-san's true colors are starting to show through. Really, he is one scary guy. He's covering it up by smiling and laughing, but it's too late. After this episode, I think Tohma-san's fans are going to diminish **RAPIDLY.** I'm going to get **PLENTY** of letters from fans complaining about this. Stuff like: "I hate him!"; "Die!"; "He's scary!"; "I always knew he was like this..."

Meanwhile, there will be **ABSOLUTELY NO** letters supporting me, nothing at all like: "Murakami-san, keep up the good fight!"; "Murakami-san is so wonderful!"; "You're so cool, Murakami-san!"

And then there are the letters that will go like this: "I know your secrets..."; "Stop jiggling your legs like there's an earthquake."; "Stop quaking in your boots!"; "Give back my money!"

See ya next time!

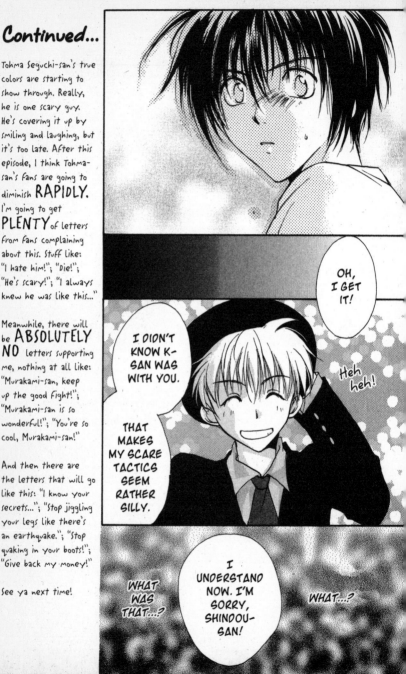

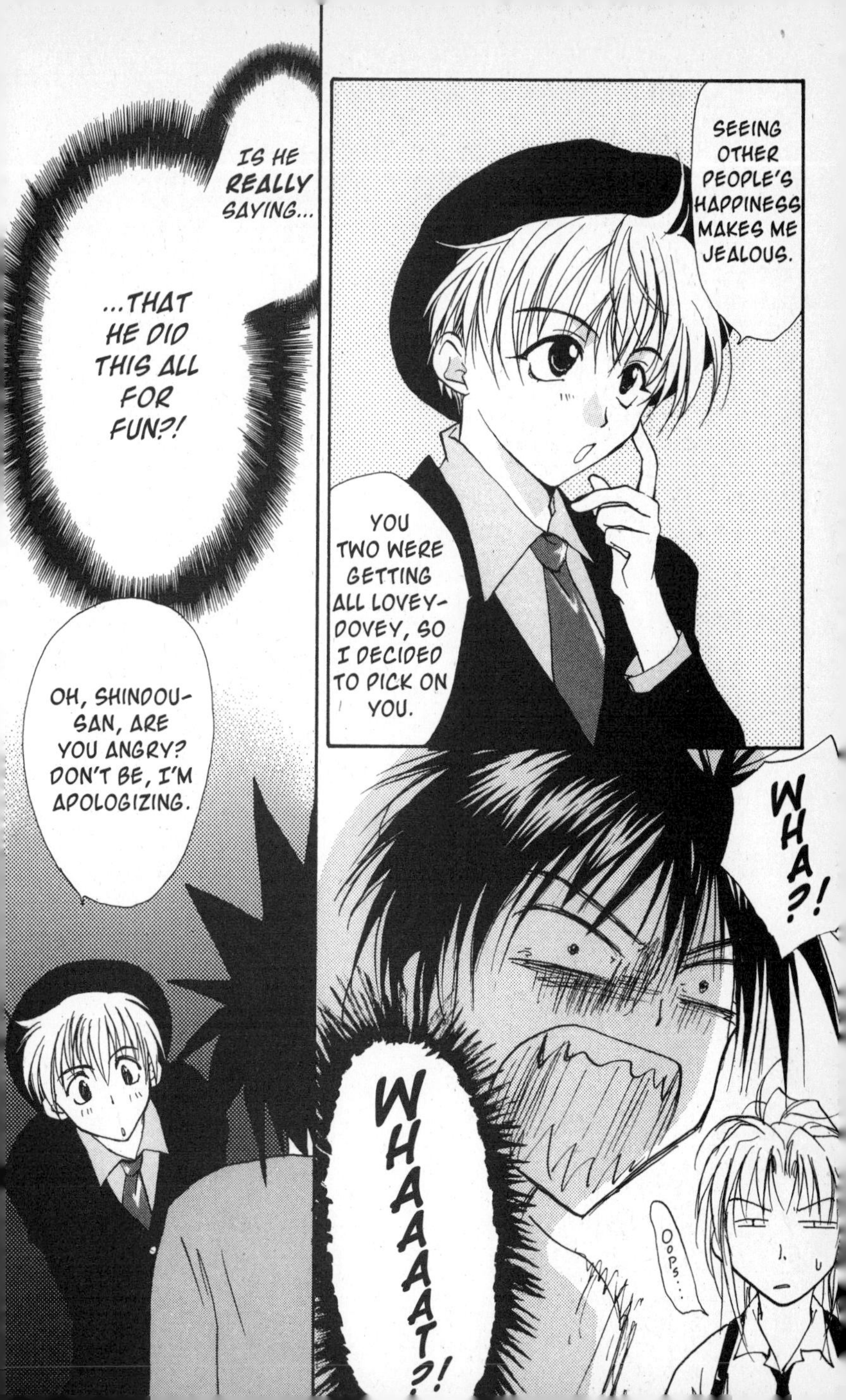
SEEING OTHER PEOPLE'S HAPPINESS MAKES ME JEALOUS.
YOU TWO WERE GETTING ALL LOVEY-DOVEY, SO I DECIDED TO PICK ON YOU.
IS HE REALLY SAYING...
...THAT HE DID THIS ALL FOR FUN?!
WHA?!
WHAAAAAT?!
Oops...
OH, SHINDOU-SAN, ARE YOU ANGRY? DON'T BE, I'M APOLOGIZING.

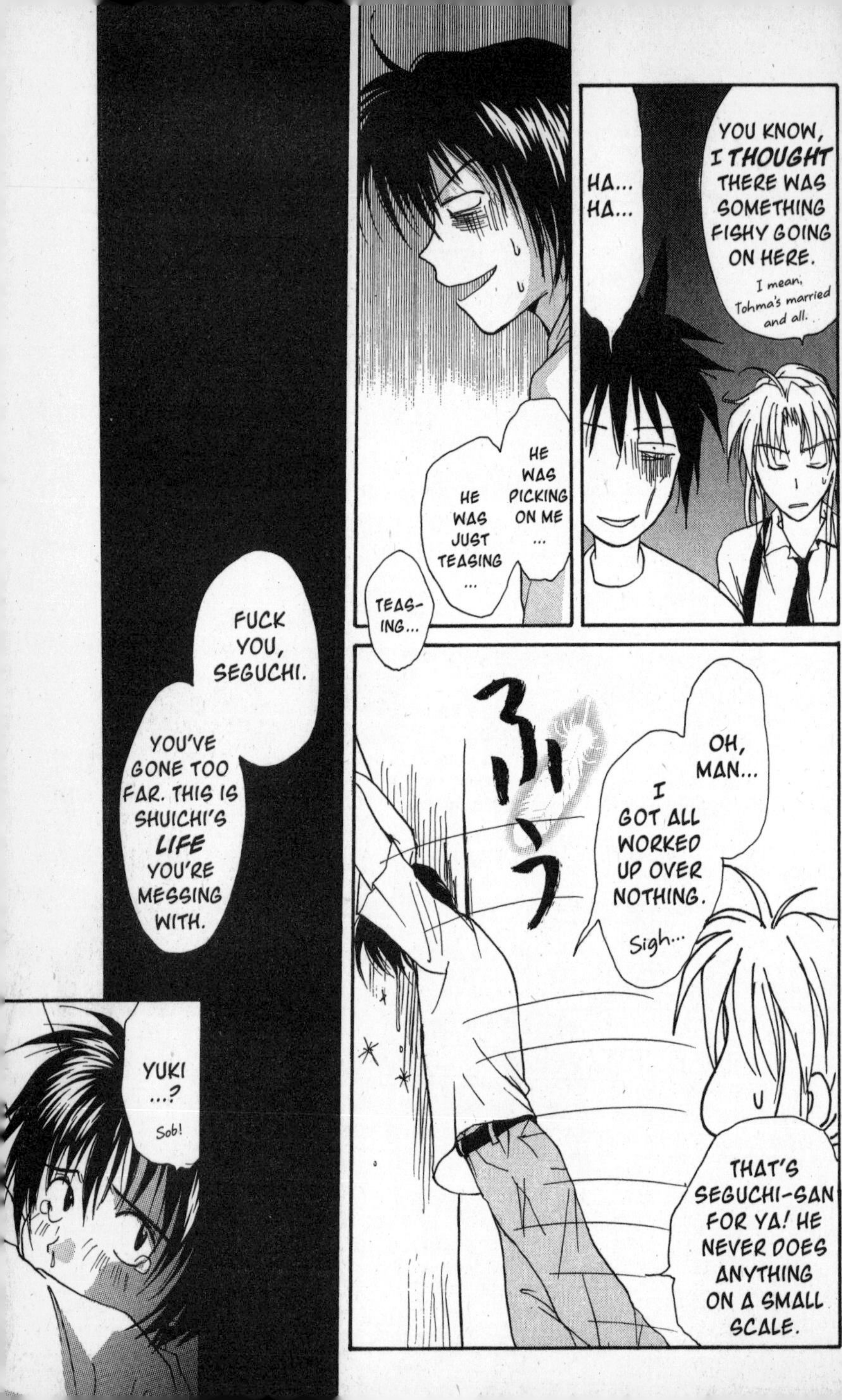
YOU KNOW, I THOUGHT THERE WAS SOMETHING FISHY GOING ON HERE.
I mean, Tohma's married and all.
HA... HA...
HE WAS PICKING ON ME ...
HE WAS JUST TEASING ...
TEAS-ING...
OH, MAN... I GOT ALL WORKED UP OVER NOTHING.
Sigh...
ふう
THAT'S SEGUCHI-SAN FOR YA! HE NEVER DOES ANYTHING ON A SMALL SCALE.
FUCK YOU, SEGUCHI.
YOU'VE GONE TOO FAR. THIS IS SHUICHI'S LIFE YOU'RE MESSING WITH.
YUKI ...?
Sob!

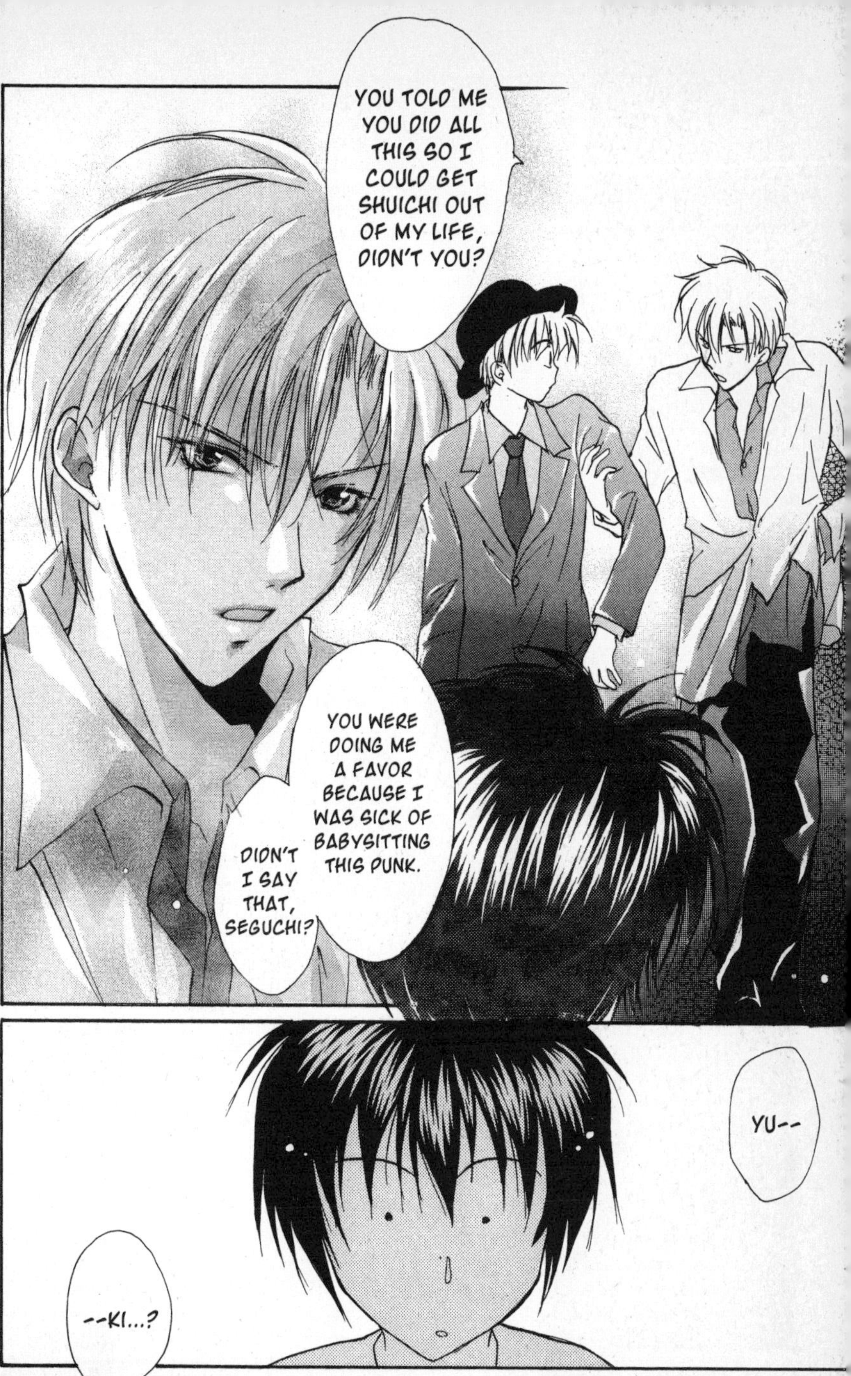
YOU TOLD ME YOU DID ALL THIS SO I COULD GET SHUICHI OUT OF MY LIFE, DIDN'T YOU?
YOU WERE DOING ME A FAVOR BECAUSE I WAS SICK OF BABYSITTING THIS PUNK.
DIDN'T I SAY THAT, SEGUCHI?
YU--
--KI...?

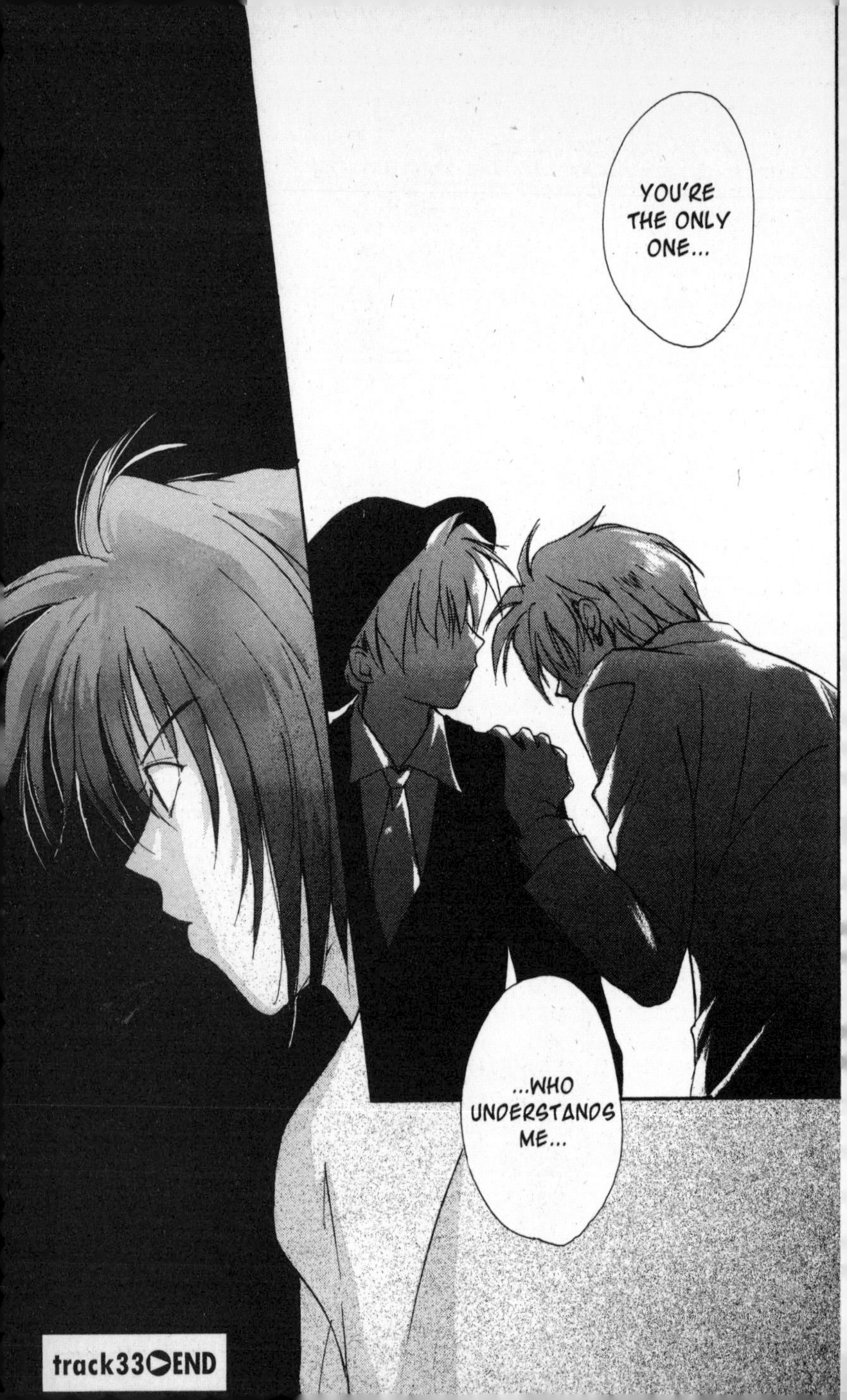
YOU'RE THE ONLY ONE...
...WHO UNDERSTANDS ME...
track33 END

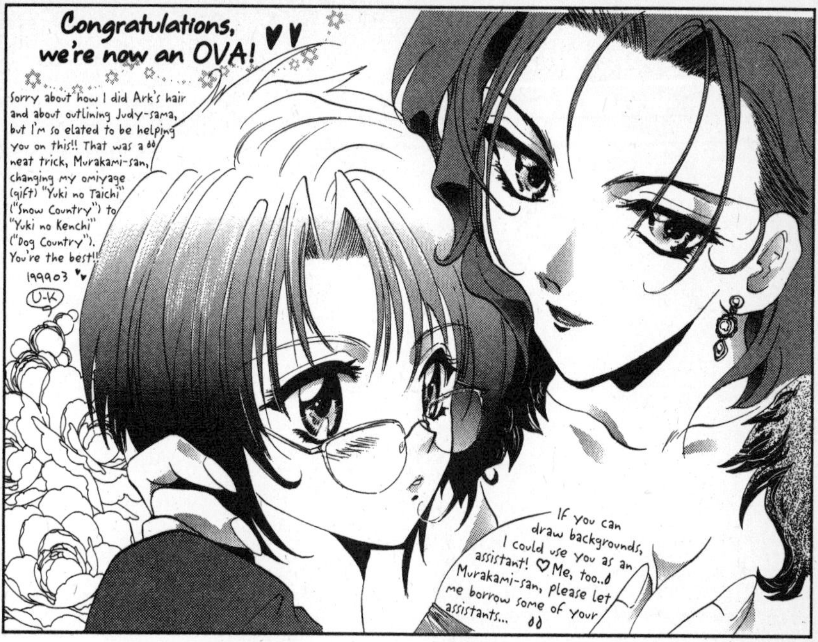
Congratulations, we're now an OVA!
Sorry about how I did Ark's hair and about outlining Judy-sama, but I'm so elated to be helping you on this!! That was a neat trick, Murakami-san, changing my omiyage (gift) "Yuki no Taichi" ("Snow Country") to "Yuki no Kenchi" ("Dog Country"). You're the best!! 199903
U-K
If you can draw backgrounds, I could use you as an assistant! ♡ Me, too.. Murakami-san, please let me borrow some of your assistants...

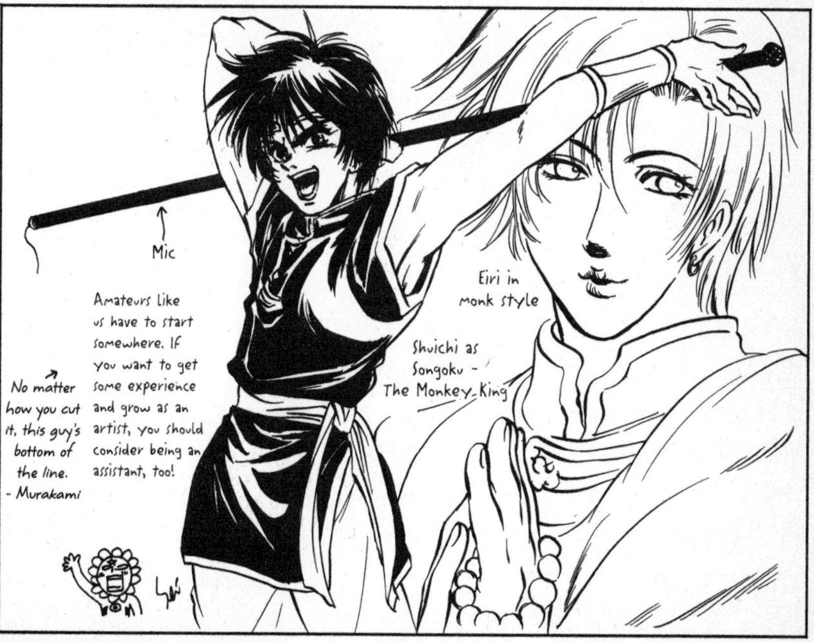
Eiri in monk style
Shuichi as Songoku - The Monkey King
Mic
Amateurs like us have to start somewhere. If you want to get some experience and grow as an artist, you should consider being an assistant, too!
No matter how you cut it, this guy's bottom of the line. - Murakami

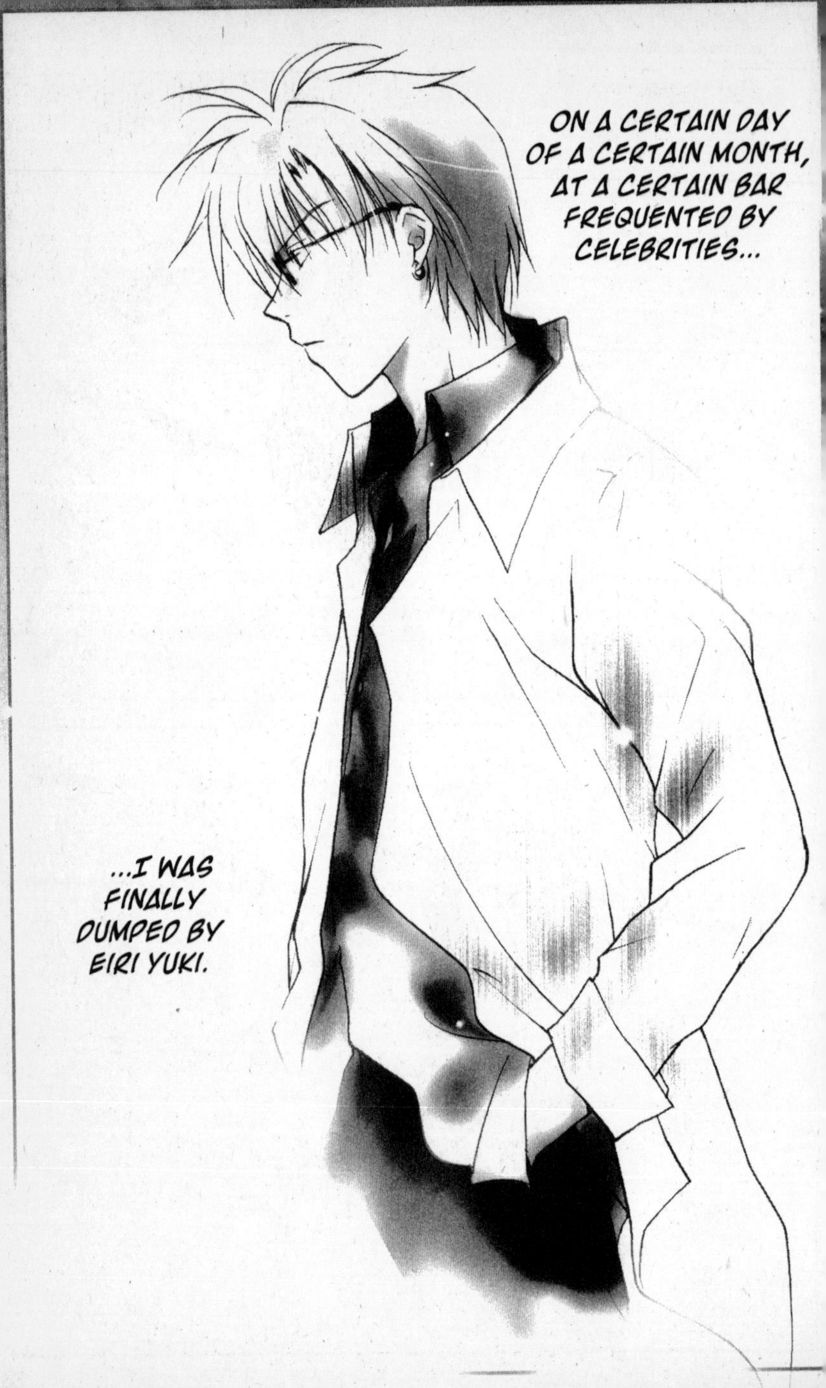
ON A CERTAIN DAY OF A CERTAIN MONTH, AT A CERTAIN BAR FREQUENTED BY CELEBRITIES...
...I WAS FINALLY DUMPED BY EIRI YUKI.

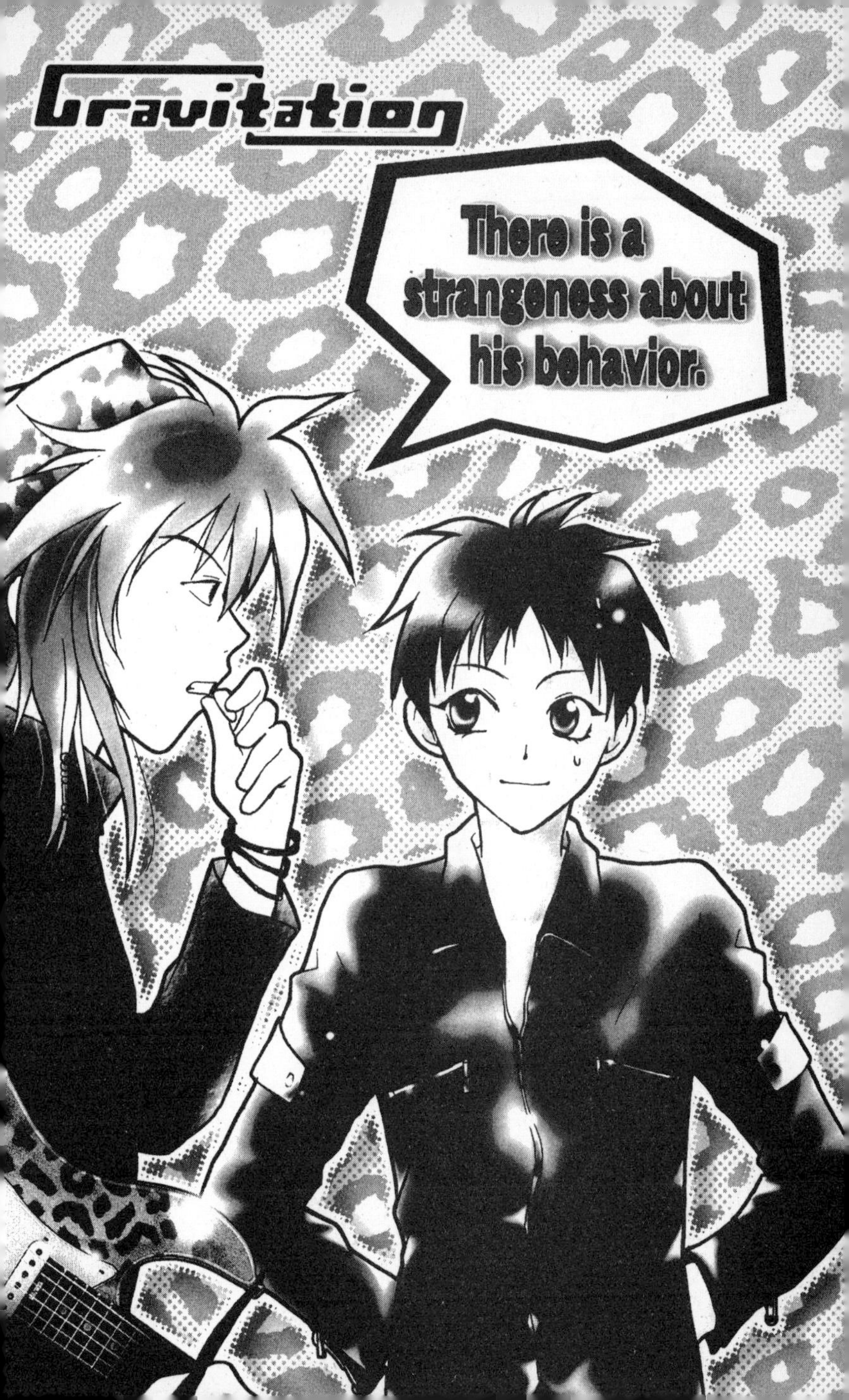
Gravitation
There is a strangeness about his behavior.

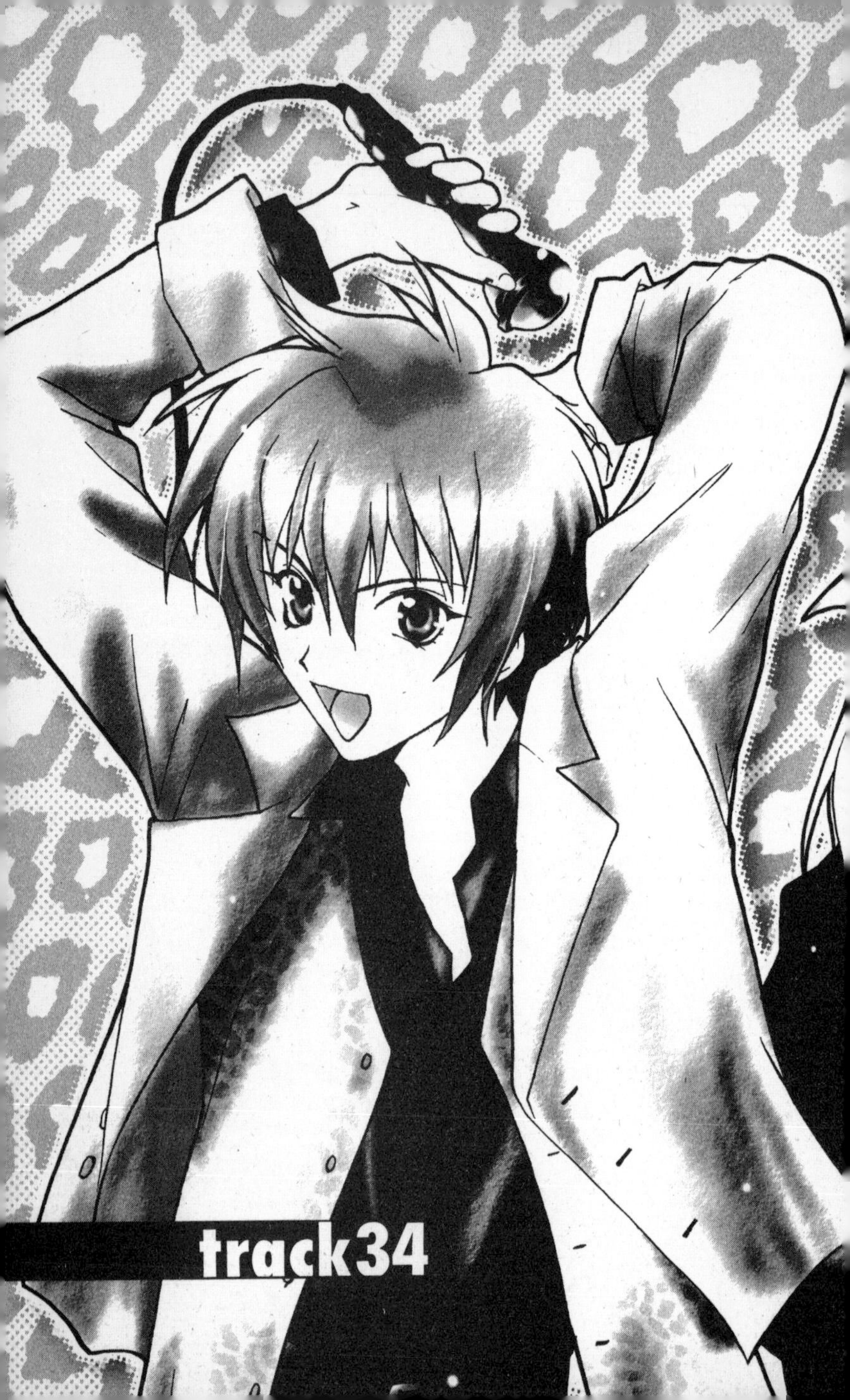
track 34

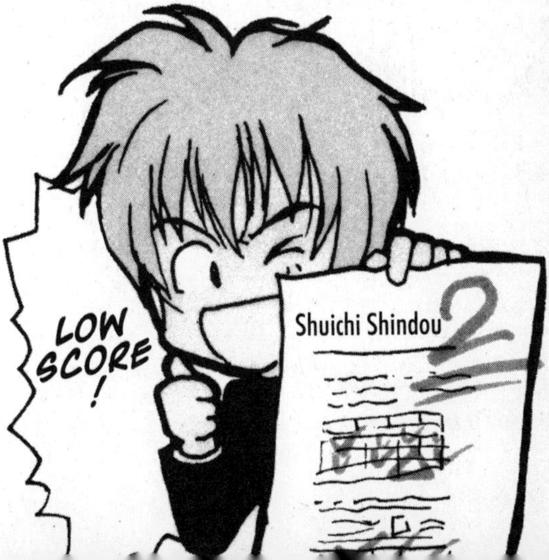
LOW SCORE!
Shuichi Shindou
2

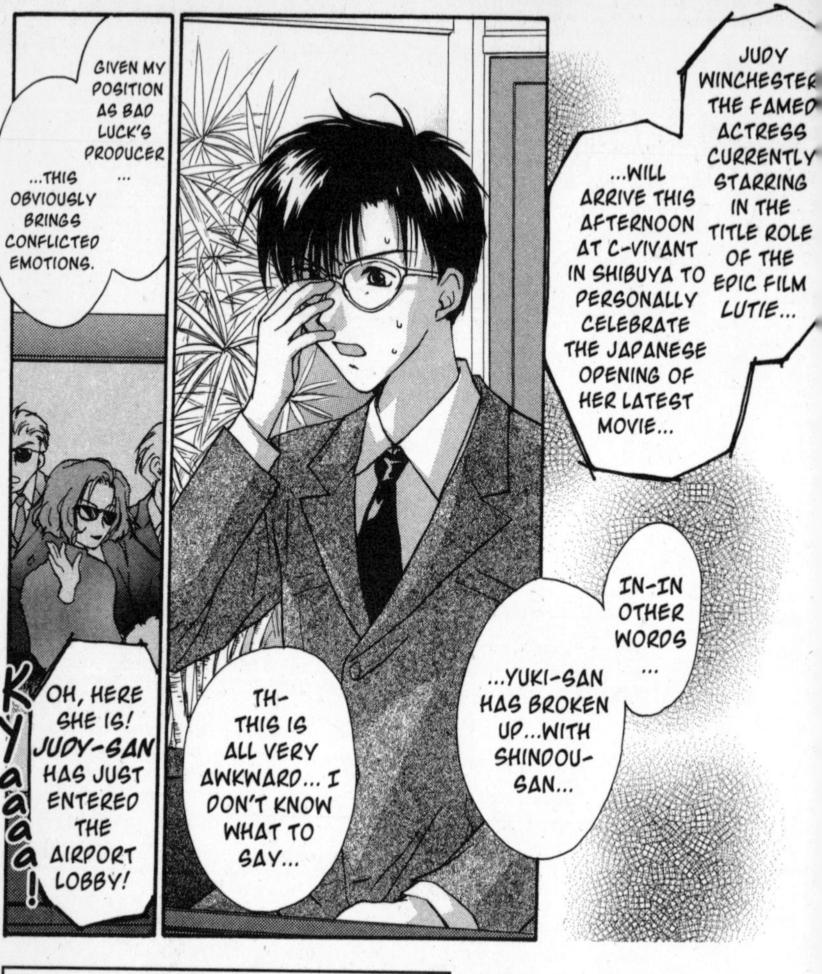
JUDY WINCHESTER THE FAMED ACTRESS CURRENTLY STARRING IN THE TITLE ROLE OF THE EPIC FILM LUTIE...
...WILL ARRIVE THIS AFTERNOON AT C-VIVANT IN SHIBUYA TO PERSONALLY CELEBRATE THE JAPANESE OPENING OF HER LATEST MOVIE...
IN-IN OTHER WORDS ...
...YUKI-SAN HAS BROKEN UP...WITH SHINDOU-SAN...
TH- THIS IS ALL VERY AWKWARD... I DON'T KNOW WHAT TO SAY...
GIVEN MY POSITION AS BAD LUCK'S PRODUCER ...
...THIS OBVIOUSLY BRINGS CONFLICTED EMOTIONS.
OH, HERE SHE IS! JUDY-SAN HAS JUST ENTERED THE AIRPORT LOBBY!
Kyaaaa!

ABOUT GRAVITATION TRACK 34

We're here at chapter 34! This time around, I've hired an assistant from a young boy's manga magazine!! He's really good with those speed lines, it's amazing. And as a special treat, I'm sliding some new characters in!! If you want to know why, it's because the story has gotten pretty thin (sorry, I'm being honest)!! A lot of unbelievable things happen in this episode, so if you try to skim through it, you might not understand where we end up later. I hope you'll read this installment carefully and pay attention to the dialogue. I mean it, it gets that complicated. I may have tried to cram too much in all at once...

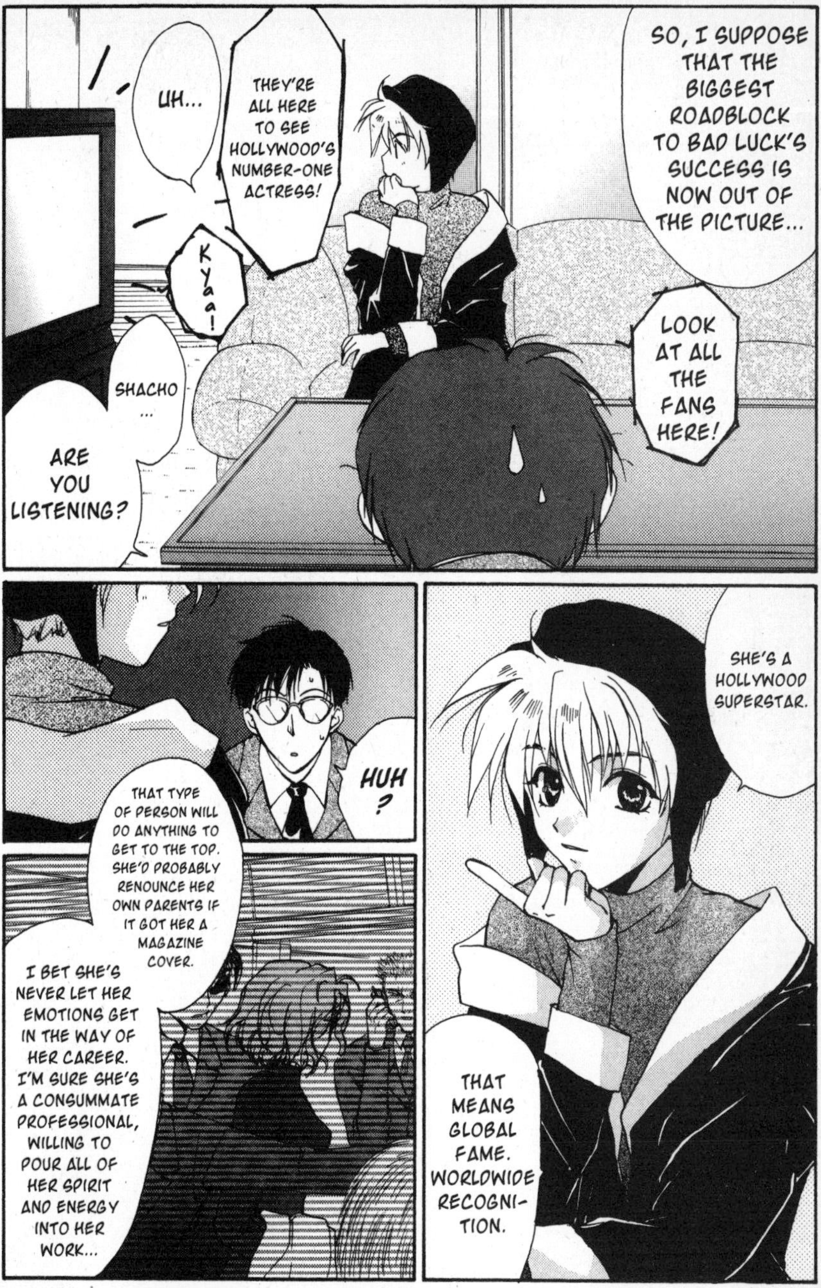
SO, I SUPPOSE THAT THE BIGGEST ROADBLOCK TO BAD LUCK'S SUCCESS IS NOW OUT OF THE PICTURE...
LOOK AT ALL THE FANS HERE!
THEY'RE ALL HERE TO SEE HOLLYWOOD'S NUMBER-ONE ACTRESS!
UH...
Kyaa!
SHACHO...
ARE YOU LISTENING?
SHE'S A HOLLYWOOD SUPERSTAR.
THAT MEANS GLOBAL FAME. WORLDWIDE RECOGNI-TION.
HUH?
THAT TYPE OF PERSON WILL DO ANYTHING TO GET TO THE TOP. SHE'D PROBABLY RENOUNCE HER OWN PARENTS IF IT GOT HER A MAGAZINE COVER.
I BET SHE'S NEVER LET HER EMOTIONS GET IN THE WAY OF HER CAREER. I'M SURE SHE'S A CONSUMMATE PROFESSIONAL, WILLING TO POUR ALL OF HER SPIRIT AND ENERGY INTO HER WORK...

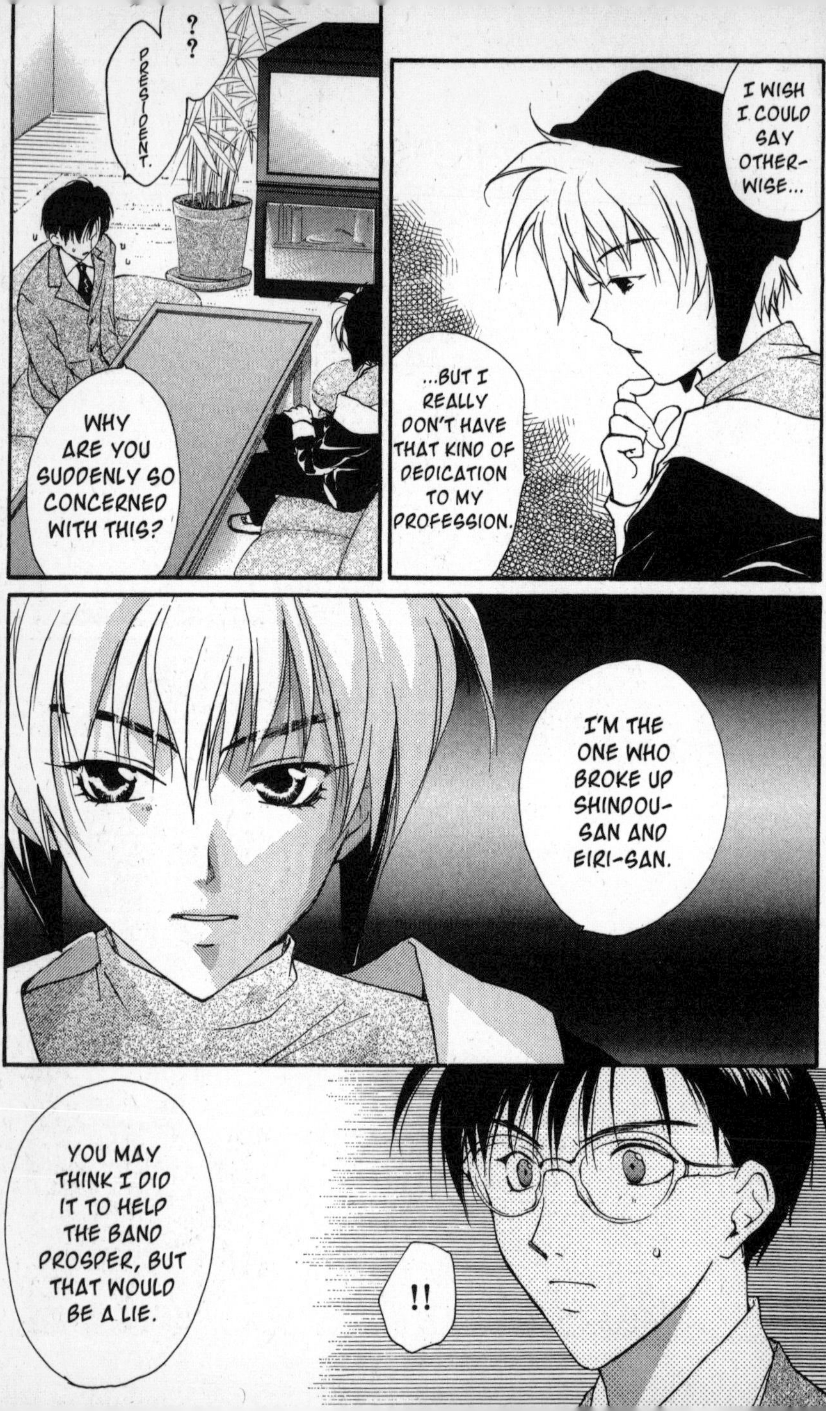
I WISH I COULD SAY OTHER-WISE...
...BUT I REALLY DON'T HAVE THAT KIND OF DEDICATION TO MY PROFESSION.
??
PRESIDENT.
WHY ARE YOU SUDDENLY SO CONCERNED WITH THIS?
I'M THE ONE WHO BROKE UP SHINDOU-SAN AND EIRI-SAN.
!!
YOU MAY THINK I DID IT TO HELP THE BAND PROSPER, BUT THAT WOULD BE A LIE.

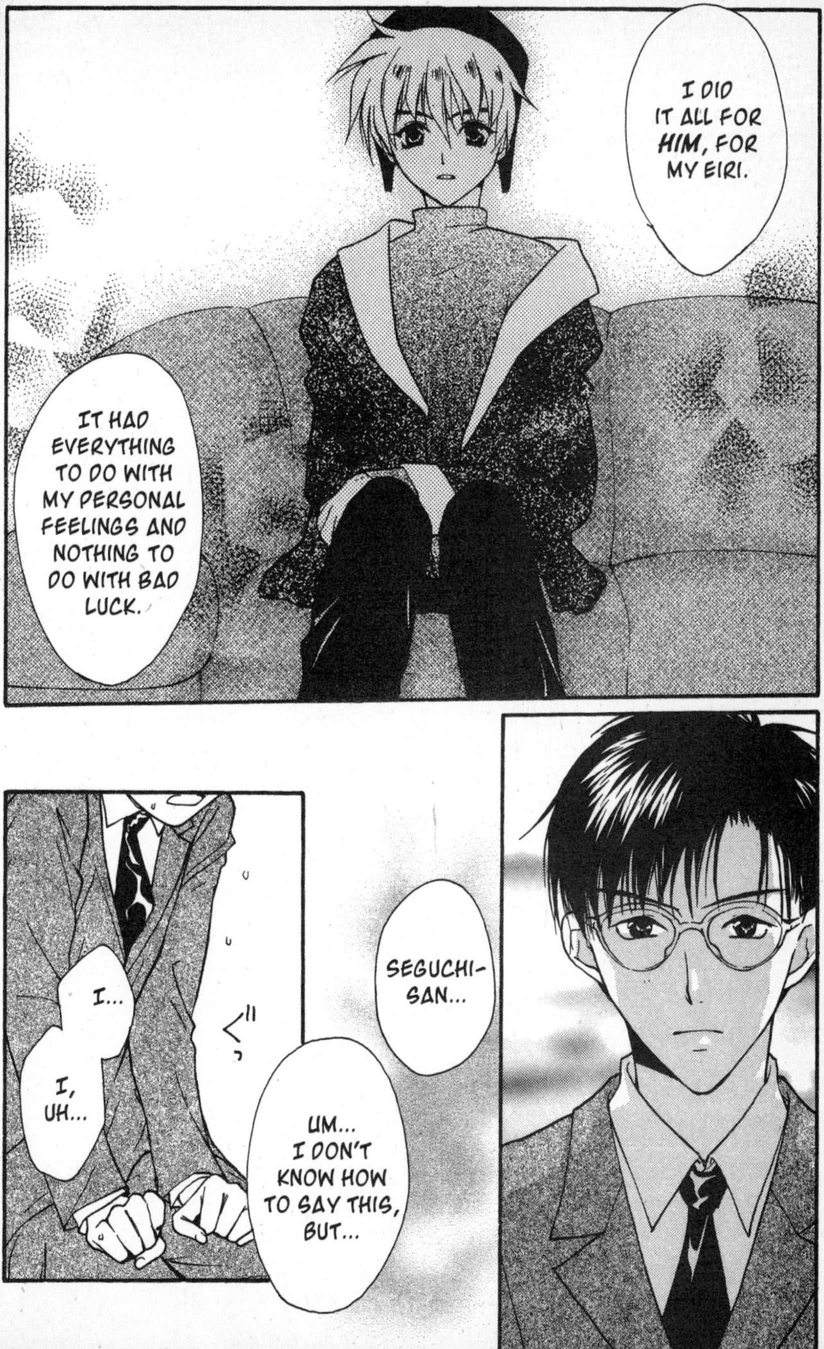
I DID IT ALL FOR HIM, FOR MY EIRI.
IT HAD EVERYTHING TO DO WITH MY PERSONAL FEELINGS AND NOTHING TO DO WITH BAD LUCK.
SEGUCHI-SAN...
UM... I DON'T KNOW HOW TO SAY THIS, BUT...
I...
I, UH...

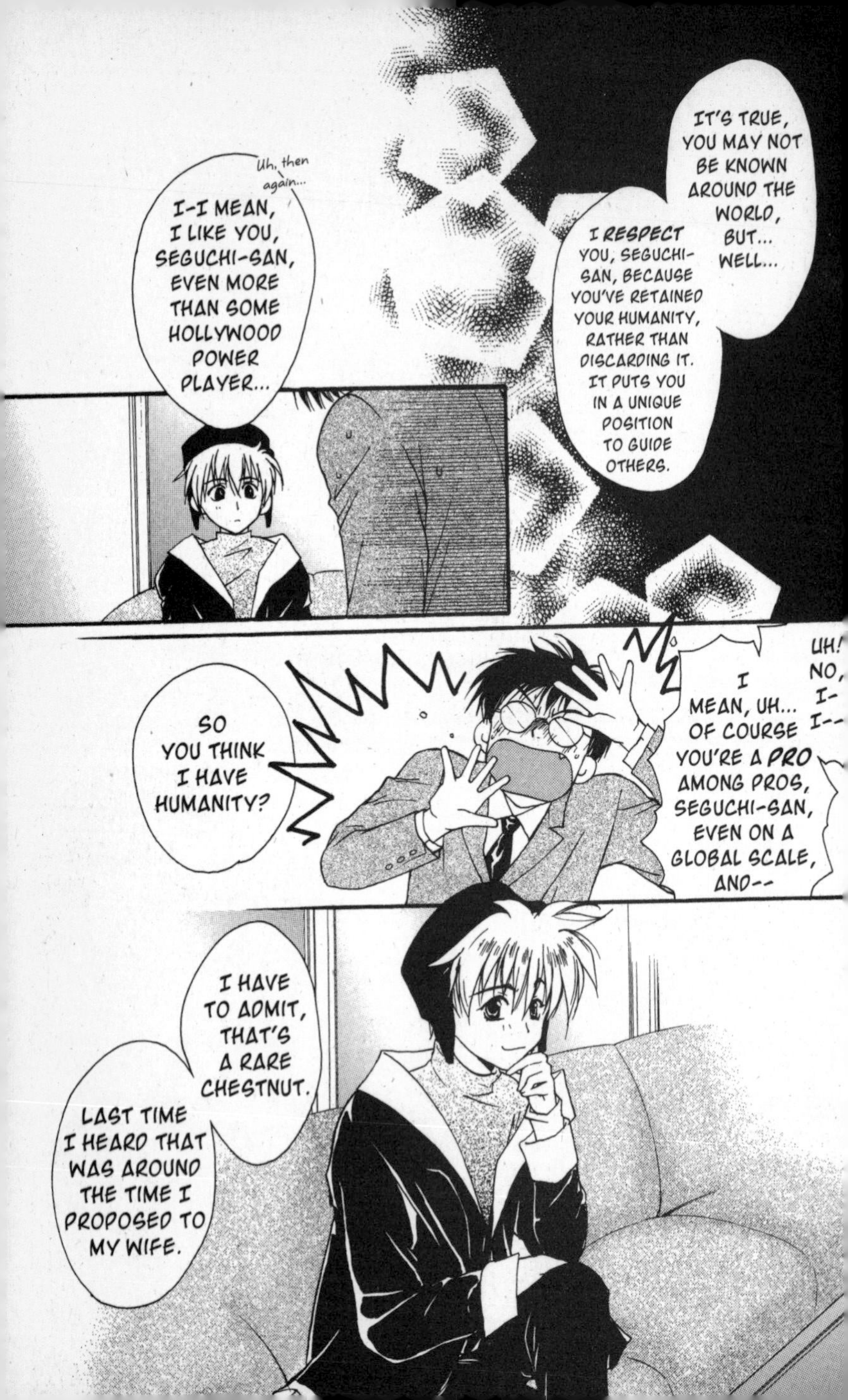
IT'S TRUE, YOU MAY NOT BE KNOWN AROUND THE WORLD, BUT... WELL...
I *RESPECT* YOU, SEGUCHI-SAN, BECAUSE YOU'VE RETAINED YOUR HUMANITY, RATHER THAN DISCARDING IT. IT PUTS YOU IN A UNIQUE POSITION TO GUIDE OTHERS.
Uh, then again...
I-I MEAN, I LIKE YOU, SEGUCHI-SAN, EVEN MORE THAN SOME HOLLYWOOD POWER PLAYER...
UH! NO, I- I--
I MEAN, UH... OF COURSE YOU'RE A *PRO* AMONG PROS, SEGUCHI-SAN, EVEN ON A GLOBAL SCALE, AND--
SO YOU THINK I HAVE HUMANITY?
I HAVE TO ADMIT, THAT'S A RARE CHESTNUT.
LAST TIME I HEARD THAT WAS AROUND THE TIME I PROPOSED TO MY WIFE.

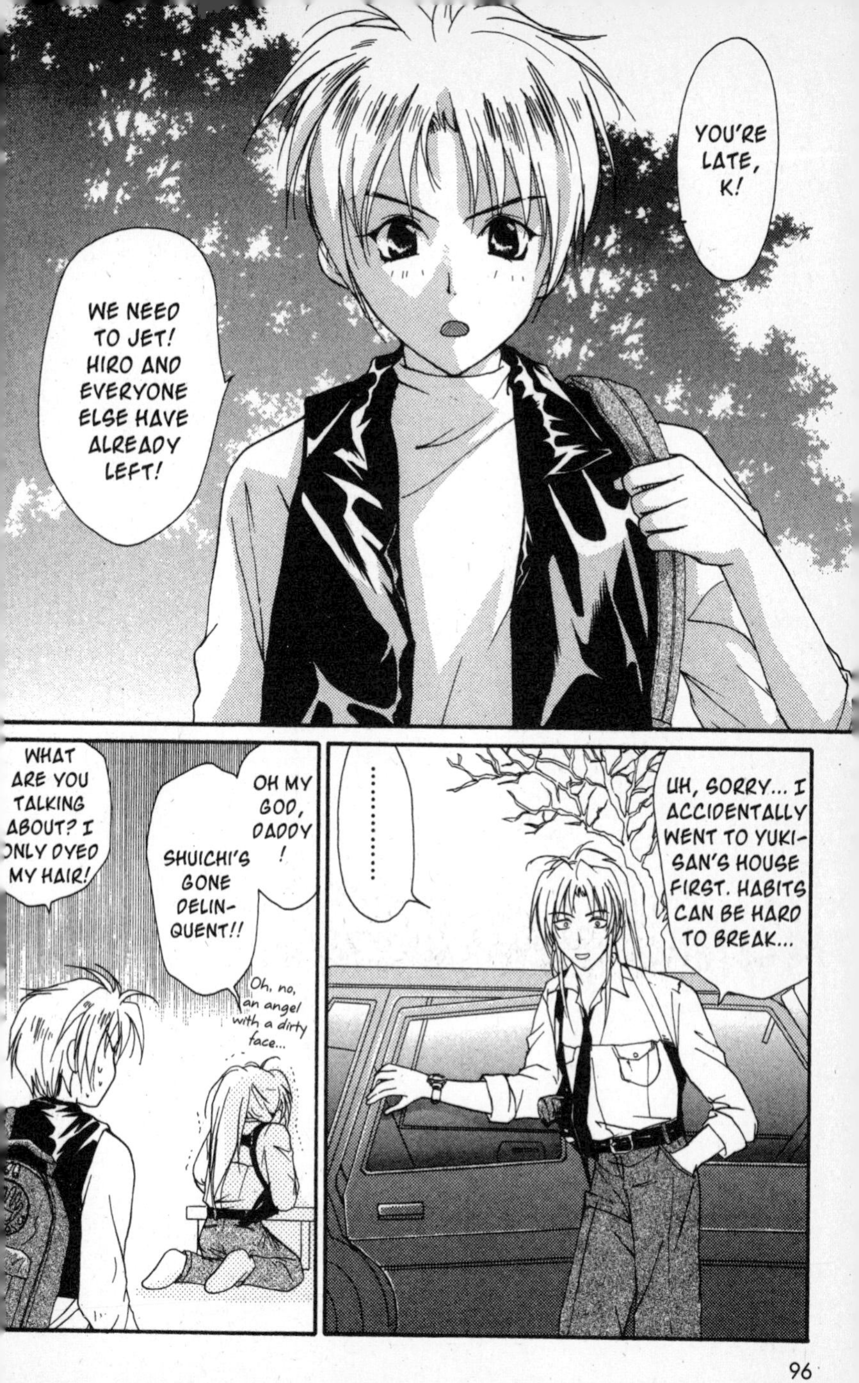
YOU'RE LATE, K!
WE NEED TO JET! HIRO AND EVERYONE ELSE HAVE ALREADY LEFT!
UH, SORRY... I ACCIDENTALLY WENT TO YUKI-SAN'S HOUSE FIRST. HABITS CAN BE HARD TO BREAK...
....
OH MY GOD, DADDY!
SHUICHI'S GONE DELIN-QUENT!!
Oh, no, an angel with a dirty face...
WHAT ARE YOU TALKING ABOUT? I ONLY DYED MY HAIR!

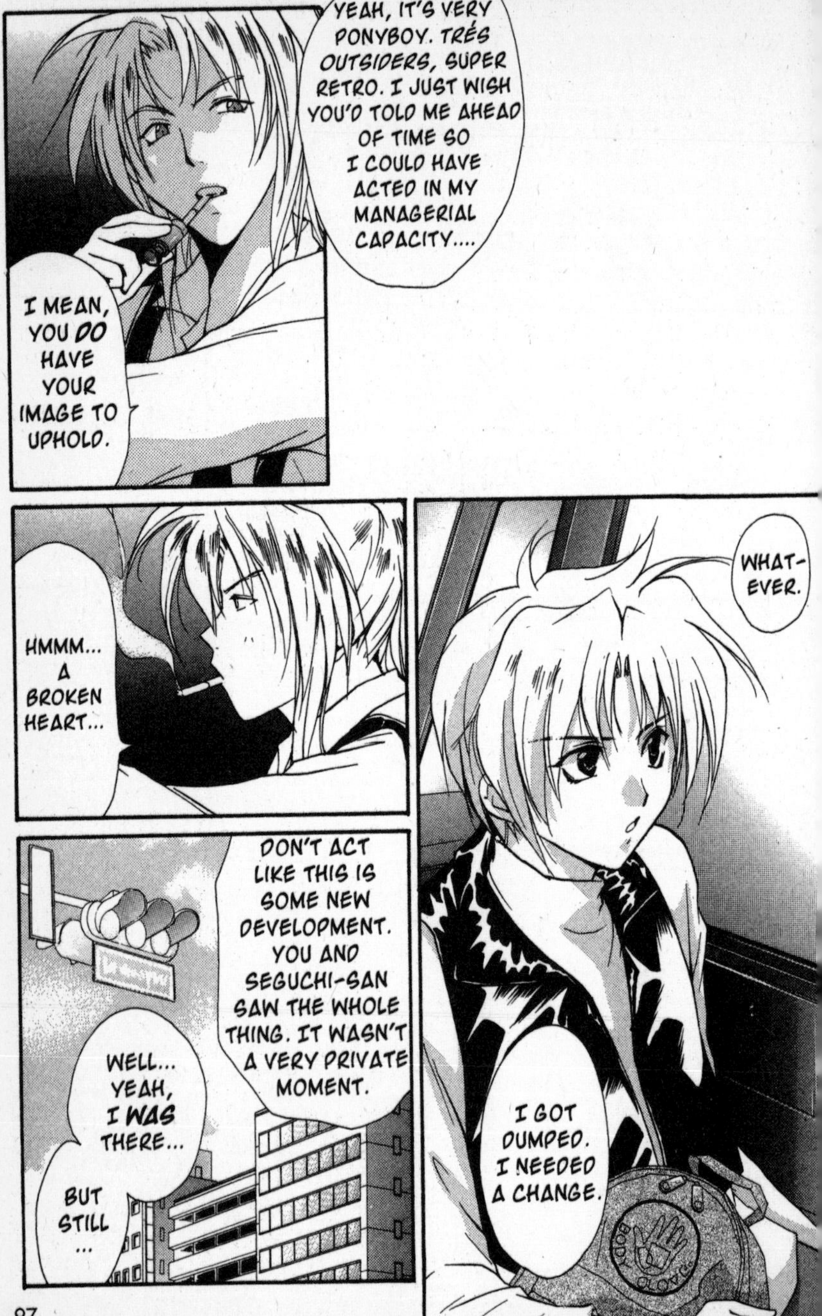
YEAH, IT'S VERY PONYBOY. TRÉS OUTSIDERS, SUPER RETRO. I JUST WISH YOU'D TOLD ME AHEAD OF TIME SO I COULD HAVE ACTED IN MY MANAGERIAL CAPACITY....
I MEAN, YOU *DO* HAVE YOUR IMAGE TO UPHOLD.
WHAT-EVER.
I GOT DUMPED. I NEEDED A CHANGE.
HMMM... A BROKEN HEART...
DON'T ACT LIKE THIS IS SOME NEW DEVELOPMENT. YOU AND SEGUCHI-SAN SAW THE WHOLE THING. IT WASN'T A VERY PRIVATE MOMENT.
WELL... YEAH, **I WAS** THERE...
BUT STILL ...

Continuance...

As you've probably noticed, these spaces are used to give a sneak peek at the next month's features in the anthology that serializes *Gravitation*. And this time, this space is in the OPPOSITE position of where it normally is.

That's right, usually it's on the left page, but this time it's on the opposite side.

In other words, I just made a mistake. I'm an idiot.

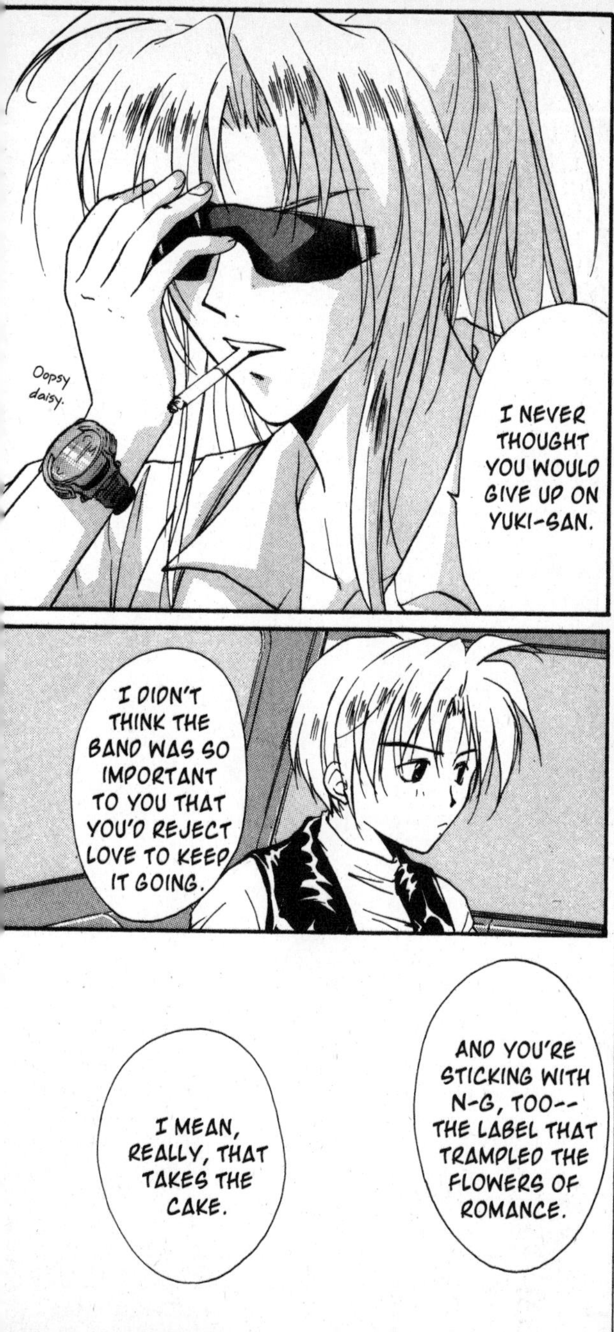

I NEVER THOUGHT YOU WOULD GIVE UP ON YUKI-SAN.
Oopsy daisy.
I DIDN'T THINK THE BAND WAS SO IMPORTANT TO YOU THAT YOU'D REJECT LOVE TO KEEP IT GOING.
AND YOU'RE STICKING WITH N-G, TOO-- THE LABEL THAT TRAMPLED THE FLOWERS OF ROMANCE.
I MEAN, REALLY, THAT TAKES THE CAKE.

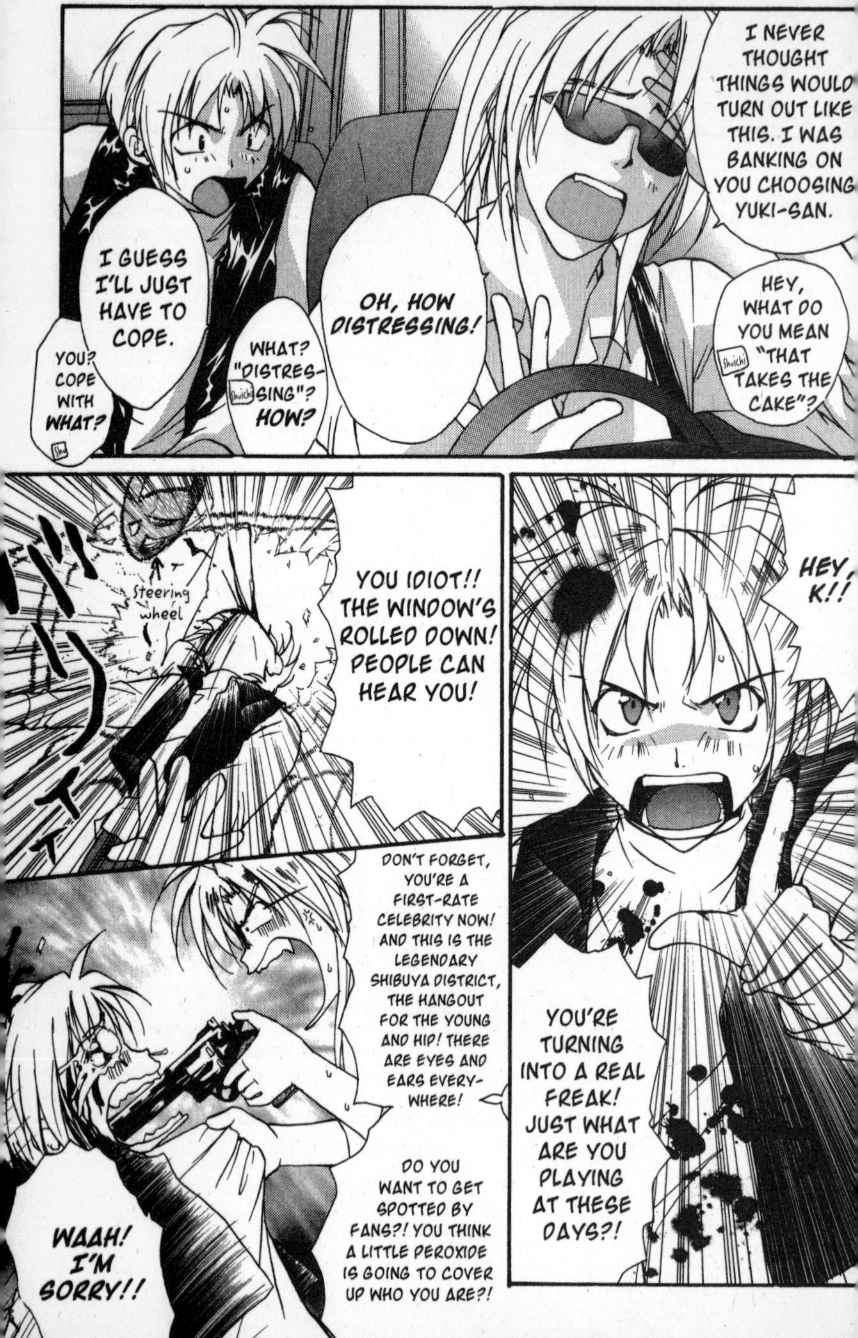
I NEVER THOUGHT THINGS WOULD TURN OUT LIKE THIS. I WAS BANKING ON YOU CHOOSING YUKI-SAN.
HEY, WHAT DO YOU MEAN "THAT TAKES THE CAKE"?
OH, HOW DISTRESSING!
WHAT? "DISTRES-SING"? HOW?
I GUESS I'LL JUST HAVE TO COPE.
YOU? COPE WITH WHAT?
HEY, K!!
YOU'RE TURNING INTO A REAL FREAK! JUST WHAT ARE YOU PLAYING AT THESE DAYS?!
YOU IDIOT!! THE WINDOW'S ROLLED DOWN! PEOPLE CAN HEAR YOU!
Steering wheel
DON'T FORGET, YOU'RE A FIRST-RATE CELEBRITY NOW! AND THIS IS THE LEGENDARY SHIBUYA DISTRICT, THE HANGOUT FOR THE YOUNG AND HIP! THERE ARE EYES AND EARS EVERY-WHERE!
DO YOU WANT TO GET SPOTTED BY FANS?! YOU THINK A LITTLE PEROXIDE IS GOING TO COVER UP WHO YOU ARE?!
WAAH! I'M SORRY!!

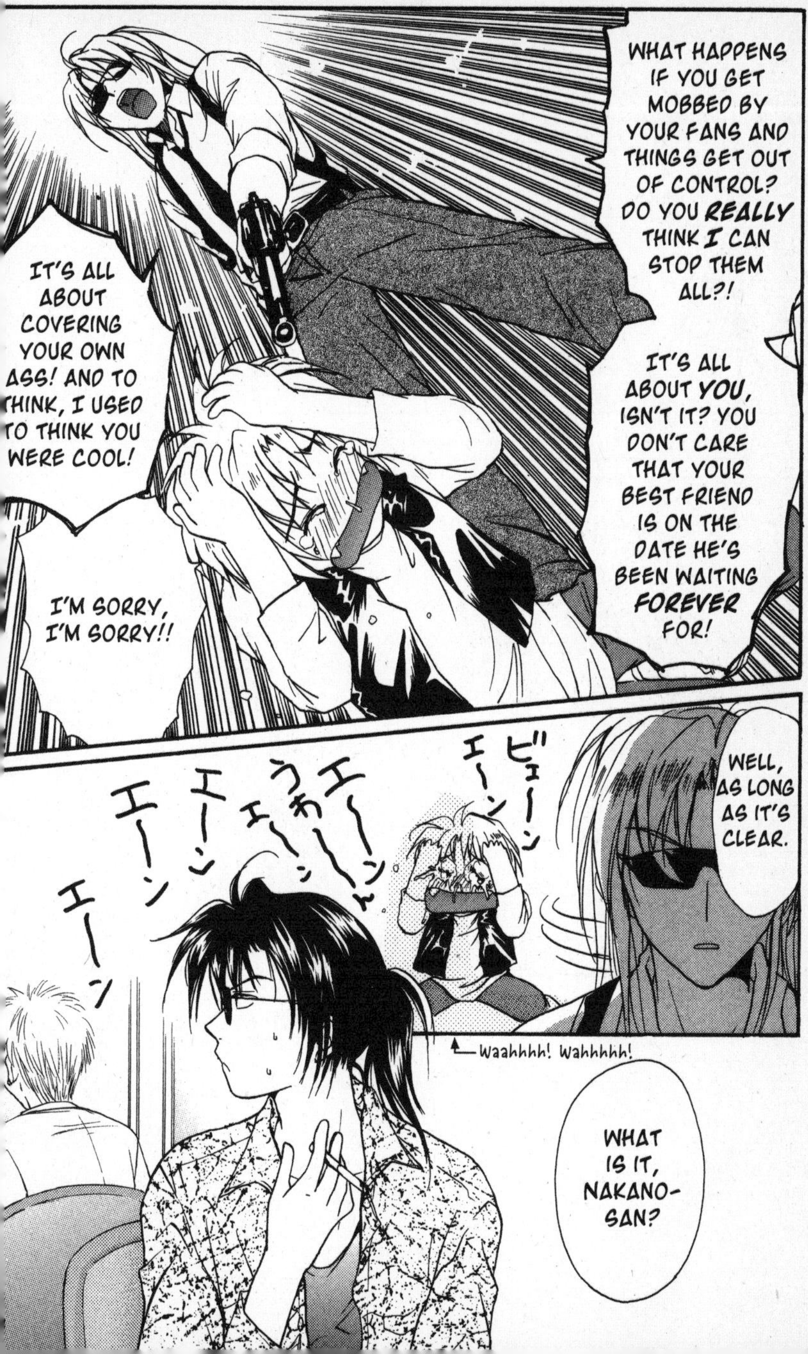
WHAT HAPPENS IF YOU GET MOBBED BY YOUR FANS AND THINGS GET OUT OF CONTROL? DO YOU **REALLY** THINK **I** CAN STOP THEM ALL?!
IT'S ALL ABOUT **YOU**, ISN'T IT? YOU DON'T CARE THAT YOUR BEST FRIEND IS ON THE DATE HE'S BEEN WAITING **FOREVER** FOR!
IT'S ALL ABOUT COVERING YOUR OWN ASS! AND TO THINK, I USED TO THINK YOU WERE COOL!
I'M SORRY, I'M SORRY!!
WELL, AS LONG AS IT'S CLEAR.
ビェーン
エーン
Waahhhh! Wahhhhh!
WHAT IS IT, NAKANO-SAN?

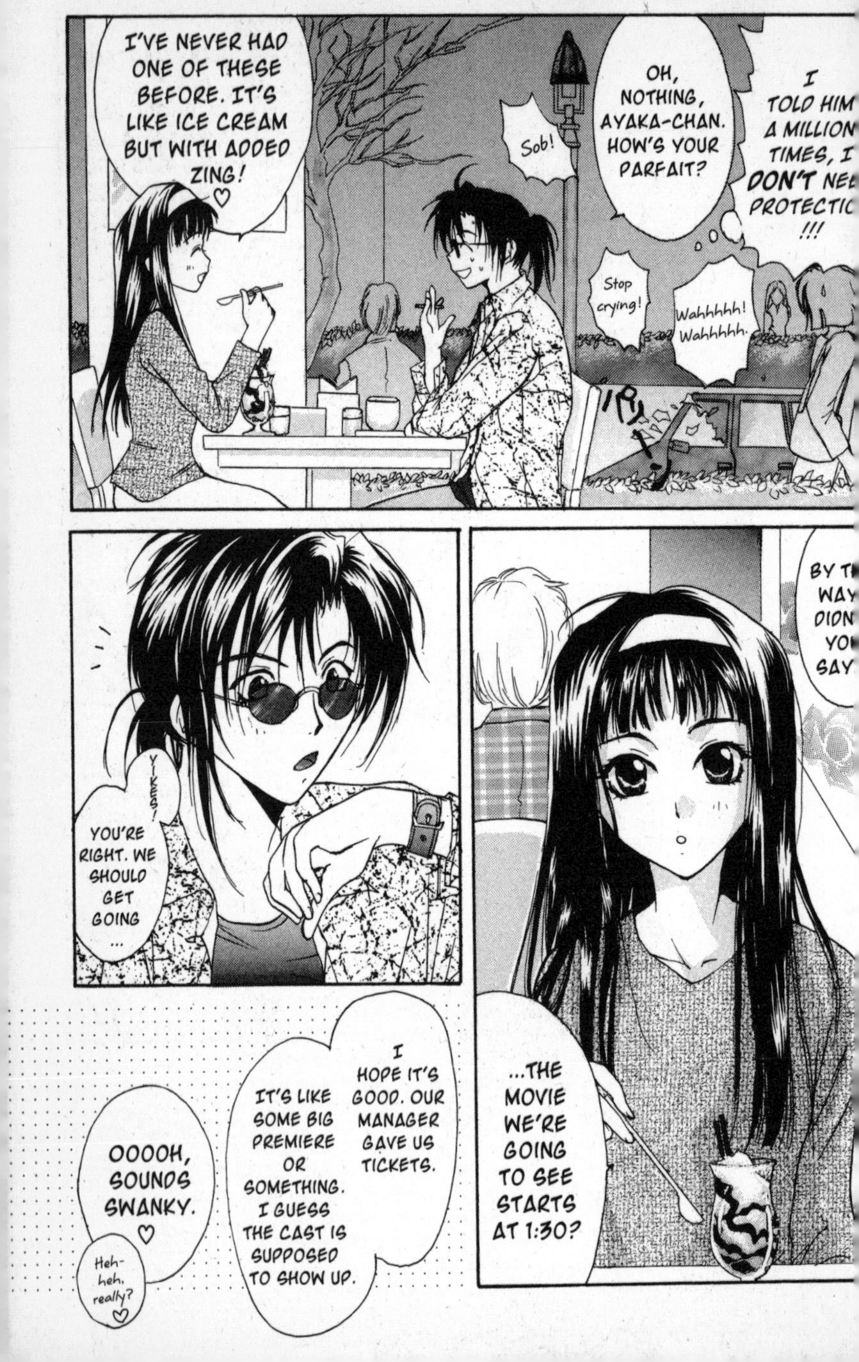
I TOLD HIM A MILLION TIMES, I DON'T NE PROTECTI !!!
Wahhhhh! Wahhhhh.
Stop crying!
OH, NOTHING, AYAKA-CHAN. HOW'S YOUR PARFAIT?
Sob!
I'VE NEVER HAD ONE OF THESE BEFORE. IT'S LIKE ICE CREAM BUT WITH ADDED ZING! ♡
BY T WAY DION YO SAY
...THE MOVIE WE'RE GOING TO SEE STARTS AT 1:30?
YIKES!
YOU'RE RIGHT. WE SHOULD GET GOING ...
I HOPE IT'S GOOD. OUR MANAGER GAVE US TICKETS.
IT'S LIKE SOME BIG PREMIERE OR SOMETHING. I GUESS THE CAST IS SUPPOSED TO SHOW UP.
OOOOH, SOUNDS SWANKY. ♡
Heh-heh, really? ♡

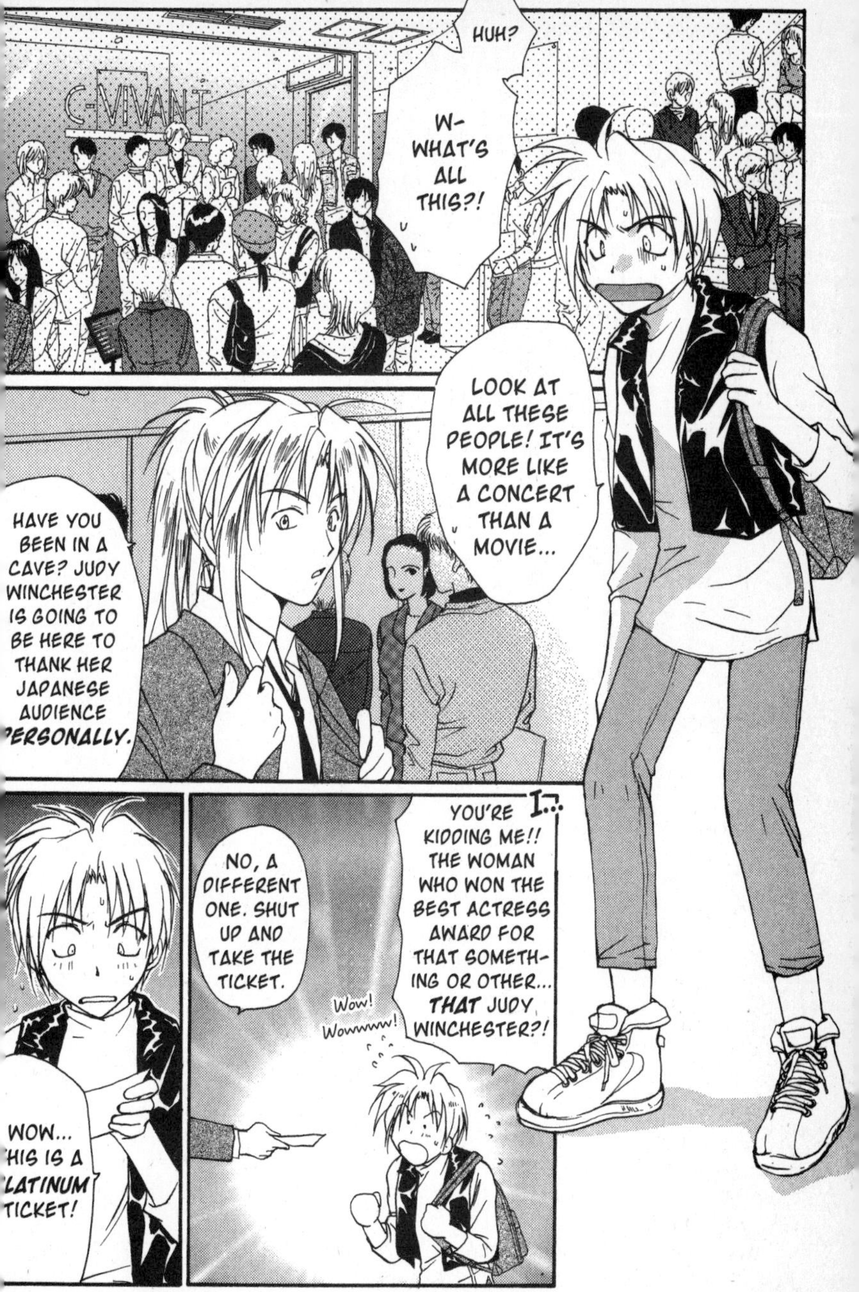
HUH?
W-WHAT'S ALL THIS?!
LOOK AT ALL THESE PEOPLE! IT'S MORE LIKE A CONCERT THAN A MOVIE...
HAVE YOU BEEN IN A CAVE? JUDY WINCHESTER IS GOING TO BE HERE TO THANK HER JAPANESE AUDIENCE PERSONALLY.
I...
YOU'RE KIDDING ME!! THE WOMAN WHO WON THE BEST ACTRESS AWARD FOR THAT SOMETHING OR OTHER... THAT JUDY WINCHESTER?!
NO, A DIFFERENT ONE. SHUT UP AND TAKE THE TICKET.
Wow! Wowwww!
WOW... HIS IS A LATINUM TICKET!
C-VIVANT

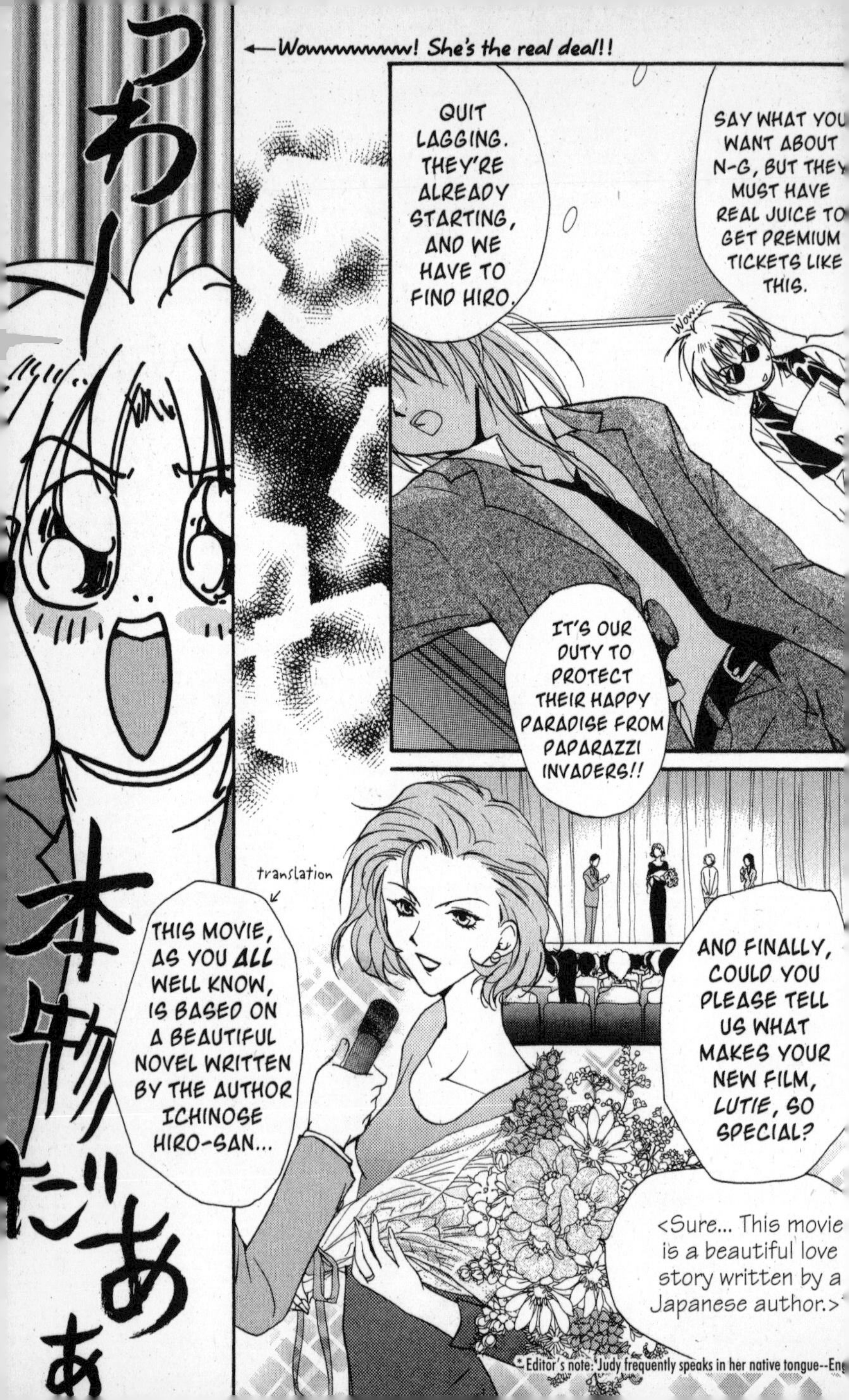
SAY WHAT YOU WANT ABOUT N-G, BUT THEY MUST HAVE REAL JUICE TO GET PREMIUM TICKETS LIKE THIS.
QUIT LAGGING. THEY'RE ALREADY STARTING, AND WE HAVE TO FIND HIRO.
Wow...
IT'S OUR DUTY TO PROTECT THEIR HAPPY PARADISE FROM PAPARAZZI INVADERS!!
AND FINALLY, COULD YOU PLEASE TELL US WHAT MAKES YOUR NEW FILM, LUTIE, SO SPECIAL?
<Sure... This movie is a beautiful love story written by a Japanese author.>
translation
THIS MOVIE, AS YOU ALL WELL KNOW, IS BASED ON A BEAUTIFUL NOVEL WRITTEN BY THE AUTHOR ICHINOSE HIRO-SAN...
* Editor's note: Judy frequently speaks in her native tongue--Eng
わ～～本物だああ
← Wowwwwwww! She's the real deal!!

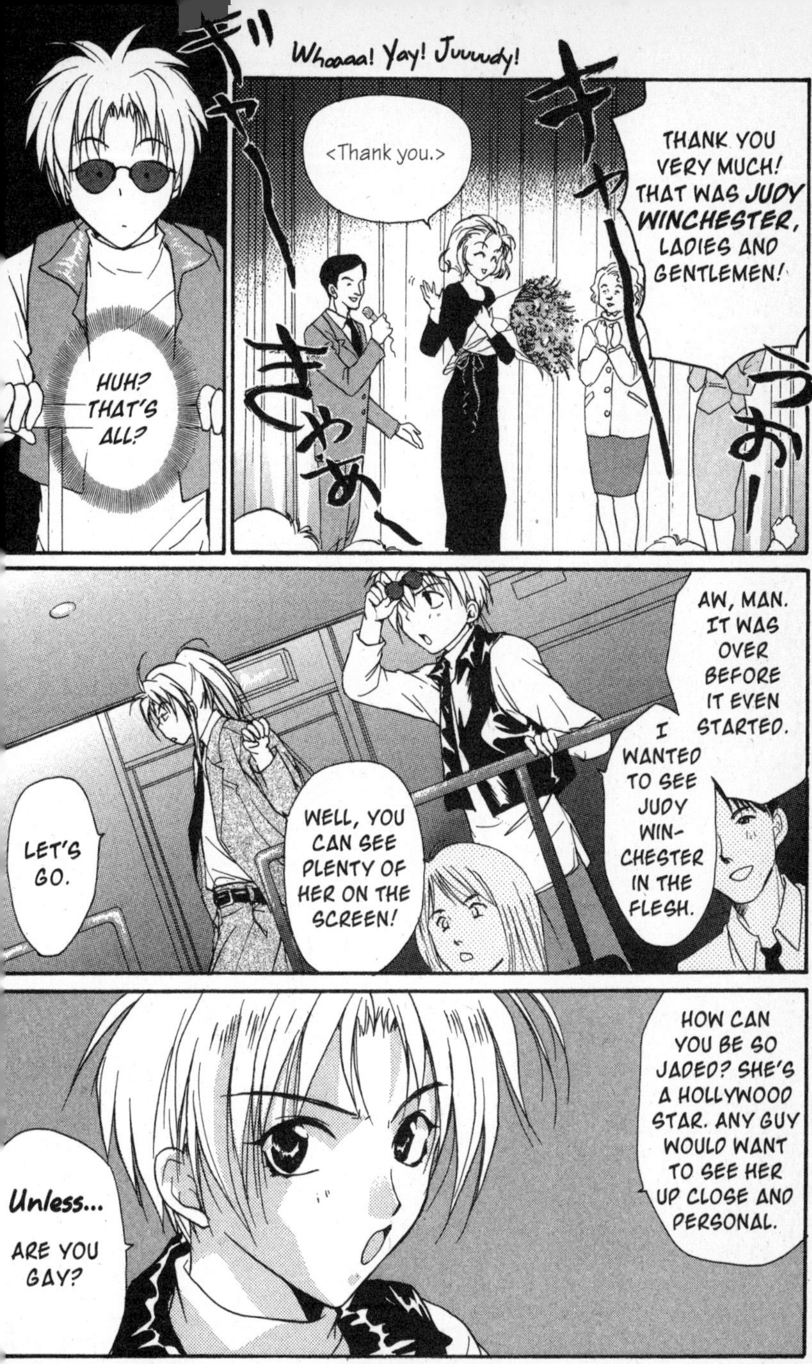

Whoaaa! Yay! Juuuudy!
THANK YOU VERY MUCH! THAT WAS **JUDY WINCHESTER**, LADIES AND GENTLEMEN!
<Thank you.>
HUH? THAT'S ALL?
AW, MAN. IT WAS OVER BEFORE IT EVEN STARTED.
I WANTED TO SEE JUDY WIN-CHESTER IN THE FLESH.
WELL, YOU CAN SEE PLENTY OF HER ON THE SCREEN!
LET'S GO.
HOW CAN YOU BE SO JADED? SHE'S A HOLLYWOOD STAR. ANY GUY WOULD WANT TO SEE HER UP CLOSE AND PERSONAL.
Unless...
ARE YOU GAY?

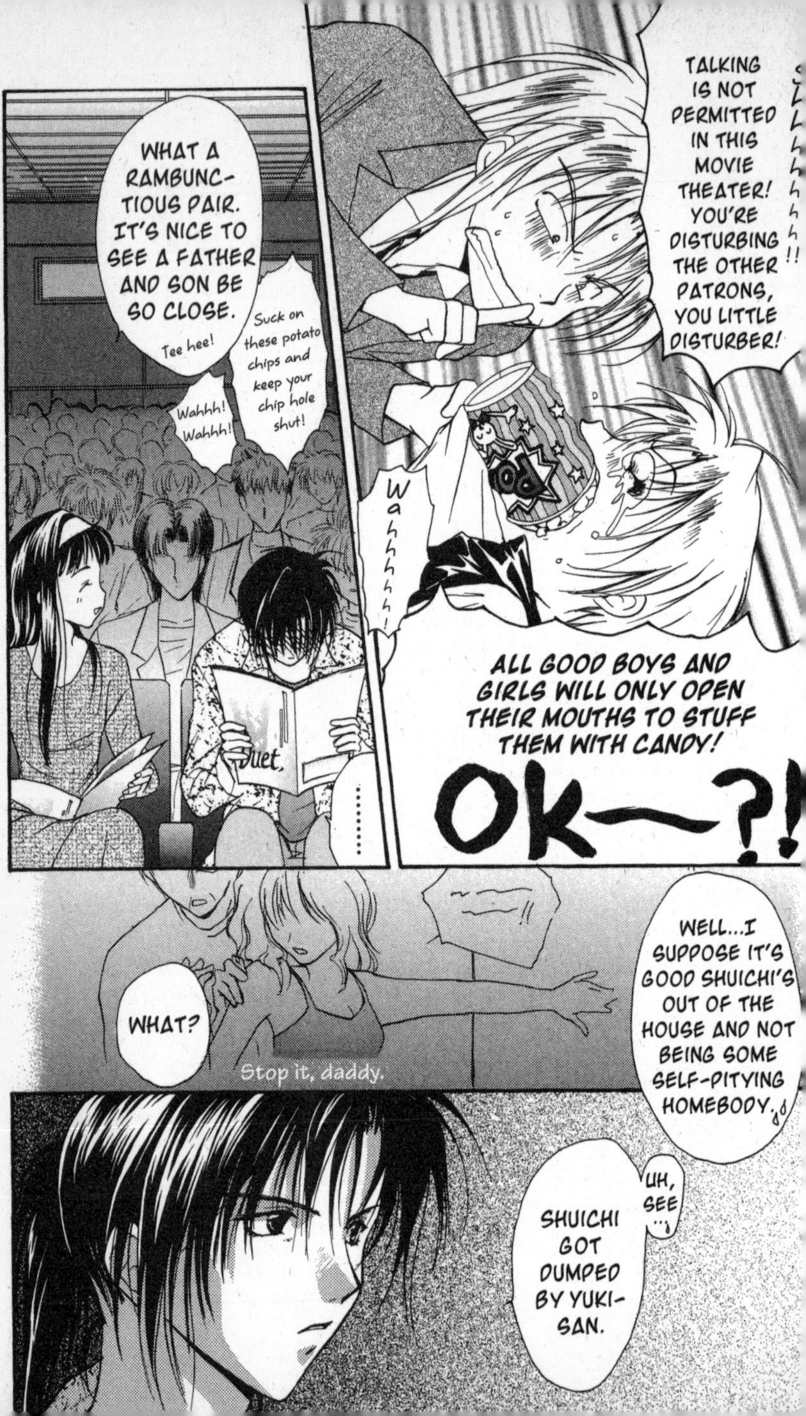

TALKING IS NOT PERMITTED IN THIS MOVIE THEATER! YOU'RE DISTURBING THE OTHER PATRONS, YOU LITTLE DISTURBER!
Shhhhhhhh!!
Wahhhhhh!
ALL GOOD BOYS AND GIRLS WILL ONLY OPEN THEIR MOUTHS TO STUFF THEM WITH CANDY!
OK—?!
WHAT A RAMBUNCTIOUS PAIR. IT'S NICE TO SEE A FATHER AND SON BE SO CLOSE.
Tee hee!
Suck on these potato chips and keep your chip hole shut!
Wahhh! Wahhh!
Duet
WELL...I SUPPOSE IT'S GOOD SHUICHI'S OUT OF THE HOUSE AND NOT BEING SOME SELF-PITYING HOMEBODY.
WHAT?
Stop it, daddy.
UH, SEE...
SHUICHI GOT DUMPED BY YUKI-SAN.

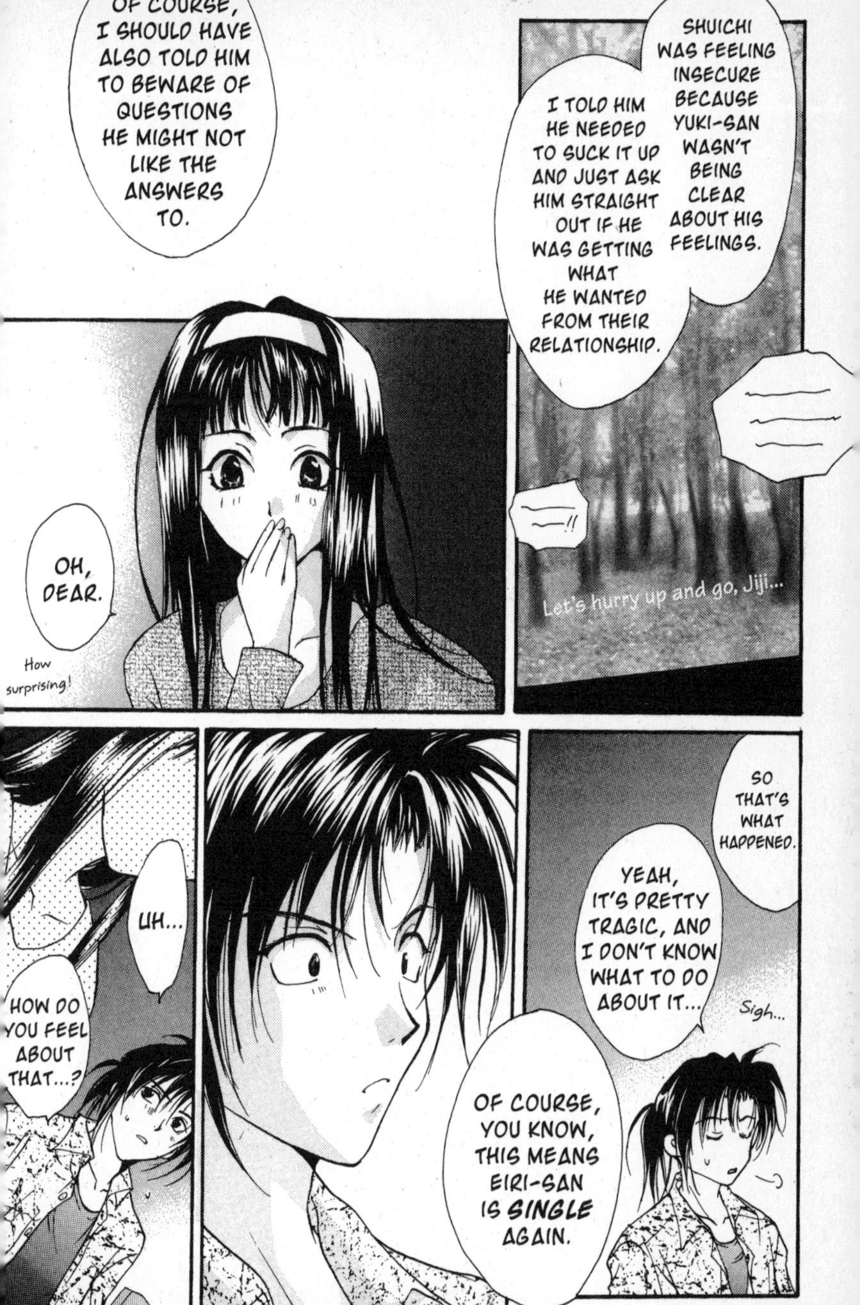
SHUICHI WAS FEELING INSECURE BECAUSE YUKI-SAN WASN'T BEING CLEAR ABOUT HIS FEELINGS.
I TOLD HIM HE NEEDED TO SUCK IT UP AND JUST ASK HIM STRAIGHT OUT IF HE WAS GETTING WHAT HE WANTED FROM THEIR RELATIONSHIP.
——
——!!
Let's hurry up and go, Jiji...
OF COURSE, I SHOULD HAVE ALSO TOLD HIM TO BEWARE OF QUESTIONS HE MIGHT NOT LIKE THE ANSWERS TO.
OH, DEAR.
How surprising!
SO THAT'S WHAT HAPPENED.
YEAH, IT'S PRETTY TRAGIC, AND I DON'T KNOW WHAT TO DO ABOUT IT...
Sigh...
OF COURSE, YOU KNOW, THIS MEANS EIRI-SAN IS **SINGLE** AGAIN.
UH...
HOW DO YOU FEEL ABOUT THAT...?

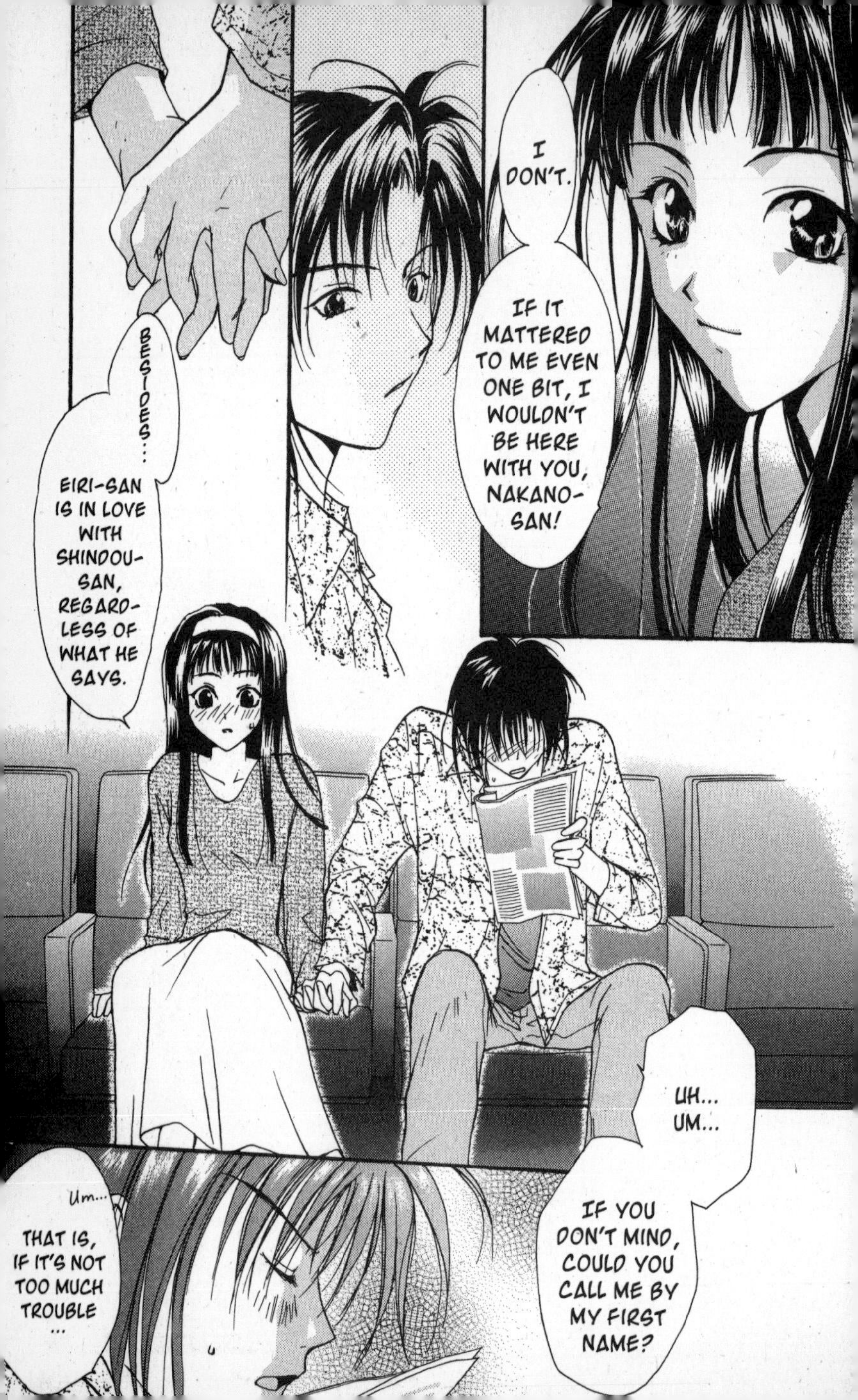
I DON'T.
IF IT MATTERED TO ME EVEN ONE BIT, I WOULDN'T BE HERE WITH YOU, NAKANO-SAN!
BESIDES...
EIRI-SAN IS IN LOVE WITH SHINDOU-SAN, REGARDLESS OF WHAT HE SAYS.
UH... UM...
IF YOU DON'T MIND, COULD YOU CALL ME BY MY FIRST NAME?
Um...
THAT IS, IF IT'S NOT TOO MUCH TROUBLE ...

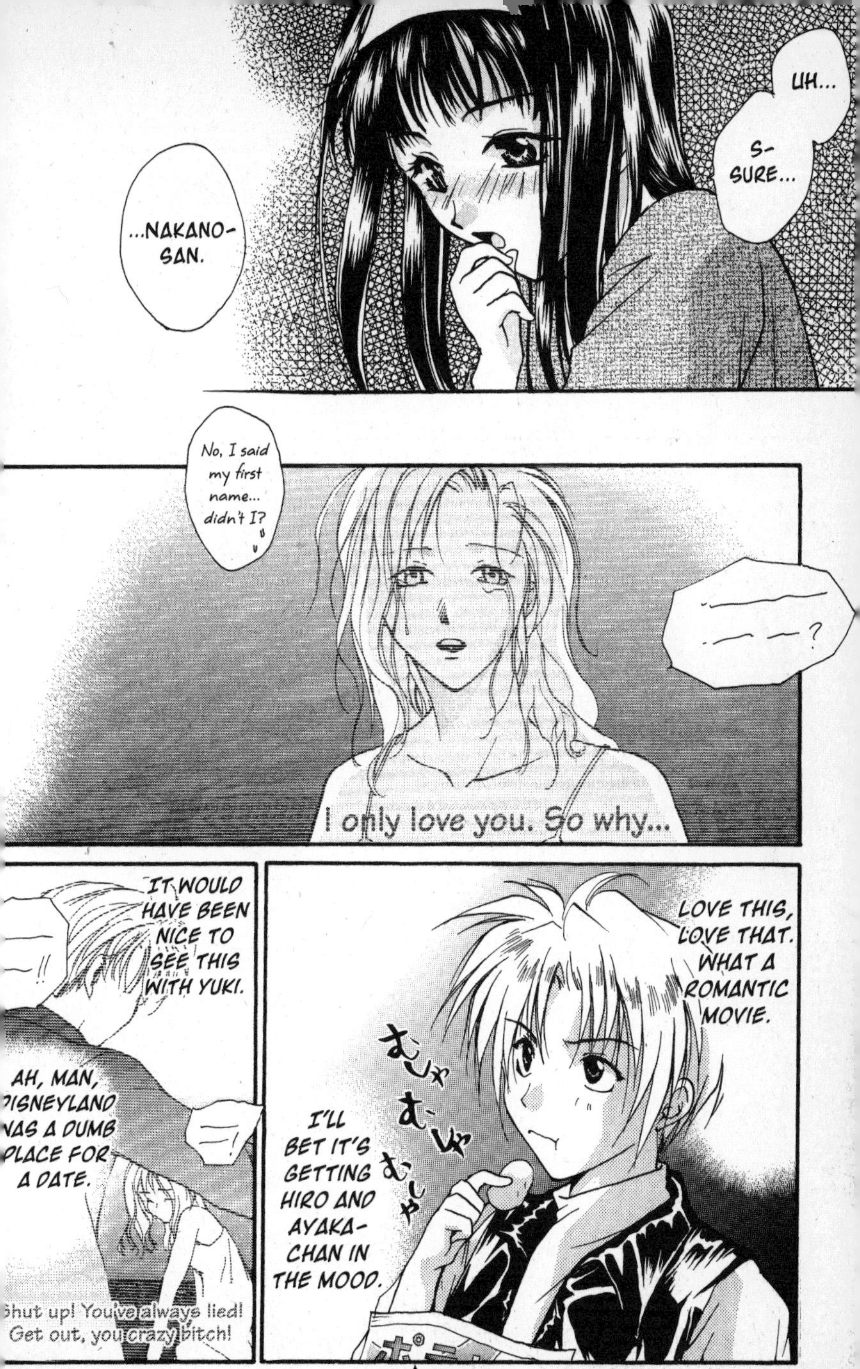
UH... S-SURE...
...NAKANO-SAN.
—— ——?
No, I said my first name... didn't I?
I only love you. So why...
LOVE THIS, LOVE THAT. WHAT A ROMANTIC MOVIE.
I'LL BET IT'S GETTING HIRO AND AYAKA-CHAN IN THE MOOD.
munch munch munch
IT WOULD HAVE BEEN NICE TO SEE THIS WITH YUKI.
!!
—!
AH, MAN, DISNEYLAND WAS A DUMB PLACE FOR A DATE.
Shut up! You've always lied! Get out, you crazy bitch!

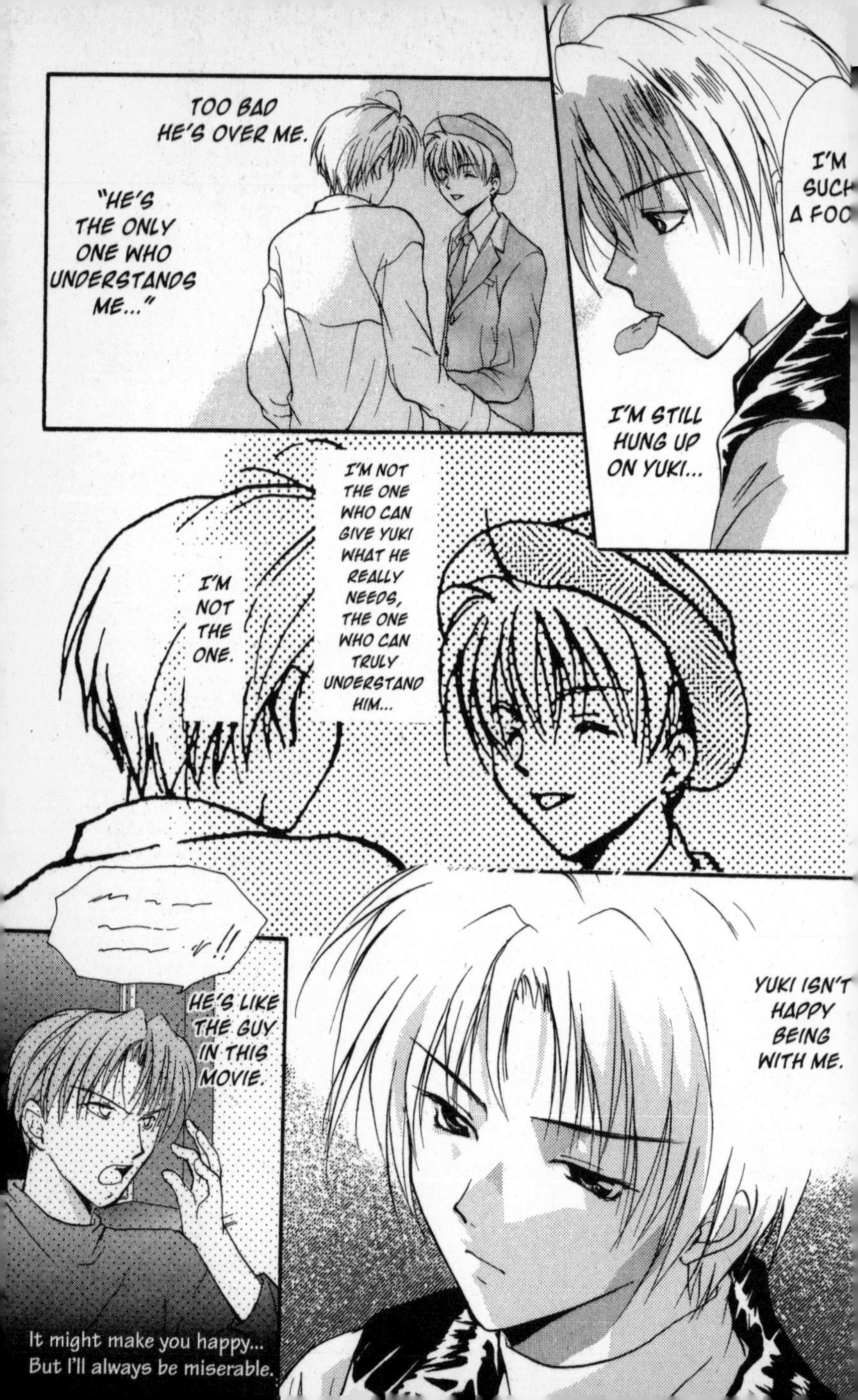
I'M SUCH A FOO
I'M STILL HUNG UP ON YUKI...
TOO BAD HE'S OVER ME.
"HE'S THE ONLY ONE WHO UNDERSTANDS ME..."
I'M NOT THE ONE WHO CAN GIVE YUKI WHAT HE REALLY NEEDS, THE ONE WHO CAN TRULY UNDERSTAND HIM...
I'M NOT THE ONE.
YUKI ISN'T HAPPY BEING WITH ME.
HE'S LIKE THE GUY IN THIS MOVIE.
It might make you happy...
But I'll always be miserable.

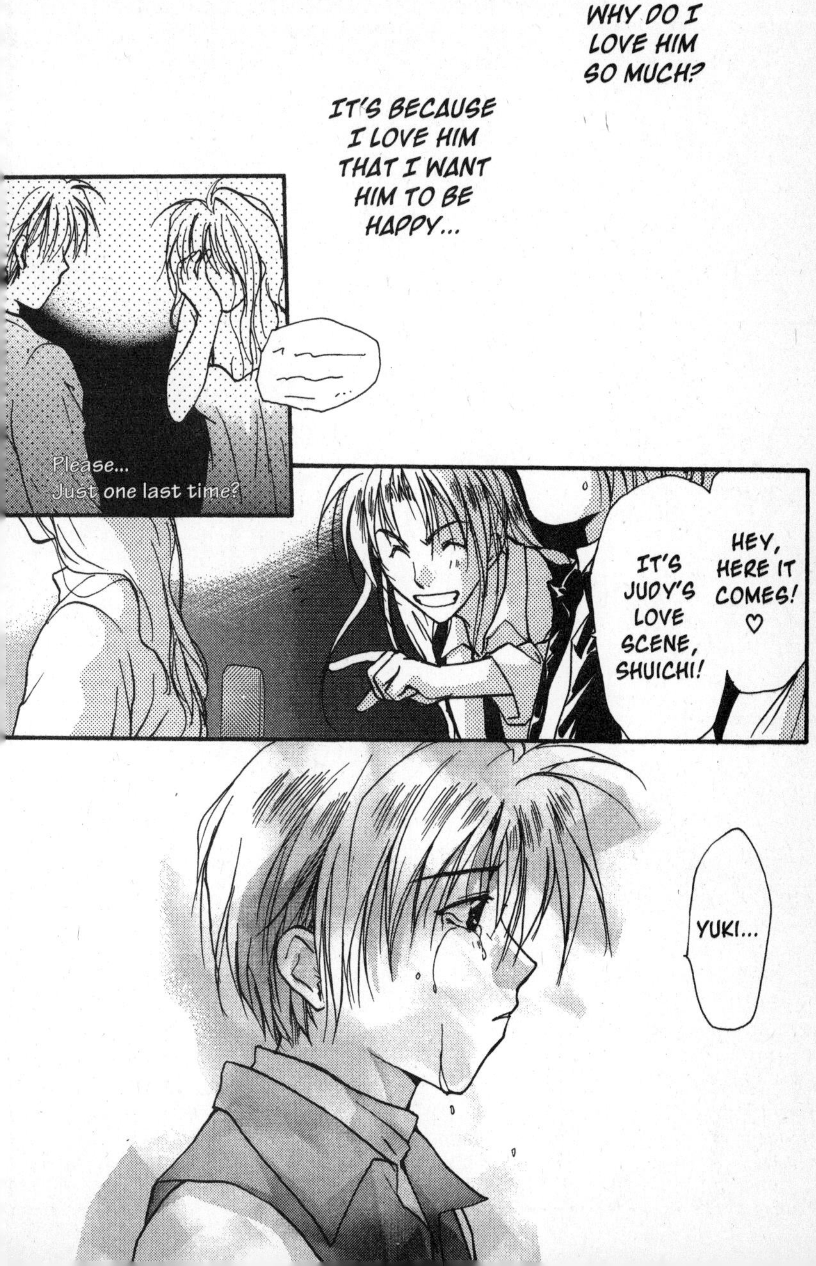
WHY DO I LOVE HIM SO MUCH?
IT'S BECAUSE I LOVE HIM THAT I WANT HIM TO BE HAPPY...
Please... Just one last time?
HEY, HERE IT COMES! ♡
IT'S JUDY'S LOVE SCENE, SHUICHI!
YUKI...

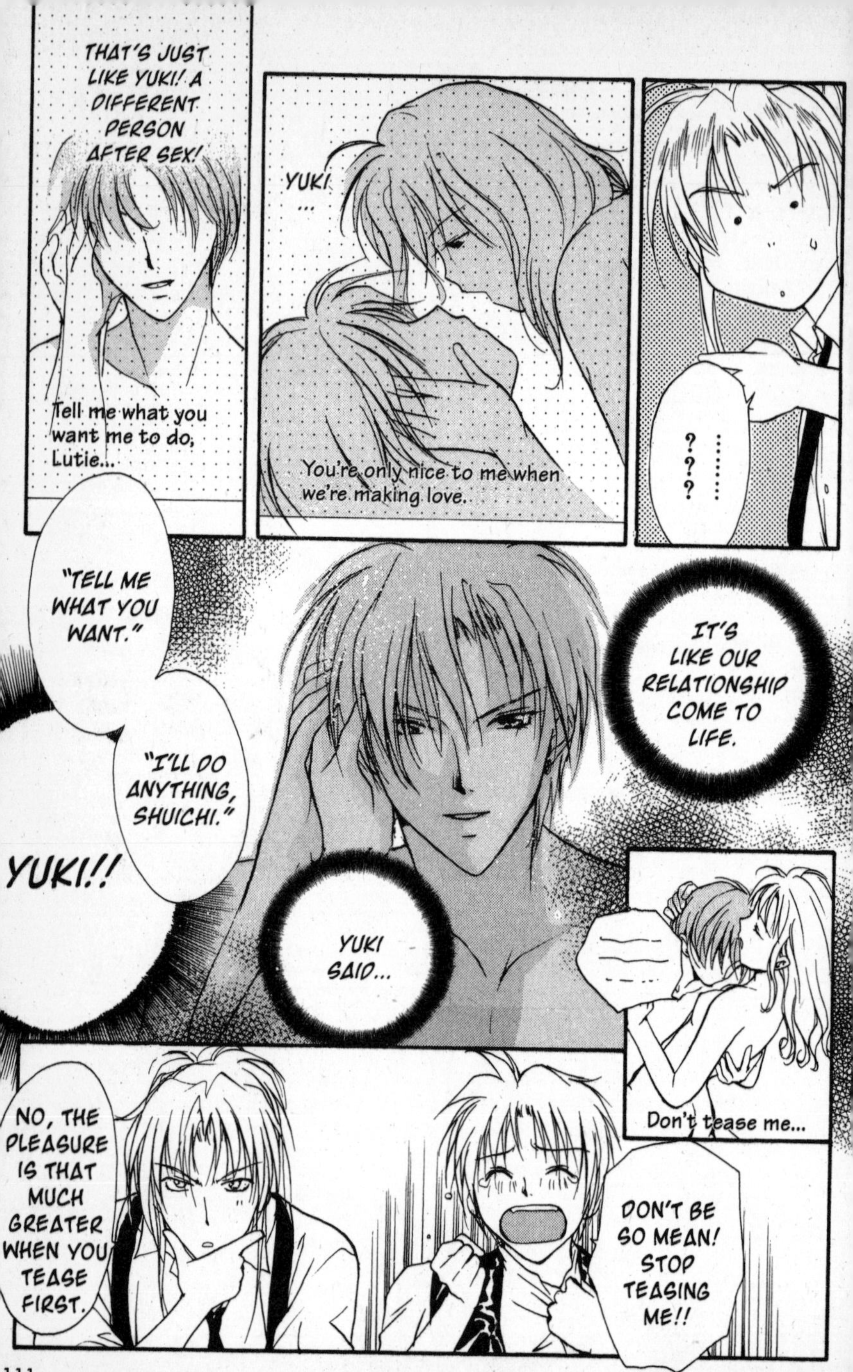

??? ......
YUKI ...
You're only nice to me when we're making love.
THAT'S JUST LIKE YUKI! A DIFFERENT PERSON AFTER SEX!
Tell me what you want me to do, Lutie...
IT'S LIKE OUR RELATIONSHIP COME TO LIFE.
Don't tease me...
YUKI SAID...
"TELL ME WHAT YOU WANT."
"I'LL DO ANYTHING, SHUICHI."
YUKI!!
DON'T BE SO MEAN! STOP TEASING ME!!
NO, THE PLEASURE IS THAT MUCH GREATER WHEN YOU TEASE FIRST.

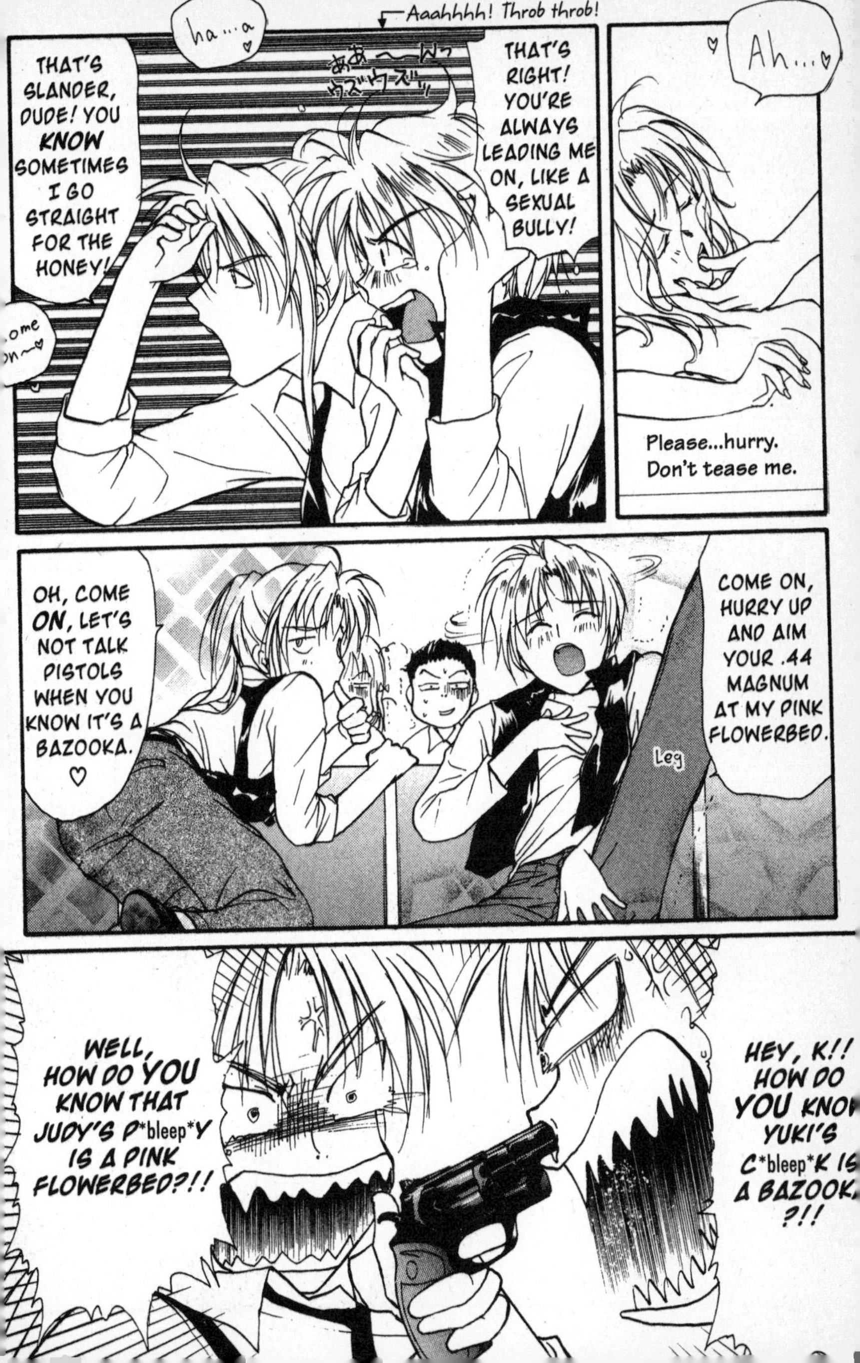
Ah...♥
Please...hurry. Don't tease me.
Aaahhhh! Throb throb!
THAT'S RIGHT! YOU'RE ALWAYS LEADING ME ON, LIKE A SEXUAL BULLY!
ha...a♥
THAT'S SLANDER, DUDE! YOU KNOW SOMETIMES I GO STRAIGHT FOR THE HONEY!
.ome on~♥
COME ON, HURRY UP AND AIM YOUR .44 MAGNUM AT MY PINK FLOWERBED.
Leg
OH, COME ON, LET'S NOT TALK PISTOLS WHEN YOU KNOW IT'S A BAZOOKA. ♡
HEY, K!! HOW DO YOU KNOW YUKI'S C*bleep*K IS A BAZOOKA ?!!
WELL, HOW DO YOU KNOW THAT JUDY'S P*bleep*Y IS A PINK FLOWERBED?!!

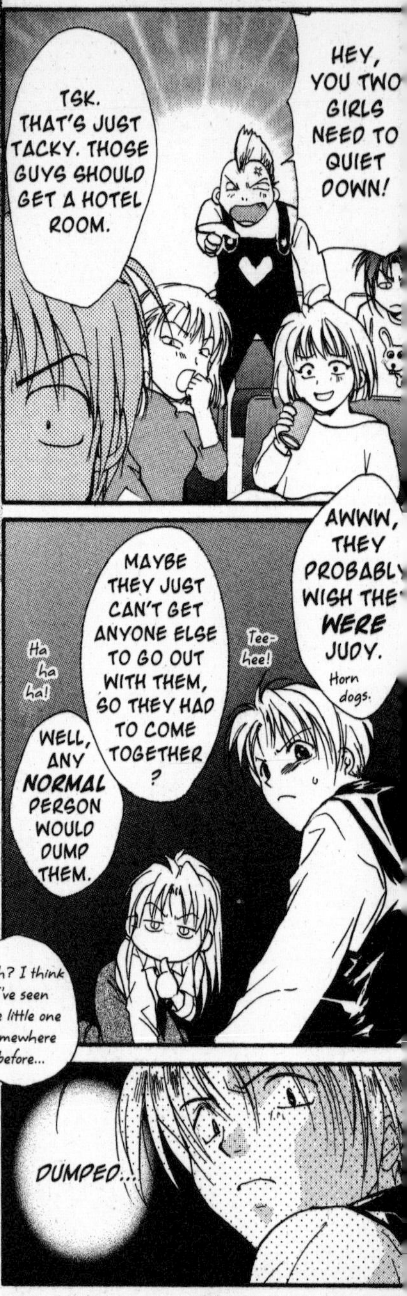
HEY, YOU TWO GIRLS NEED TO QUIET DOWN!
TSK. THAT'S JUST TACKY. THOSE GUYS SHOULD GET A HOTEL ROOM.
AWWW, THEY PROBABL WISH THE WERE JUDY.
Horn dogs.
Tee-hee!
MAYBE THEY JUST CAN'T GET ANYONE ELSE TO GO OUT WITH THEM, SO THEY HAD TO COME TOGETHER?
Ha ha ha!
WELL, ANY NORMAL PERSON WOULD DUMP THEM.
Huh? I think I've seen the little one somewhere before...
DUMPED...

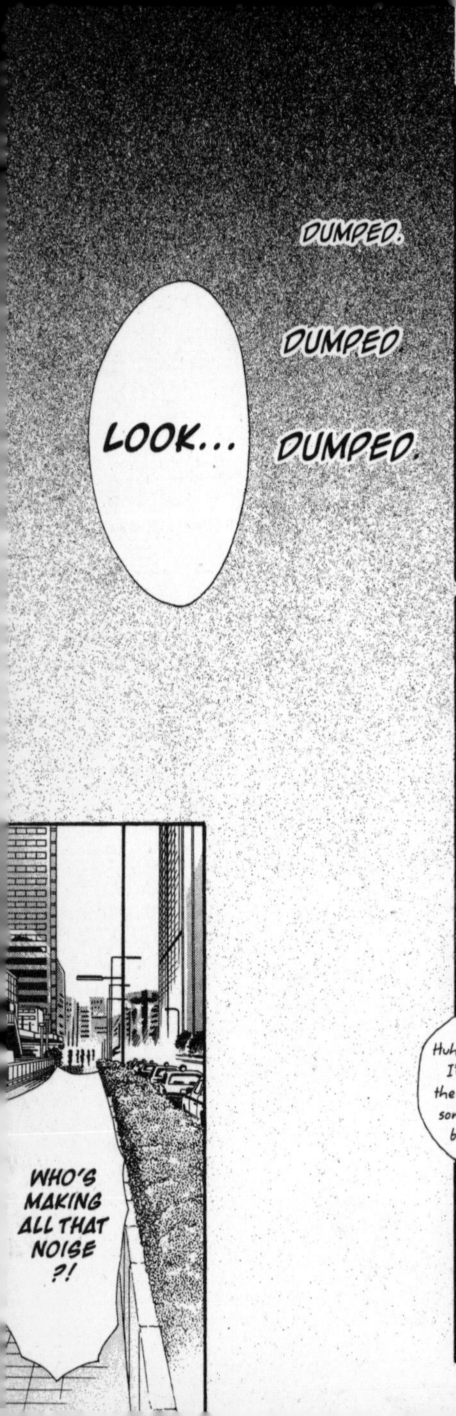
DUMPED.
DUMPED
DUMPED.
LOOK...
WHO'S MAKING ALL THAT NOISE ?!

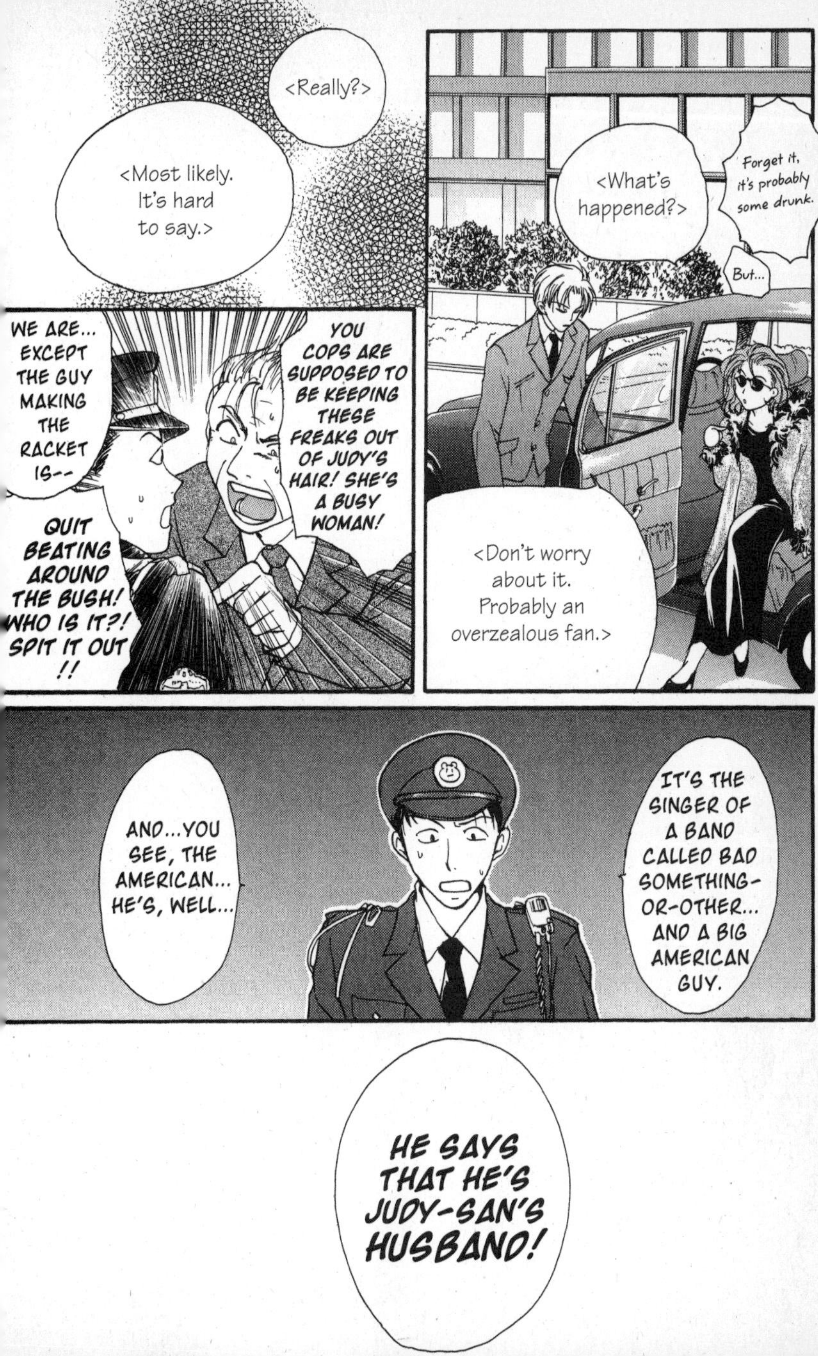
Forget it, it's probably some drunk.
<What's happened?>
But...
<Don't worry about it. Probably an overzealous fan.>
<Really?>
<Most likely. It's hard to say.>
YOU COPS ARE SUPPOSED TO BE KEEPING THESE FREAKS OUT OF JUDY'S HAIR! SHE'S A BUSY WOMAN!
WE ARE... EXCEPT THE GUY MAKING THE RACKET IS--
QUIT BEATING AROUND THE BUSH! WHO IS IT?! SPIT IT OUT !!
IT'S THE SINGER OF A BAND CALLED BAD SOMETHING-OR-OTHER... AND A BIG AMERICAN GUY.
AND...YOU SEE, THE AMERICAN... HE'S, WELL...
HE SAYS THAT HE'S JUDY-SAN'S HUSBAND!

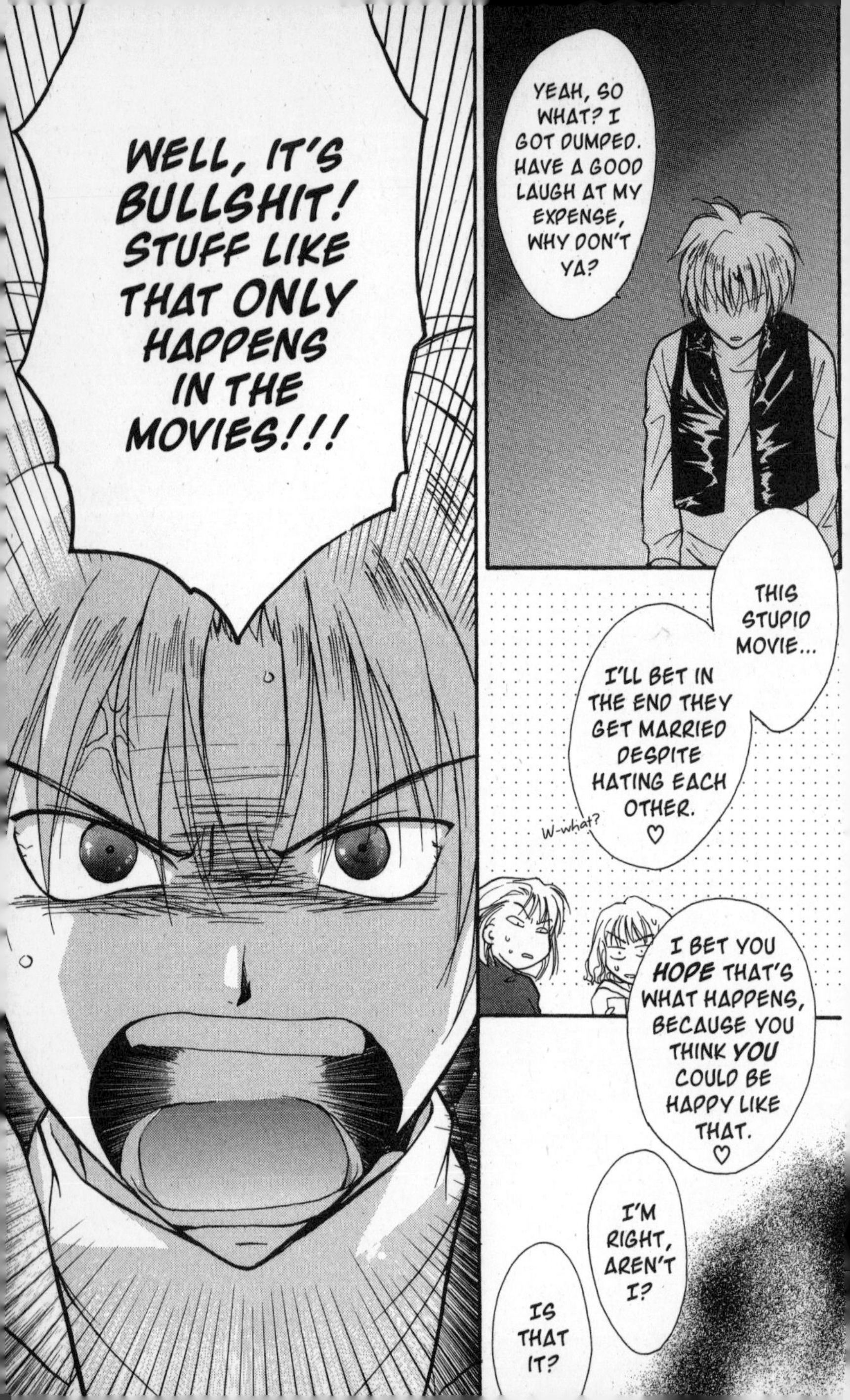
YEAH, SO WHAT? I GOT DUMPED. HAVE A GOOD LAUGH AT MY EXPENSE, WHY DON'T YA?
THIS STUPID MOVIE...
I'LL BET IN THE END THEY GET MARRIED DESPITE HATING EACH OTHER. ♡
W-what?
I BET YOU *HOPE* THAT'S WHAT HAPPENS, BECAUSE YOU THINK *YOU* COULD BE HAPPY LIKE THAT. ♡
I'M RIGHT, AREN'T I?
IS THAT IT?
WELL, IT'S BULLSHIT! STUFF LIKE THAT ONLY HAPPENS IN THE MOVIES!!!

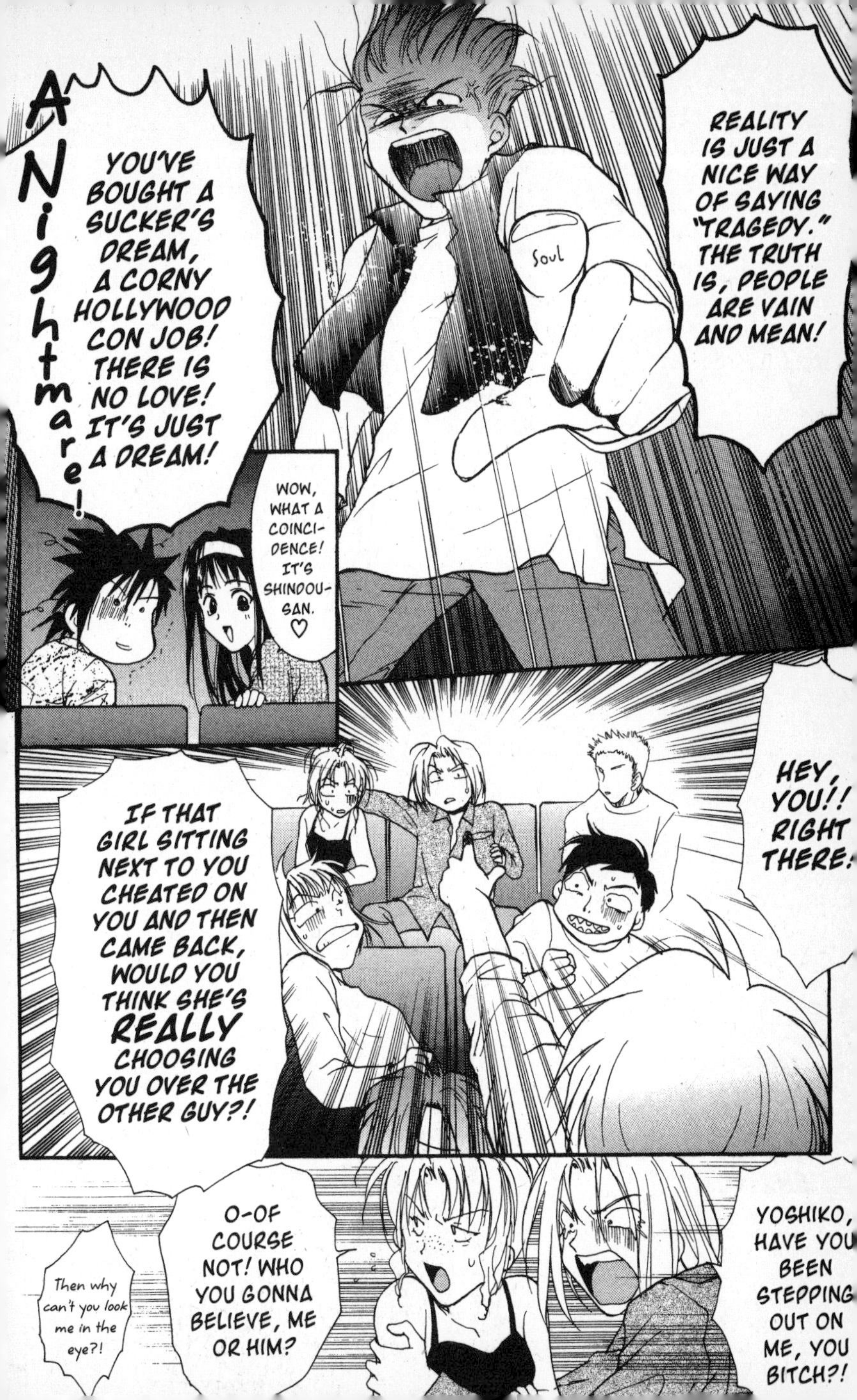
REALITY IS JUST A NICE WAY OF SAYING "TRAGEDY." THE TRUTH IS, PEOPLE ARE VAIN AND MEAN!
YOU'VE BOUGHT A SUCKER'S DREAM, A CORNY HOLLYWOOD CON JOB! THERE IS NO LOVE! IT'S JUST A DREAM!
A Nightmare!
WOW, WHAT A COINCI-DENCE! IT'S SHINDOU-SAN. ♡
HEY, YOU!! RIGHT THERE!
IF THAT GIRL SITTING NEXT TO YOU CHEATED ON YOU AND THEN CAME BACK, WOULD YOU THINK SHE'S REALLY CHOOSING YOU OVER THE OTHER GUY?!
YOSHIKO, HAVE YOU BEEN STEPPING OUT ON ME, YOU BITCH?!
O-OF COURSE NOT! WHO YOU GONNA BELIEVE, ME OR HIM?
Then why can't you look me in the eye?!

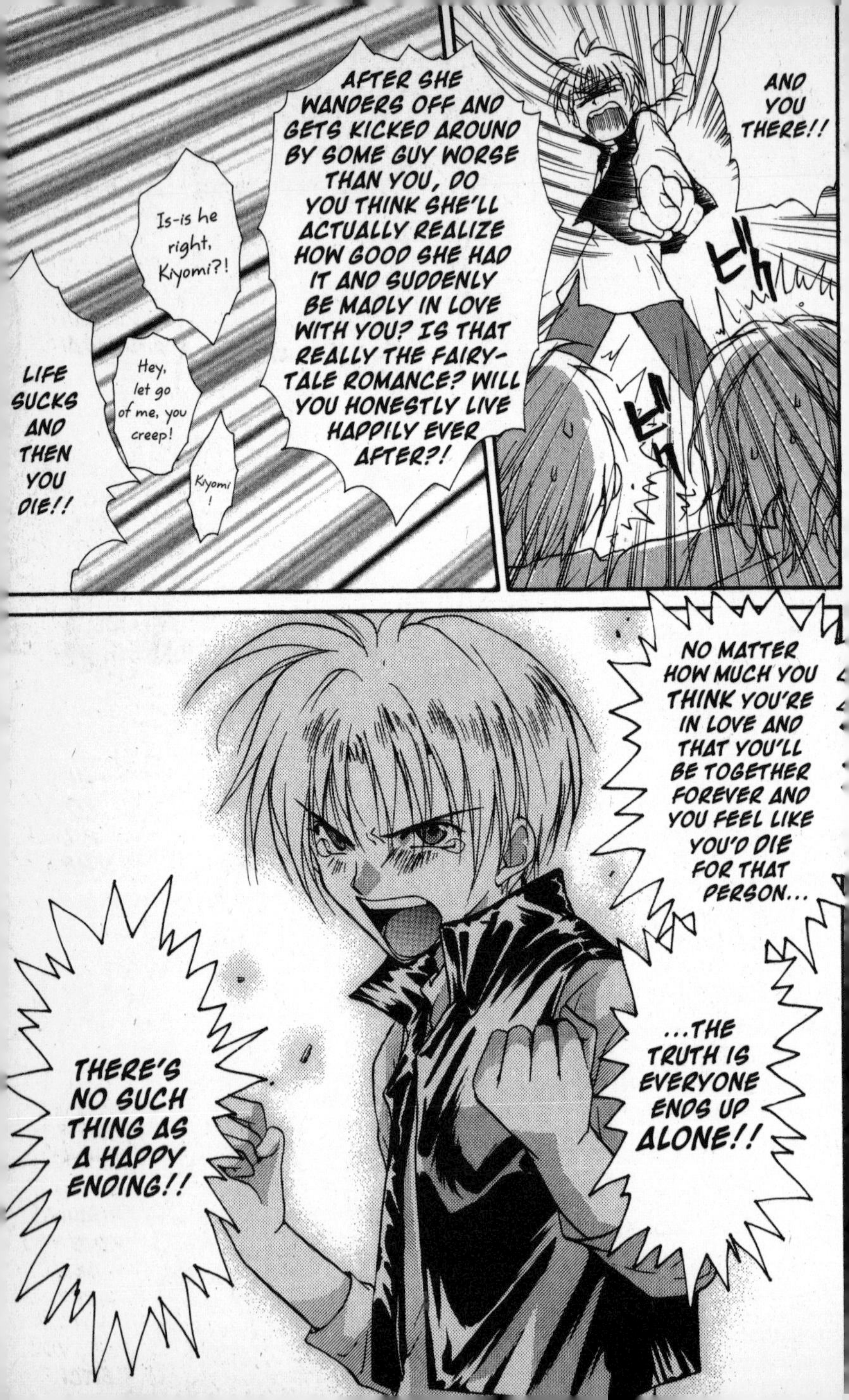
AND YOU THERE!!
AFTER SHE WANDERS OFF AND GETS KICKED AROUND BY SOME GUY WORSE THAN YOU, DO YOU THINK SHE'LL ACTUALLY REALIZE HOW GOOD SHE HAD IT AND SUDDENLY BE MADLY IN LOVE WITH YOU? IS THAT REALLY THE FAIRY-TALE ROMANCE? WILL YOU HONESTLY LIVE HAPPILY EVER AFTER?!
Is-is he right, Kiyomi?!
Hey, let go of me, you creep!
Kiyomi!
LIFE SUCKS AND THEN YOU DIE!!
NO MATTER HOW MUCH YOU THINK YOU'RE IN LOVE AND THAT YOU'LL BE TOGETHER FOREVER AND YOU FEEL LIKE YOU'D DIE FOR THAT PERSON...
...THE TRUTH IS EVERYONE ENDS UP ALONE!!
THERE'S NO SUCH THING AS A HAPPY ENDING!!

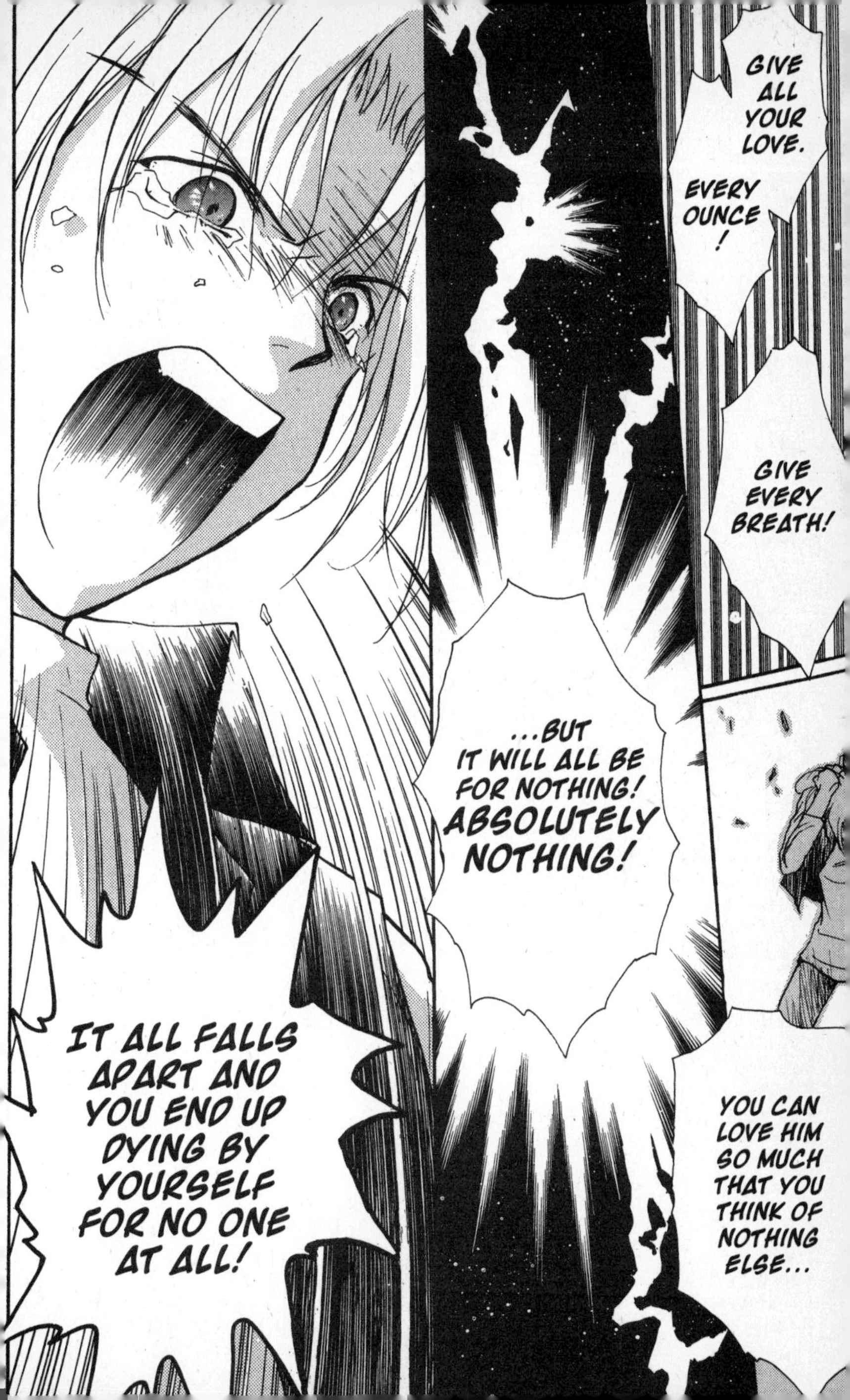
GIVE ALL YOUR LOVE.
EVERY OUNCE!
GIVE EVERY BREATH!
YOU CAN LOVE HIM SO MUCH THAT YOU THINK OF NOTHING ELSE...
...BUT IT WILL ALL BE FOR NOTHING! ABSOLUTELY NOTHING!
IT ALL FALLS APART AND YOU END UP DYING BY YOURSELF FOR NO ONE AT ALL!

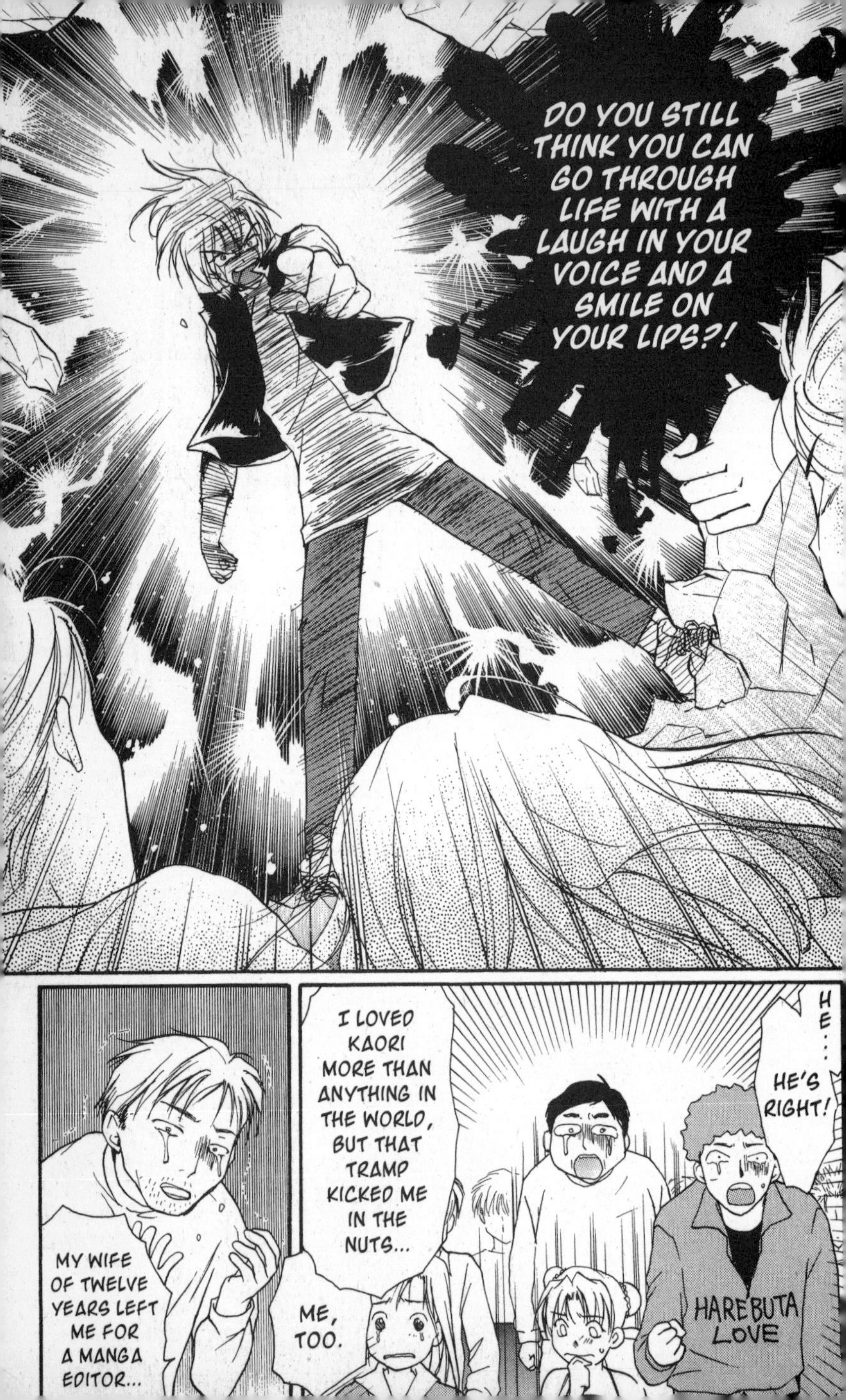
DO YOU STILL THINK YOU CAN GO THROUGH LIFE WITH A LAUGH IN YOUR VOICE AND A SMILE ON YOUR LIPS?!
HE...
HE'S RIGHT!
I LOVED KAORI MORE THAN ANYTHING IN THE WORLD, BUT THAT TRAMP KICKED ME IN THE NUTS...
HAREBUTA LOVE
ME, TOO.
MY WIFE OF TWELVE YEARS LEFT ME FOR A MANGA EDITOR...

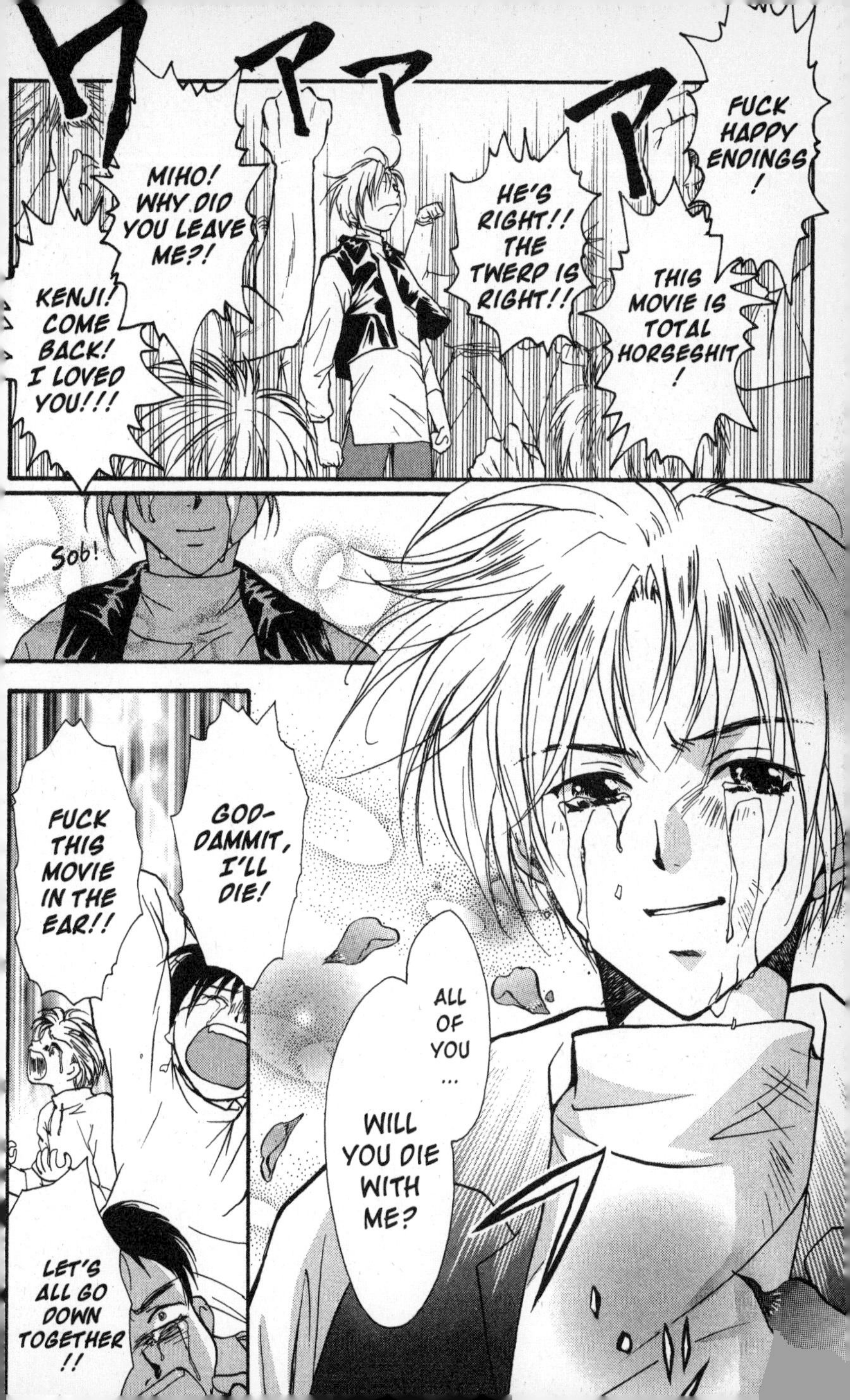
FUCK HAPPY ENDINGS!
THIS MOVIE IS TOTAL HORSESHIT!
HE'S RIGHT!! THE TWERP IS RIGHT!!
MIHO! WHY DID YOU LEAVE ME?!
KENJI! COME BACK! I LOVED YOU!!!
ALL OF YOU ...
WILL YOU DIE WITH ME?
Sob!
GOD-DAMMIT, I'LL DIE!
FUCK THIS MOVIE IN THE EAR!!
LET'S ALL GO DOWN TOGETHER!!

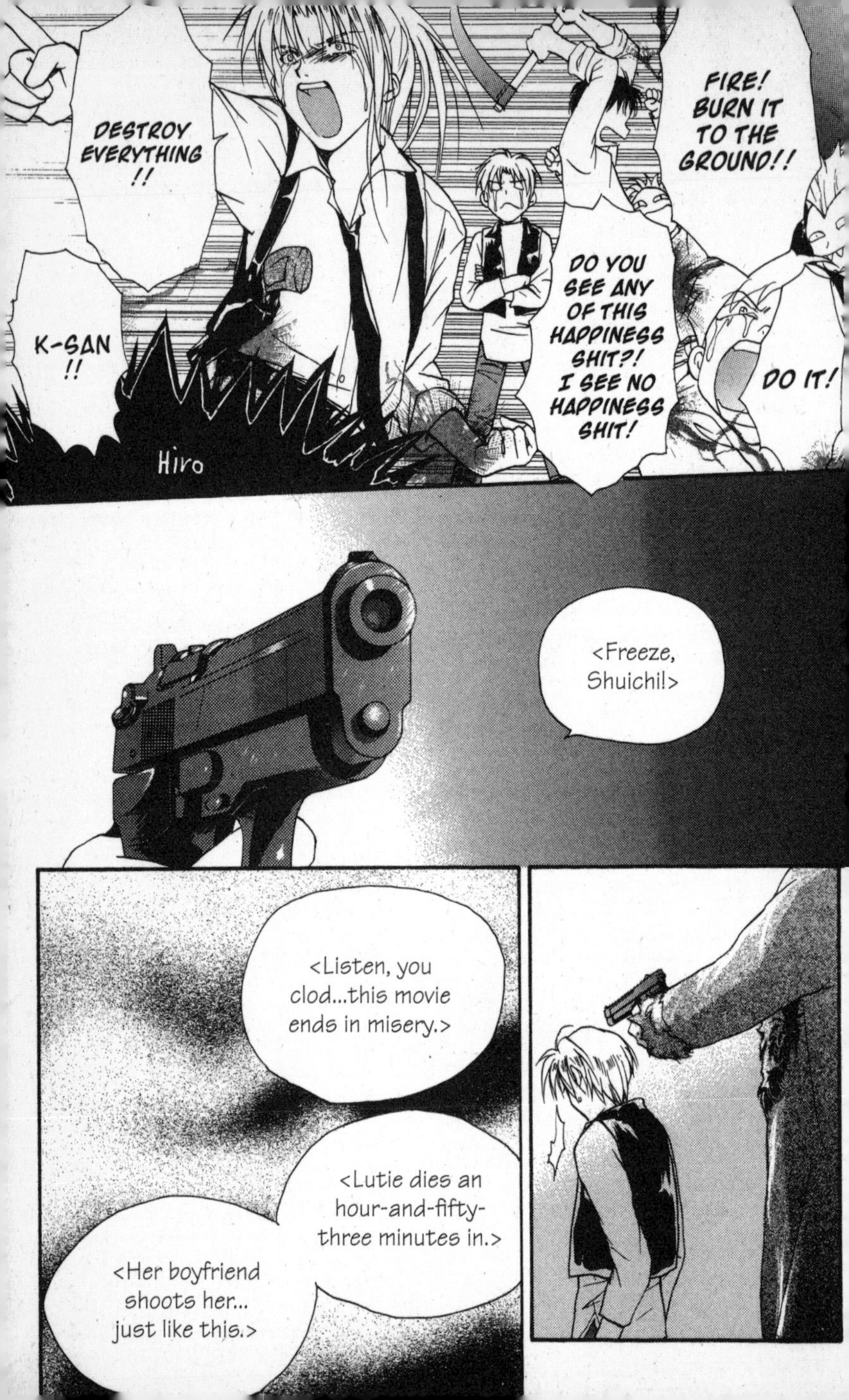
FIRE! BURN IT TO THE GROUND!!
DESTROY EVERYTHING!!
DO YOU SEE ANY OF THIS HAPPINESS SHIT?! I SEE NO HAPPINESS SHIT!
DO IT!
K-SAN!!
Hiro
<Freeze, Shuichi!>
<Listen, you clod...this movie ends in misery.>
<Lutie dies an hour-and-fifty-three minutes in.>
<Her boyfriend shoots her... just like this.>

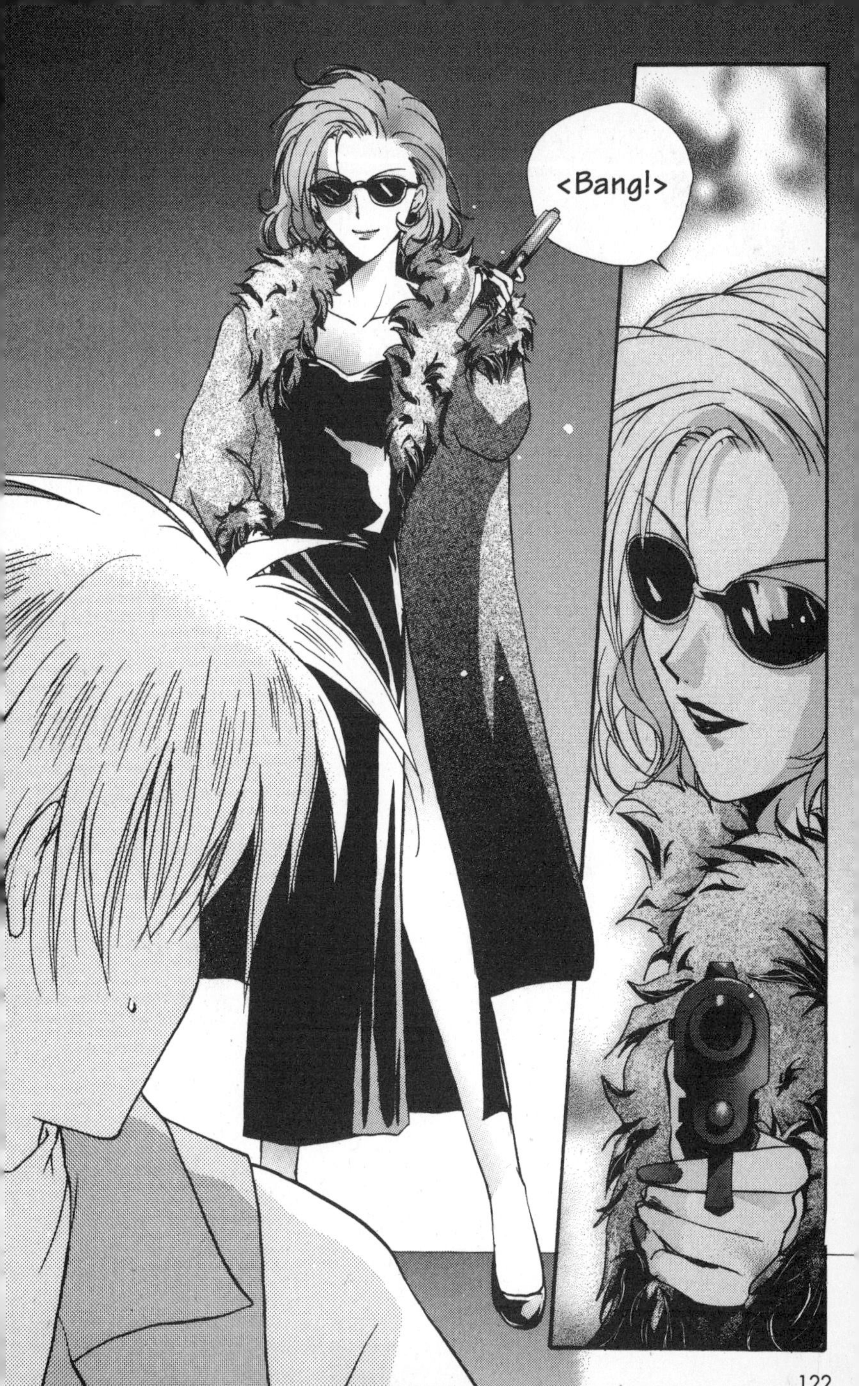
<Bang!>

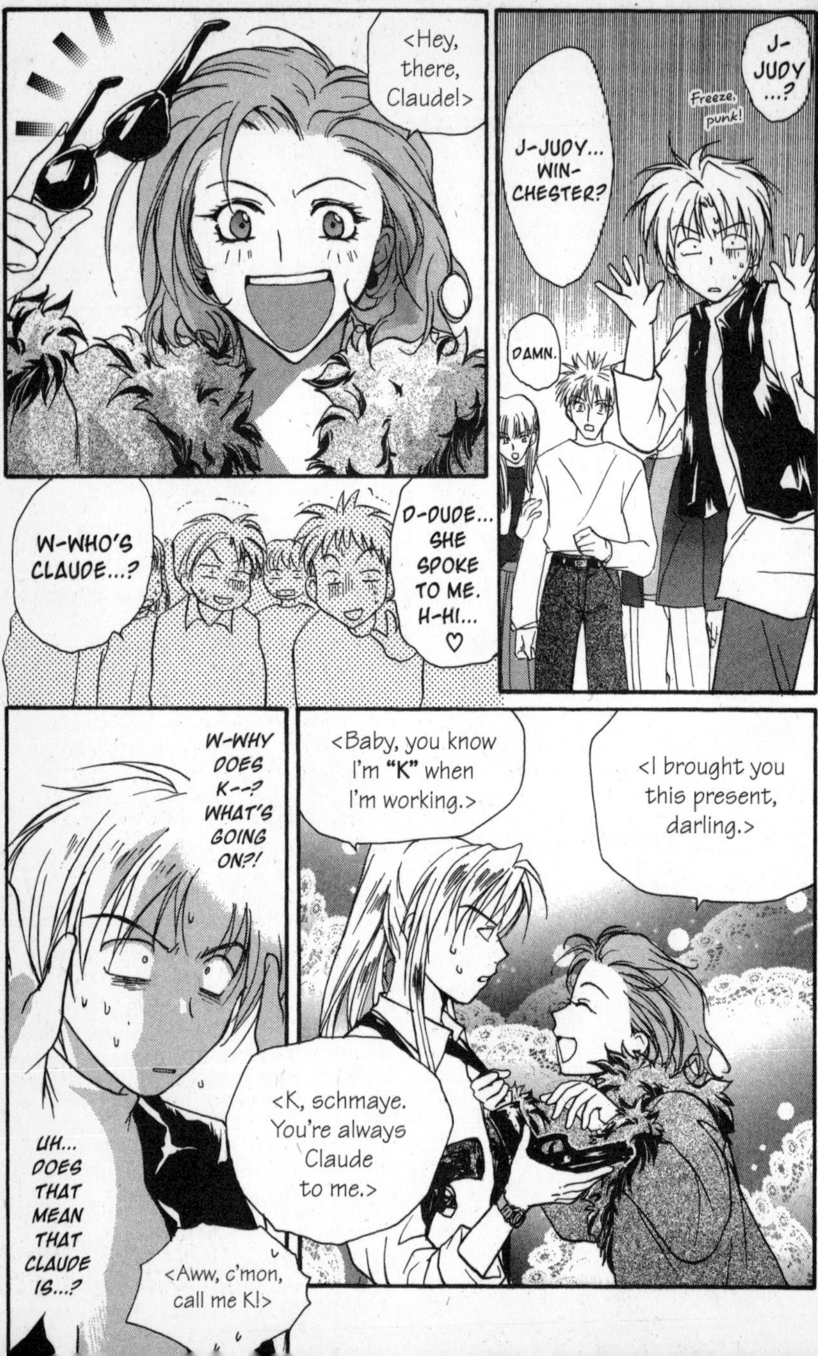
J-JUDY ...?
Freeze, punk!
J-JUDY... WIN-CHESTER?
DAMN.
<Hey, there, Claude!>
D-DUDE... SHE SPOKE TO ME. H-HI... ♡
W-WHO'S CLAUDE...?
<I brought you this present, darling.>
<Baby, you know I'm "K" when I'm working.>
<K, schmaye. You're always Claude to me.>
W-WHY DOES K--? WHAT'S GOING ON?!
UH... DOES THAT MEAN THAT CLAUDE IS...?
<Aww, c'mon, call me K!>

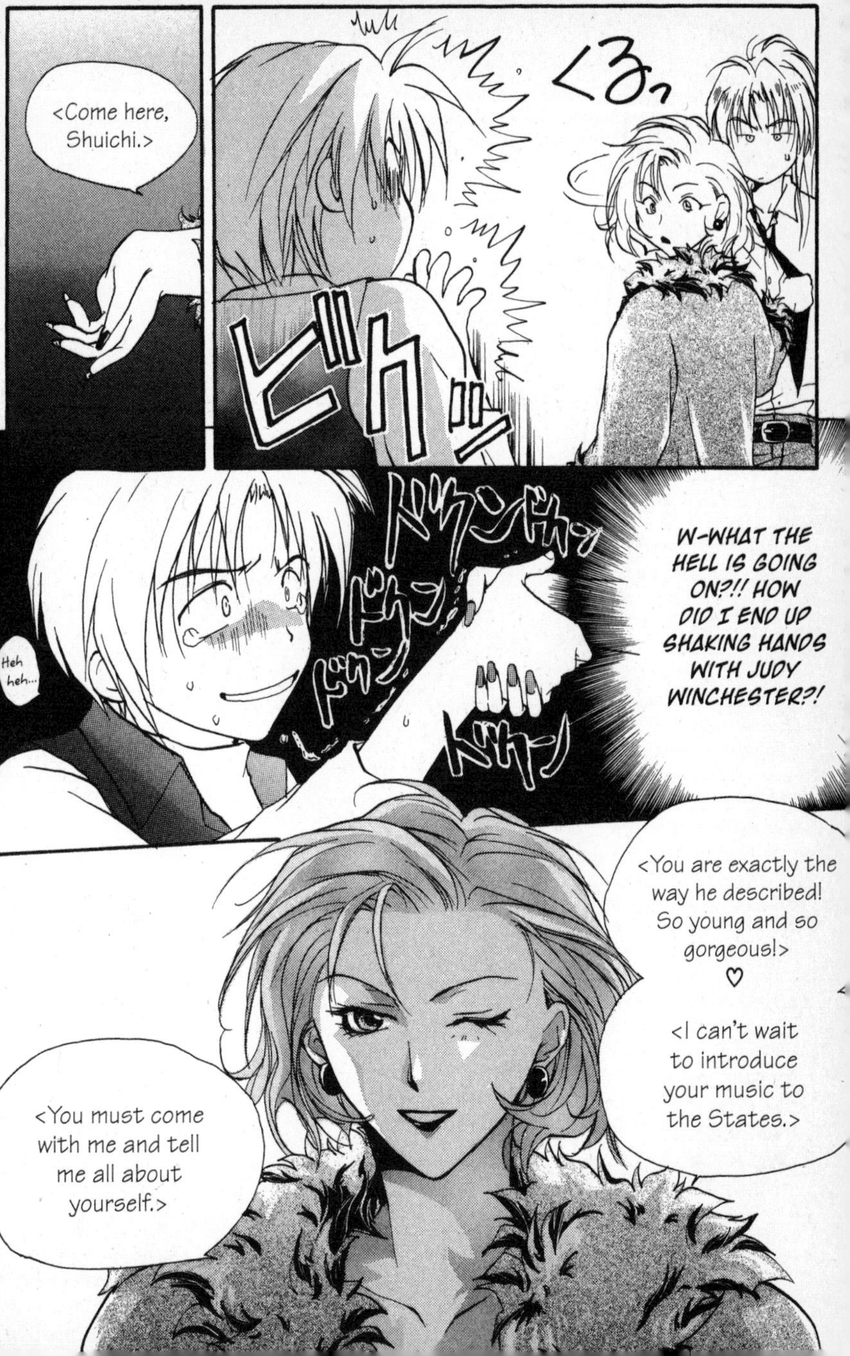

くるっ
ビクッ
<Come here, Shuichi.>
W-WHAT THE HELL IS GOING ON?!! HOW DID I END UP SHAKING HANDS WITH JUDY WINCHESTER?!
ドクン
Heh heh...
<You are exactly the way he described! So young and so gorgeous!> ♡
<I can't wait to introduce your music to the States.>
<You must come with me and tell me all about yourself.>

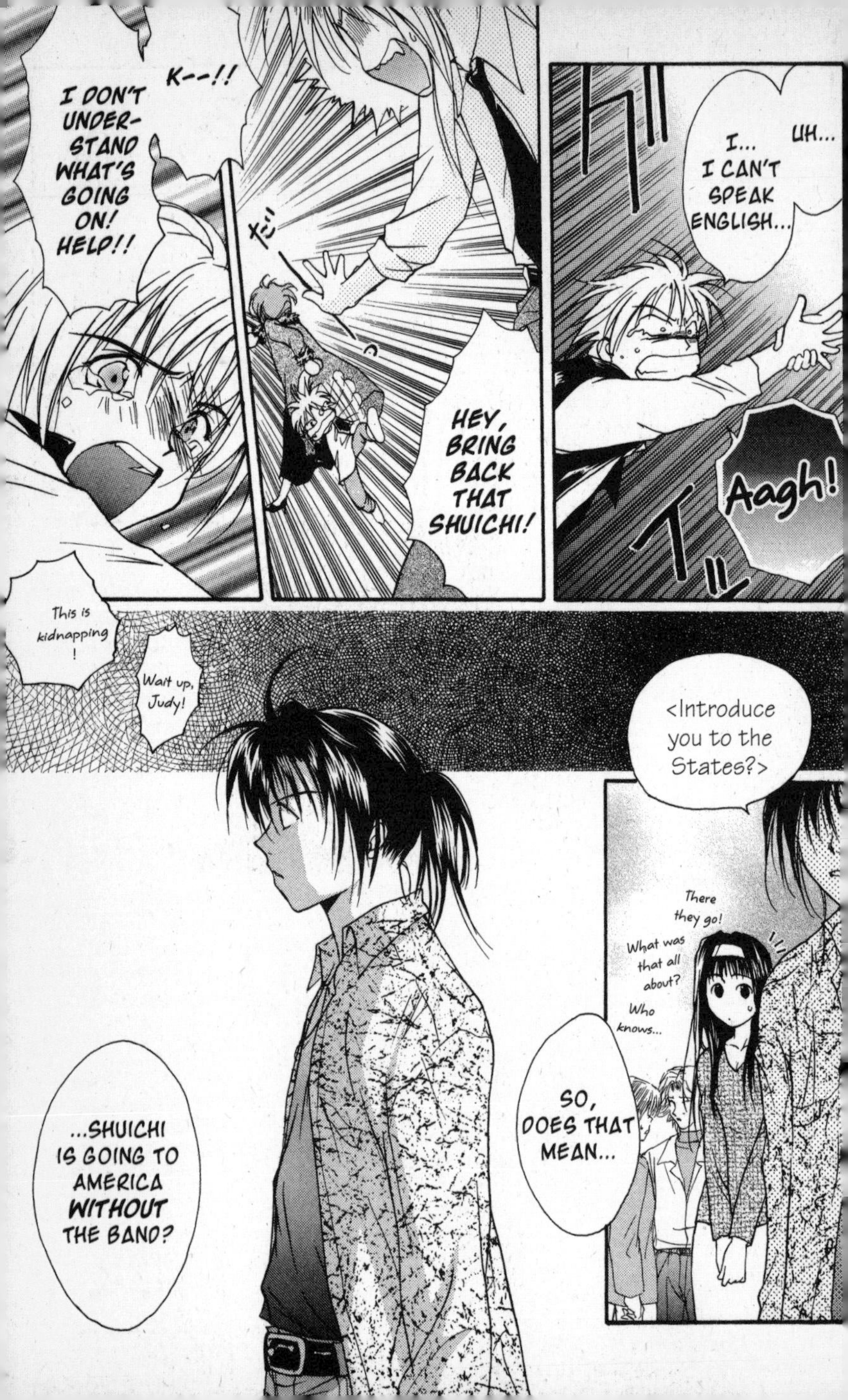
UH...
I... I CAN'T SPEAK ENGLISH...
Aagh!
HEY, BRING BACK THAT SHUICHI!
K--!!
I DON'T UNDER-STAND WHAT'S GOING ON! HELP!!
This is kidnapping!
Wait up, Judy!
<Introduce you to the States?>
There they go!
What was that all about?
Who knows...
SO, DOES THAT MEAN...
...SHUICHI IS GOING TO AMERICA WITHOUT THE BAND?

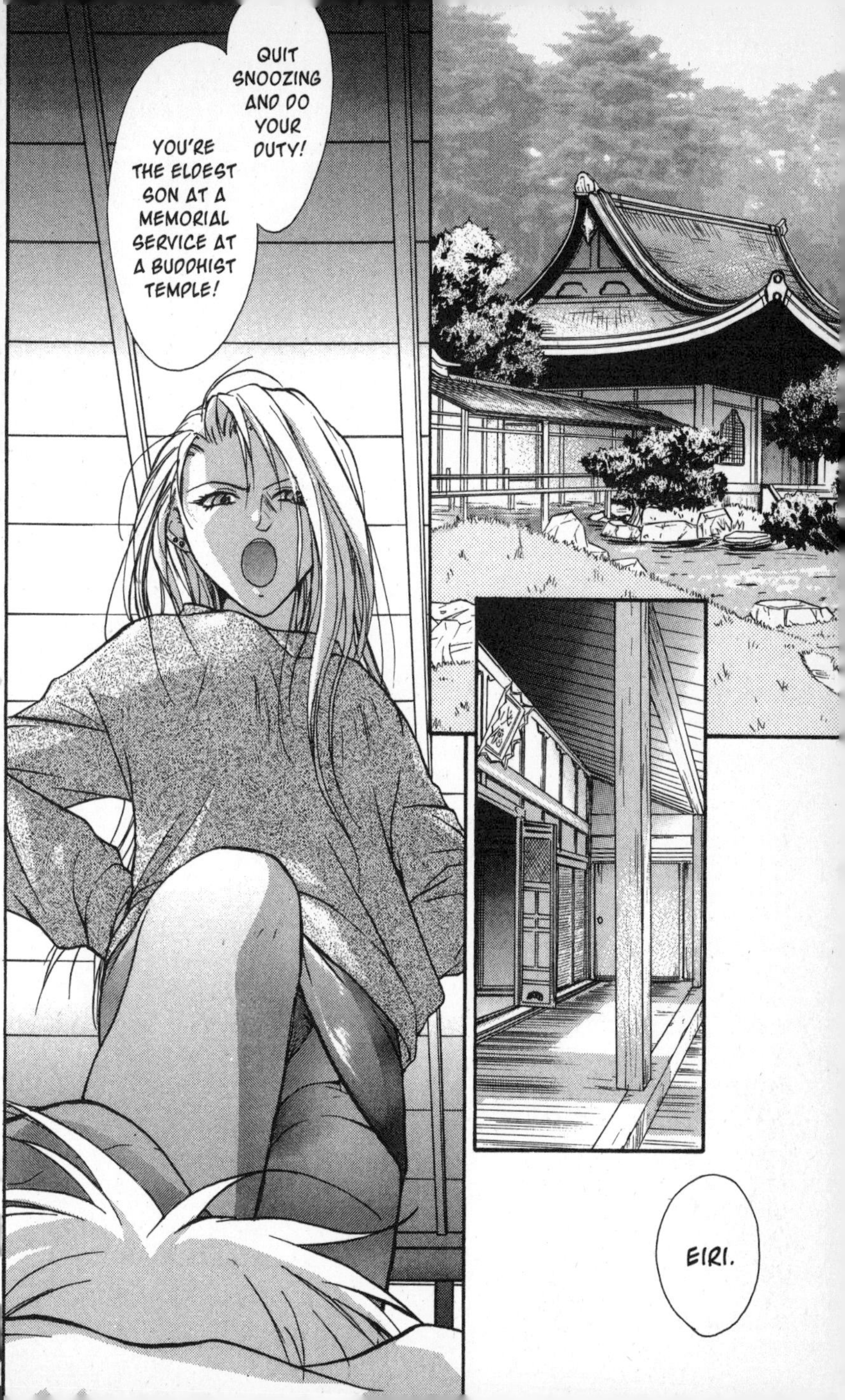
EIRI.
QUIT SNOOZING AND DO YOUR DUTY!
YOU'RE THE ELDEST SON AT A MEMORIAL SERVICE AT A BUDDHIST TEMPLE!

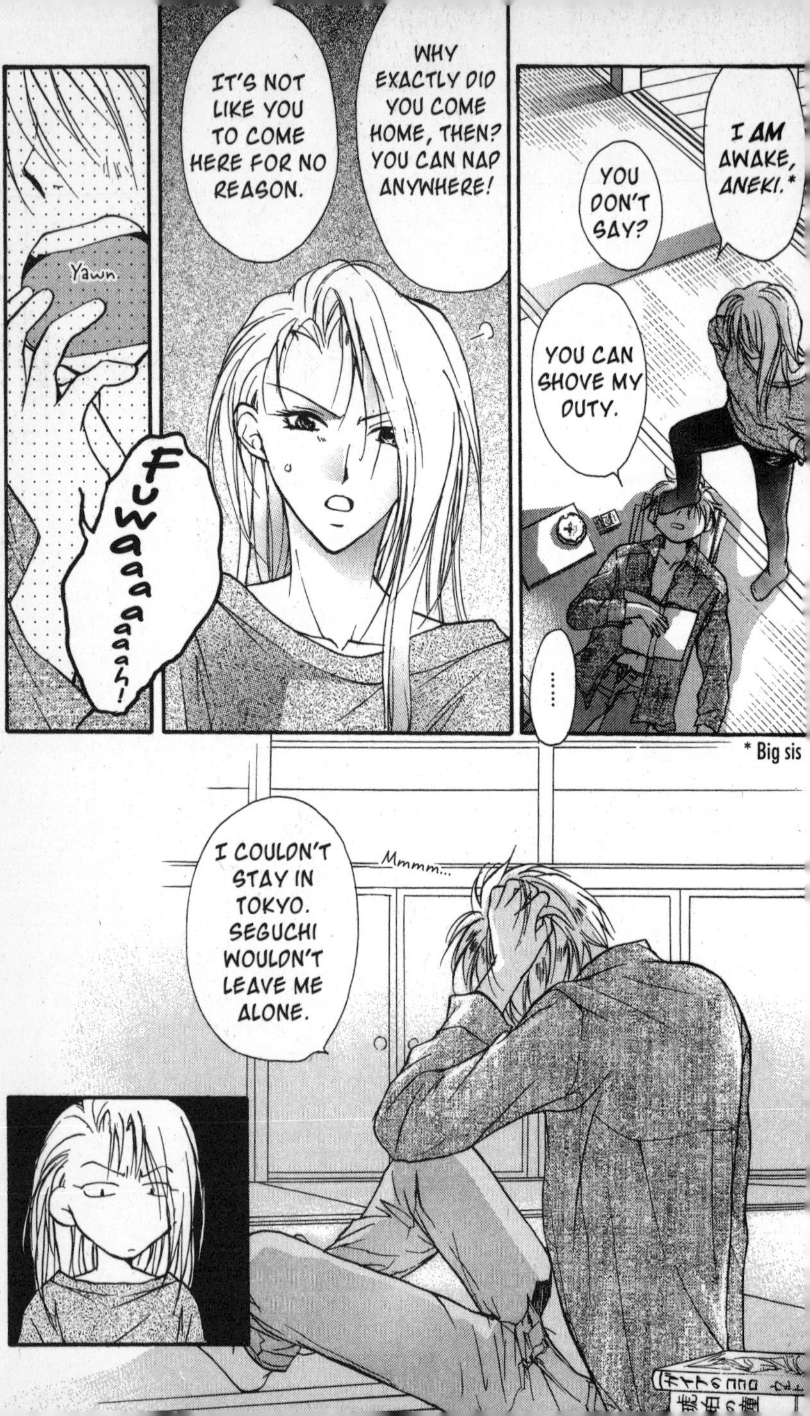
I AM AWAKE, ANEKI.*
YOU DON'T SAY?
YOU CAN SHOVE MY DUTY.
......
WHY EXACTLY DID YOU COME HOME, THEN? YOU CAN NAP ANYWHERE!
IT'S NOT LIKE YOU TO COME HERE FOR NO REASON.
Yawn.
Fuwaaaaaaaaah!
Mmmm...
I COULDN'T STAY IN TOKYO. SEGUCHI WOULDN'T LEAVE ME ALONE.

* Big sis

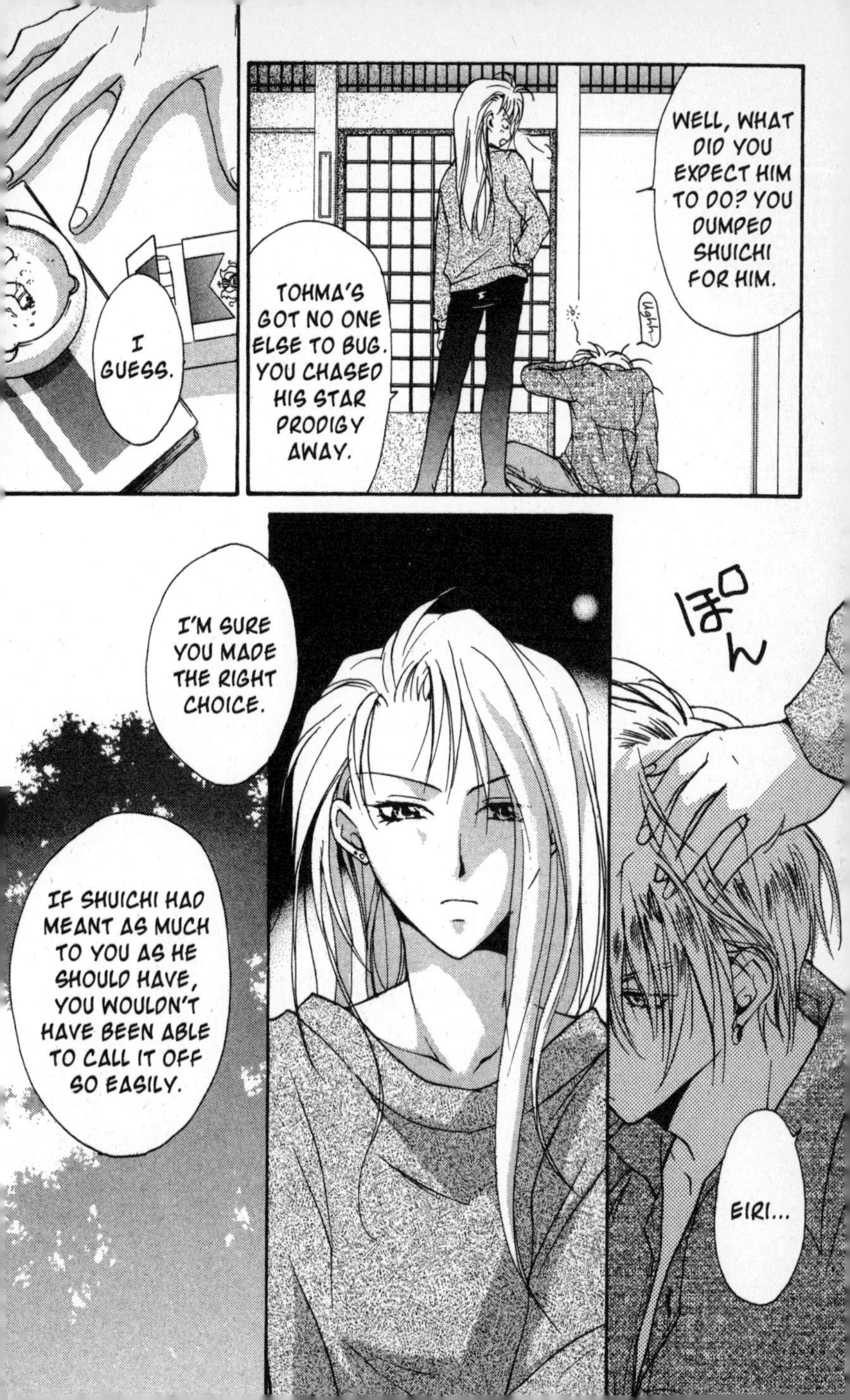
WELL, WHAT DID YOU EXPECT HIM TO DO? YOU DUMPED SHUICHI FOR HIM.
Ughh...
TOHMA'S GOT NO ONE ELSE TO BUG. YOU CHASED HIS STAR PRODIGY AWAY.
I GUESS.
ぽん
EIRI...
I'M SURE YOU MADE THE RIGHT CHOICE.
IF SHUICHI HAD MEANT AS MUCH TO YOU AS HE SHOULD HAVE, YOU WOULDN'T HAVE BEEN ABLE TO CALL IT OFF SO EASILY.

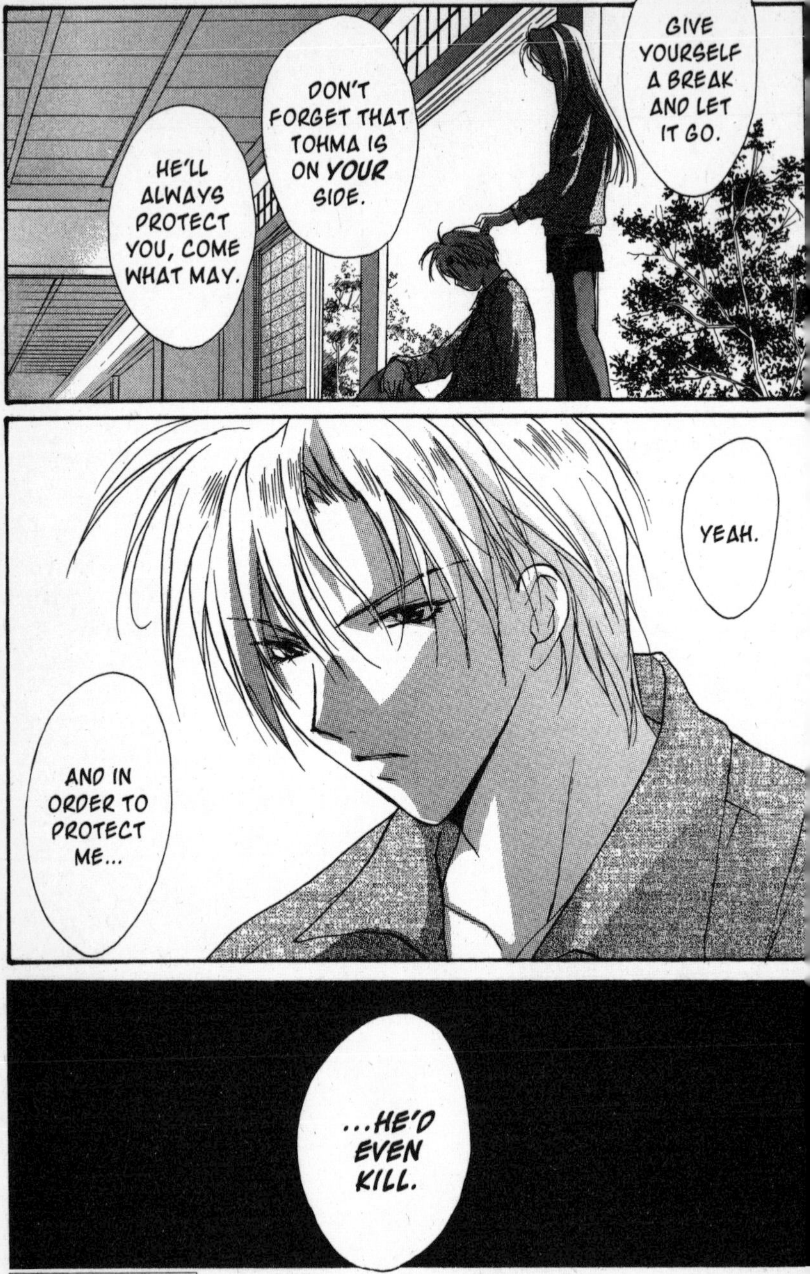
GIVE YOURSELF A BREAK AND LET IT GO.
DON'T FORGET THAT TOHMA IS ON *YOUR* SIDE.
HE'LL ALWAYS PROTECT YOU, COME WHAT MAY.
YEAH.
AND IN ORDER TO PROTECT ME...
...HE'D EVEN KILL.

track34▶END

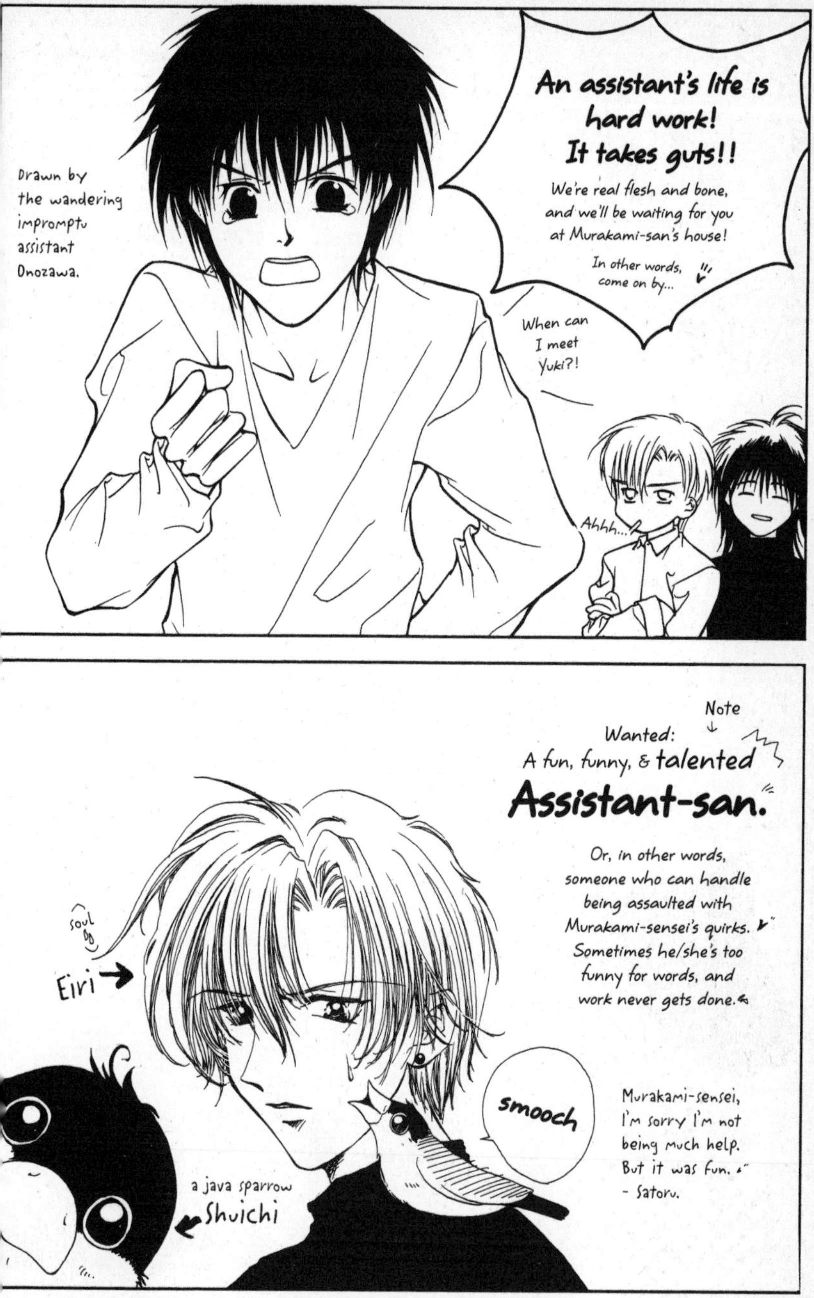
An assistant's life is hard work! It takes guts!!
We're real flesh and bone, and we'll be waiting for you at Murakami-san's house!
In other words, come on by...
When can I meet Yuki?!
Ahhh...
Drawn by the wandering impromptu assistant Onozawa.
Note
Wanted: A fun, funny, & talented Assistant-san.
Or, in other words, someone who can handle being assaulted with Murakami-sensei's quirks. Sometimes he/she's too funny for words, and work never gets done.
Murakami-sensei, I'm sorry I'm not being much help. But it was fun. - Satoru.
smooch
soul
Eiri
a java sparrow Shuichi

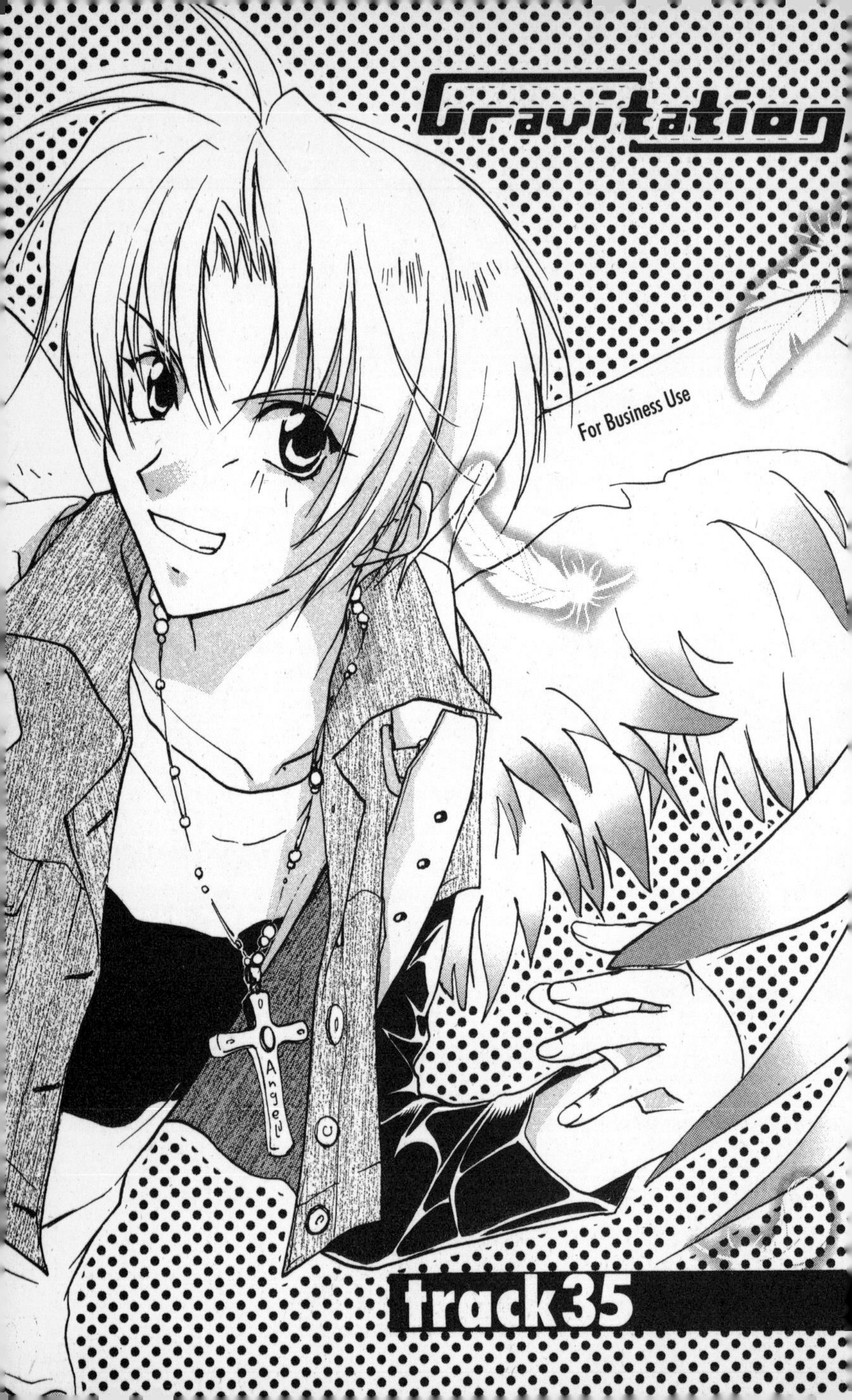
Gravitation
For Business Use
Angel
track35

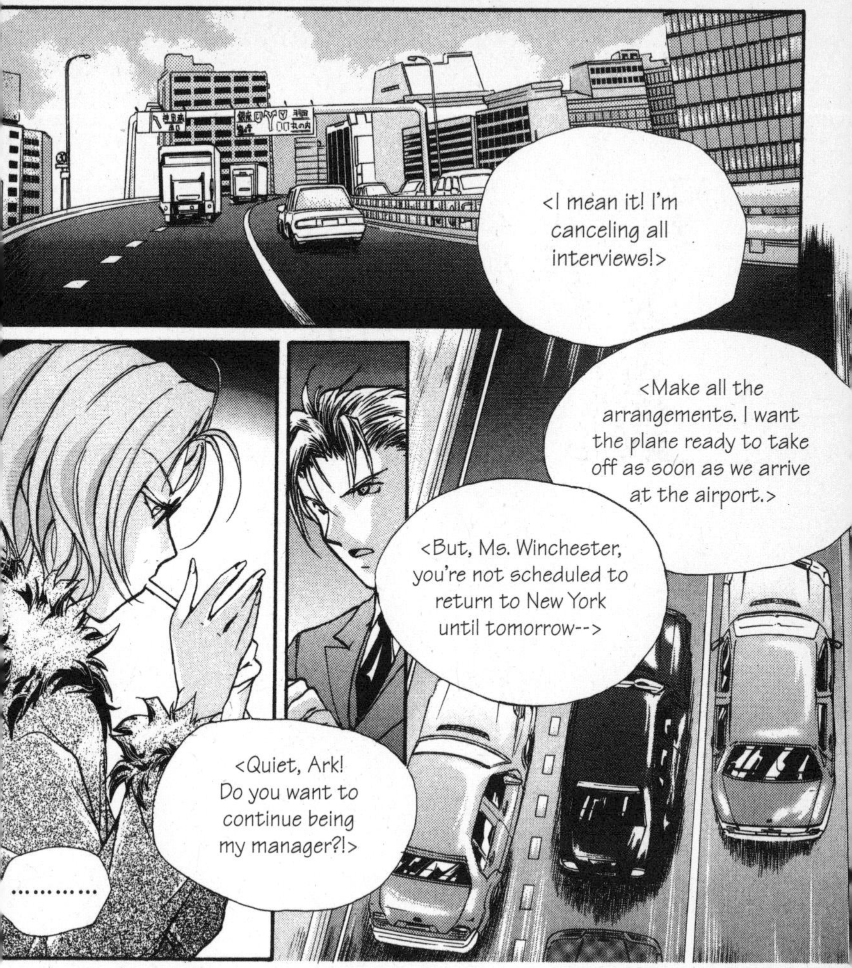
<I mean it! I'm canceling all interviews!>
<Make all the arrangements. I want the plane ready to take off as soon as we arrive at the airport.>
<But, Ms. Winchester, you're not scheduled to return to New York until tomorrow-->
<Quiet, Ark! Do you want to continue being my manager?!>
....

ABOUT GRAVITATION TRACK 35

In this author's opinion, Volume 8 marks the appearance of the most high-scoring point getter, a man whose name and face do not fit each other at all: the gorilla-bumpkin macho manager Ark!! Too bad he's only a supporting character!! Whether or not he takes on a more major role the way K did, someone who turns into a big-time player light years beyond the position he debuted in... well, that's up to you, my dear readers.

So, anyway, in this episode, I went through the trouble of bringing over some big guns from the mainland. They're going to set up some intense trials by fire for our boy. So expect lots of fun!

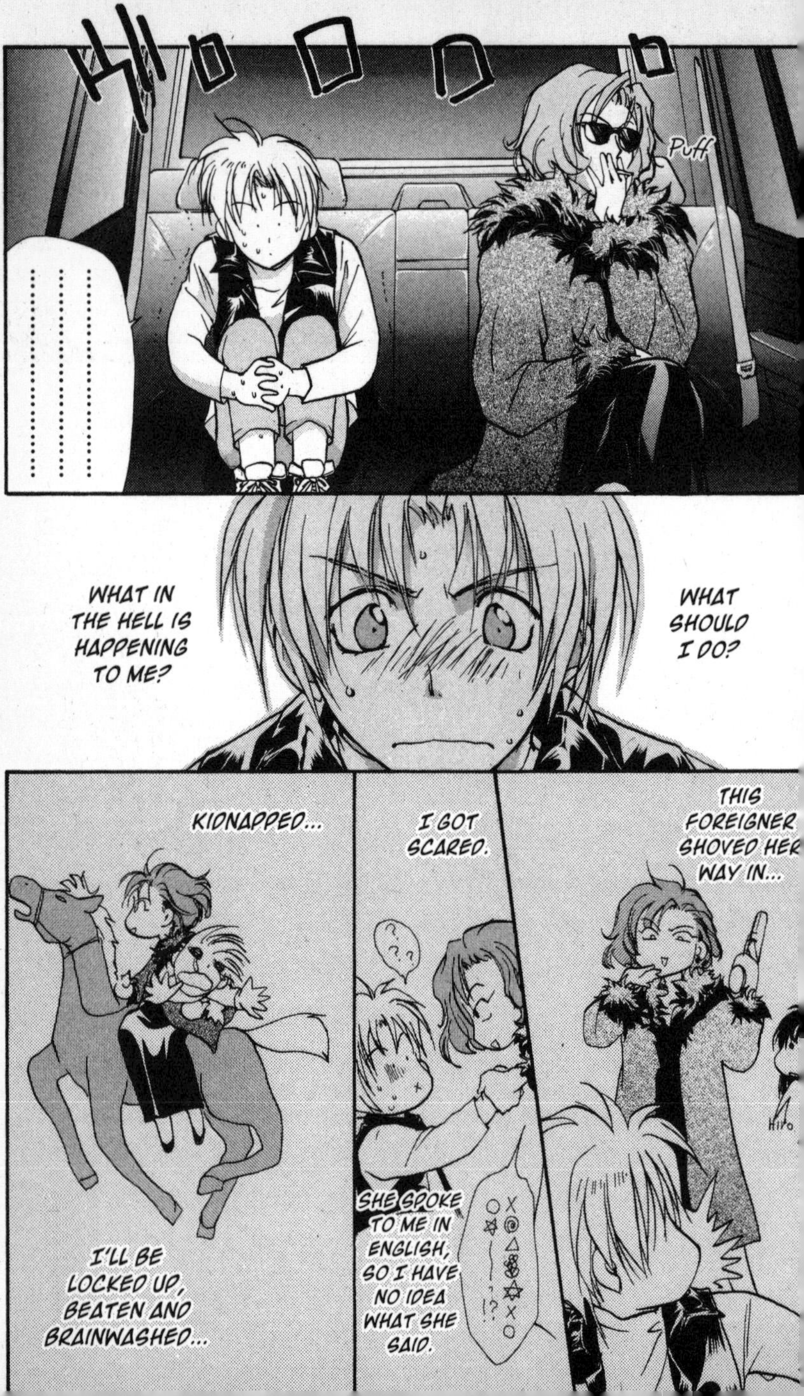
Puff
......
WHAT SHOULD I DO?
WHAT IN THE HELL IS HAPPENING TO ME?
THIS FOREIGNER SHOVED HER WAY IN...
Hiro
I GOT SCARED.
SHE SPOKE TO ME IN ENGLISH, SO I HAVE NO IDEA WHAT SHE SAID.
KIDNAPPED...
I'LL BE LOCKED UP, BEATEN AND BRAINWASHED...

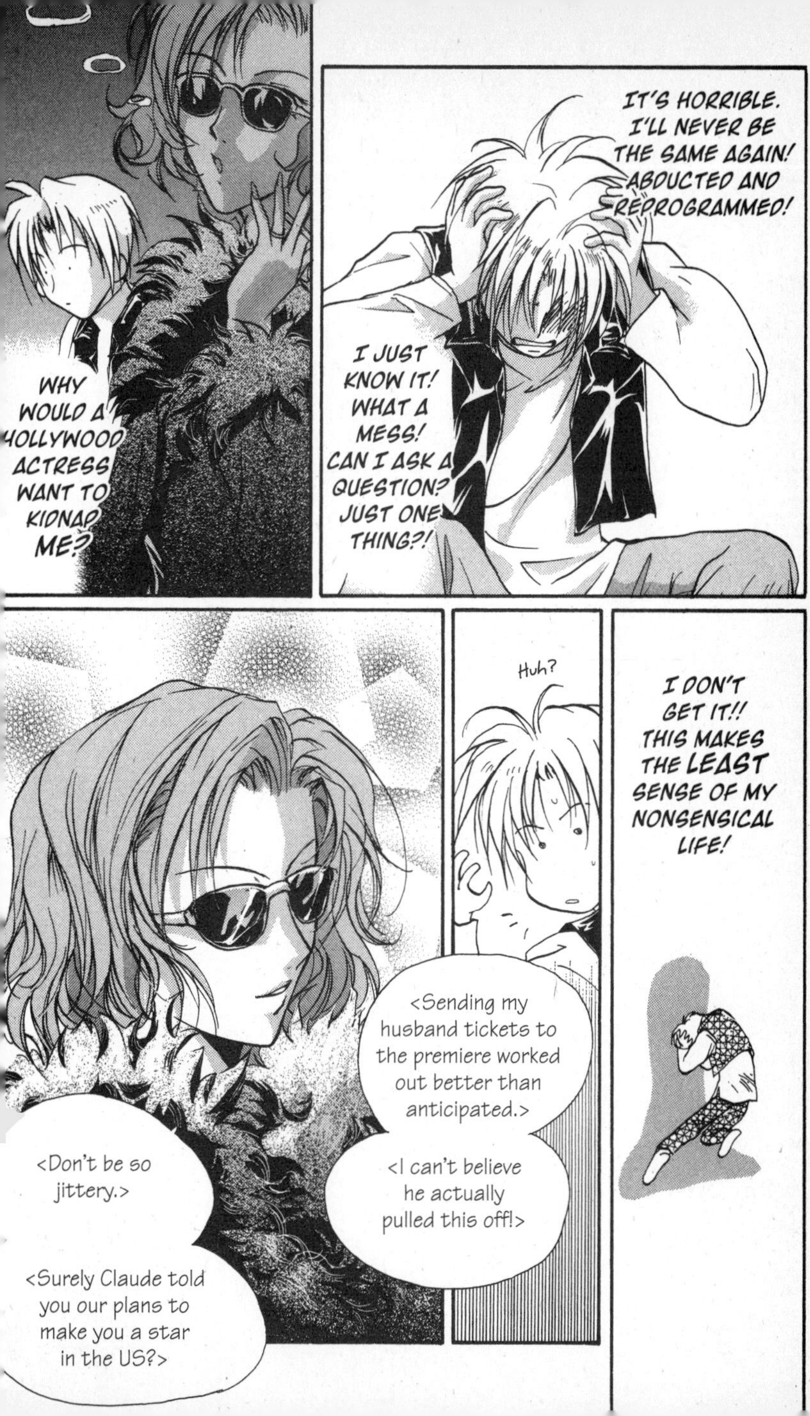
IT'S HORRIBLE. I'LL NEVER BE THE SAME AGAIN! ABDUCTED AND REPROGRAMMED!
I JUST KNOW IT! WHAT A MESS! CAN I ASK A QUESTION? JUST ONE THING?!
WHY WOULD A HOLLYWOOD ACTRESS WANT TO KIDNAP ME?
I DON'T GET IT!! THIS MAKES THE LEAST SENSE OF MY NONSENSICAL LIFE!
Huh?
<Sending my husband tickets to the premiere worked out better than anticipated.>
<I can't believe he actually pulled this off!>
<Don't be so jittery.>
<Surely Claude told you our plans to make you a star in the US?>

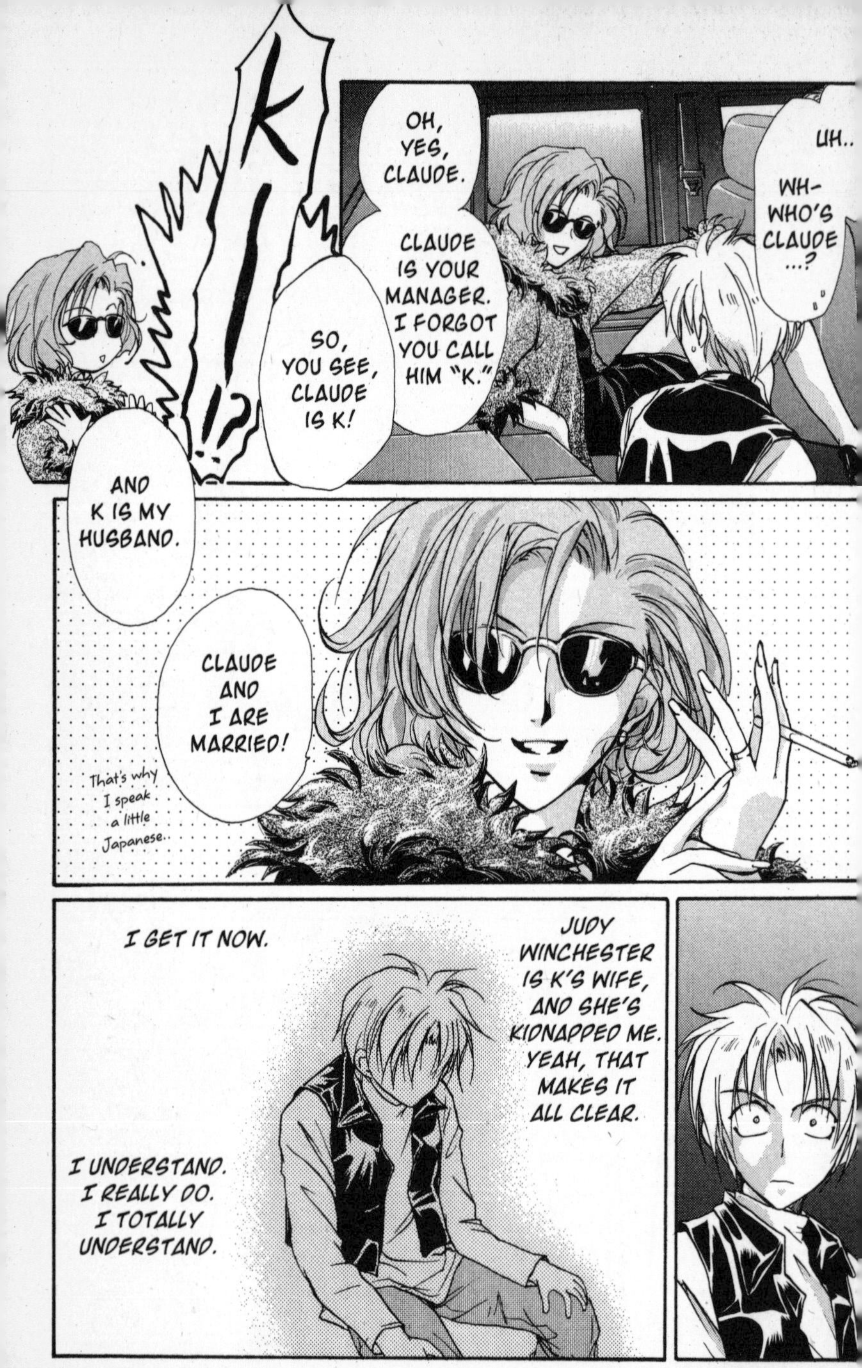
UH..
WH-WHO'S CLAUDE ...?
OH, YES, CLAUDE.
CLAUDE IS YOUR MANAGER. I FORGOT YOU CALL HIM "K."
SO, YOU SEE, CLAUDE IS K!
K!!?
AND K IS MY HUSBAND.
CLAUDE AND I ARE MARRIED!
That's why I speak a little Japanese..
JUDY WINCHESTER IS K'S WIFE, AND SHE'S KIDNAPPED ME. YEAH, THAT MAKES IT ALL CLEAR.
I GET IT NOW.
I UNDERSTAND. I REALLY DO. I TOTALLY UNDERSTAND.

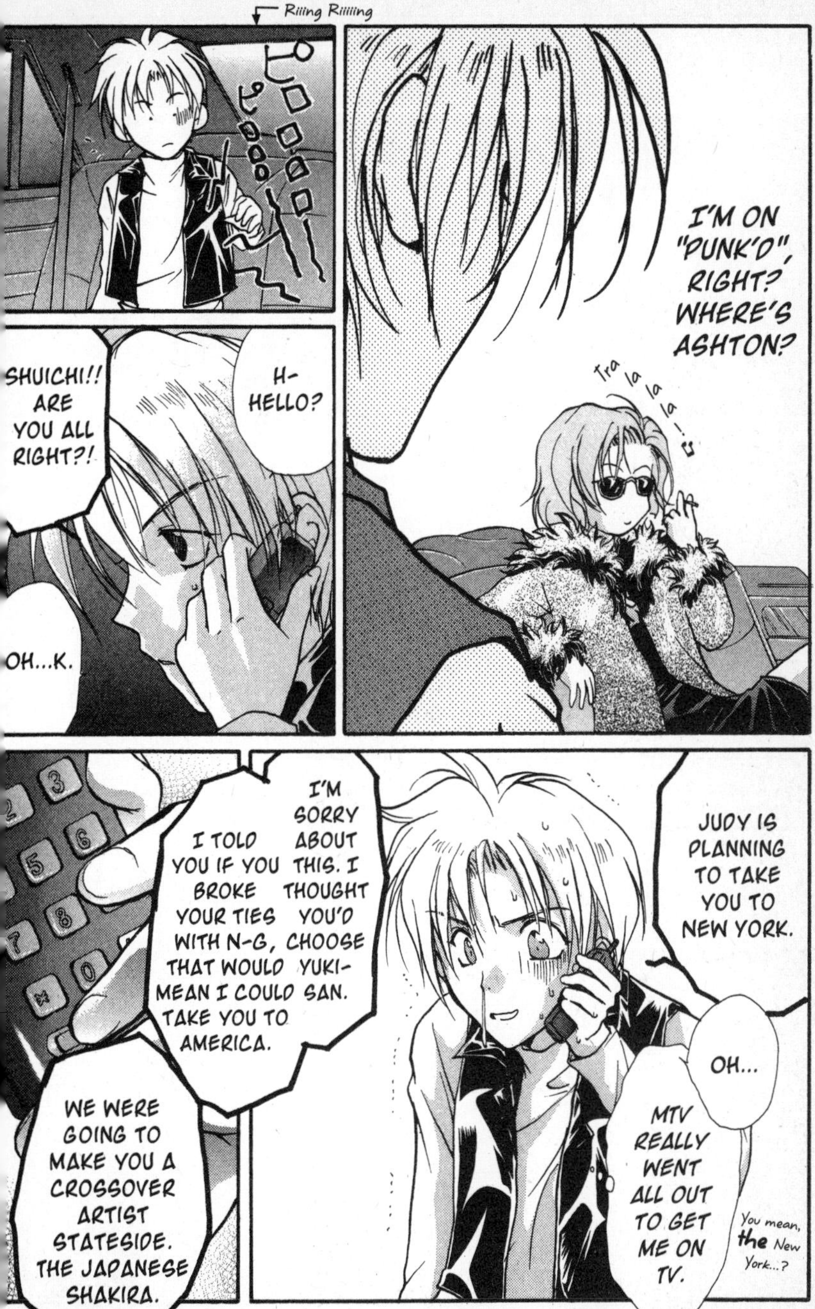
I'M ON "PUNK'D", RIGHT? WHERE'S ASHTON?
Tra la la la~!
Riiing Riiiiing
H-HELLO?
SHUICHI!! ARE YOU ALL RIGHT?!
OH...K.
JUDY IS PLANNING TO TAKE YOU TO NEW YORK.
OH...
MTV REALLY WENT ALL OUT TO GET ME ON TV.
You mean, the New York...?
I'M SORRY ABOUT THIS. I THOUGHT YOU'D CHOOSE YUKI-SAN.
I TOLD YOU IF YOU BROKE YOUR TIES WITH N-G, THAT WOULD MEAN I COULD TAKE YOU TO AMERICA.
WE WERE GOING TO MAKE YOU A CROSSOVER ARTIST STATESIDE. THE JAPANESE SHAKIRA.

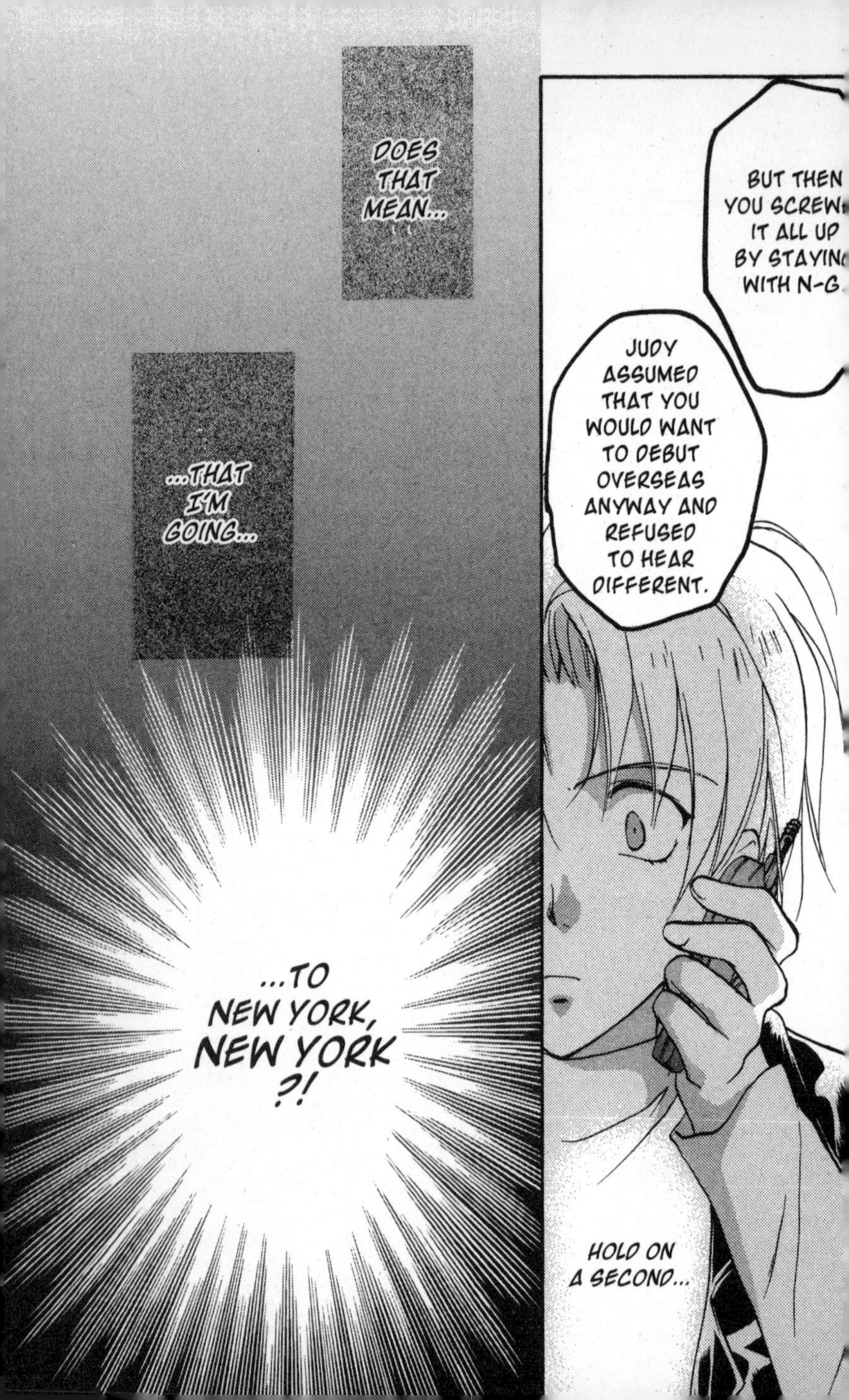
BUT THEN YOU SCREW IT ALL UP BY STAYIN WITH N-G
JUDY ASSUMED THAT YOU WOULD WANT TO DEBUT OVERSEAS ANYWAY AND REFUSED TO HEAR DIFFERENT.
HOLD ON A SECOND...
DOES THAT MEAN...
...THAT I'M GOING...
...TO NEW YORK, NEW YORK ?!

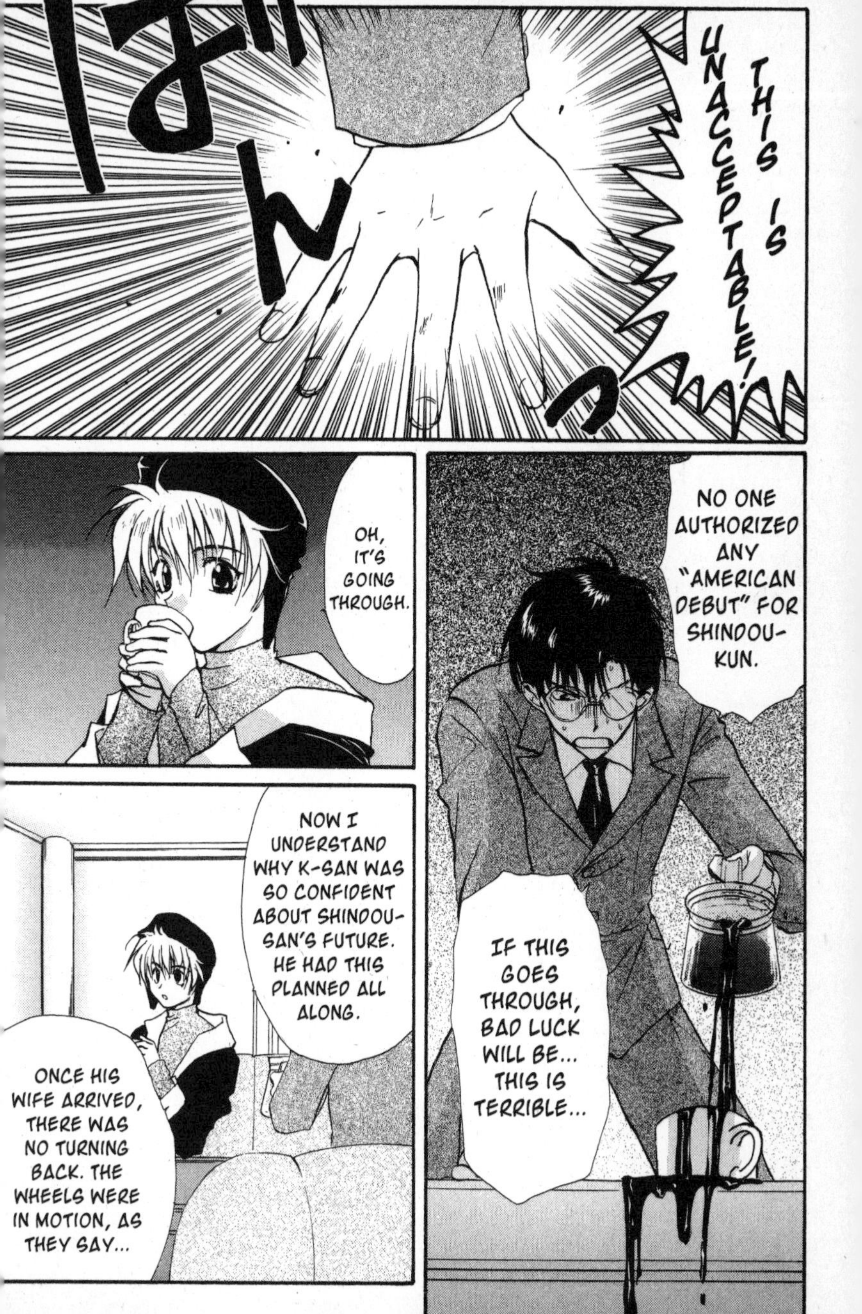
ばんっ
THIS IS UNACCEPTABLE!
NO ONE AUTHORIZED ANY "AMERICAN DEBUT" FOR SHINDOU-KUN.
IF THIS GOES THROUGH, BAD LUCK WILL BE... THIS IS TERRIBLE...
OH, IT'S GOING THROUGH.
NOW I UNDERSTAND WHY K-SAN WAS SO CONFIDENT ABOUT SHINDOU-SAN'S FUTURE. HE HAD THIS PLANNED ALL ALONG.
ONCE HIS WIFE ARRIVED, THERE WAS NO TURNING BACK. THE WHEELS WERE IN MOTION, AS THEY SAY...

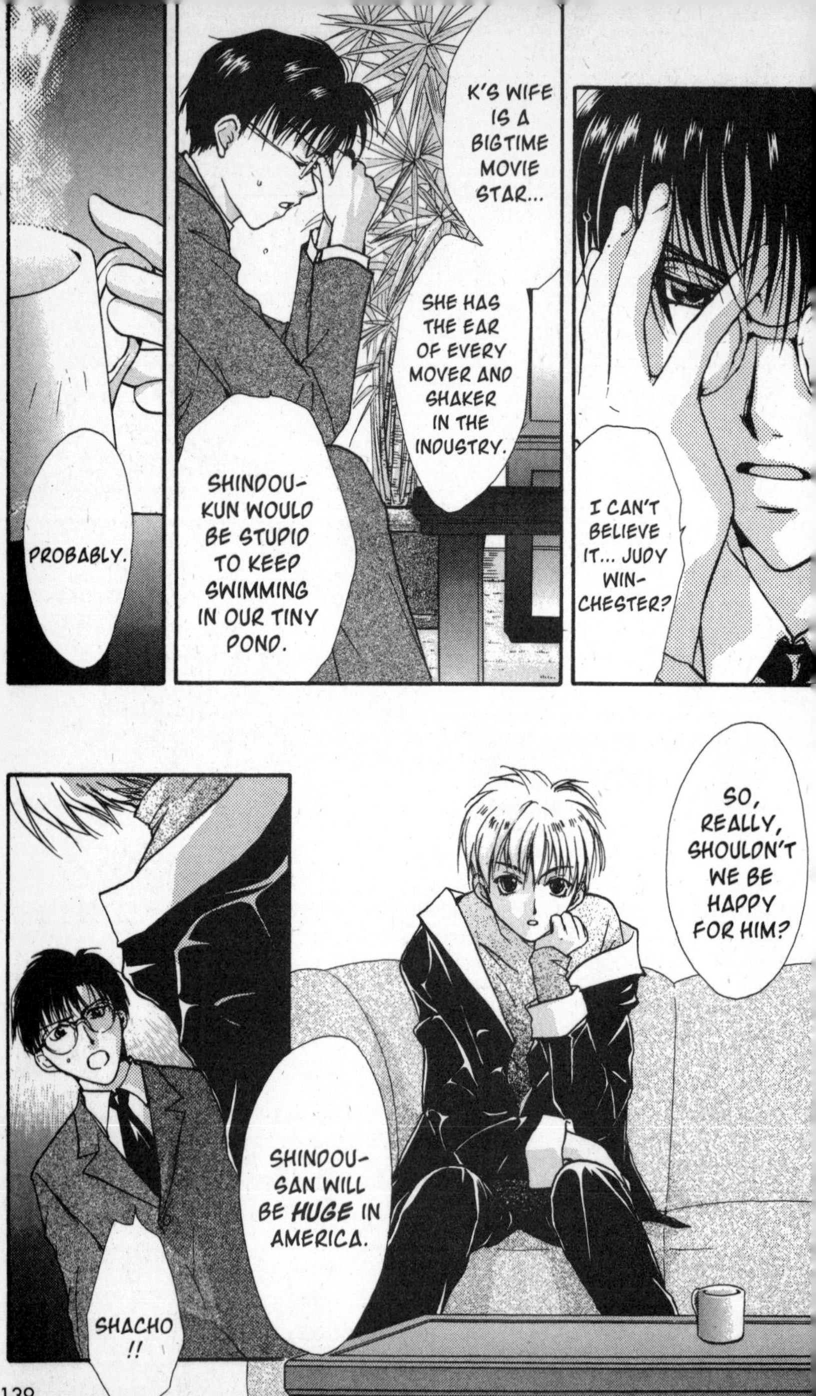
I CAN'T BELIEVE IT... JUDY WIN-CHESTER?
K'S WIFE IS A BIGTIME MOVIE STAR...
SHE HAS THE EAR OF EVERY MOVER AND SHAKER IN THE INDUSTRY.
SHINDOU-KUN WOULD BE STUPID TO KEEP SWIMMING IN OUR TINY POND.
PROBABLY.
SO, REALLY, SHOULDN'T WE BE HAPPY FOR HIM?
SHINDOU-SAN WILL BE *HUGE* IN AMERICA.
SHACHO!!

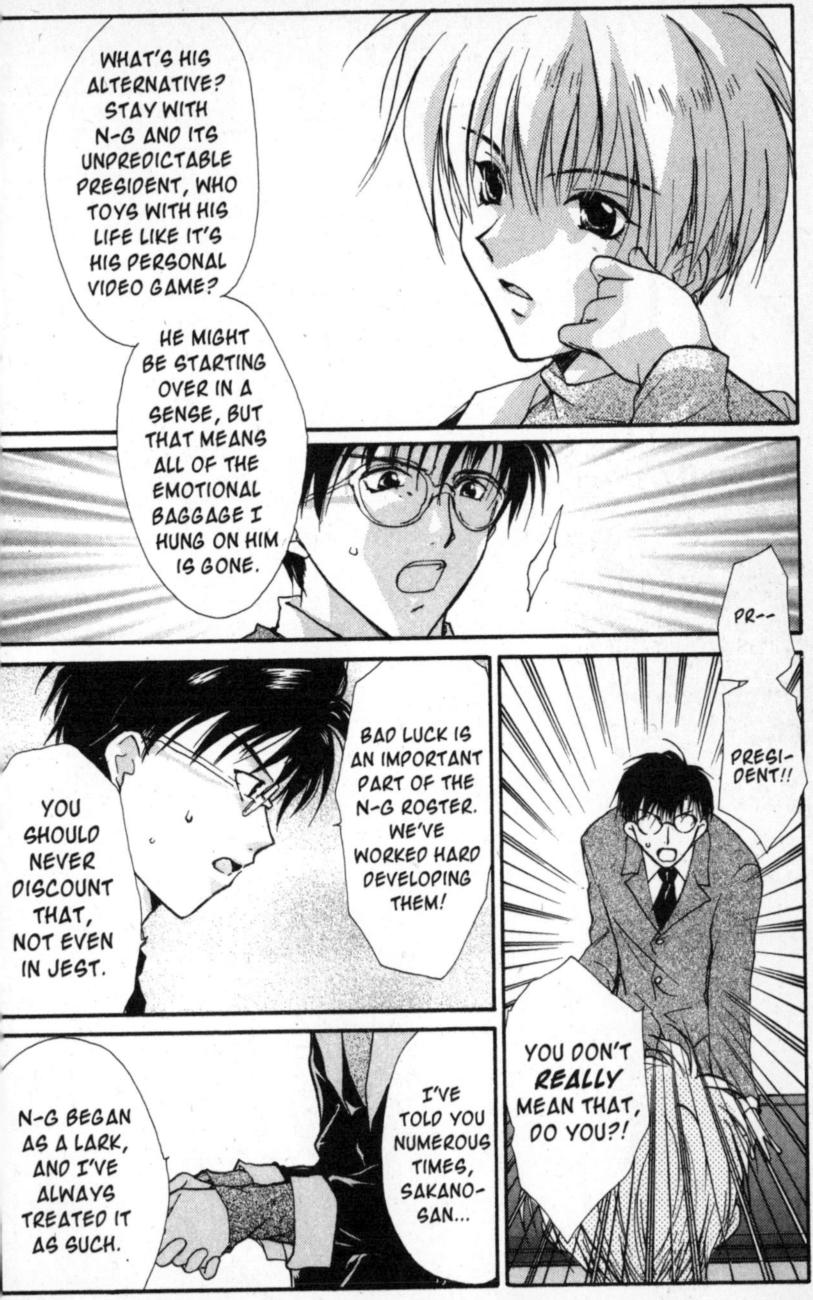
WHAT'S HIS ALTERNATIVE? STAY WITH N-G AND ITS UNPREDICTABLE PRESIDENT, WHO TOYS WITH HIS LIFE LIKE IT'S HIS PERSONAL VIDEO GAME?
HE MIGHT BE STARTING OVER IN A SENSE, BUT THAT MEANS ALL OF THE EMOTIONAL BAGGAGE I HUNG ON HIM IS GONE.
PR--
PRESI-DENT!!
YOU DON'T **REALLY** MEAN THAT, DO YOU?!
BAD LUCK IS AN IMPORTANT PART OF THE N-G ROSTER. WE'VE WORKED HARD DEVELOPING THEM!
YOU SHOULD NEVER DISCOUNT THAT, NOT EVEN IN JEST.
I'VE TOLD YOU NUMEROUS TIMES, SAKANO-SAN...
N-G BEGAN AS A LARK, AND I'VE ALWAYS TREATED IT AS SUCH.

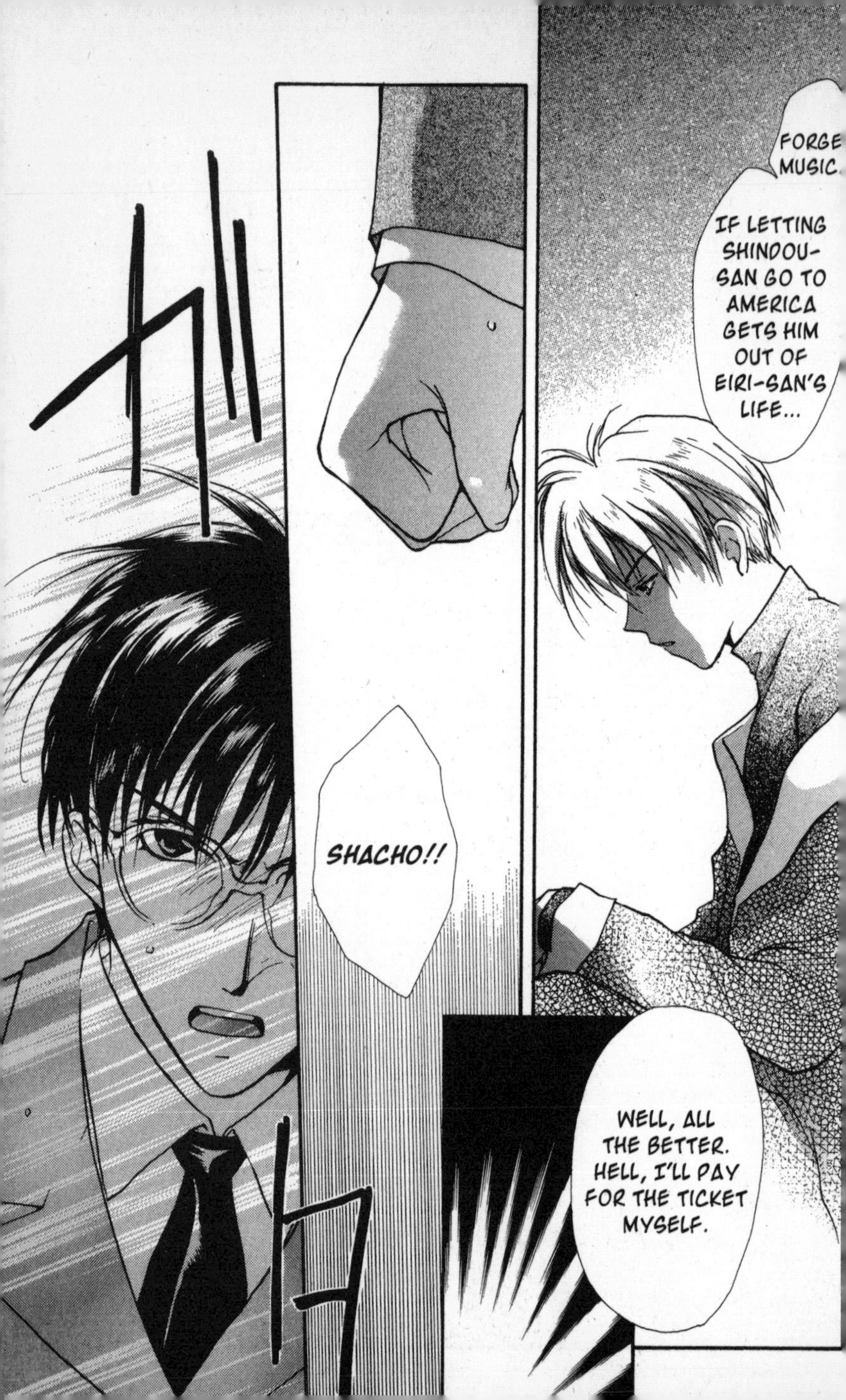
FORGE MUSIC.
IF LETTING SHINDOU-SAN GO TO AMERICA GETS HIM OUT OF EIRI-SAN'S LIFE...
SHACHO!!
WELL, ALL THE BETTER. HELL, I'LL PAY FOR THE TICKET MYSELF.

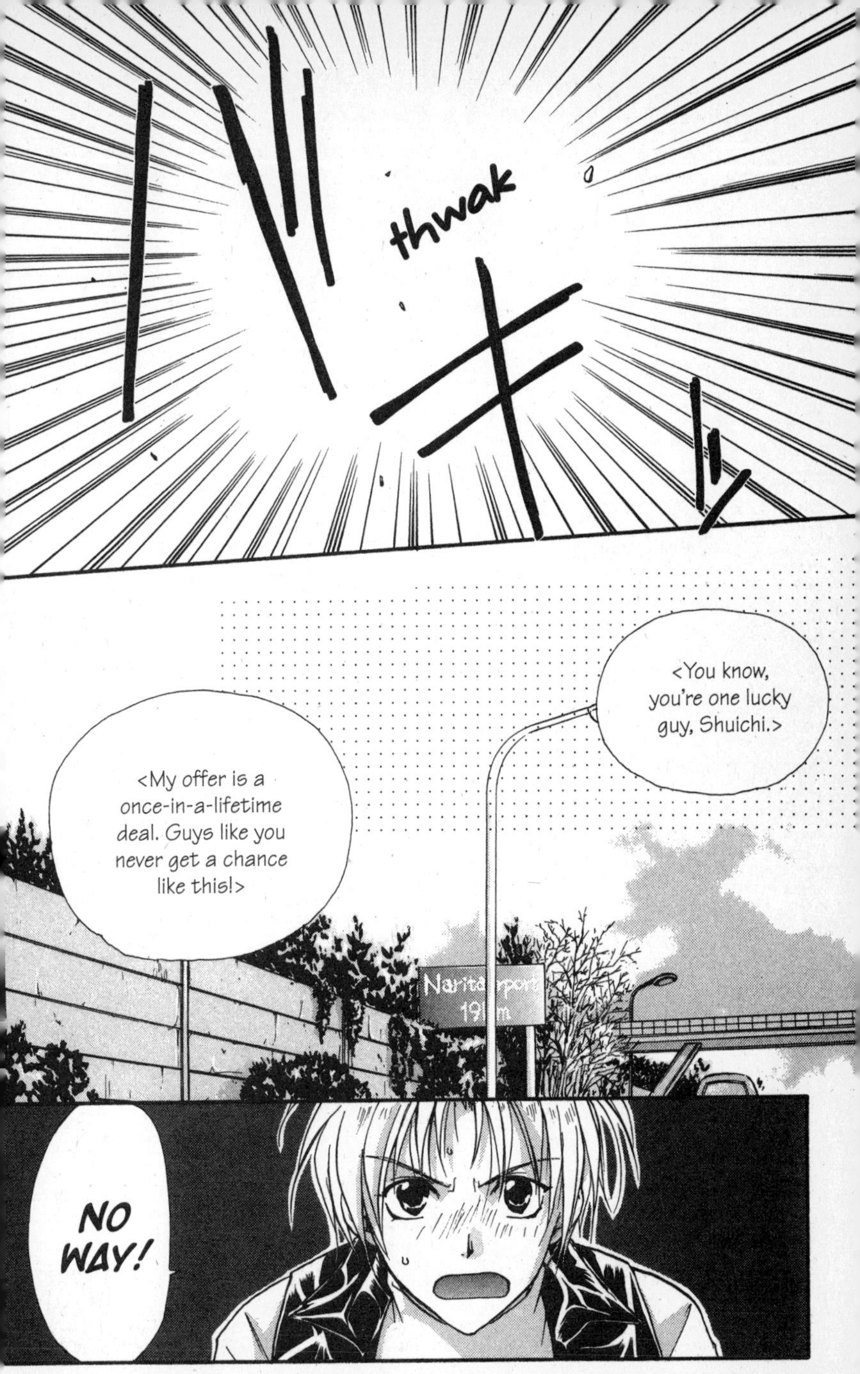
thwak
<You know, you're one lucky guy, Shuichi.>
<My offer is a once-in-a-lifetime deal. Guys like you never get a chance like this!>
NO WAY!

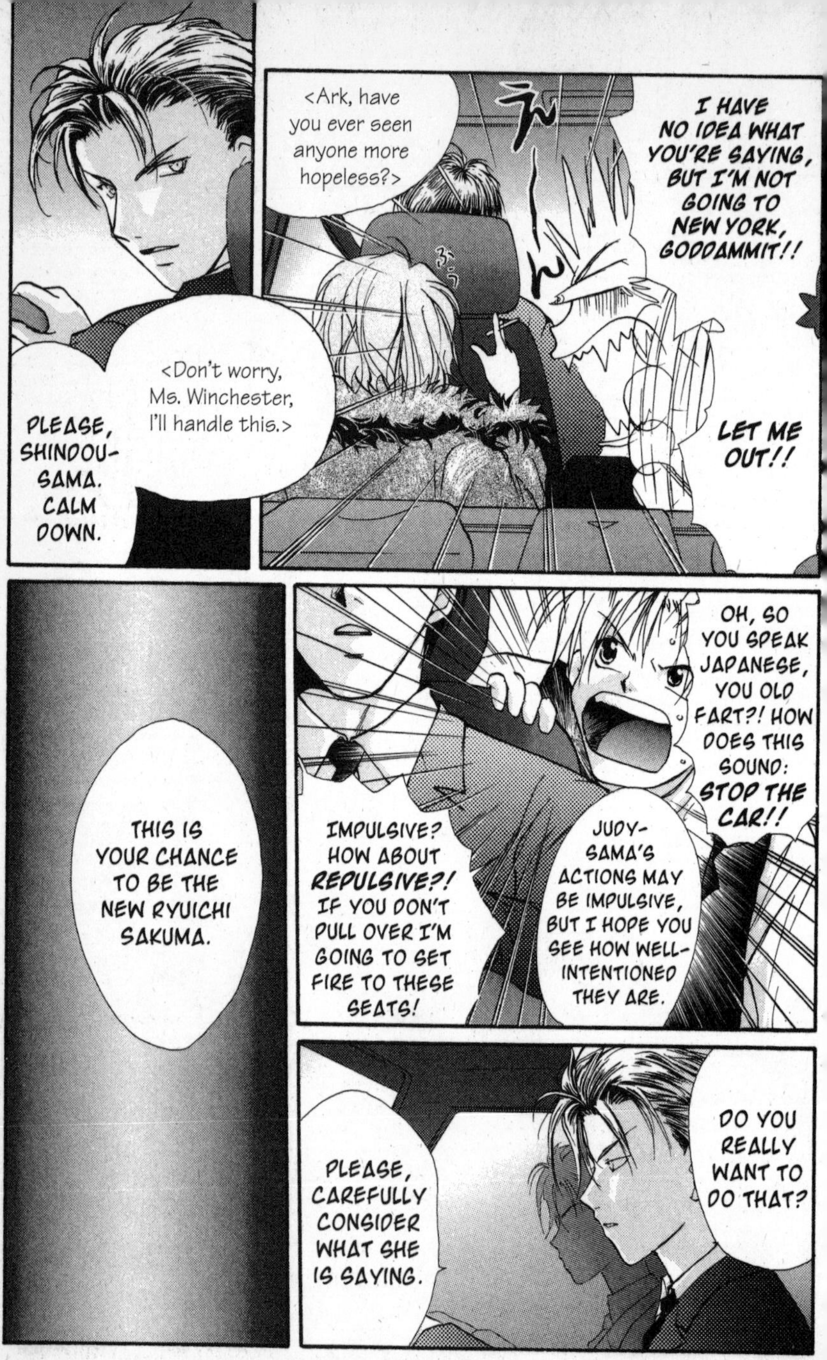
I HAVE NO IDEA WHAT YOU'RE SAYING, BUT I'M NOT GOING TO NEW YORK, GODDAMMIT!!
<Ark, have you ever seen anyone more hopeless?>
LET ME OUT!!
<Don't worry, Ms. Winchester, I'll handle this.>
PLEASE, SHINDOU-SAMA. CALM DOWN.
OH, SO YOU SPEAK JAPANESE, YOU OLD FART?! HOW DOES THIS SOUND: STOP THE CAR!!
JUDY-SAMA'S ACTIONS MAY BE IMPULSIVE, BUT I HOPE YOU SEE HOW WELL-INTENTIONED THEY ARE.
IMPULSIVE? HOW ABOUT REPULSIVE?! IF YOU DON'T PULL OVER I'M GOING TO SET FIRE TO THESE SEATS!
DO YOU REALLY WANT TO DO THAT?
PLEASE, CAREFULLY CONSIDER WHAT SHE IS SAYING.
THIS IS YOUR CHANCE TO BE THE NEW RYUICHI SAKUMA.

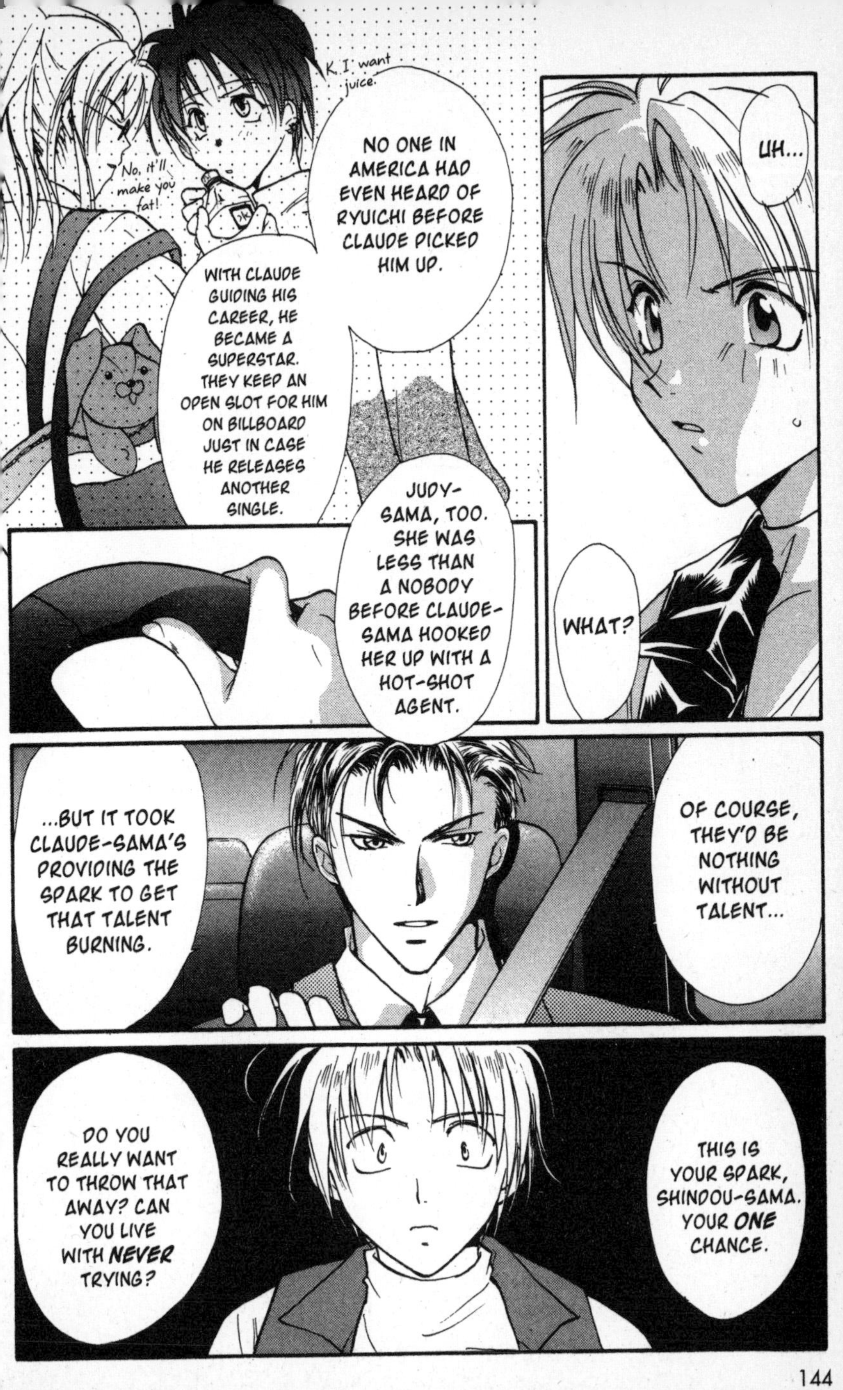
UH...
WHAT?
K. I want juice.
No, it'll make you fat!
NO ONE IN AMERICA HAD EVEN HEARD OF RYUICHI BEFORE CLAUDE PICKED HIM UP.
WITH CLAUDE GUIDING HIS CAREER, HE BECAME A SUPERSTAR. THEY KEEP AN OPEN SLOT FOR HIM ON BILLBOARD JUST IN CASE HE RELEASES ANOTHER SINGLE.
JUDY-SAMA, TOO. SHE WAS LESS THAN A NOBODY BEFORE CLAUDE-SAMA HOOKED HER UP WITH A HOT-SHOT AGENT.
OF COURSE, THEY'D BE NOTHING WITHOUT TALENT...
...BUT IT TOOK CLAUDE-SAMA'S PROVIDING THE SPARK TO GET THAT TALENT BURNING.
THIS IS YOUR SPARK, SHINDOU-SAMA. YOUR ***ONE*** CHANCE.
DO YOU REALLY WANT TO THROW THAT AWAY? CAN YOU LIVE WITH ***NEVER*** TRYING?

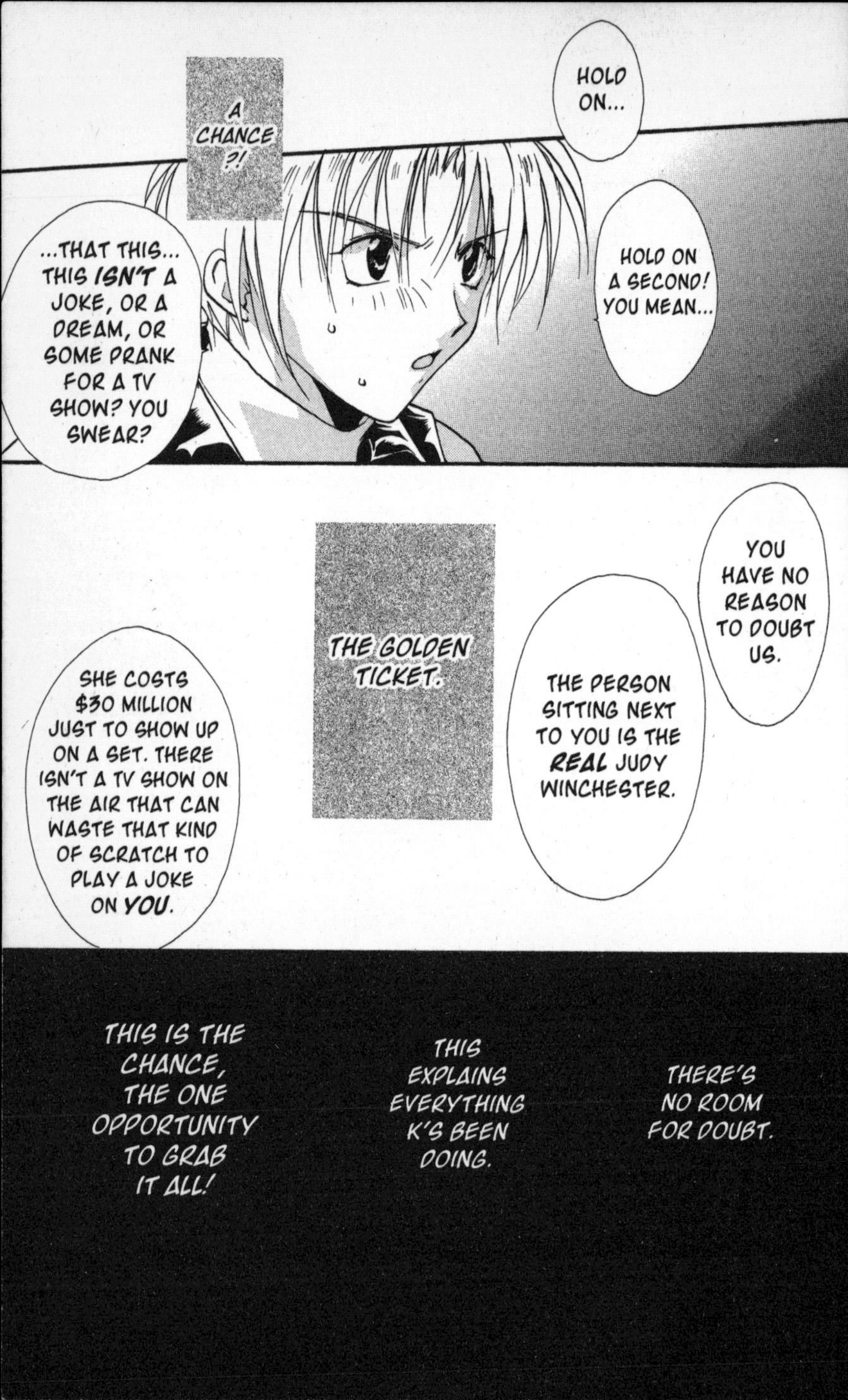
HOLD ON...
HOLD ON A SECOND! YOU MEAN...
A CHANCE ?!
...THAT THIS... THIS ISN'T A JOKE, OR A DREAM, OR SOME PRANK FOR A TV SHOW? YOU SWEAR?
YOU HAVE NO REASON TO DOUBT US.
THE PERSON SITTING NEXT TO YOU IS THE REAL JUDY WINCHESTER.
THE GOLDEN TICKET.
SHE COSTS $30 MILLION JUST TO SHOW UP ON A SET. THERE ISN'T A TV SHOW ON THE AIR THAT CAN WASTE THAT KIND OF SCRATCH TO PLAY A JOKE ON YOU.
THERE'S NO ROOM FOR DOUBT.
THIS EXPLAINS EVERYTHING K'S BEEN DOING.
THIS IS THE CHANCE, THE ONE OPPORTUNITY TO GRAB IT ALL!

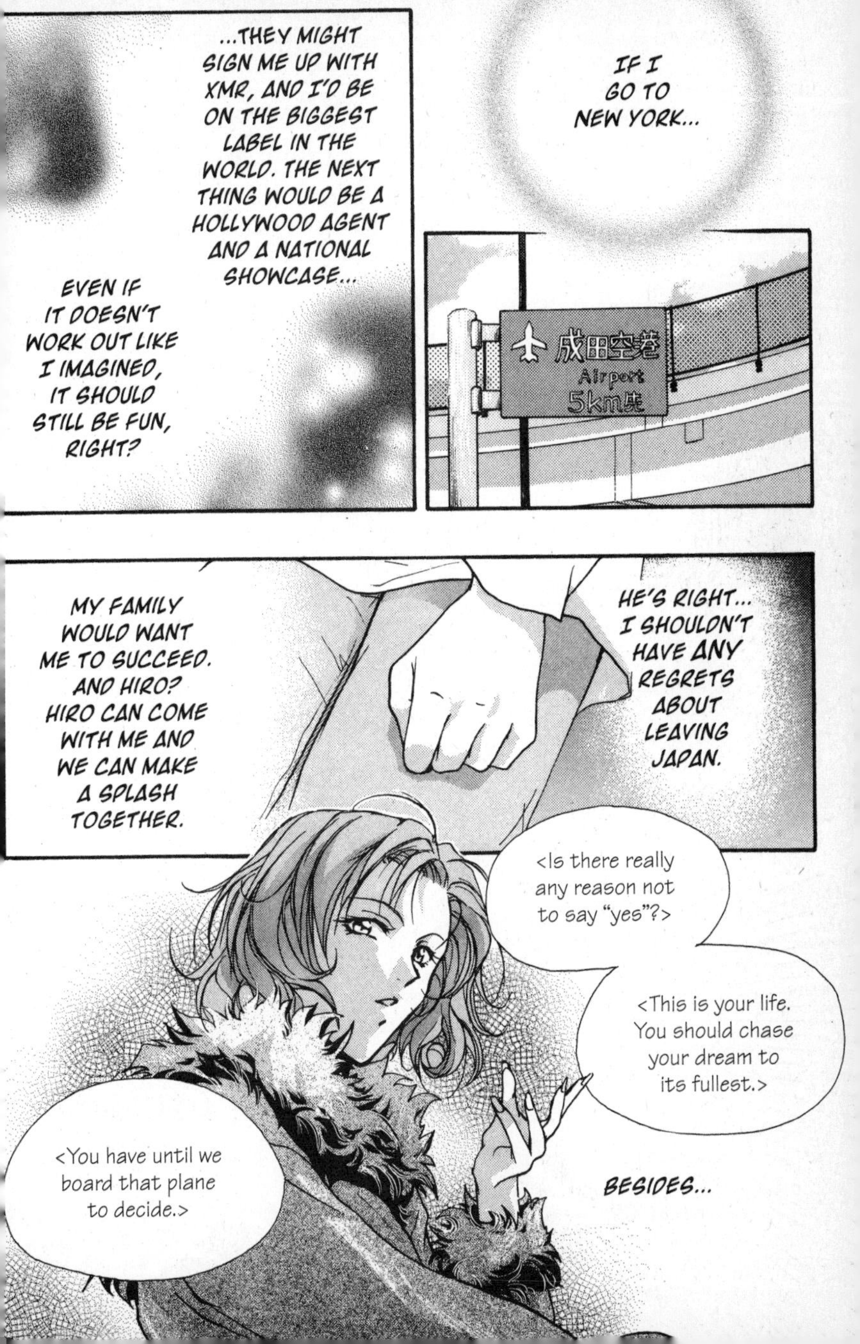
IF I GO TO NEW YORK...
成田空港
Airport
5km先
...THEY MIGHT SIGN ME UP WITH XMR, AND I'D BE ON THE BIGGEST LABEL IN THE WORLD. THE NEXT THING WOULD BE A HOLLYWOOD AGENT AND A NATIONAL SHOWCASE...
EVEN IF IT DOESN'T WORK OUT LIKE I IMAGINED, IT SHOULD STILL BE FUN, RIGHT?
HE'S RIGHT... I SHOULDN'T HAVE ANY REGRETS ABOUT LEAVING JAPAN.
MY FAMILY WOULD WANT ME TO SUCCEED. AND HIRO? HIRO CAN COME WITH ME AND WE CAN MAKE A SPLASH TOGETHER.
<Is there really any reason not to say "yes"?>
<This is your life. You should chase your dream to its fullest.>
<You have until we board that plane to decide.>
BESIDES...

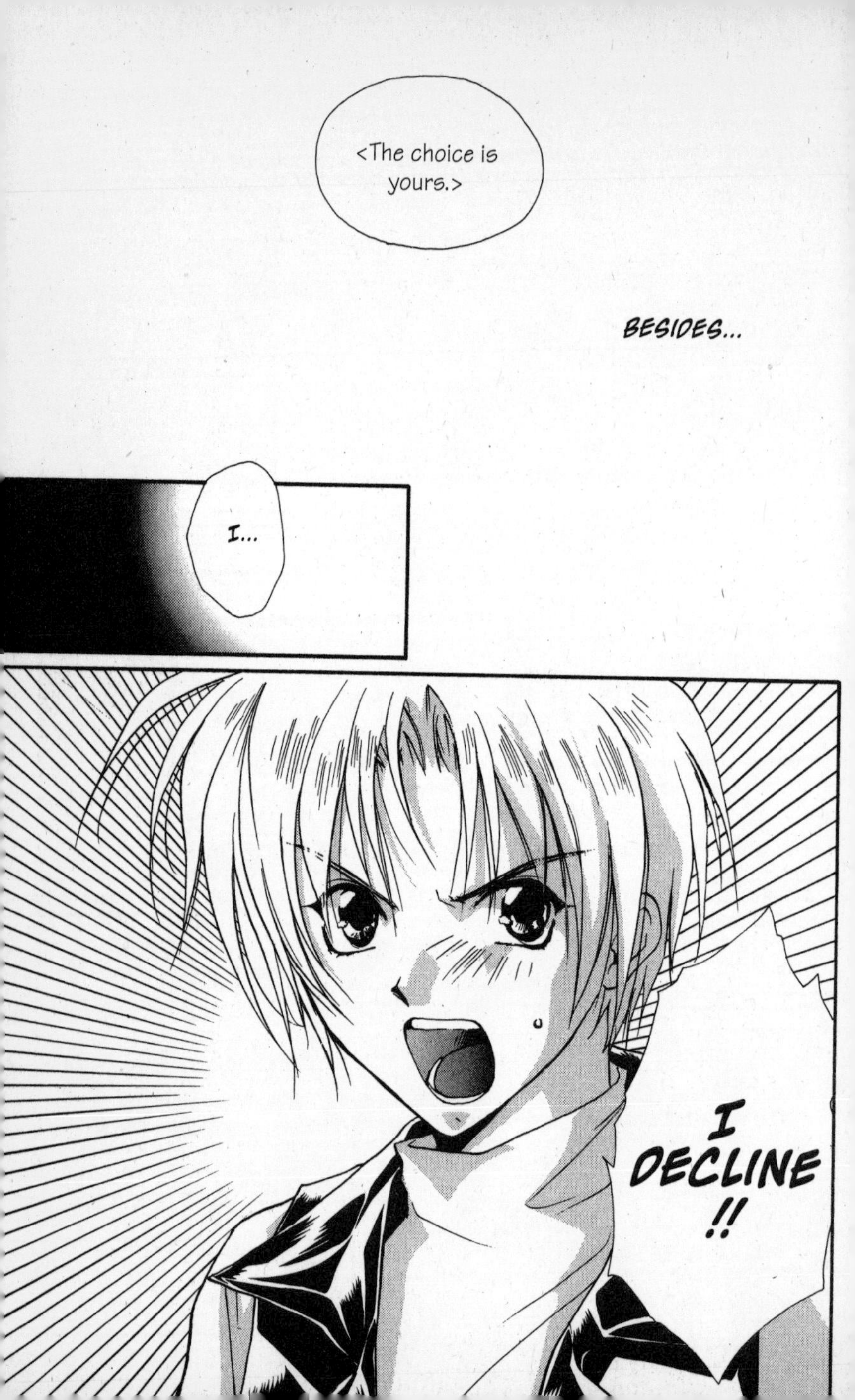
<The choice is yours.>
BESIDES...
I...
I DECLINE!!

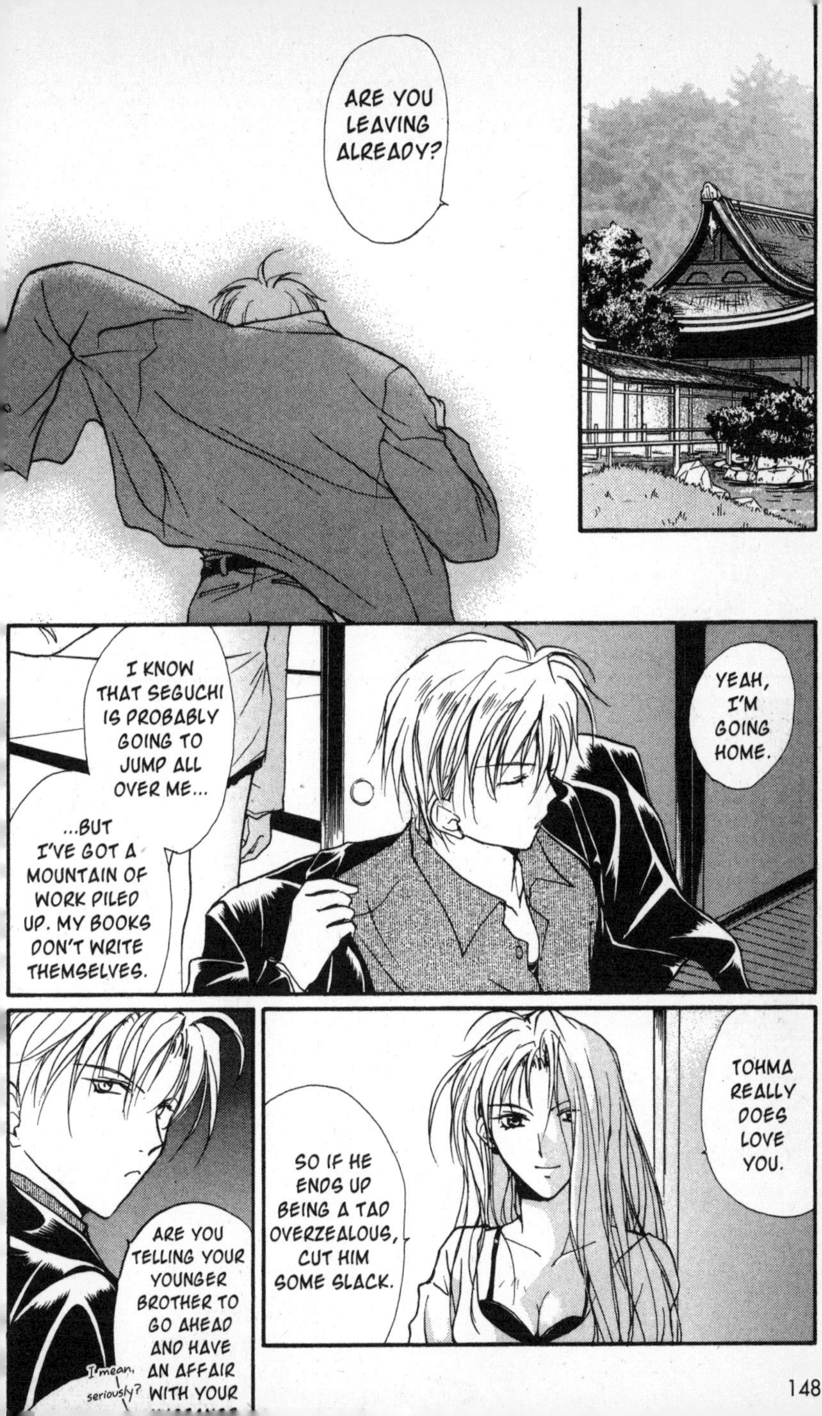

ARE YOU LEAVING ALREADY?
YEAH, I'M GOING HOME.
I KNOW THAT SEGUCHI IS PROBABLY GOING TO JUMP ALL OVER ME...
...BUT I'VE GOT A MOUNTAIN OF WORK PILED UP. MY BOOKS DON'T WRITE THEMSELVES.
TOHMA REALLY DOES LOVE YOU.
SO IF HE ENDS UP BEING A TAD OVERZEALOUS, CUT HIM SOME SLACK.
ARE YOU TELLING YOUR YOUNGER BROTHER TO GO AHEAD AND HAVE AN AFFAIR WITH YOUR
I mean, seriously?

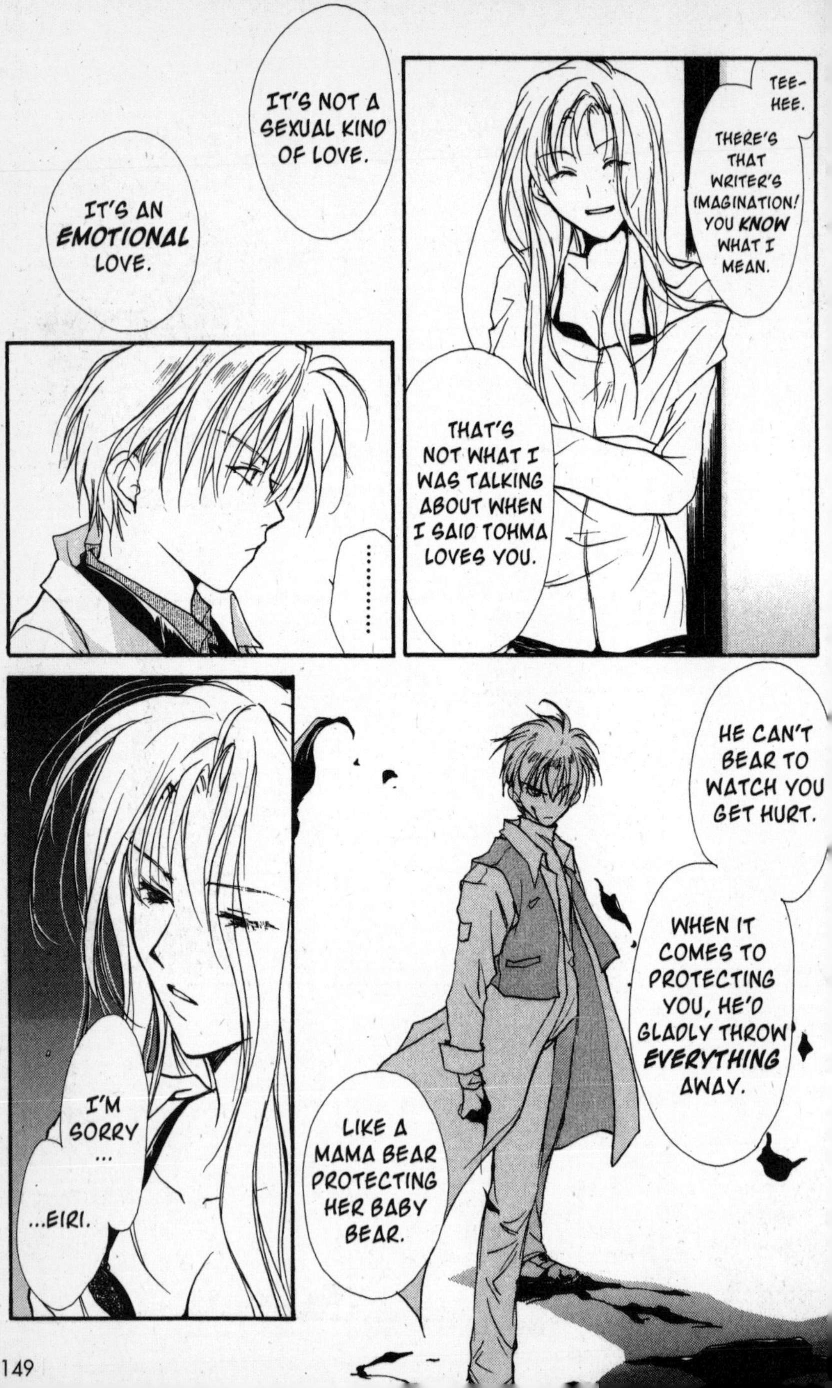
TEE-HEE.
THERE'S THAT WRITER'S IMAGINATION! YOU *KNOW* WHAT I MEAN.
THAT'S NOT WHAT I WAS TALKING ABOUT WHEN I SAID TOHMA LOVES YOU.
IT'S NOT A SEXUAL KIND OF LOVE.
IT'S AN *EMOTIONAL* LOVE.
....
HE CAN'T BEAR TO WATCH YOU GET HURT.
WHEN IT COMES TO PROTECTING YOU, HE'D GLADLY THROW *EVERYTHING* AWAY.
LIKE A MAMA BEAR PROTECTING HER BABY BEAR.
I'M SORRY ...
...EIRI.

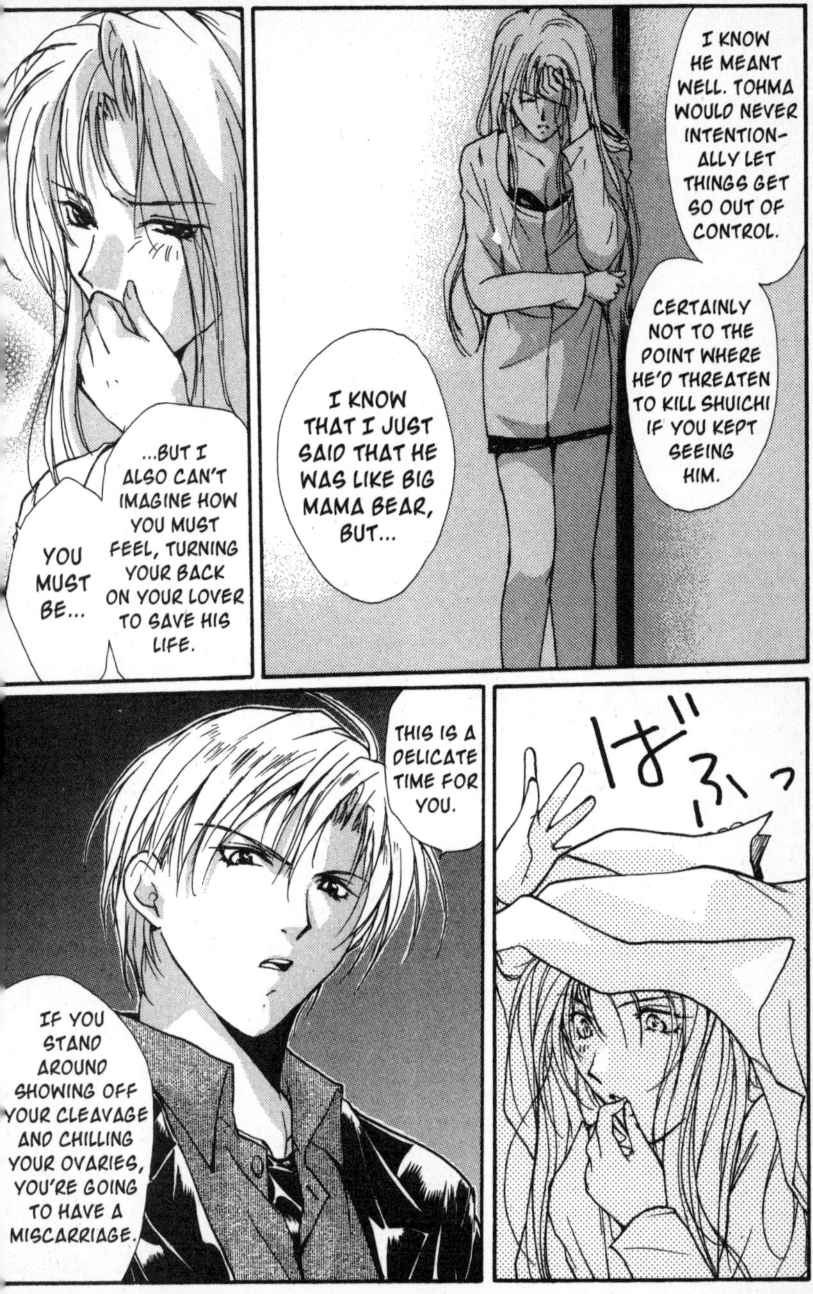
I KNOW HE MEANT WELL. TOHMA WOULD NEVER INTENTION-ALLY LET THINGS GET SO OUT OF CONTROL.
CERTAINLY NOT TO THE POINT WHERE HE'D THREATEN TO KILL SHUICHI IF YOU KEPT SEEING HIM.
I KNOW THAT I JUST SAID THAT HE WAS LIKE BIG MAMA BEAR, BUT...
...BUT I ALSO CAN'T IMAGINE HOW YOU MUST FEEL, TURNING YOUR BACK ON YOUR LOVER TO SAVE HIS LIFE.
YOU MUST BE...
ばふっ
THIS IS A DELICATE TIME FOR YOU.
IF YOU STAND AROUND SHOWING OFF YOUR CLEAVAGE AND CHILLING YOUR OVARIES, YOU'RE GOING TO HAVE A MISCARRIAGE.

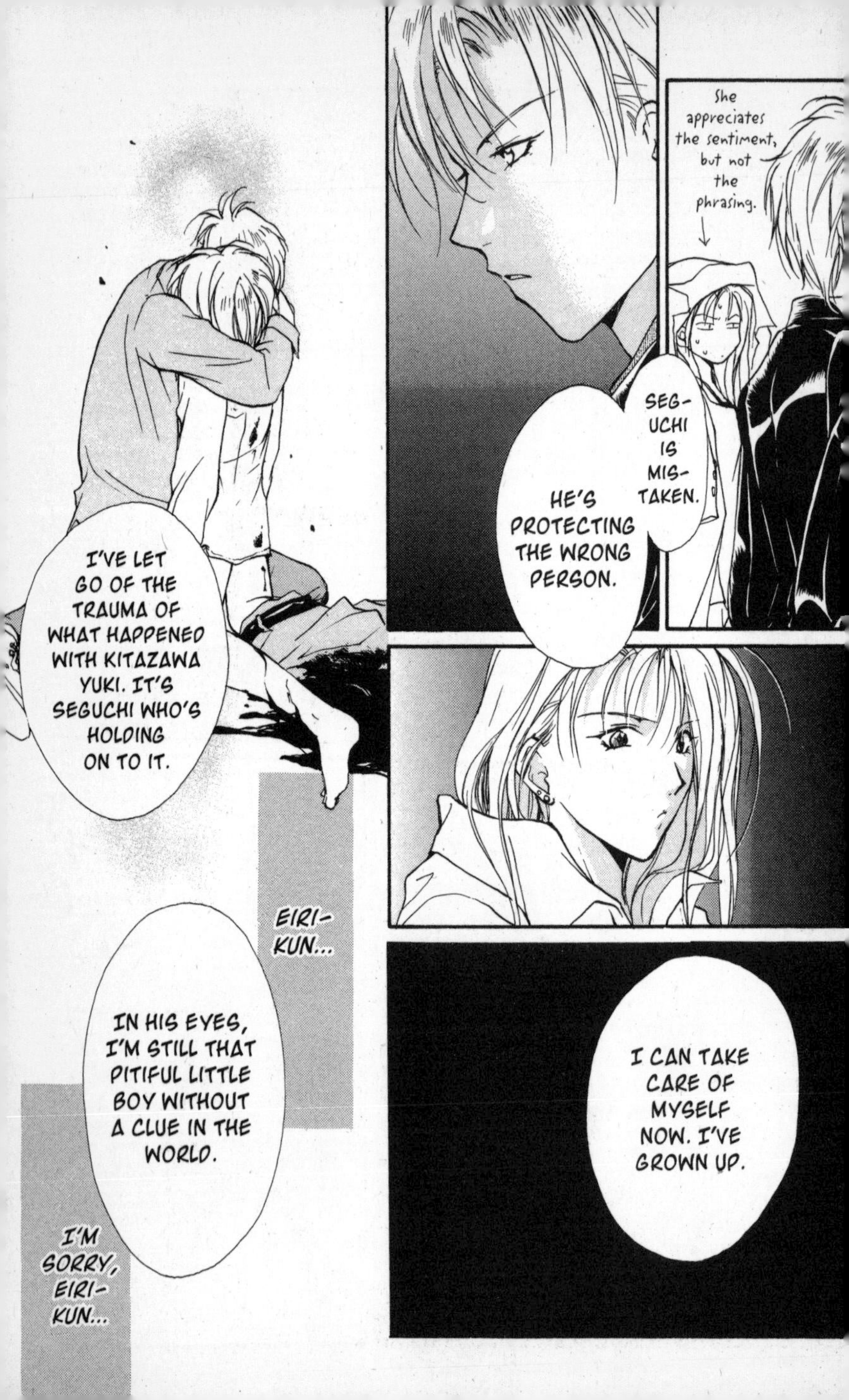
She appreciates the sentiment, but not the phrasing.
SEGUCHI IS MISTAKEN.
HE'S PROTECTING THE WRONG PERSON.
I CAN TAKE CARE OF MYSELF NOW. I'VE GROWN UP.
I'VE LET GO OF THE TRAUMA OF WHAT HAPPENED WITH KITAZAWA YUKI. IT'S SEGUCHI WHO'S HOLDING ON TO IT.
EIRI-KUN...
IN HIS EYES, I'M STILL THAT PITIFUL LITTLE BOY WITHOUT A CLUE IN THE WORLD.
I'M SORRY, EIRI-KUN...

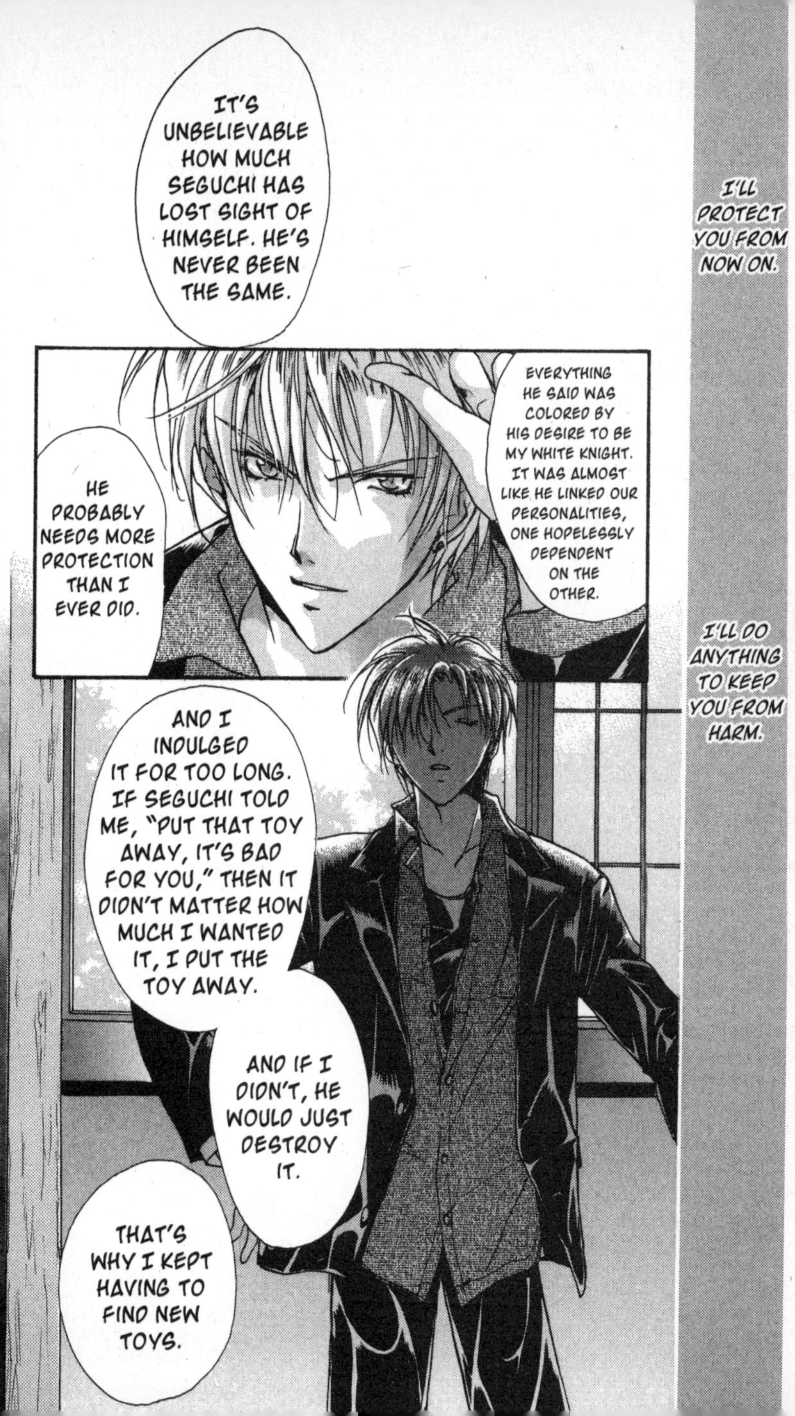
I'LL PROTECT YOU FROM NOW ON.
I'LL DO ANYTHING TO KEEP YOU FROM HARM.
IT'S UNBELIEVABLE HOW MUCH SEGUCHI HAS LOST SIGHT OF HIMSELF. HE'S NEVER BEEN THE SAME.
EVERYTHING HE SAID WAS COLORED BY HIS DESIRE TO BE MY WHITE KNIGHT. IT WAS ALMOST LIKE HE LINKED OUR PERSONALITIES, ONE HOPELESSLY DEPENDENT ON THE OTHER.
HE PROBABLY NEEDS MORE PROTECTION THAN I EVER DID.
AND I INDULGED IT FOR TOO LONG. IF SEGUCHI TOLD ME, "PUT THAT TOY AWAY, IT'S BAD FOR YOU," THEN IT DIDN'T MATTER HOW MUCH I WANTED IT, I PUT THE TOY AWAY.
AND IF I DIDN'T, HE WOULD JUST DESTROY IT.
THAT'S WHY I KEPT HAVING TO FIND NEW TOYS.

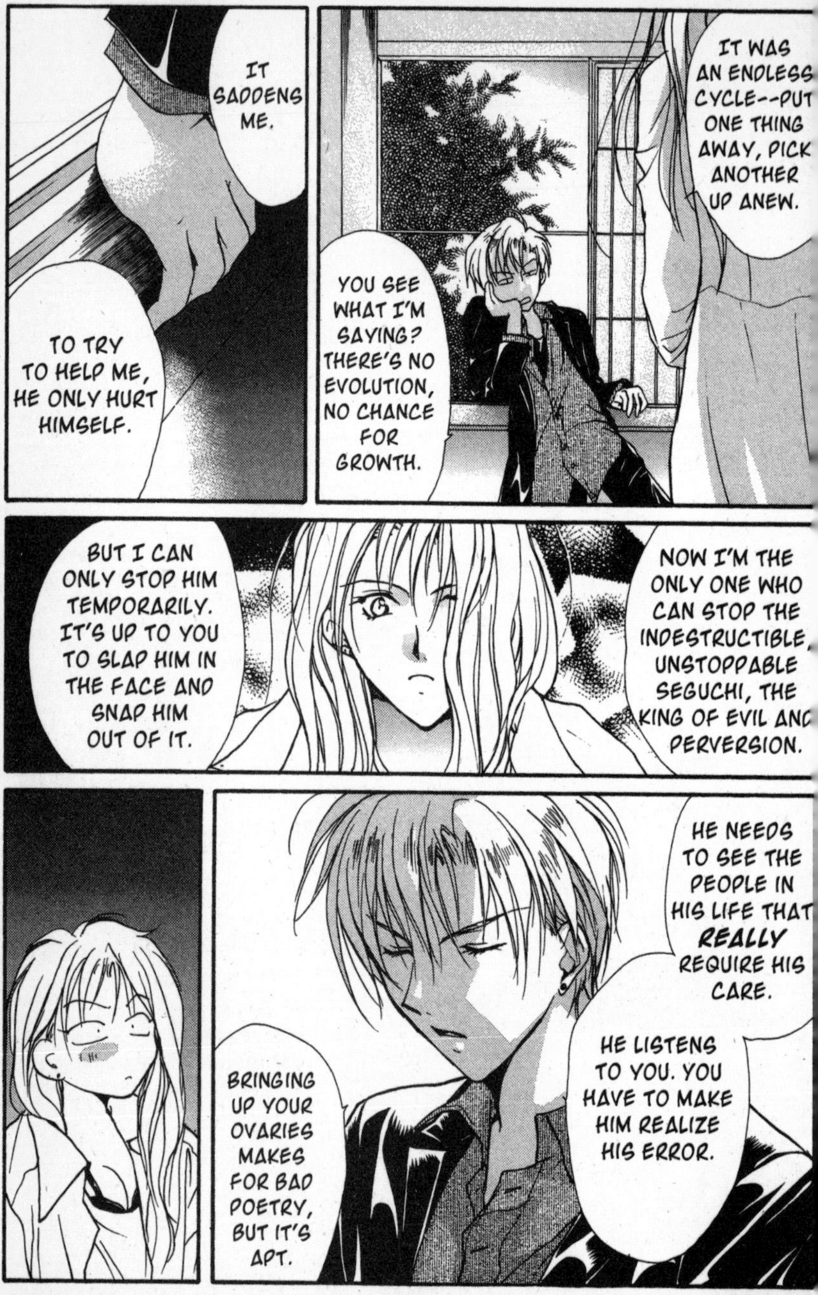
IT WAS AN ENDLESS CYCLE--PUT ONE THING AWAY, PICK ANOTHER UP ANEW.
YOU SEE WHAT I'M SAYING? THERE'S NO EVOLUTION, NO CHANCE FOR GROWTH.
IT SADDENS ME.
TO TRY TO HELP ME, HE ONLY HURT HIMSELF.
NOW I'M THE ONLY ONE WHO CAN STOP THE INDESTRUCTIBLE, UNSTOPPABLE SEGUCHI, THE KING OF EVIL AND PERVERSION.
BUT I CAN ONLY STOP HIM TEMPORARILY. IT'S UP TO YOU TO SLAP HIM IN THE FACE AND SNAP HIM OUT OF IT.
HE NEEDS TO SEE THE PEOPLE IN HIS LIFE THAT ***REALLY*** REQUIRE HIS CARE.
HE LISTENS TO YOU. YOU HAVE TO MAKE HIM REALIZE HIS ERROR.
BRINGING UP YOUR OVARIES MAKES FOR BAD POETRY, BUT IT'S APT.

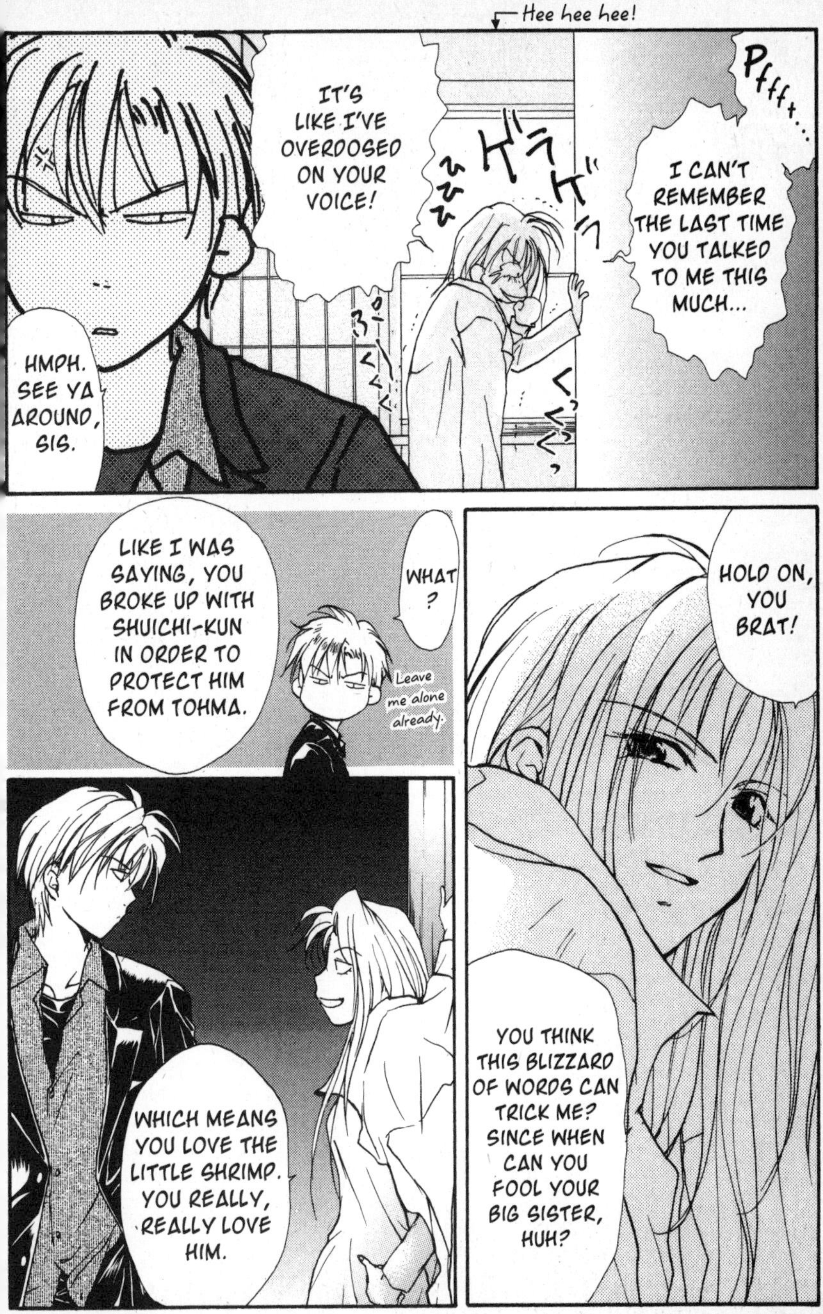
Hee hee hee!
Pffft...
I CAN'T REMEMBER THE LAST TIME YOU TALKED TO ME THIS MUCH...
IT'S LIKE I'VE OVERDOSED ON YOUR VOICE!
HMPH. SEE YA AROUND, SIS.
HOLD ON, YOU BRAT!
YOU THINK THIS BLIZZARD OF WORDS CAN TRICK ME? SINCE WHEN CAN YOU FOOL YOUR BIG SISTER, HUH?
WHAT?
LIKE I WAS SAYING, YOU BROKE UP WITH SHUICHI-KUN IN ORDER TO PROTECT HIM FROM TOHMA.
Leave me alone already.
WHICH MEANS YOU LOVE THE LITTLE SHRIMP. YOU REALLY, REALLY LOVE HIM.

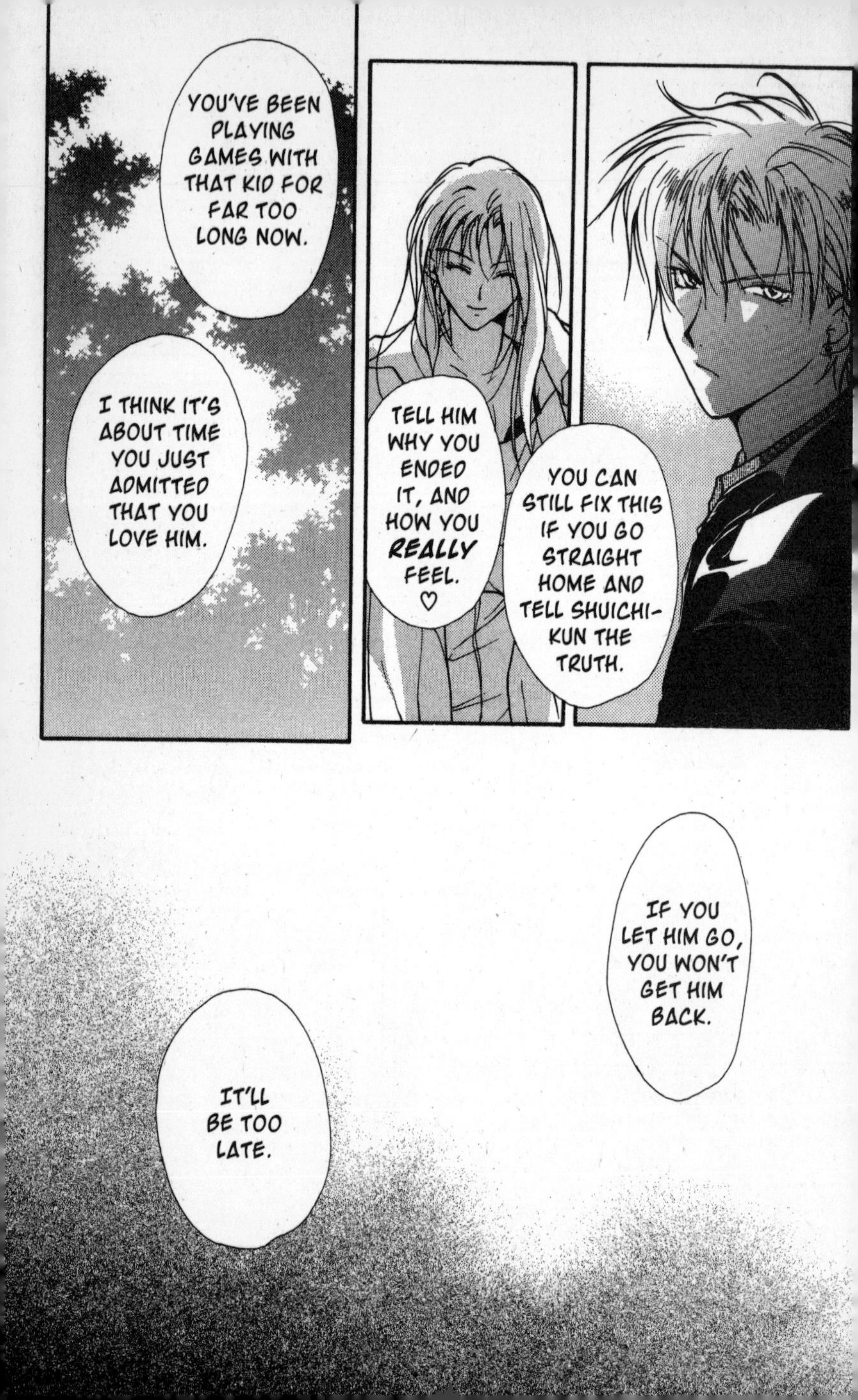
YOU CAN STILL FIX THIS IF YOU GO STRAIGHT HOME AND TELL SHUICHI-KUN THE TRUTH.
TELL HIM WHY YOU ENDED IT, AND HOW YOU **REALLY** FEEL. ♡
YOU'VE BEEN PLAYING GAMES WITH THAT KID FOR FAR TOO LONG NOW.
I THINK IT'S ABOUT TIME YOU JUST ADMITTED THAT YOU LOVE HIM.
IF YOU LET HIM GO, YOU WON'T GET HIM BACK.
IT'LL BE TOO LATE.

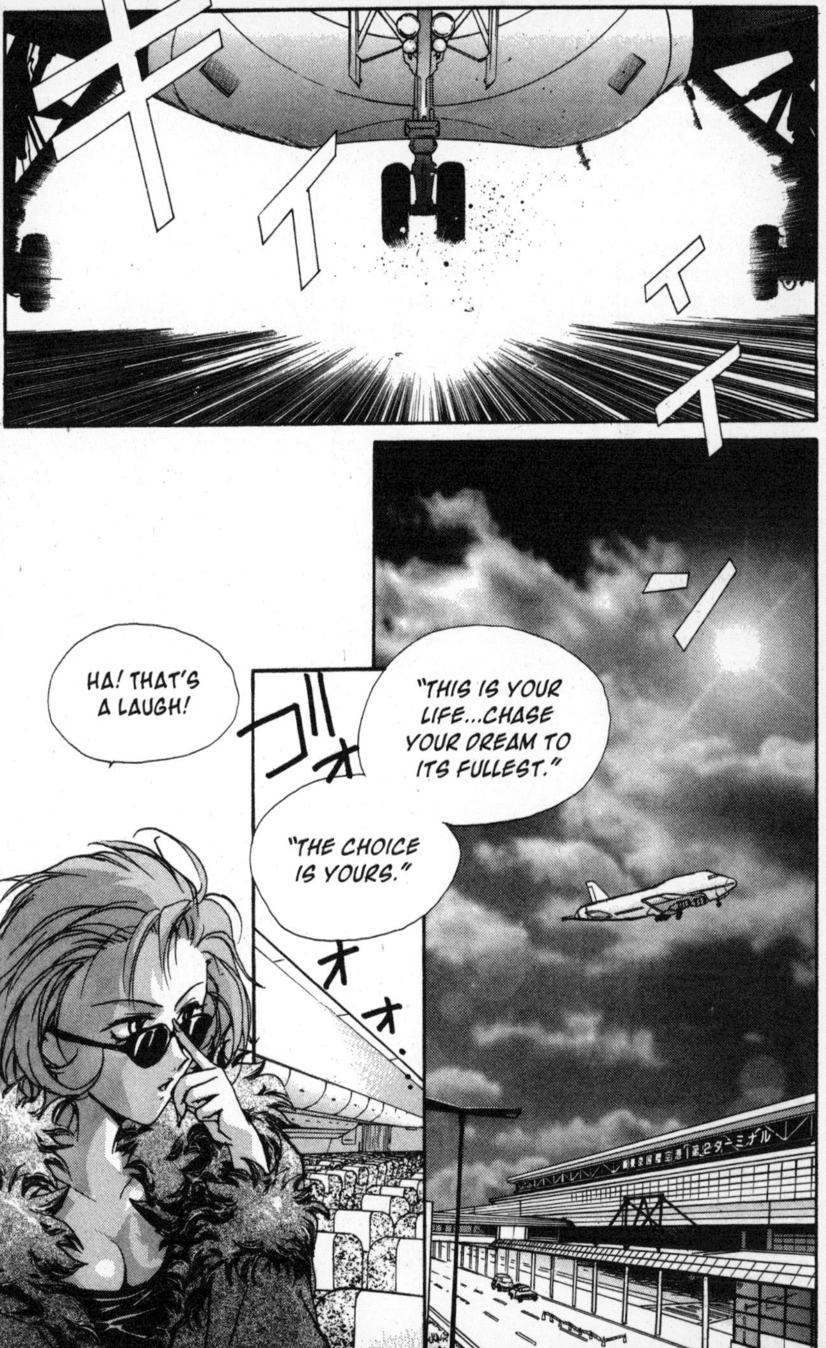
"THIS IS YOUR LIFE...CHASE YOUR DREAM TO ITS FULLEST."
"THE CHOICE IS YOURS."
HA! THAT'S A LAUGH!

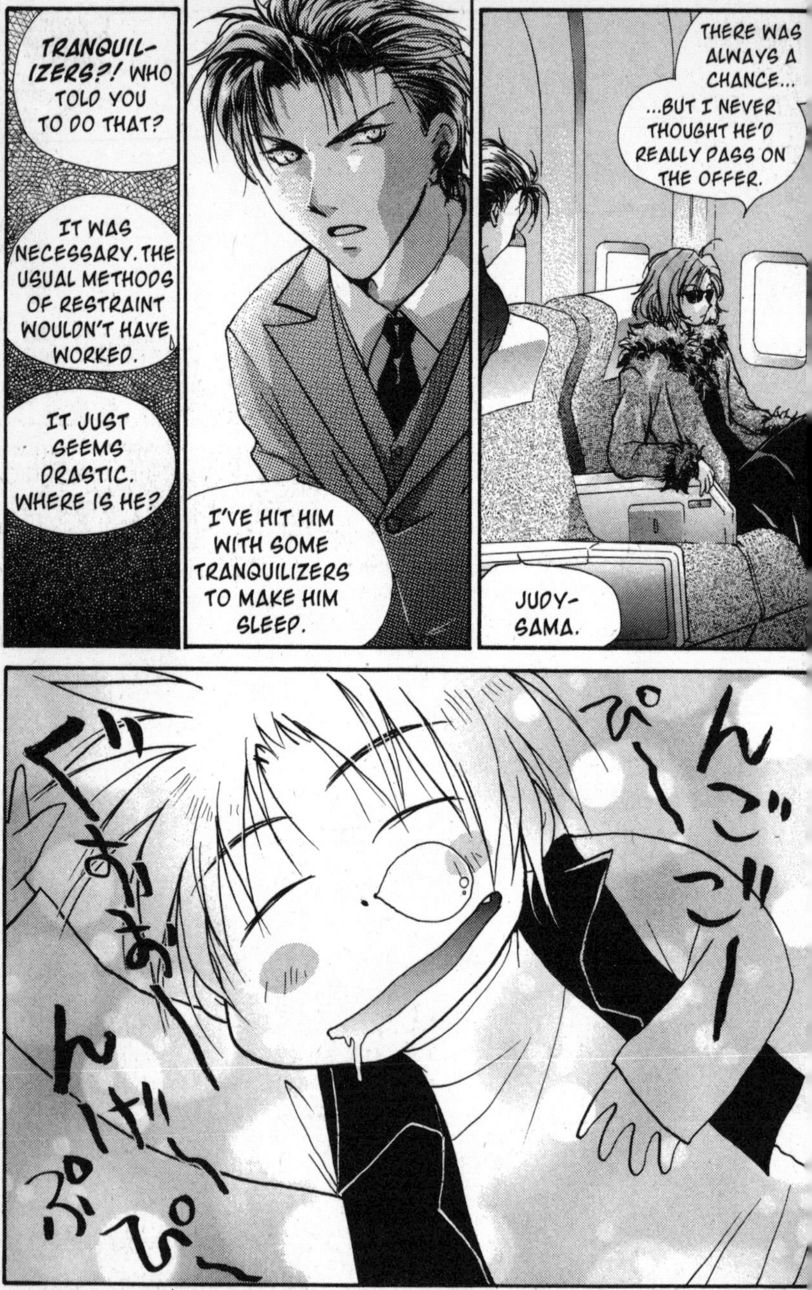
THERE WAS ALWAYS A CHANCE...
...BUT I NEVER THOUGHT HE'D REALLY PASS ON THE OFFER.
JUDY-SAMA.
I'VE HIT HIM WITH SOME TRANQUILIZERS TO MAKE HIM SLEEP.
TRANQUIL-IZERS?! WHO TOLD YOU TO DO THAT?
IT WAS NECESSARY. THE USUAL METHODS OF RESTRAINT WOULDN'T HAVE WORKED.
IT JUST SEEMS DRASTIC. WHERE IS HE?
ぴ〜
snore zzzzzz

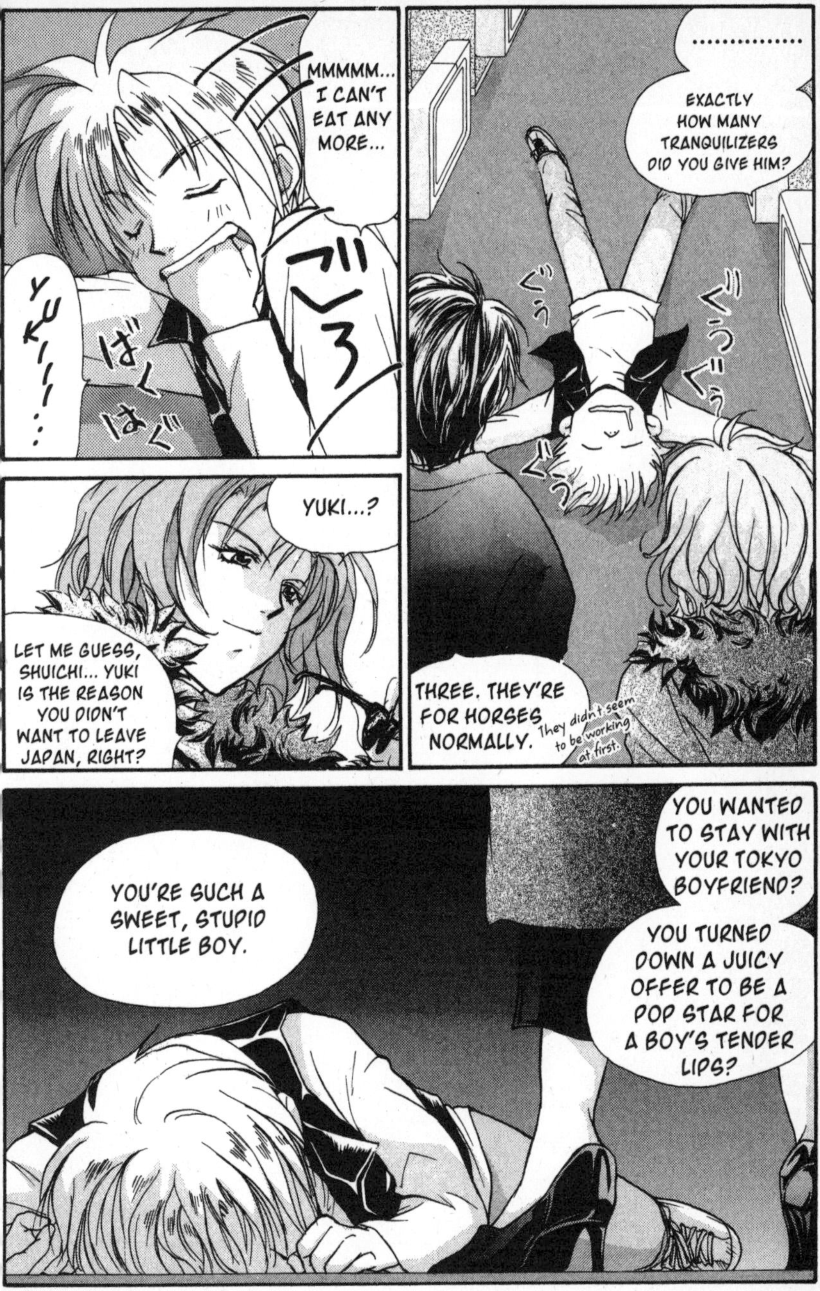
....
EXACTLY HOW MANY TRANQUILIZERS DID YOU GIVE HIM?
THREE. THEY'RE FOR HORSES NORMALLY.
They didn't seem to be working at first.
MMMMM... I CAN'T EAT ANY MORE...
YUKI------...
YUKI...?
LET ME GUESS, SHUICHI... YUKI IS THE REASON YOU DIDN'T WANT TO LEAVE JAPAN, RIGHT?
YOU WANTED TO STAY WITH YOUR TOKYO BOYFRIEND?
YOU TURNED DOWN A JUICY OFFER TO BE A POP STAR FOR A BOY'S TENDER LIPS?
YOU'RE SUCH A SWEET, STUPID LITTLE BOY.

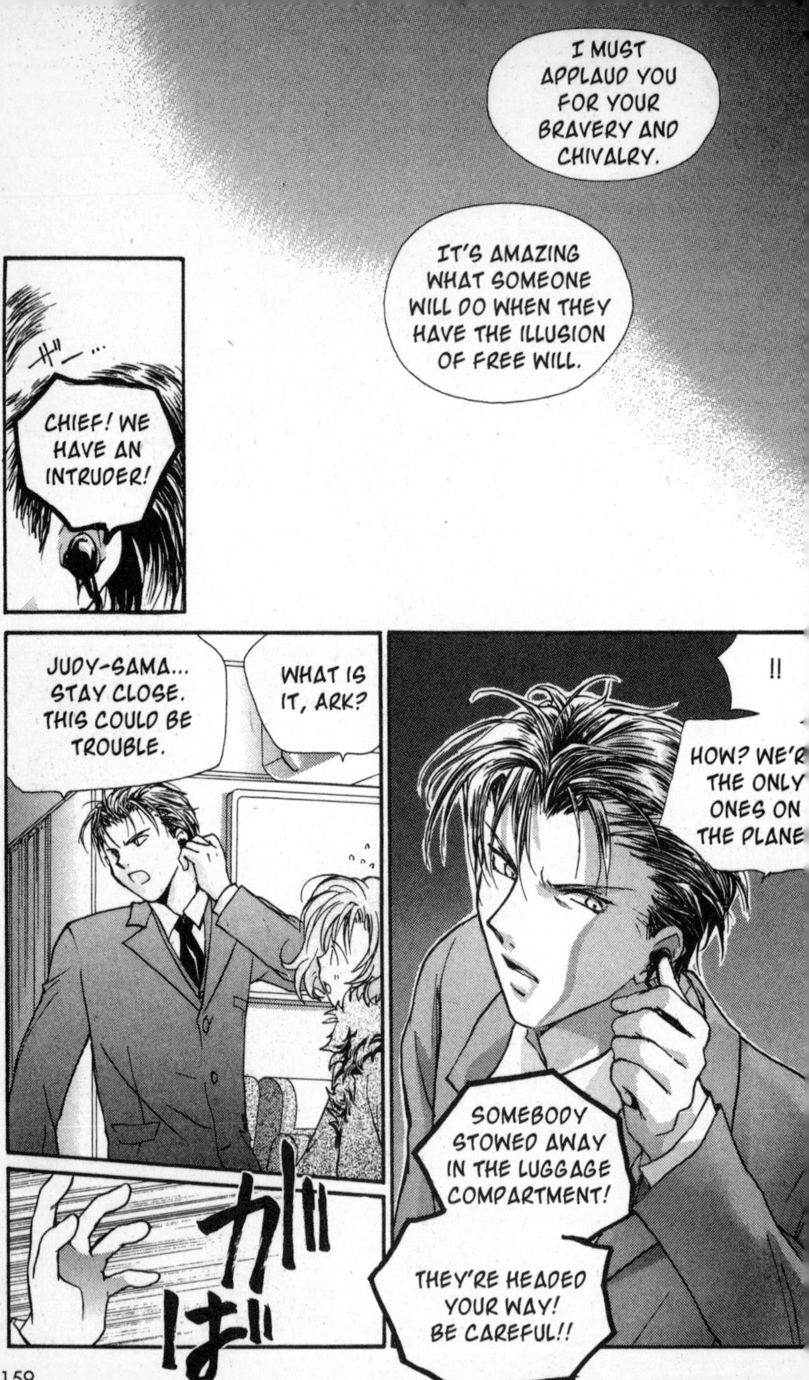
I MUST APPLAUD YOU FOR YOUR BRAVERY AND CHIVALRY.
IT'S AMAZING WHAT SOMEONE WILL DO WHEN THEY HAVE THE ILLUSION OF FREE WILL.
ギー…
CHIEF! WE HAVE AN INTRUDER!
!!
HOW? WE'R THE ONLY ONES ON THE PLANE
SOMEBODY STOWED AWAY IN THE LUGGAGE COMPARTMENT!
THEY'RE HEADED YOUR WAY! BE CAREFUL!!
WHAT IS IT, ARK?
JUDY-SAMA... STAY CLOSE. THIS COULD BE TROUBLE.
がば

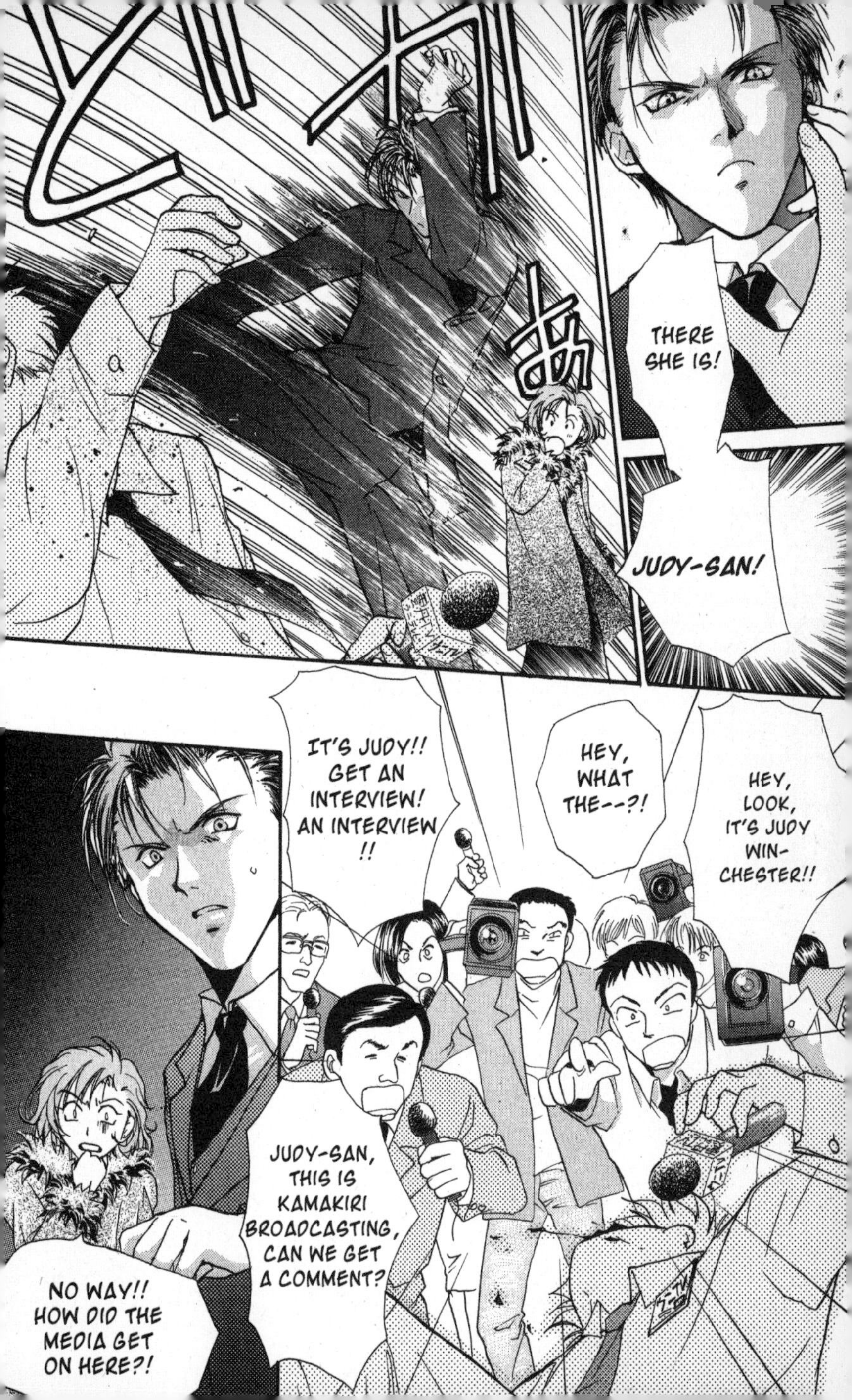
THERE SHE IS!
JUDY-SAN!
あ
HEY, LOOK, IT'S JUDY WIN-CHESTER!!
HEY, WHAT THE--?!
IT'S JUDY!! GET AN INTERVIEW! AN INTERVIEW!!
JUDY-SAN, THIS IS KAMAKIRI BROADCASTING, CAN WE GET A COMMENT?
NO WAY!! HOW DID THE MEDIA GET ON HERE?!

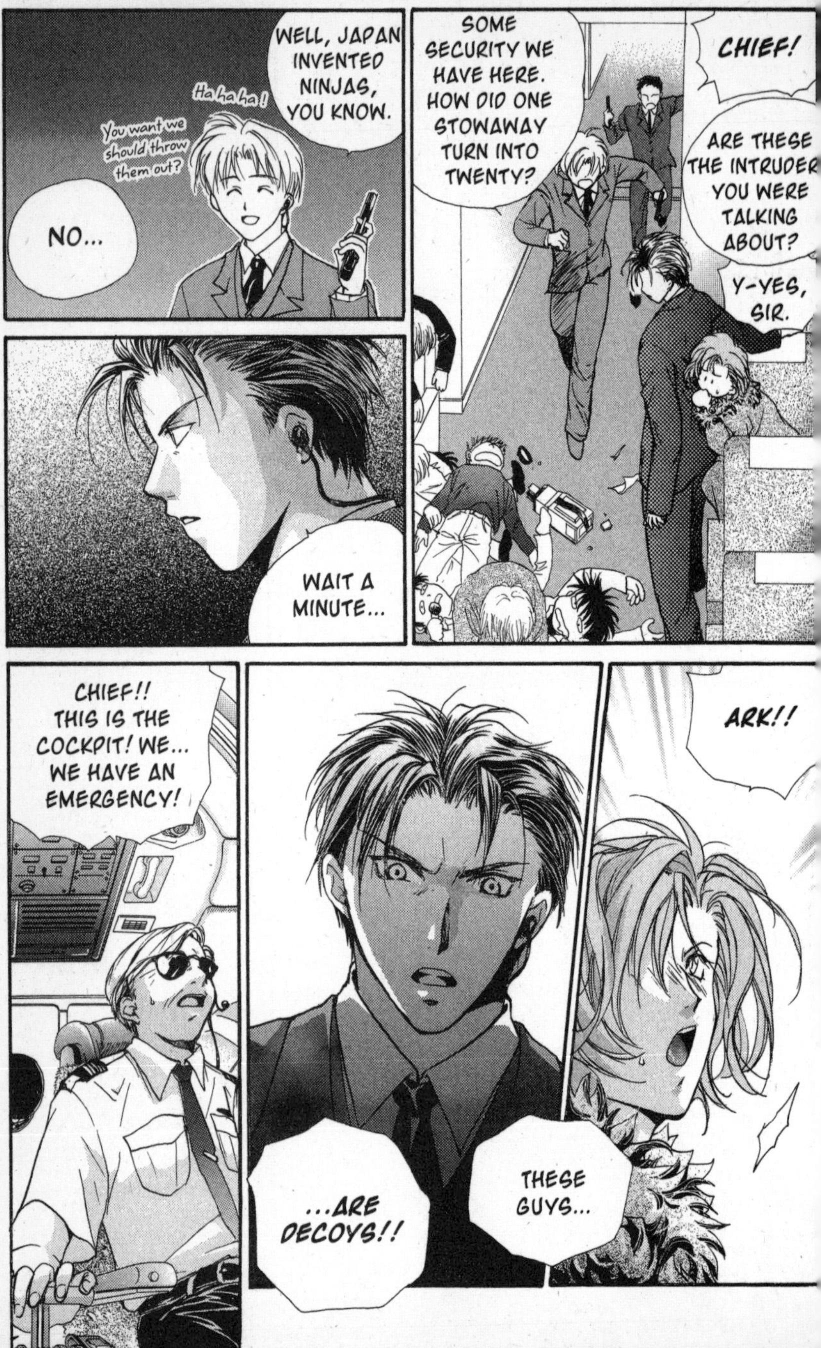
CHIEF!
SOME SECURITY WE HAVE HERE. HOW DID ONE STOWAWAY TURN INTO TWENTY?
ARE THESE THE INTRUDER YOU WERE TALKING ABOUT?
Y-YES, SIR.
WELL, JAPAN INVENTED NINJAS, YOU KNOW.
Ha ha ha!
You want we should throw them out?
NO...
WAIT A MINUTE...
ARK!!
THESE GUYS...
...ARE DECOYS!!
CHIEF!! THIS IS THE COCKPIT! WE... WE HAVE AN EMERGENCY!

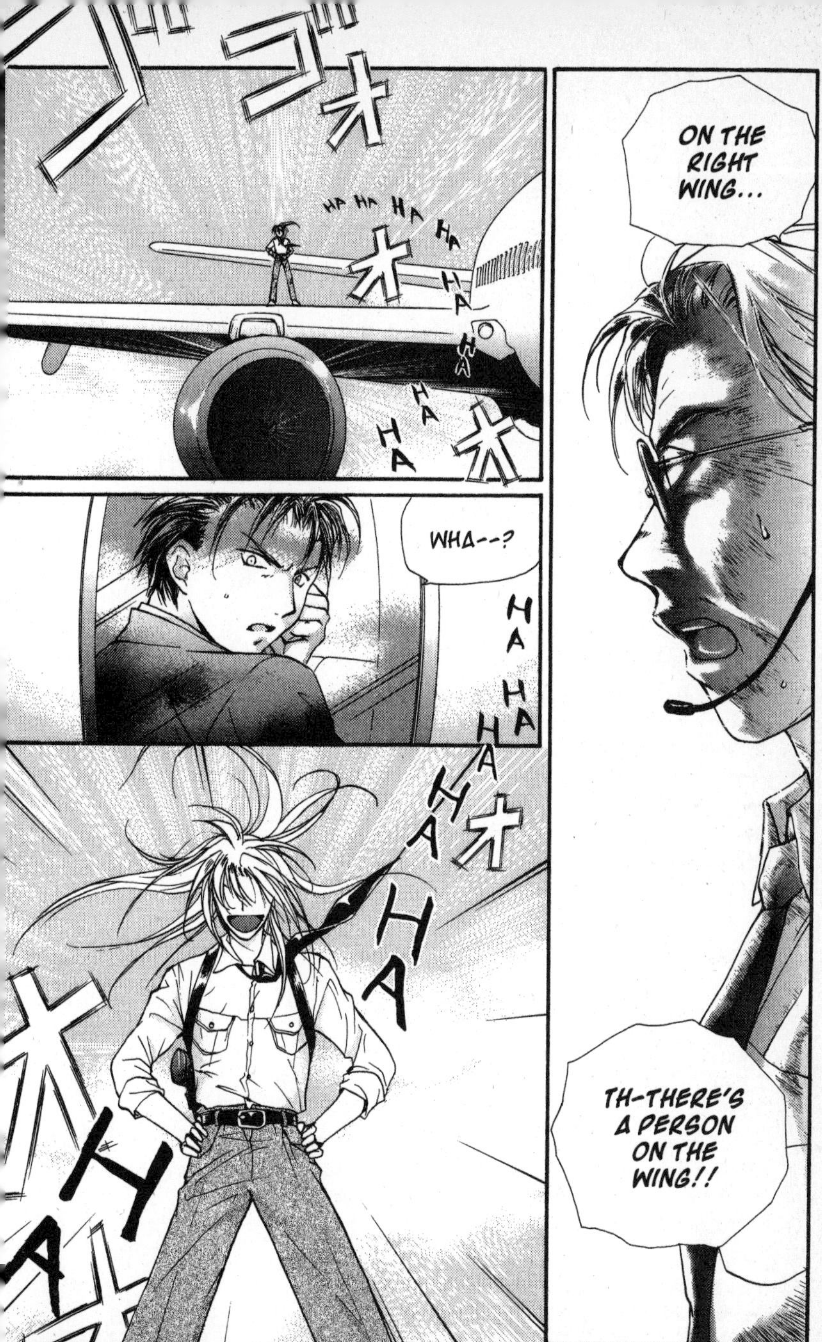
ON THE RIGHT WING...
TH-THERE'S A PERSON ON THE WING!!
HA HA HA HA HA HA HA HA HA
WHA--?
HA HA HA HA HA HA HA HA HA

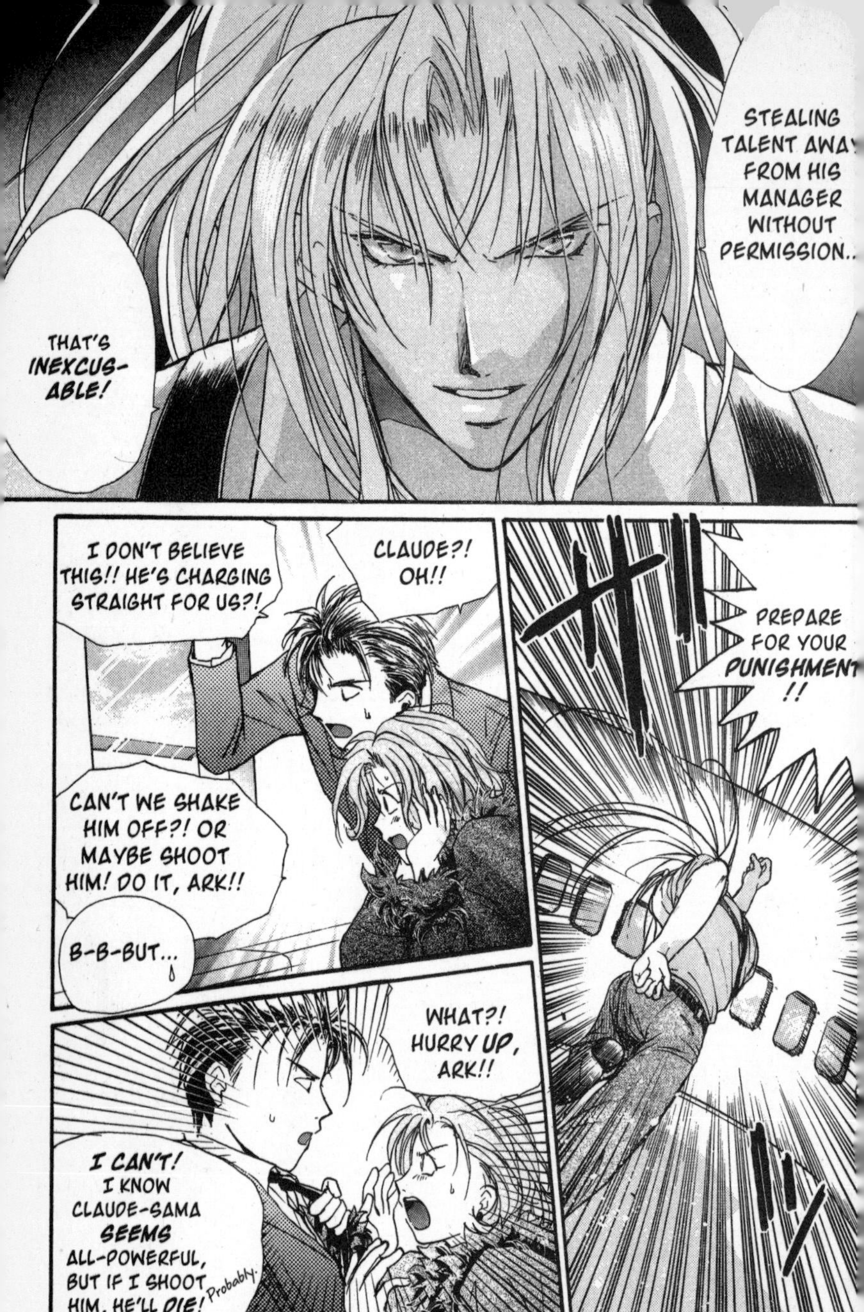
STEALING TALENT AWAY FROM HIS MANAGER WITHOUT PERMISSION...
THAT'S INEXCUSABLE!
PREPARE FOR YOUR PUNISHMENT!!
CLAUDE?! OH!!
I DON'T BELIEVE THIS!! HE'S CHARGING STRAIGHT FOR US?!
CAN'T WE SHAKE HIM OFF?! OR MAYBE SHOOT HIM! DO IT, ARK!!
B-B-BUT...
WHAT?! HURRY UP, ARK!!
I CAN'T! I KNOW CLAUDE-SAMA SEEMS ALL-POWERFUL, BUT IF I SHOOT HIM, HE'LL DIE!
Probably.

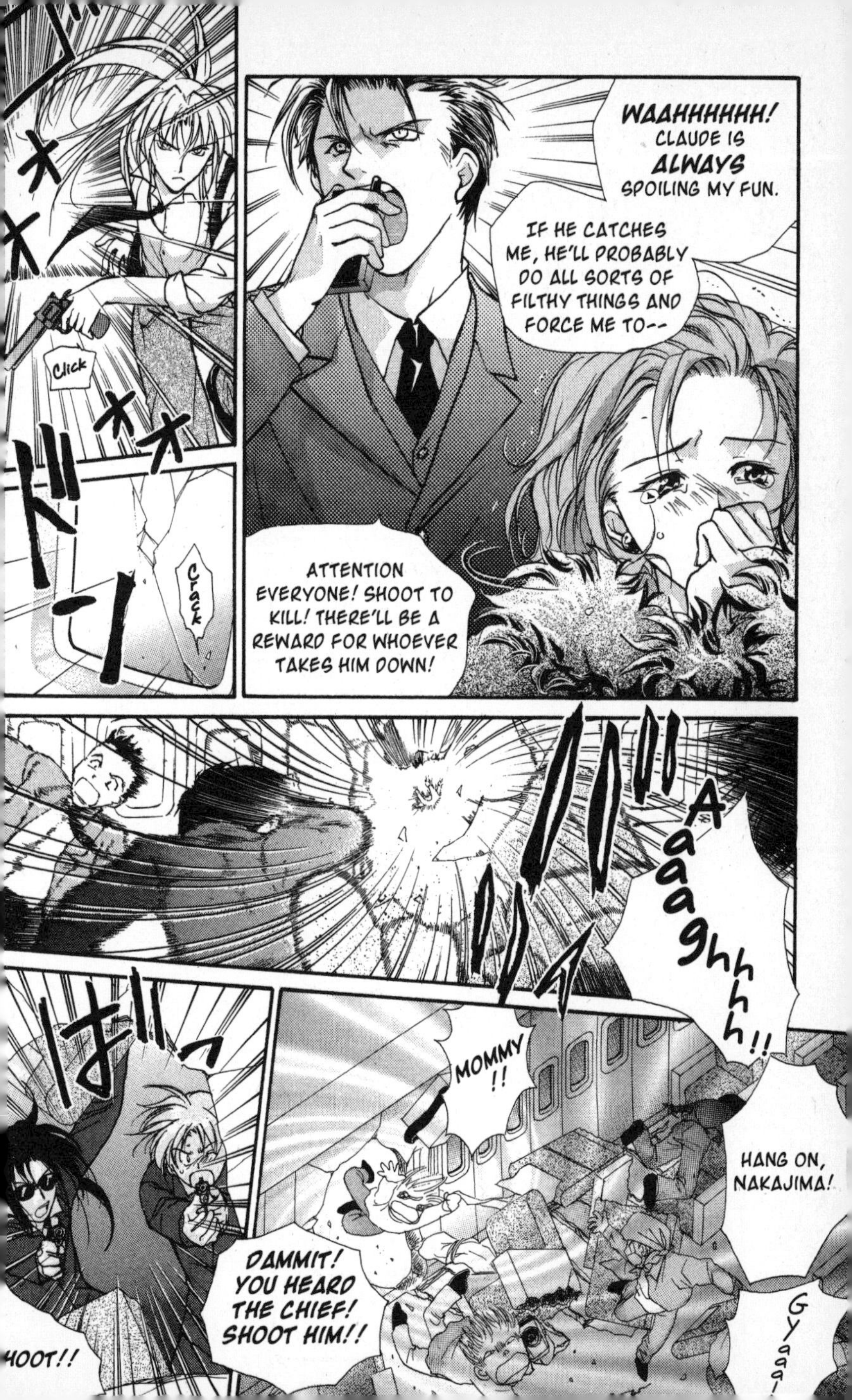
WAAHHHHHH! CLAUDE IS ALWAYS SPOILING MY FUN.
IF HE CATCHES ME, HE'LL PROBABLY DO ALL SORTS OF FILTHY THINGS AND FORCE ME TO--
ATTENTION EVERYONE! SHOOT TO KILL! THERE'LL BE A REWARD FOR WHOEVER TAKES HIM DOWN!
Click
Crack
Aaaaghhhh!!
MOMMY!!
HANG ON, NAKAJIMA!
Gyaa
DAMMIT! YOU HEARD THE CHIEF! SHOOT HIM!!
HOOT!!

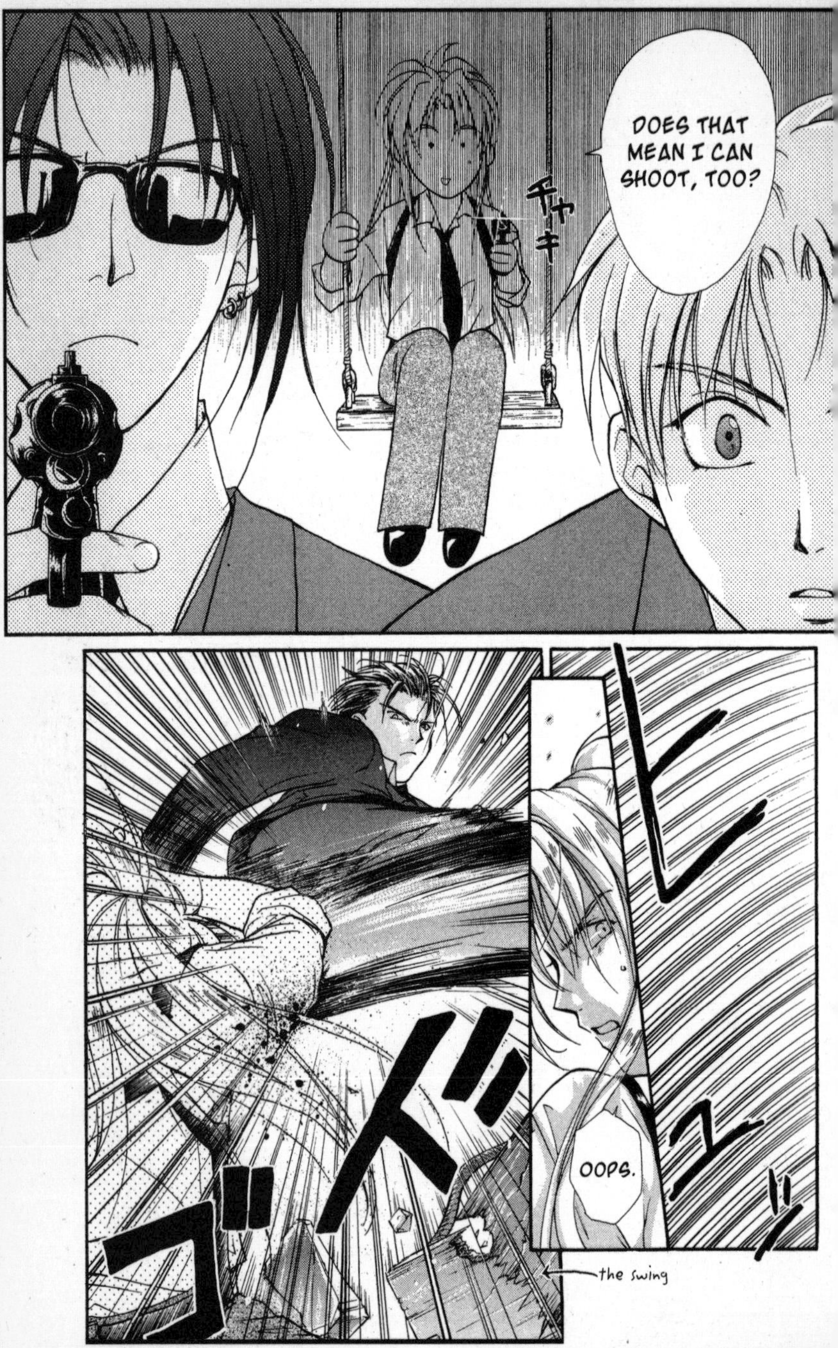
DOES THAT MEAN I CAN SHOOT, TOO?
チャキ
OOPS.
ゴッ
ド
the swing

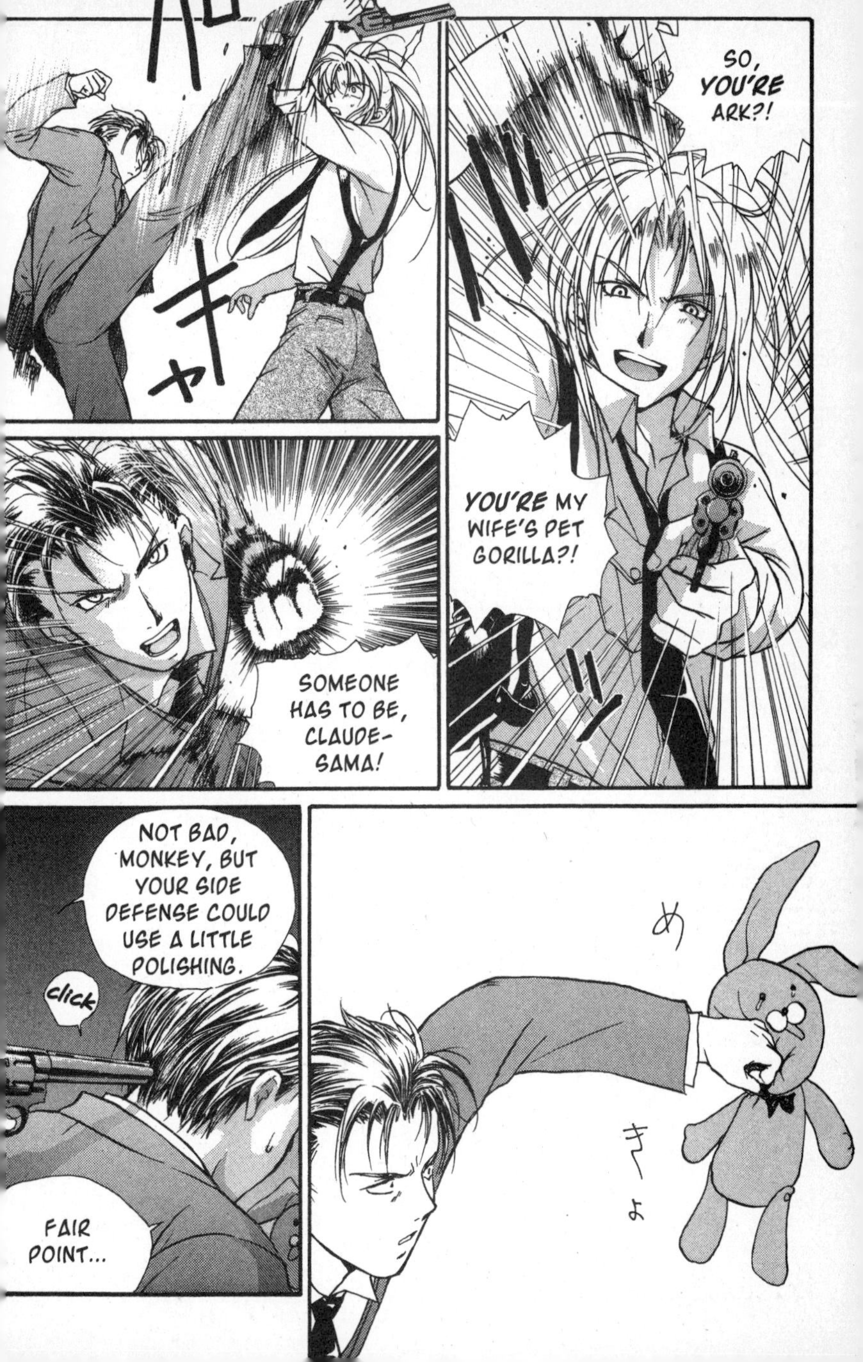

SO, YOU'RE ARK?!
YOU'RE MY WIFE'S PET GORILLA?!
ハロ
キャ
SOMEONE HAS TO BE, CLAUDE-SAMA!
めきょ
NOT BAD, MONKEY, BUT YOUR SIDE DEFENSE COULD USE A LITTLE POLISHING.
click
FAIR POINT...

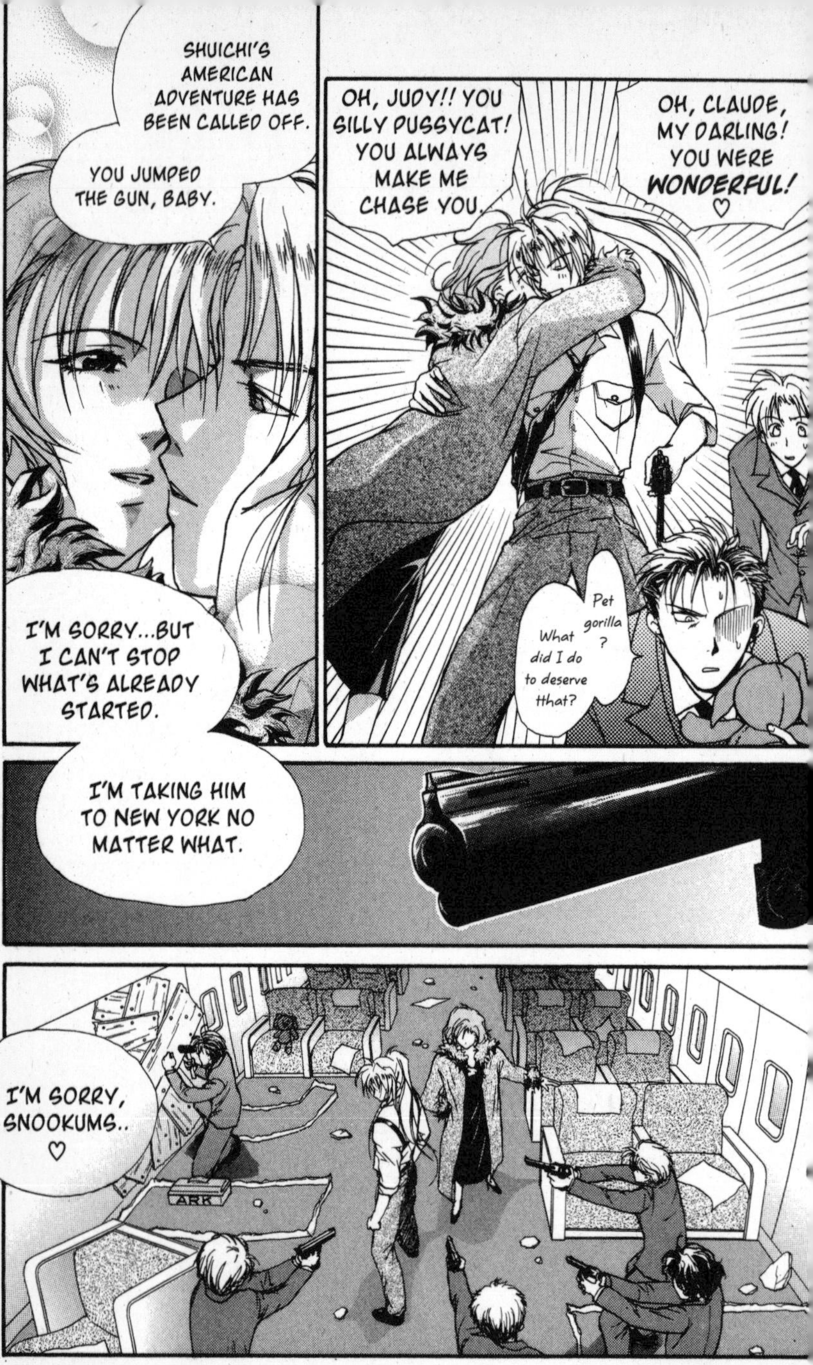

OH, CLAUDE, MY DARLING! YOU WERE **WONDERFUL!** ♡
OH, JUDY!! YOU SILLY PUSSYCAT! YOU ALWAYS MAKE ME CHASE YOU.
Pet gorilla?
What did I do to deserve that?
SHUICHI'S AMERICAN ADVENTURE HAS BEEN CALLED OFF.
YOU JUMPED THE GUN, BABY.
I'M SORRY...BUT I CAN'T STOP WHAT'S ALREADY STARTED.
I'M TAKING HIM TO NEW YORK NO MATTER WHAT.
ARK
I'M SORRY, SNOOKUMS.. ♡

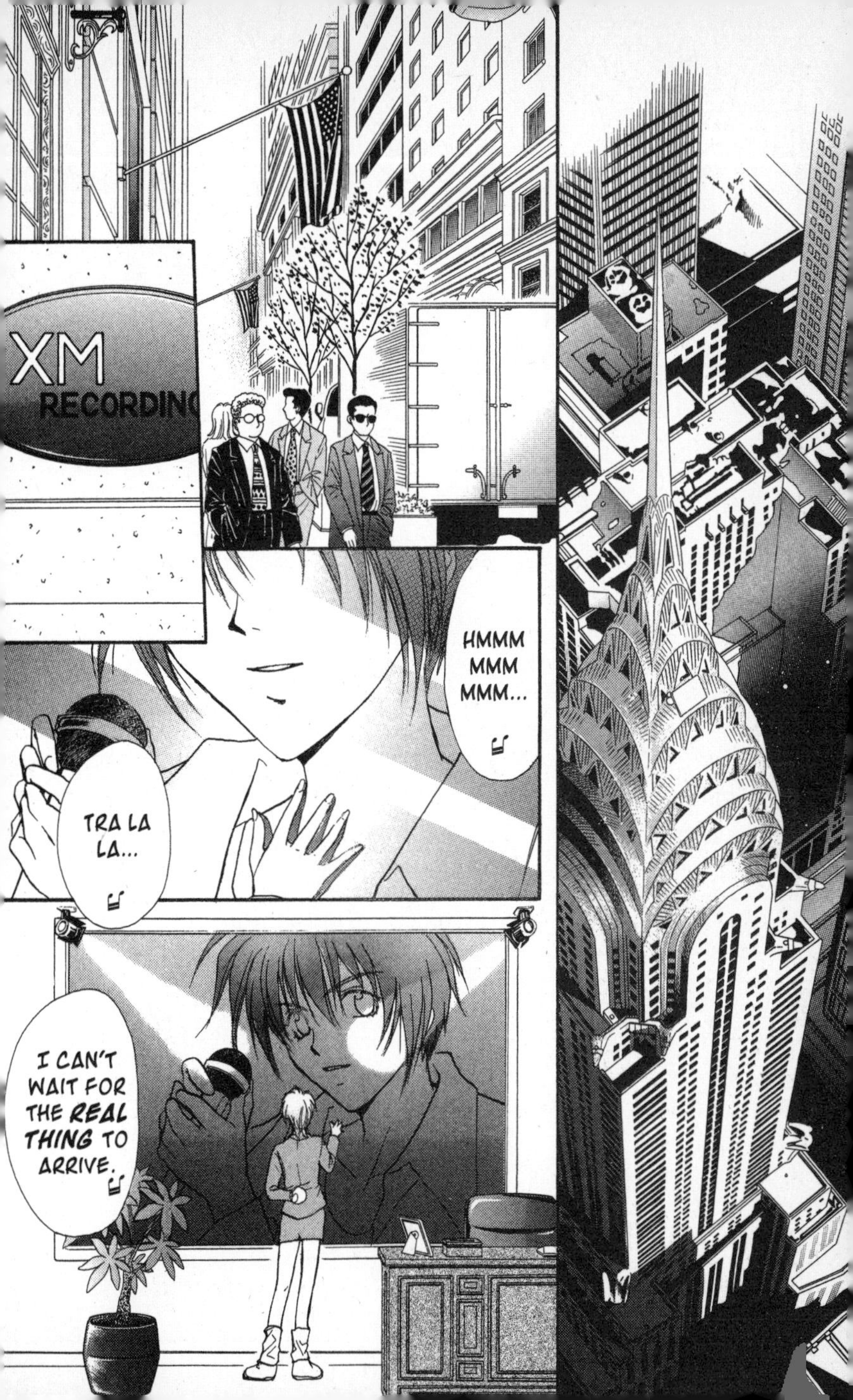
XM
RECORDING
HMMM MMM MMM... ♪
TRA LA LA... ♪
I CAN'T WAIT FOR THE *REAL THING* TO ARRIVE. ♪

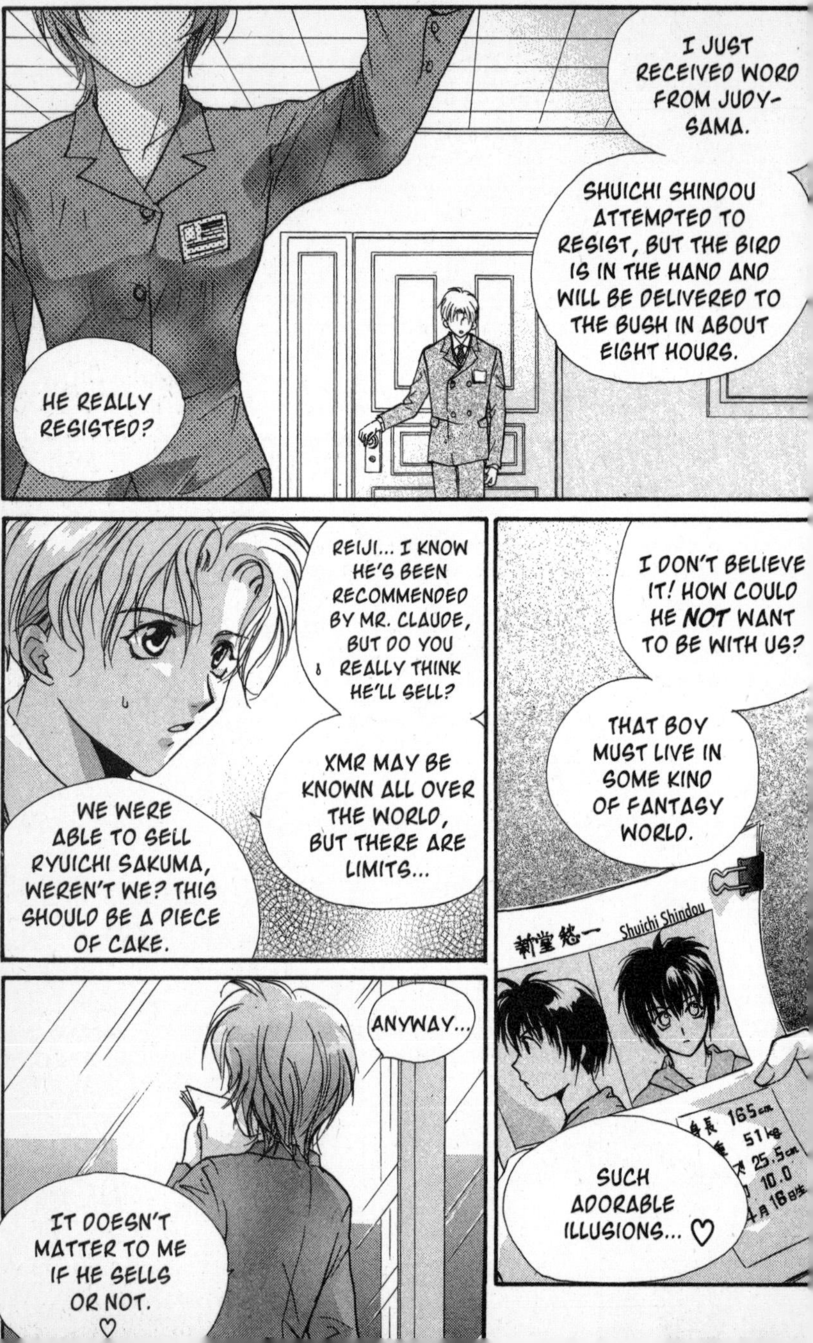
I JUST RECEIVED WORD FROM JUDY-SAMA.
SHUICHI SHINDOU ATTEMPTED TO RESIST, BUT THE BIRD IS IN THE HAND AND WILL BE DELIVERED TO THE BUSH IN ABOUT EIGHT HOURS.
HE REALLY RESISTED?
I DON'T BELIEVE IT! HOW COULD HE **NOT** WANT TO BE WITH US?
THAT BOY MUST LIVE IN SOME KIND OF FANTASY WORLD.
Shuichi Shindou
SUCH ADORABLE ILLUSIONS... ♡
REIJI... I KNOW HE'S BEEN RECOMMENDED BY MR. CLAUDE, BUT DO YOU REALLY THINK HE'LL SELL?
XMR MAY BE KNOWN ALL OVER THE WORLD, BUT THERE ARE LIMITS...
WE WERE ABLE TO SELL RYUICHI SAKUMA, WEREN'T WE? THIS SHOULD BE A PIECE OF CAKE.
ANYWAY...
IT DOESN'T MATTER TO ME IF HE SELLS OR NOT. ♡

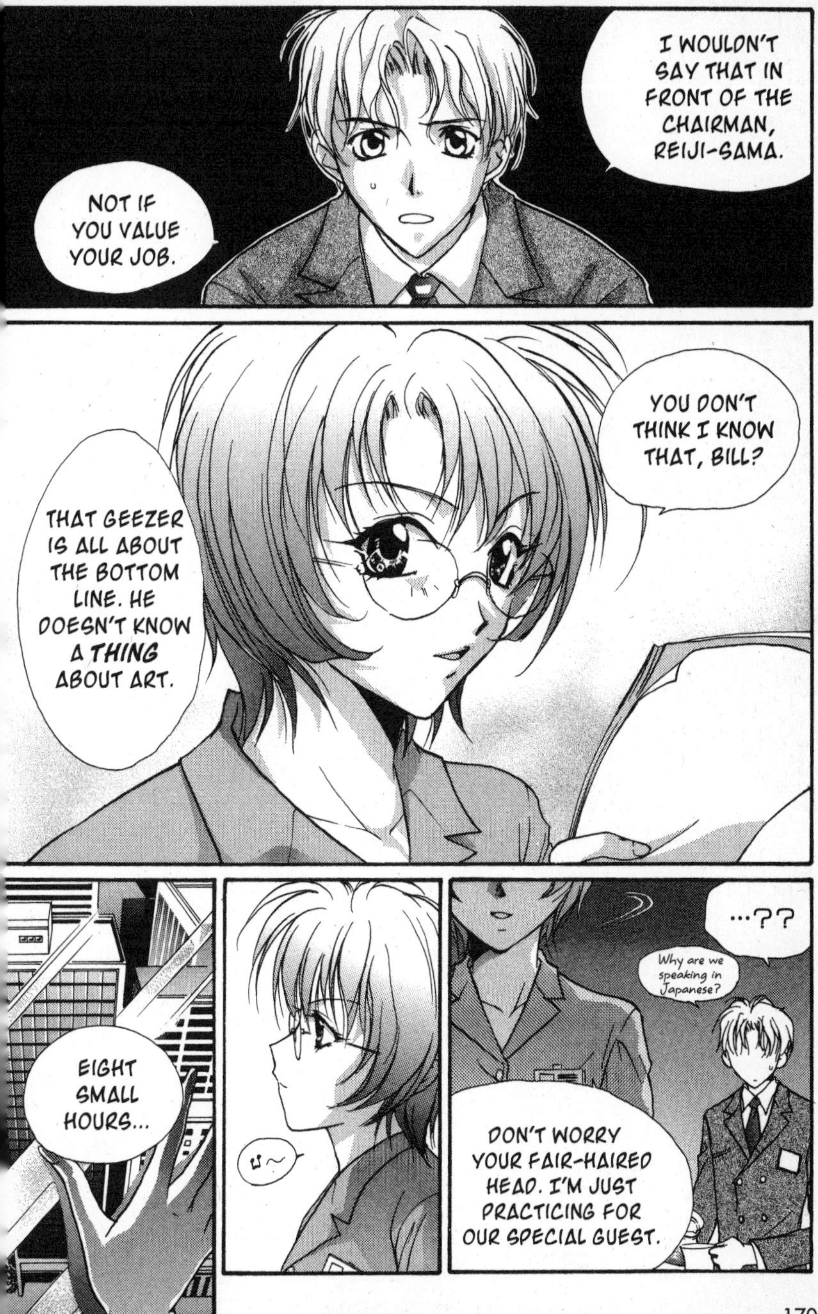
I WOULDN'T SAY THAT IN FRONT OF THE CHAIRMAN, REIJI-SAMA.
NOT IF YOU VALUE YOUR JOB.
YOU DON'T THINK I KNOW THAT, BILL?
THAT GEEZER IS ALL ABOUT THE BOTTOM LINE. HE DOESN'T KNOW A THING ABOUT ART.
...??
Why are we speaking in Japanese?
DON'T WORRY YOUR FAIR-HAIRED HEAD. I'M JUST PRACTICING FOR OUR SPECIAL GUEST.
EIGHT SMALL HOURS...

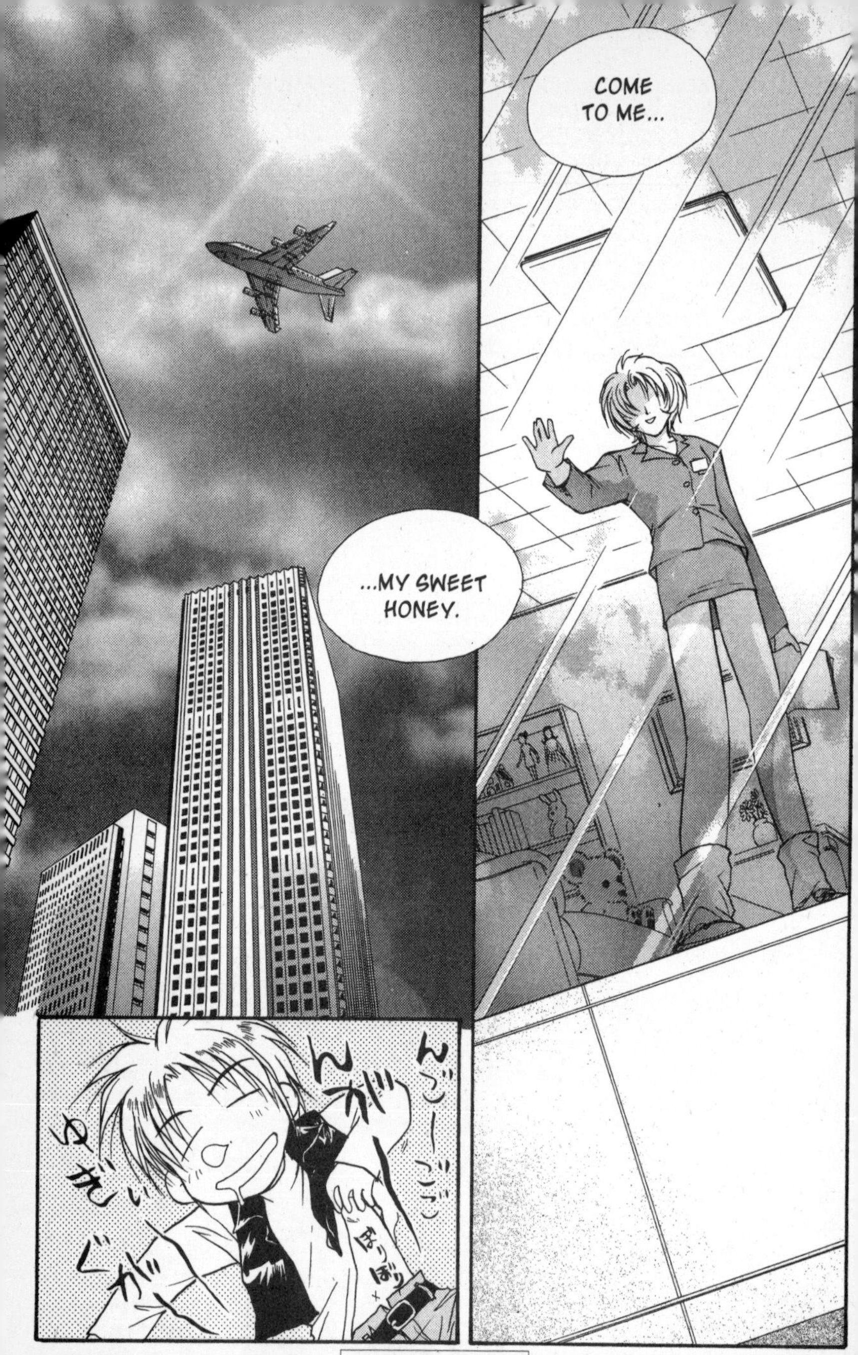
COME TO ME...
...MY SWEET HONEY.
ぽりぽり

track35▶END

Hourly rate:
One hundred million yen.

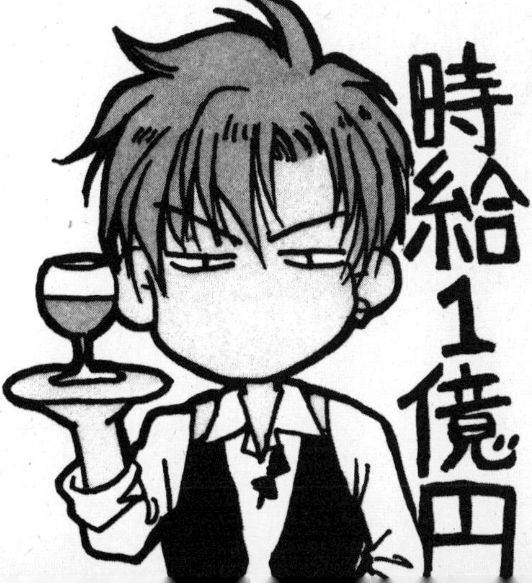
時給1億円

Gravitation

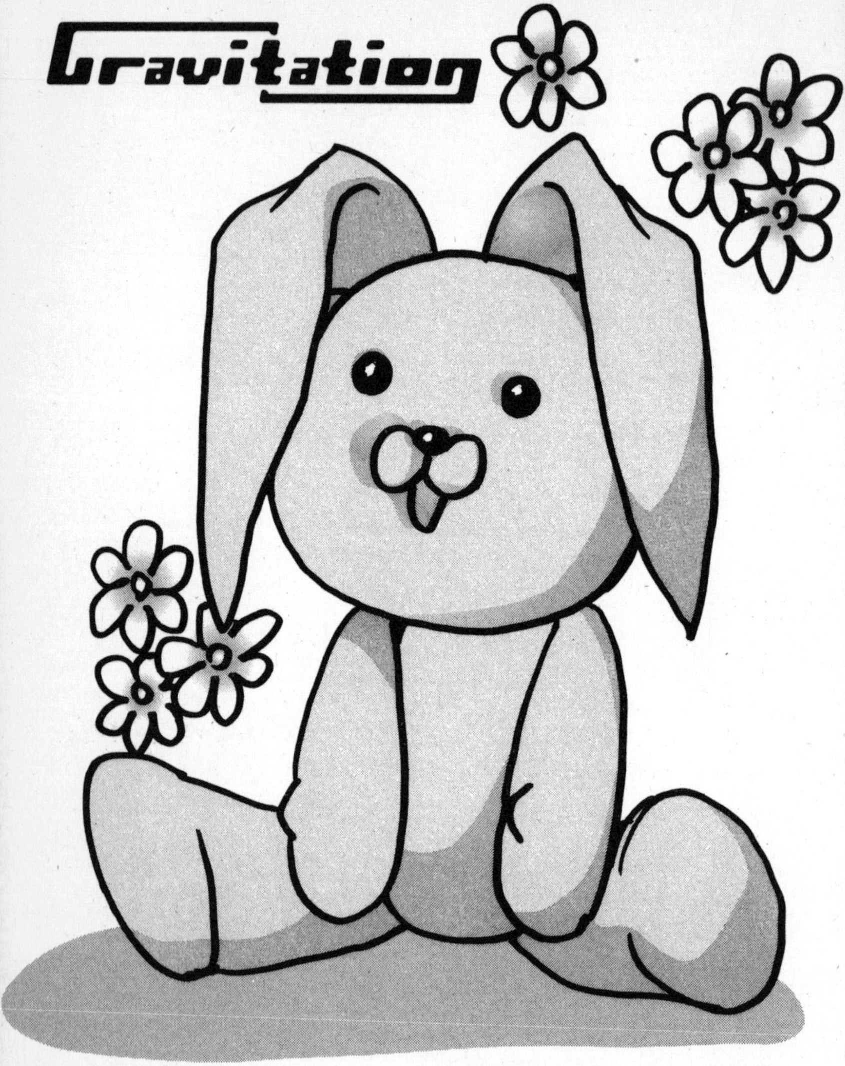

track 36

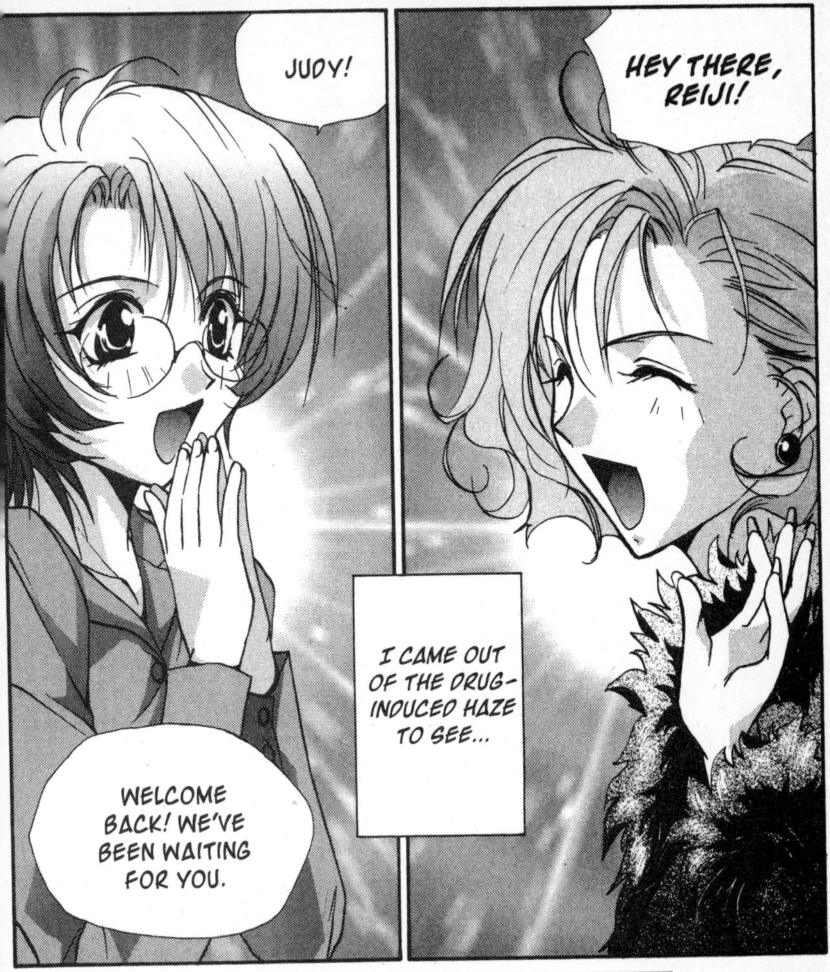
HEY THERE, REIJI!
I CAME OUT OF THE DRUG-INDUCED HAZE TO SEE...
JUDY!
WELCOME BACK! WE'VE BEEN WAITING FOR YOU.

THE SUFFERING BEHIND GRAVITATION TRACK 36

Gravitation has now gone over the edge! Hello there, everyone! Our new character is Reiji. I know, it sounds like a guy's name, but she's a girl. This is the usual sort of thing that so often happens in a girl's manga. Did you notice she wears glasses? I have a glasses fetish, so I get this nervous tingly sensation whenever I draw Reiji-san! And you've gotta focus on the story this time, because it's going more and more over the top. I took a whole bunch of pictures of Central Park to use as reference, but I ended up using them primarily to guide the way in doing the toning!! Tone-style shading has become so convenient now, it's just so wonderful!!

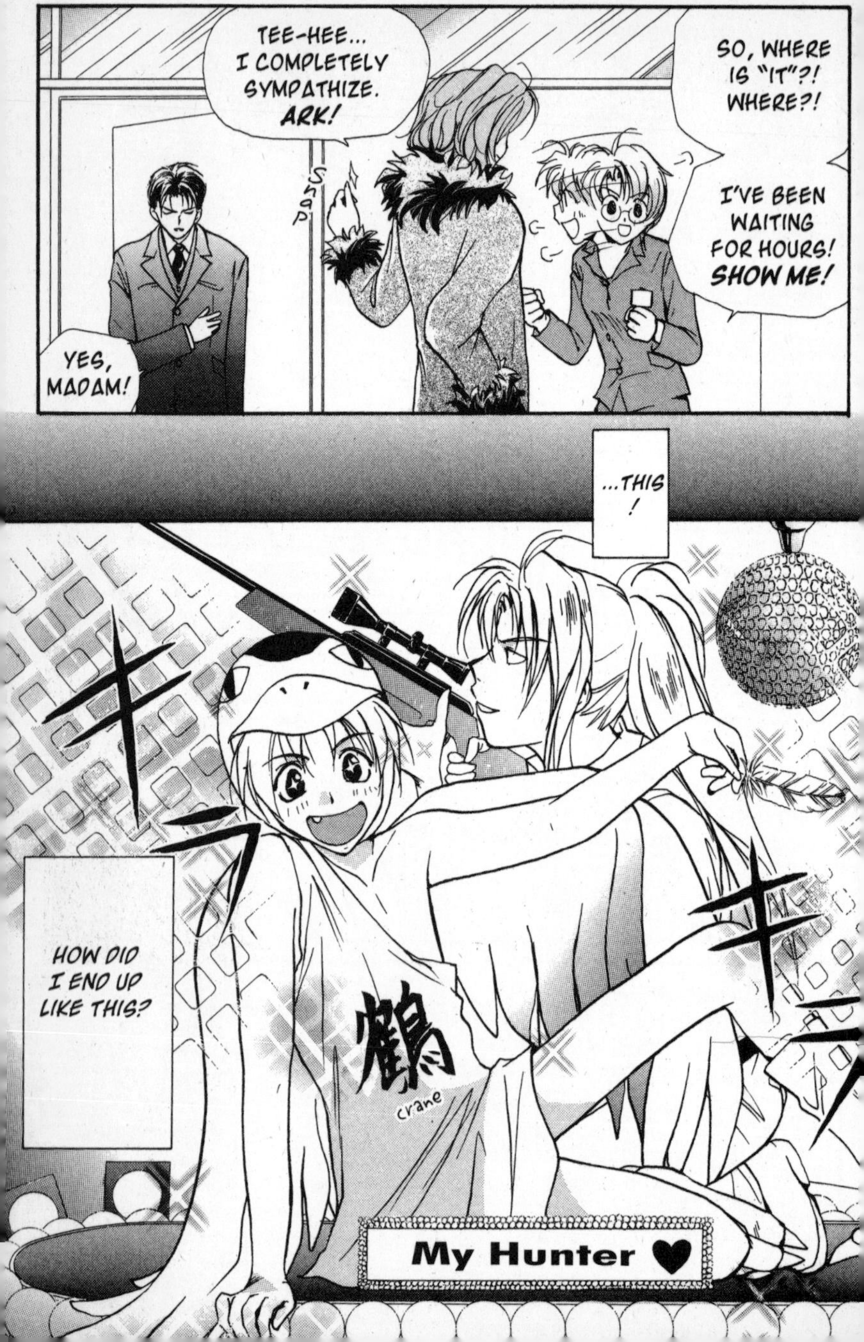

SO, WHERE IS "IT"?! WHERE?!
I'VE BEEN WAITING FOR HOURS! SHOW ME!
TEE-HEE... I COMPLETELY SYMPATHIZE. ARK!
Snap
YES, MADAM!
...THIS!
HOW DID I END UP LIKE THIS?
鶴
crane
My Hunter ♥

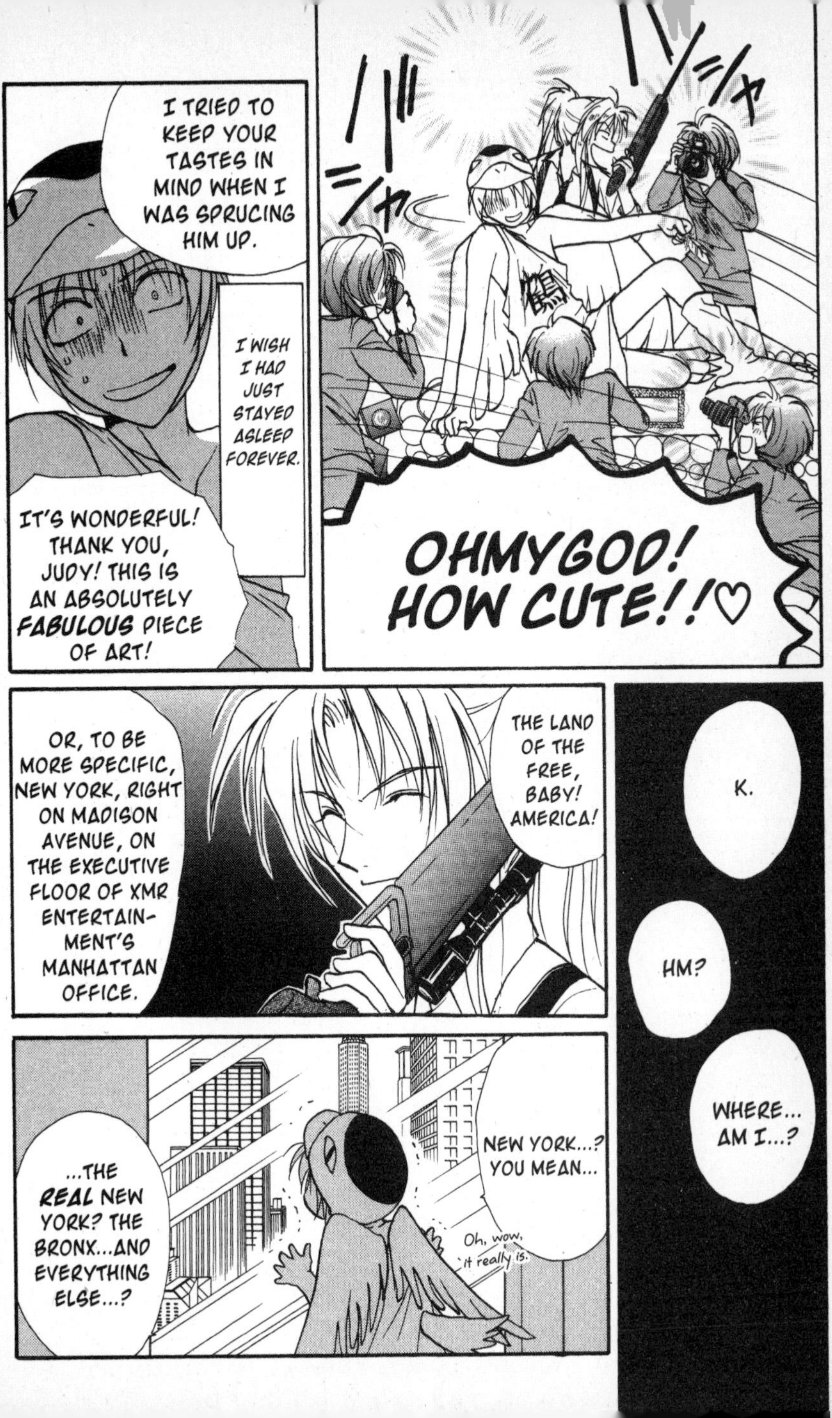

ニヤ
ニヤ
OHMYGOD! HOW CUTE!!♡
I TRIED TO KEEP YOUR TASTES IN MIND WHEN I WAS SPRUCING HIM UP.
I WISH I HAD JUST STAYED ASLEEP FOREVER.
IT'S WONDERFUL! THANK YOU, JUDY! THIS IS AN ABSOLUTELY **FABULOUS** PIECE OF ART!
K.
HM?
WHERE... AM I...?
THE LAND OF THE FREE, BABY! AMERICA!
OR, TO BE MORE SPECIFIC, NEW YORK, RIGHT ON MADISON AVENUE, ON THE EXECUTIVE FLOOR OF XMR ENTERTAIN-MENT'S MANHATTAN OFFICE.
NEW YORK...? YOU MEAN...
Oh, wow, it really is.
...THE **REAL** NEW YORK? THE BRONX...AND EVERYTHING ELSE...?

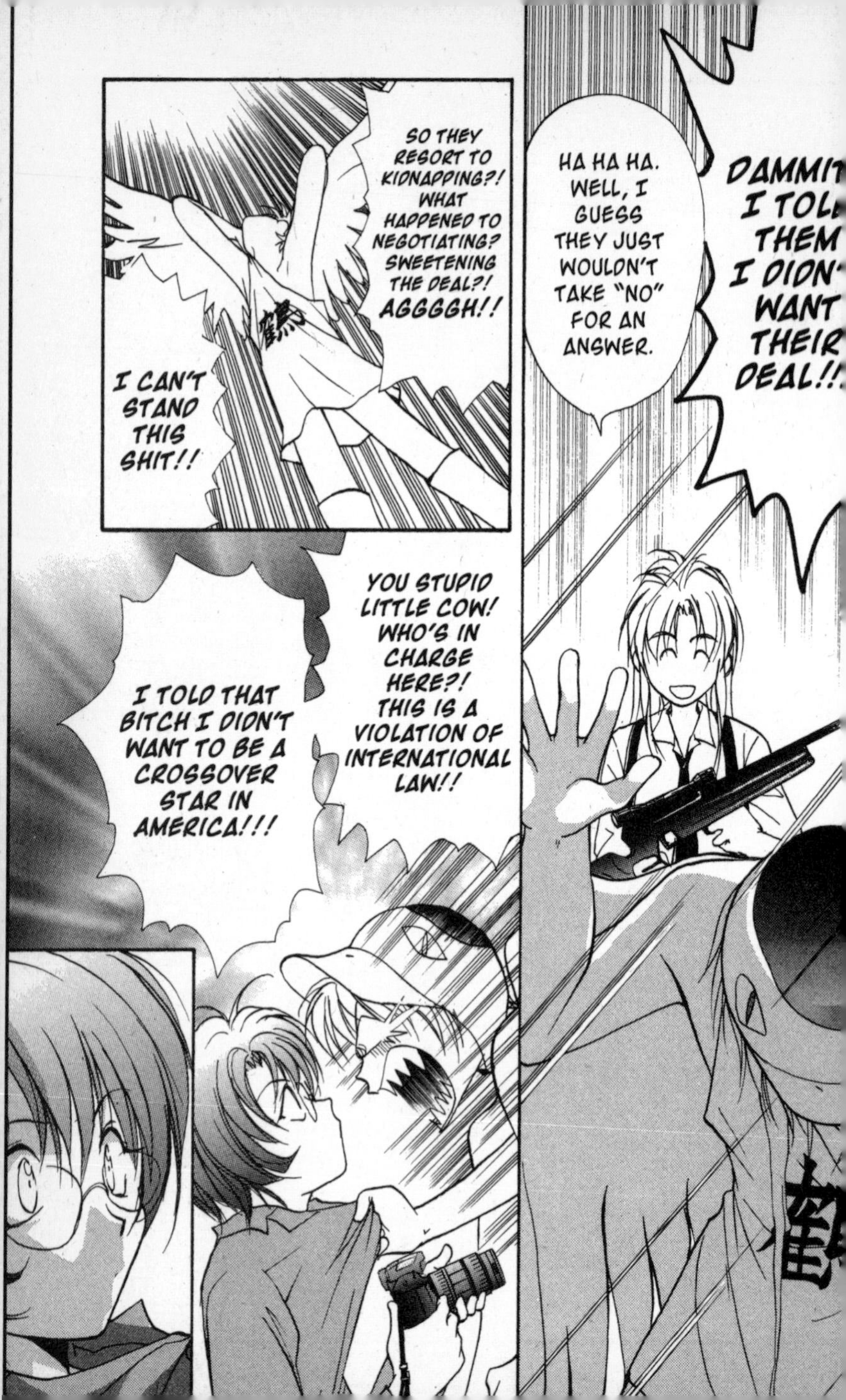
DAMMIT I TOL THEM I DIDN' WANT THEIR DEAL!!
HA HA HA. WELL, I GUESS THEY JUST WOULDN'T TAKE "NO" FOR AN ANSWER.
SO THEY RESORT TO KIDNAPPING?! WHAT HAPPENED TO NEGOTIATING? SWEETENING THE DEAL?! AGGGGH!!
I CAN'T STAND THIS SHIT!!
YOU STUPID LITTLE COW! WHO'S IN CHARGE HERE?! THIS IS A VIOLATION OF INTERNATIONAL LAW!!
I TOLD THAT BITCH I DIDN'T WANT TO BE A CROSSOVER STAR IN AMERICA!!!

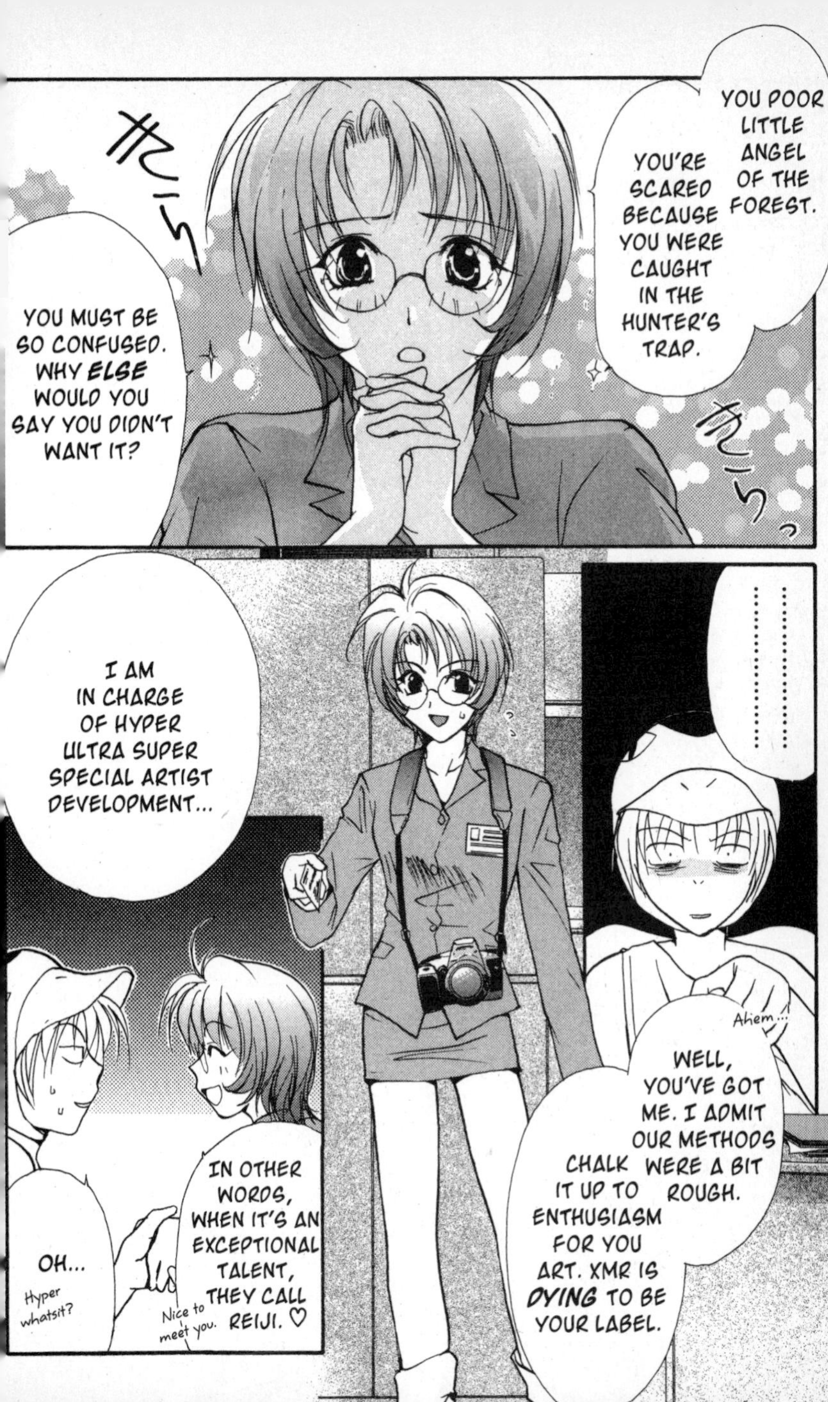
YOU POOR LITTLE ANGEL OF THE FOREST.
YOU'RE SCARED BECAUSE YOU WERE CAUGHT IN THE HUNTER'S TRAP.
YOU MUST BE SO CONFUSED. WHY *ELSE* WOULD YOU SAY YOU DIDN'T WANT IT?
......
Ahem...
WELL, YOU'VE GOT ME. I ADMIT OUR METHODS WERE A BIT ROUGH.
CHALK IT UP TO ENTHUSIASM FOR YOU ART. XMR IS *DYING* TO BE YOUR LABEL.
I AM IN CHARGE OF HYPER ULTRA SUPER SPECIAL ARTIST DEVELOPMENT...
IN OTHER WORDS, WHEN IT'S AN EXCEPTIONAL TALENT, THEY CALL REIJI. ♡
Nice to meet you.
OH...
Hyper whatsit?

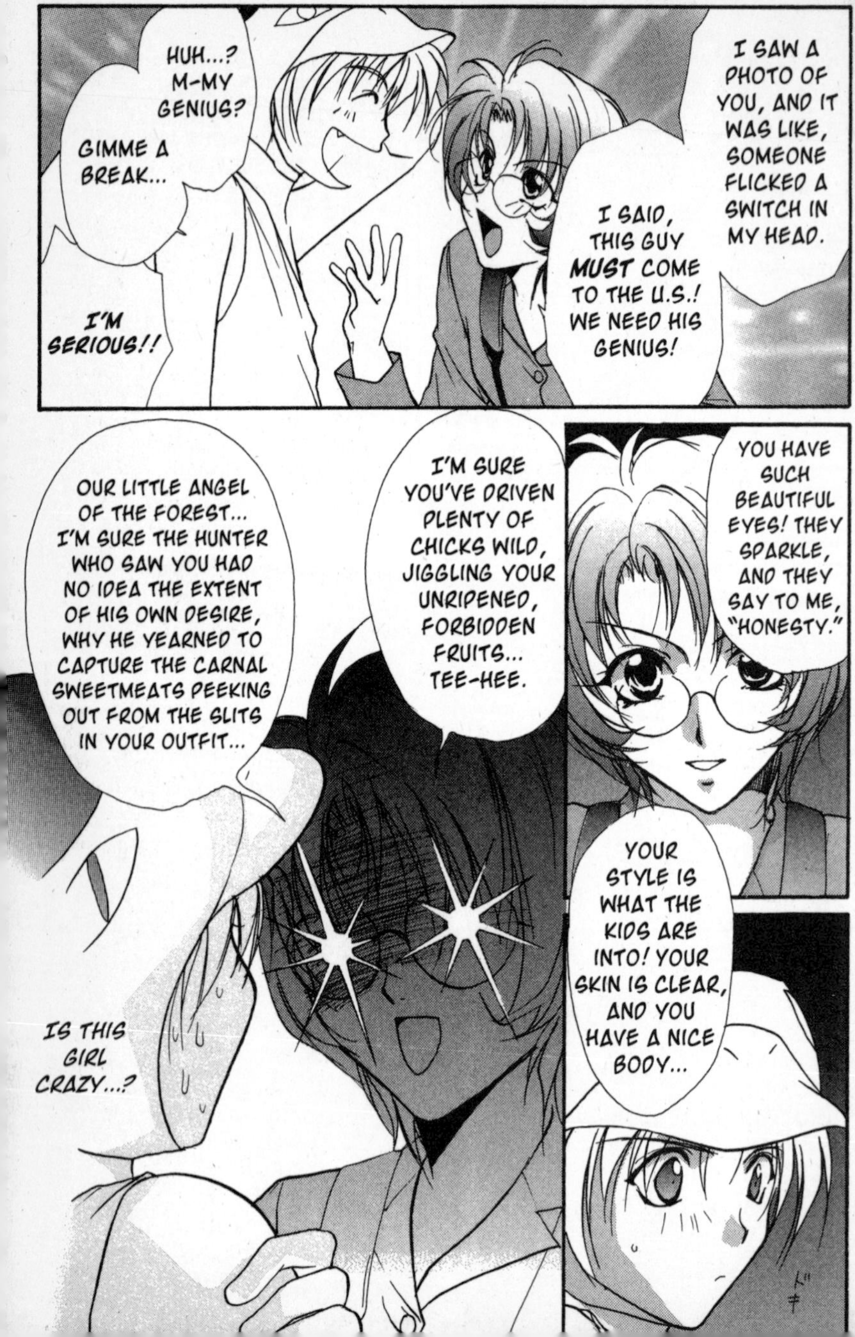
I SAW A PHOTO OF YOU, AND IT WAS LIKE, SOMEONE FLICKED A SWITCH IN MY HEAD.
I SAID, THIS GUY MUST COME TO THE U.S.! WE NEED HIS GENIUS!
HUH...? M-MY GENIUS?
GIMME A BREAK...
I'M SERIOUS!!
YOU HAVE SUCH BEAUTIFUL EYES! THEY SPARKLE, AND THEY SAY TO ME, "HONESTY."
YOUR STYLE IS WHAT THE KIDS ARE INTO! YOUR SKIN IS CLEAR, AND YOU HAVE A NICE BODY...
ドキ
I'M SURE YOU'VE DRIVEN PLENTY OF CHICKS WILD, JIGGLING YOUR UNRIPENED, FORBIDDEN FRUITS... TEE-HEE.
OUR LITTLE ANGEL OF THE FOREST... I'M SURE THE HUNTER WHO SAW YOU HAD NO IDEA THE EXTENT OF HIS OWN DESIRE, WHY HE YEARNED TO CAPTURE THE CARNAL SWEETMEATS PEEKING OUT FROM THE SLITS IN YOUR OUTFIT...
IS THIS GIRL CRAZY...?

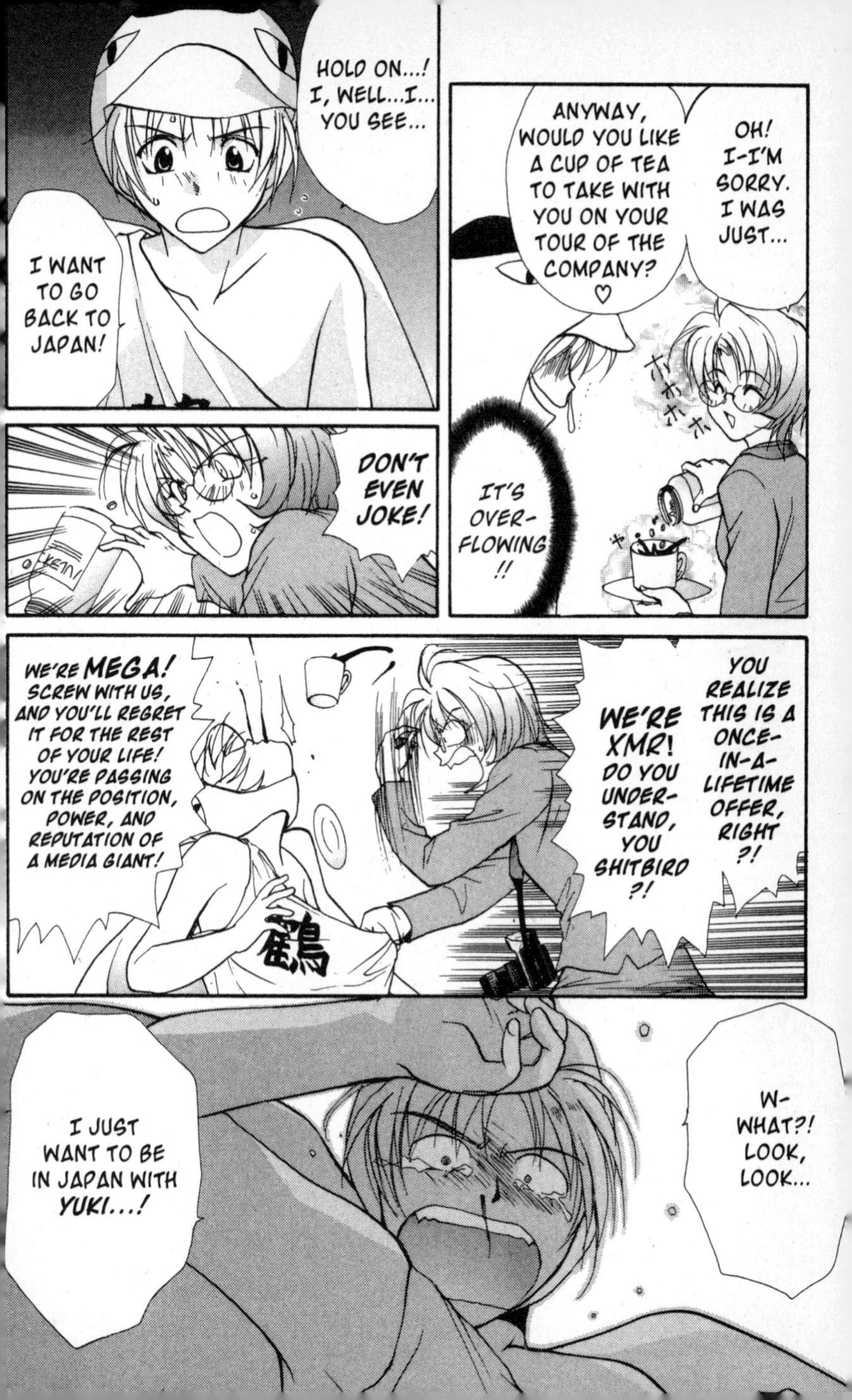
OH! I-I'M SORRY. I WAS JUST...
ANYWAY, WOULD YOU LIKE A CUP OF TEA TO TAKE WITH YOU ON YOUR TOUR OF THE COMPANY? ♡
ホホホホ
IT'S OVER-FLOWING!!
HOLD ON...! I, WELL...I... YOU SEE...
I WANT TO GO BACK TO JAPAN!
DON'T EVEN JOKE!
YOU REALIZE THIS IS A ONCE-IN-A-LIFETIME OFFER, RIGHT?!
WE'RE XMR! DO YOU UNDER-STAND, YOU SHITBIRD?!
WE'RE MEGA! SCREW WITH US, AND YOU'LL REGRET IT FOR THE REST OF YOUR LIFE! YOU'RE PASSING ON THE POSITION, POWER, AND REPUTATION OF A MEDIA GIANT!
鶴
W-WHAT?! LOOK, LOOK...
I JUST WANT TO BE IN JAPAN WITH YUKI...!

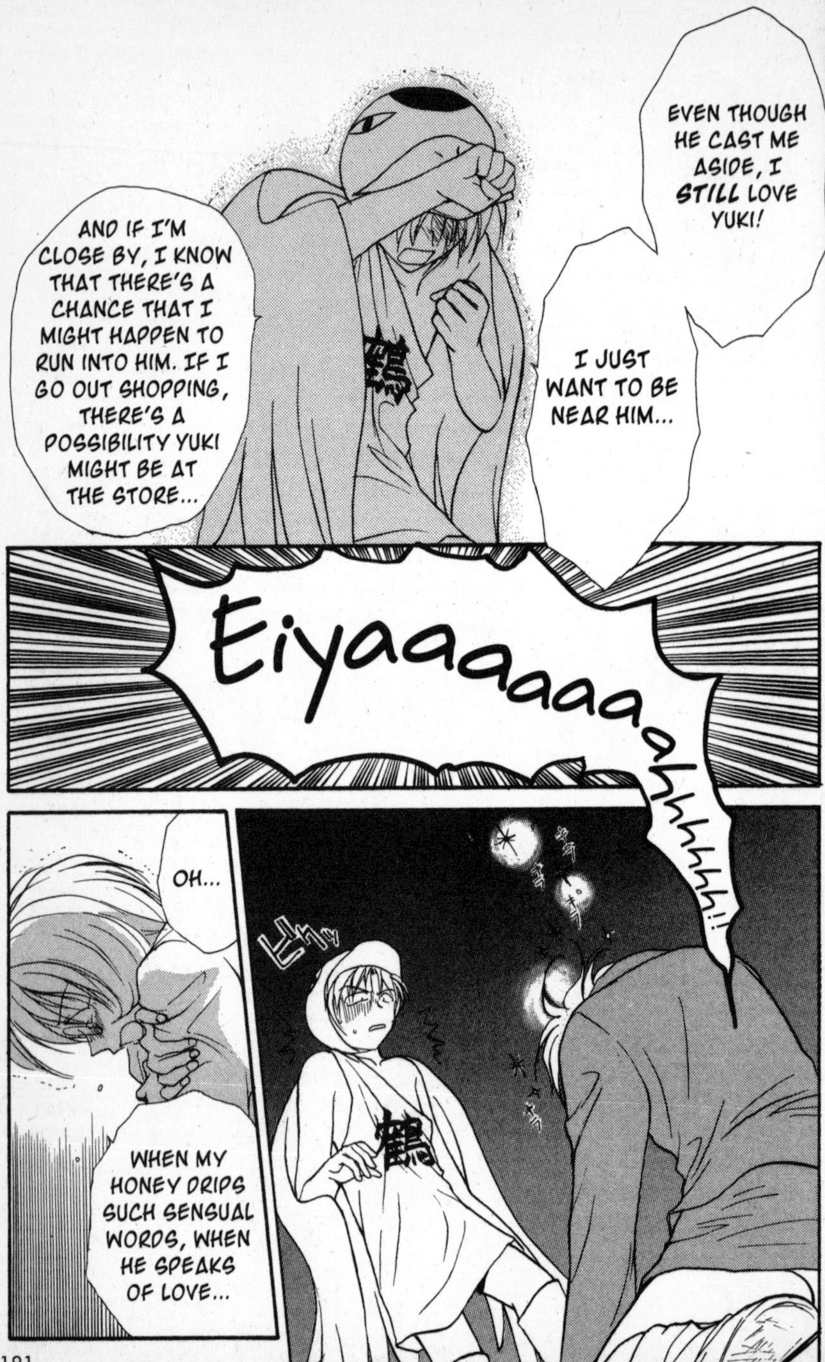
EVEN THOUGH HE CAST ME ASIDE, I **STILL** LOVE YUKI!
I JUST WANT TO BE NEAR HIM...
AND IF I'M CLOSE BY, I KNOW THAT THERE'S A CHANCE THAT I MIGHT HAPPEN TO RUN INTO HIM. IF I GO OUT SHOPPING, THERE'S A POSSIBILITY YUKI MIGHT BE AT THE STORE...
Eiyaaaaaaahhhhhh!!
OH...
WHEN MY HONEY DRIPS SUCH SENSUAL WORDS, WHEN HE SPEAKS OF LOVE...

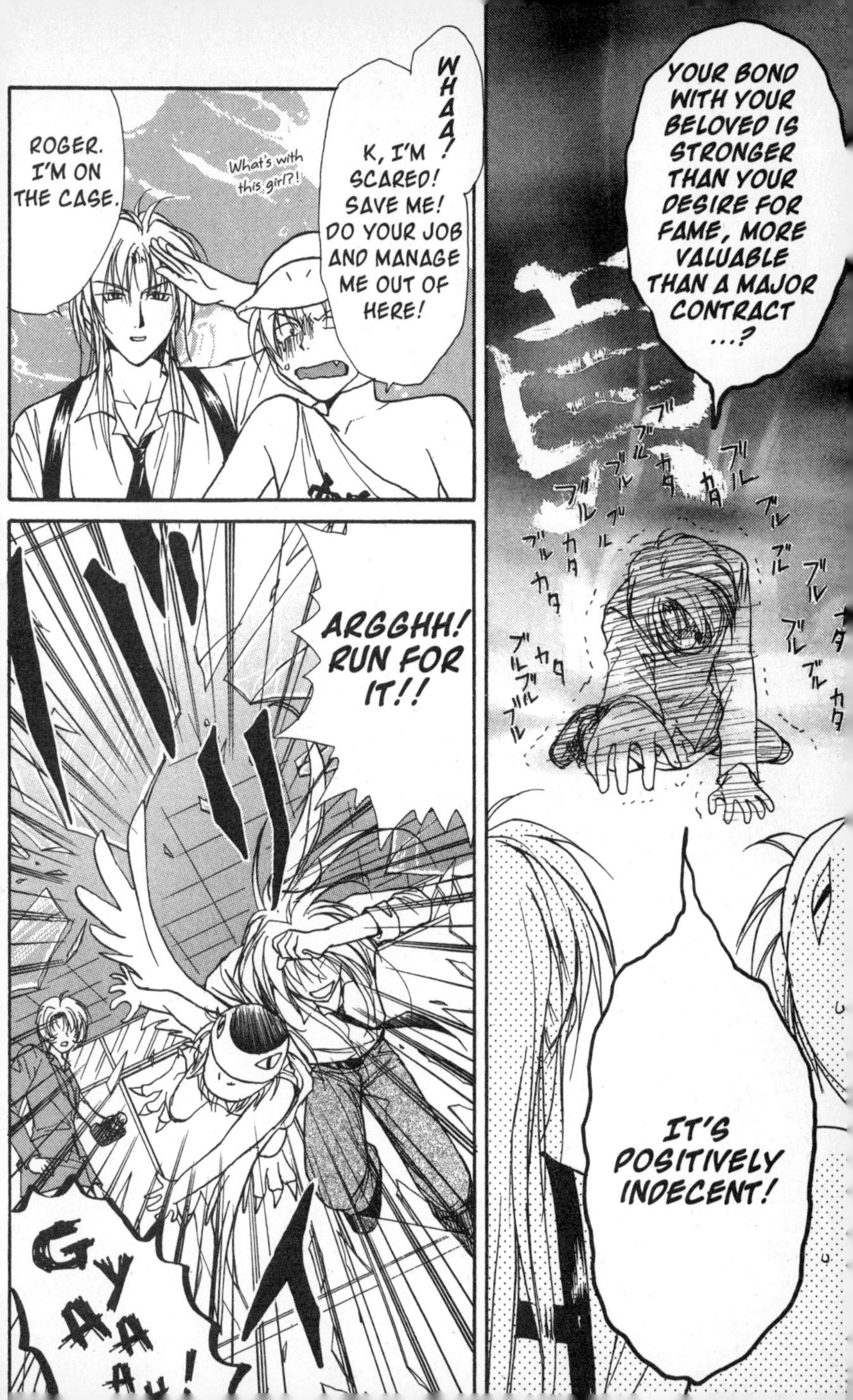
YOUR BOND WITH YOUR BELOVED IS STRONGER THAN YOUR DESIRE FOR FAME, MORE VALUABLE THAN A MAJOR CONTRACT ...?
ブルブル カタカタ
IT'S POSITIVELY INDECENT!
WHAAA!
K, I'M SCARED! SAVE ME! DO YOUR JOB AND MANAGE ME OUT OF HERE!
What's with this girl?!
ROGER. I'M ON THE CASE.
ARGGHH! RUN FOR IT!!
GYAAAH!

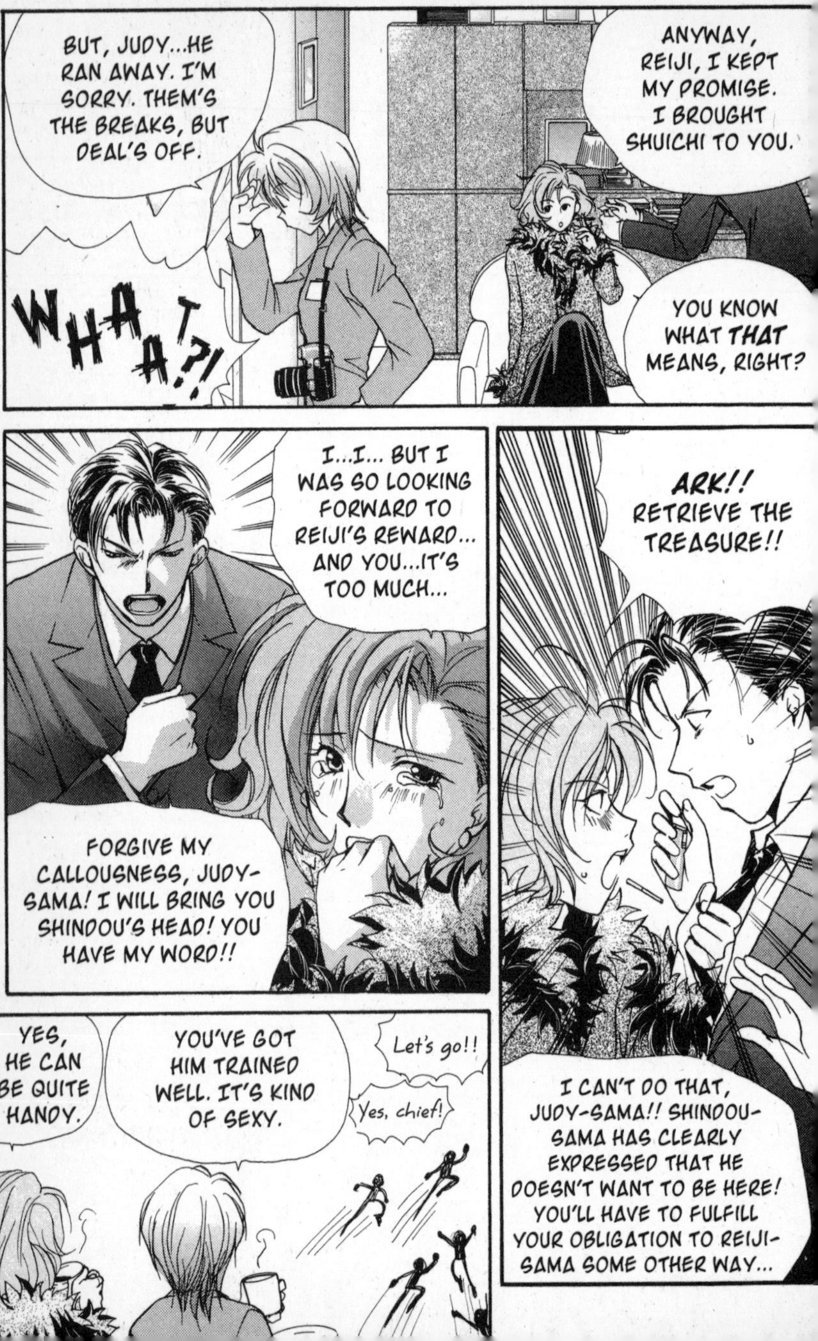
ANYWAY, REIJI, I KEPT MY PROMISE. I BROUGHT SHUICHI TO YOU.
YOU KNOW WHAT THAT MEANS, RIGHT?
BUT, JUDY...HE RAN AWAY. I'M SORRY. THEM'S THE BREAKS, BUT DEAL'S OFF.
WHAT?!
ARK!! RETRIEVE THE TREASURE!!
I CAN'T DO THAT, JUDY-SAMA!! SHINDOU-SAMA HAS CLEARLY EXPRESSED THAT HE DOESN'T WANT TO BE HERE! YOU'LL HAVE TO FULFILL YOUR OBLIGATION TO REIJI-SAMA SOME OTHER WAY...
I...I... BUT I WAS SO LOOKING FORWARD TO REIJI'S REWARD... AND YOU...IT'S TOO MUCH...
FORGIVE MY CALLOUSNESS, JUDY-SAMA! I WILL BRING YOU SHINDOU'S HEAD! YOU HAVE MY WORD!!
Let's go!!
Yes, chief!
YOU'VE GOT HIM TRAINED WELL. IT'S KIND OF SEXY.
YES, HE CAN BE QUITE HANDY.

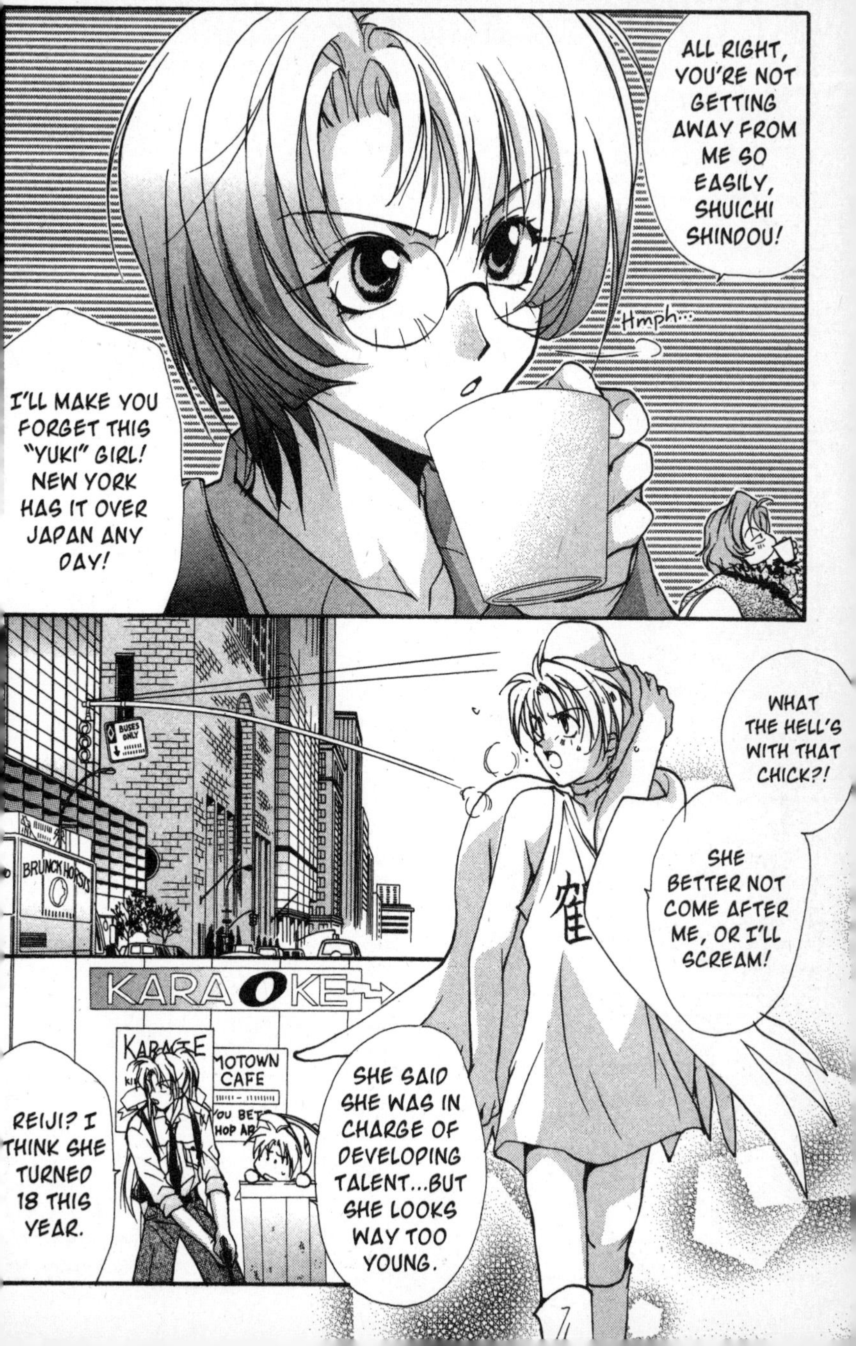
ALL RIGHT, YOU'RE NOT GETTING AWAY FROM ME SO EASILY, SHUICHI SHINDOU!
Hmph...
I'LL MAKE YOU FORGET THIS "YUKI" GIRL! NEW YORK HAS IT OVER JAPAN ANY DAY!
WHAT THE HELL'S WITH THAT CHICK?!
SHE BETTER NOT COME AFTER ME, OR I'LL SCREAM!
BUSES ONLY
KARAOKE
SHE SAID SHE WAS IN CHARGE OF DEVELOPING TALENT...BUT SHE LOOKS WAY TOO YOUNG.
REIJI? I THINK SHE TURNED 18 THIS YEAR.

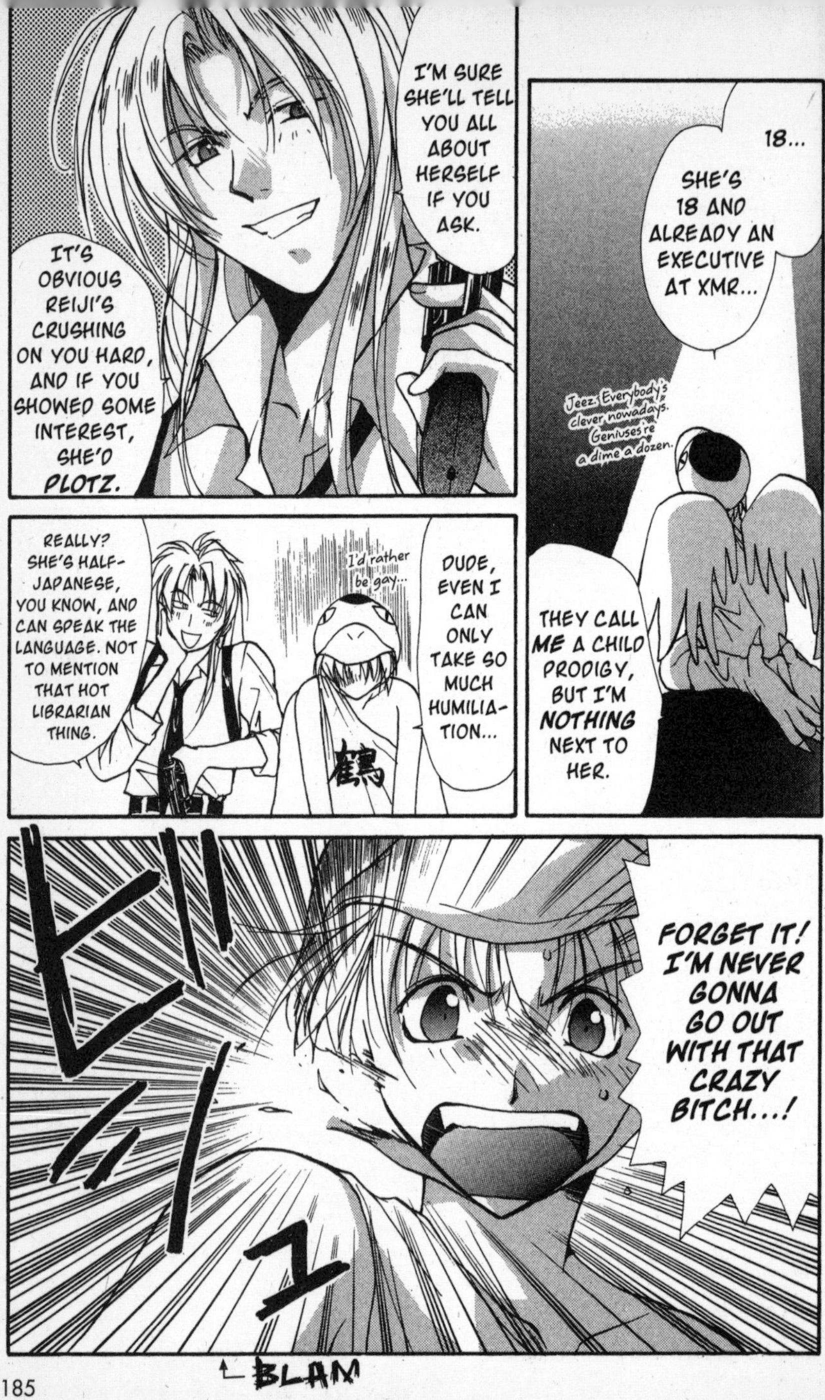
18...
SHE'S 18 AND ALREADY AN EXECUTIVE AT XMR...
Jeez. Everybody's clever nowadays. Geniuses're a dime a dozen.
THEY CALL ME A CHILD PRODIGY, BUT I'M NOTHING NEXT TO HER.
I'M SURE SHE'LL TELL YOU ALL ABOUT HERSELF IF YOU ASK.
IT'S OBVIOUS REIJI'S CRUSHING ON YOU HARD, AND IF YOU SHOWED SOME INTEREST, SHE'D PLOTZ.
DUDE, EVEN I CAN ONLY TAKE SO MUCH HUMILIATION...
I'd rather be gay...
REALLY? SHE'S HALF-JAPANESE, YOU KNOW, AND CAN SPEAK THE LANGUAGE. NOT TO MENTION THAT HOT LIBRARIAN THING.
FORGET IT! I'M NEVER GONNA GO OUT WITH THAT CRAZY BITCH...!
BLAM

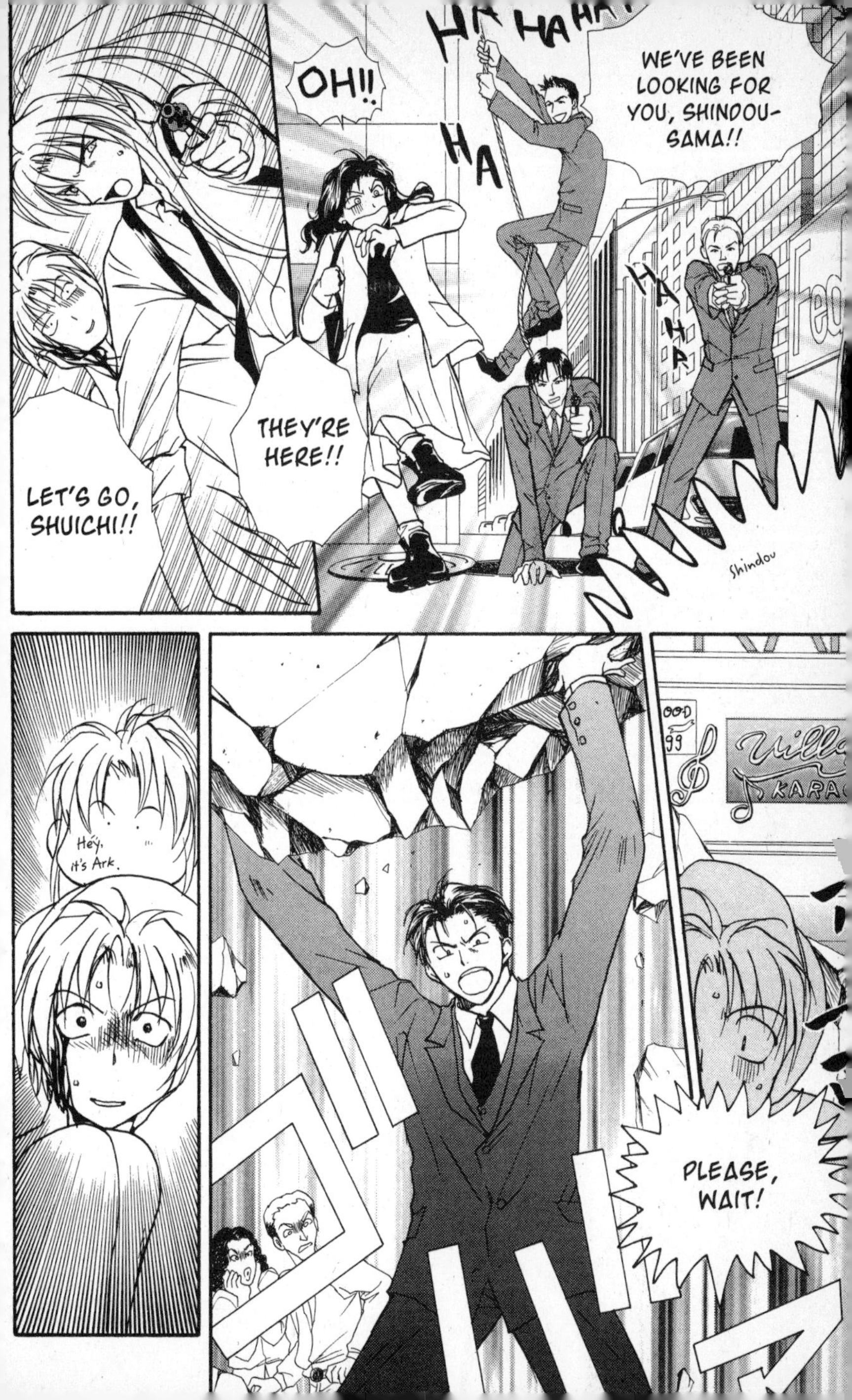

HA HA HA
WE'VE BEEN LOOKING FOR YOU, SHINDOU-SAMA!!
OH!!
HA
HA HA HA
THEY'RE HERE!!
Shindou
LET'S GO, SHUICHI!!
PLEASE, WAIT!
Hey, it's Ark.

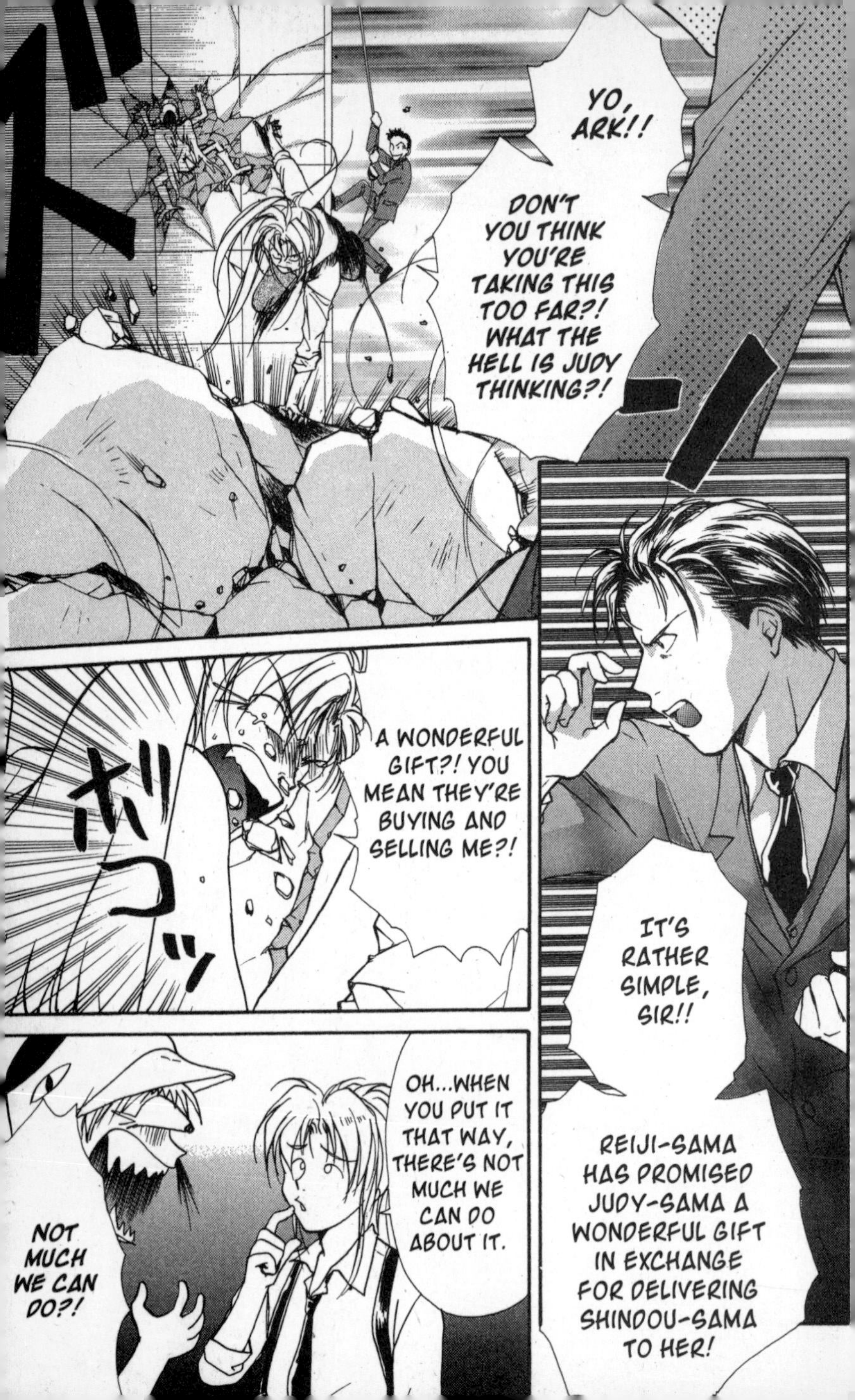
YO, ARK!!
DON'T YOU THINK YOU'RE TAKING THIS TOO FAR?! WHAT THE HELL IS JUDY THINKING?!
IT'S RATHER SIMPLE, SIR!!
REIJI-SAMA HAS PROMISED JUDY-SAMA A WONDERFUL GIFT IN EXCHANGE FOR DELIVERING SHINDOU-SAMA TO HER!
A WONDERFUL GIFT?! YOU MEAN THEY'RE BUYING AND SELLING ME?!
OH...WHEN YOU PUT IT THAT WAY, THERE'S NOT MUCH WE CAN DO ABOUT IT.
NOT MUCH WE CAN DO?!

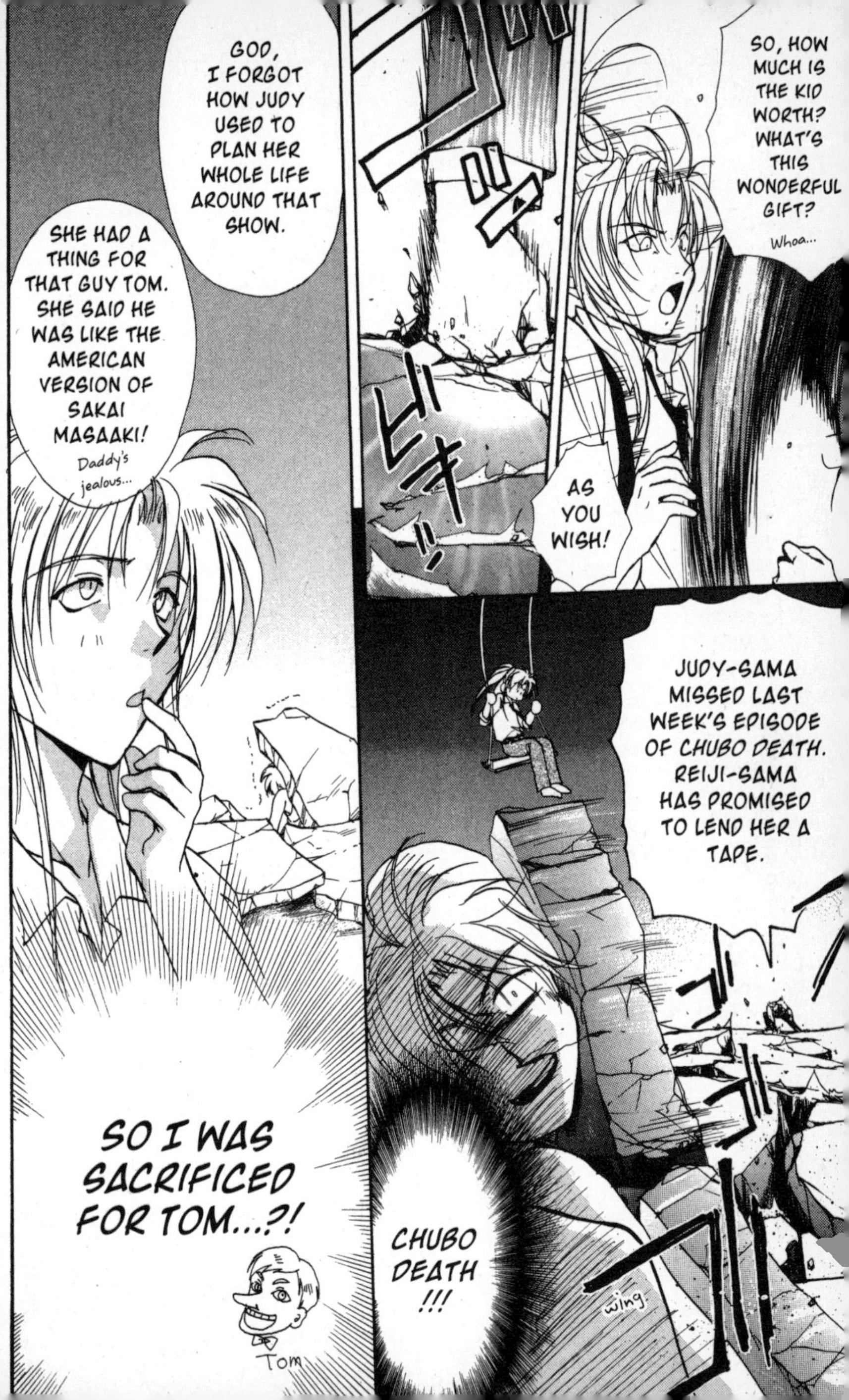
SO, HOW MUCH IS THE KID WORTH? WHAT'S THIS WONDERFUL GIFT?
Whoa...
AS YOU WISH!
JUDY-SAMA MISSED LAST WEEK'S EPISODE OF CHUBO DEATH. REIJI-SAMA HAS PROMISED TO LEND HER A TAPE.
CHUBO DEATH !!!
wing
GOD, I FORGOT HOW JUDY USED TO PLAN HER WHOLE LIFE AROUND THAT SHOW.
SHE HAD A THING FOR THAT GUY TOM. SHE SAID HE WAS LIKE THE AMERICAN VERSION OF SAKAI MASAAKI!
Daddy's jealous...
SO I WAS SACRIFICED FOR TOM...?!
Tom

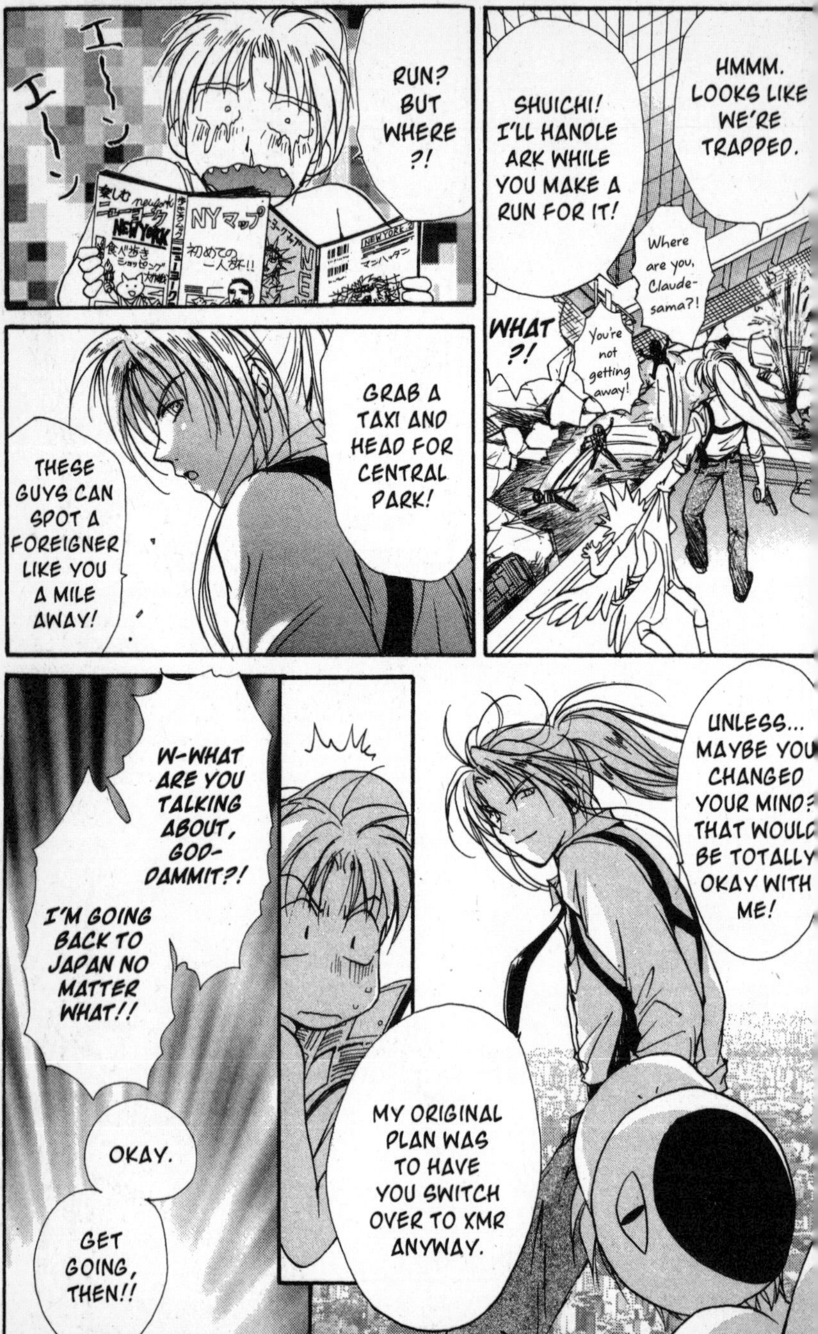
HMMM. LOOKS LIKE WE'RE TRAPPED.
SHUICHI! I'LL HANDLE ARK WHILE YOU MAKE A RUN FOR IT!
Where are you, Claude-sama?!
WHAT ?!
You're not getting away!
RUN? BUT WHERE ?!
エ〜〜ン
エ〜〜ン
NYマップ
初めての 一人旅!!
マンハッタン
GRAB A TAXI AND HEAD FOR CENTRAL PARK!
THESE GUYS CAN SPOT A FOREIGNER LIKE YOU A MILE AWAY!
UNLESS... MAYBE YOU CHANGED YOUR MIND? THAT WOULD BE TOTALLY OKAY WITH ME!
MY ORIGINAL PLAN WAS TO HAVE YOU SWITCH OVER TO XMR ANYWAY.
W-WHAT ARE YOU TALKING ABOUT, GOD-DAMMIT?!
I'M GOING BACK TO JAPAN NO MATTER WHAT!!
OKAY.
GET GOING, THEN!!

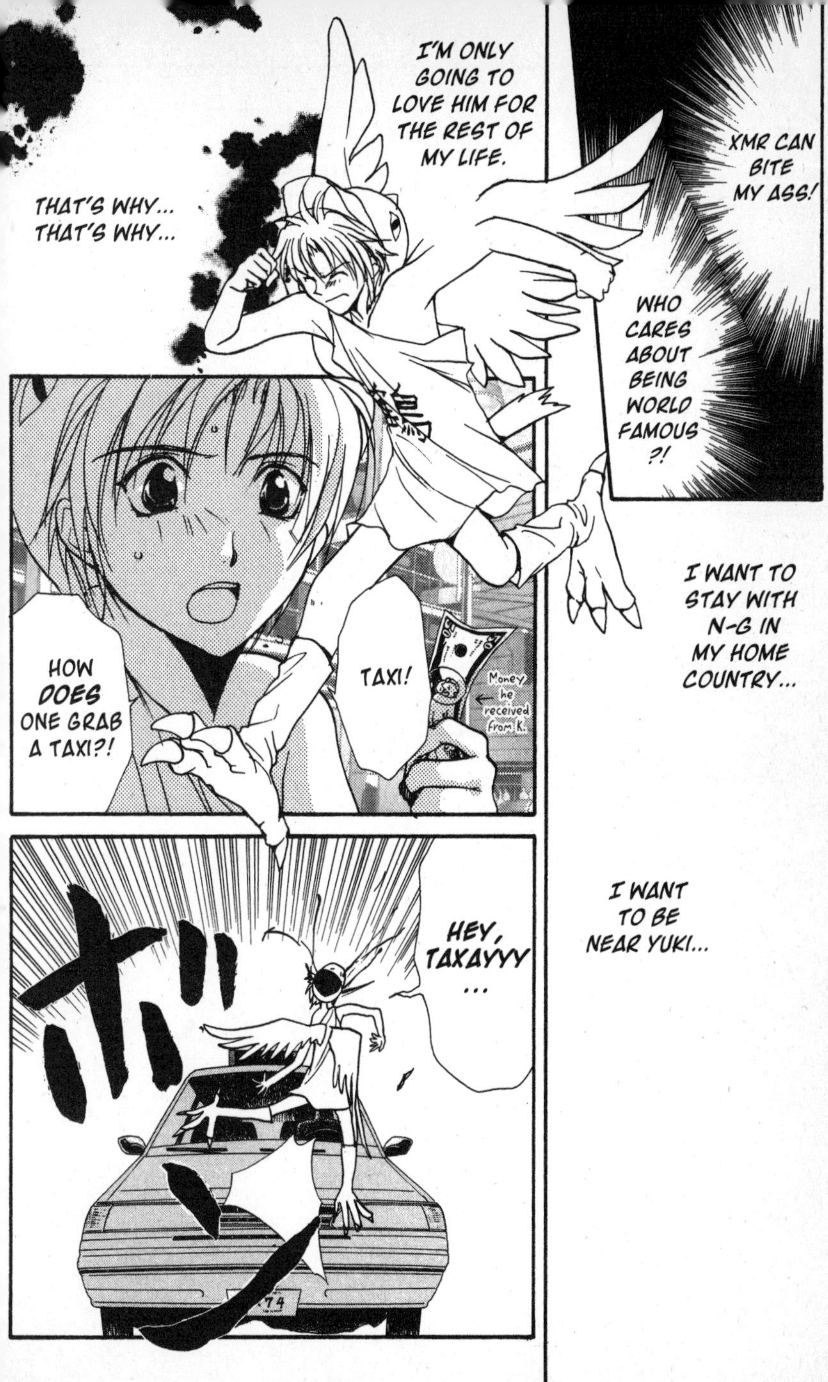
XMR CAN BITE MY ASS!
WHO CARES ABOUT BEING WORLD FAMOUS?!
I'M ONLY GOING TO LOVE HIM FOR THE REST OF MY LIFE.
THAT'S WHY... THAT'S WHY...
I WANT TO STAY WITH N-G IN MY HOME COUNTRY...
TAXI!
Money he received from K.
HOW DOES ONE GRAB A TAXI?!
I WANT TO BE NEAR YUKI...
HEY, TAXAYYY...

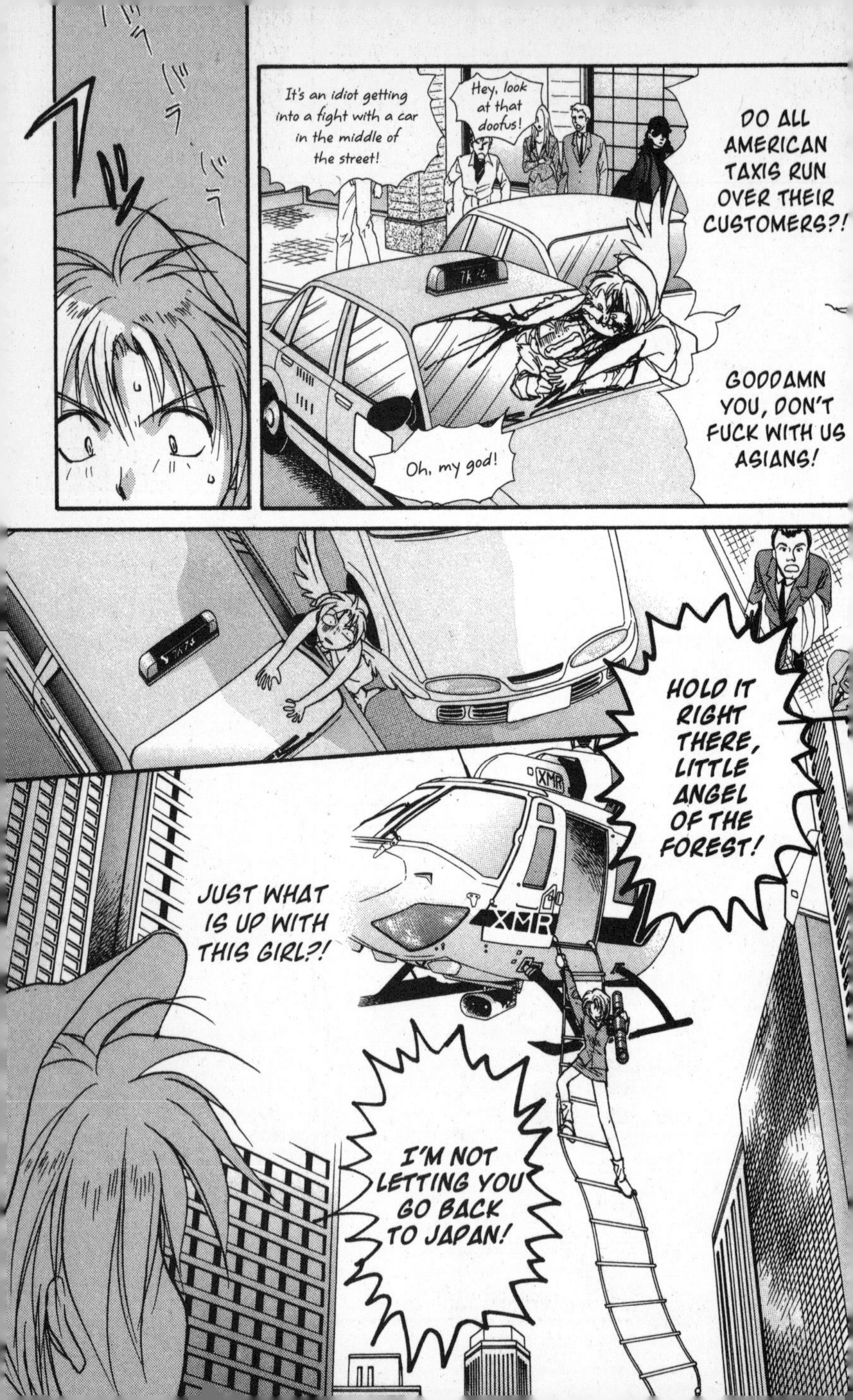
DO ALL AMERICAN TAXIS RUN OVER THEIR CUSTOMERS?!
Hey, look at that doofus!
It's an idiot getting into a fight with a car in the middle of the street!
GODDAMN YOU, DON'T FUCK WITH US ASIANS!
Oh, my god!
HOLD IT RIGHT THERE, LITTLE ANGEL OF THE FOREST!
XMR
JUST WHAT IS UP WITH THIS GIRL?!
I'M NOT LETTING YOU GO BACK TO JAPAN!

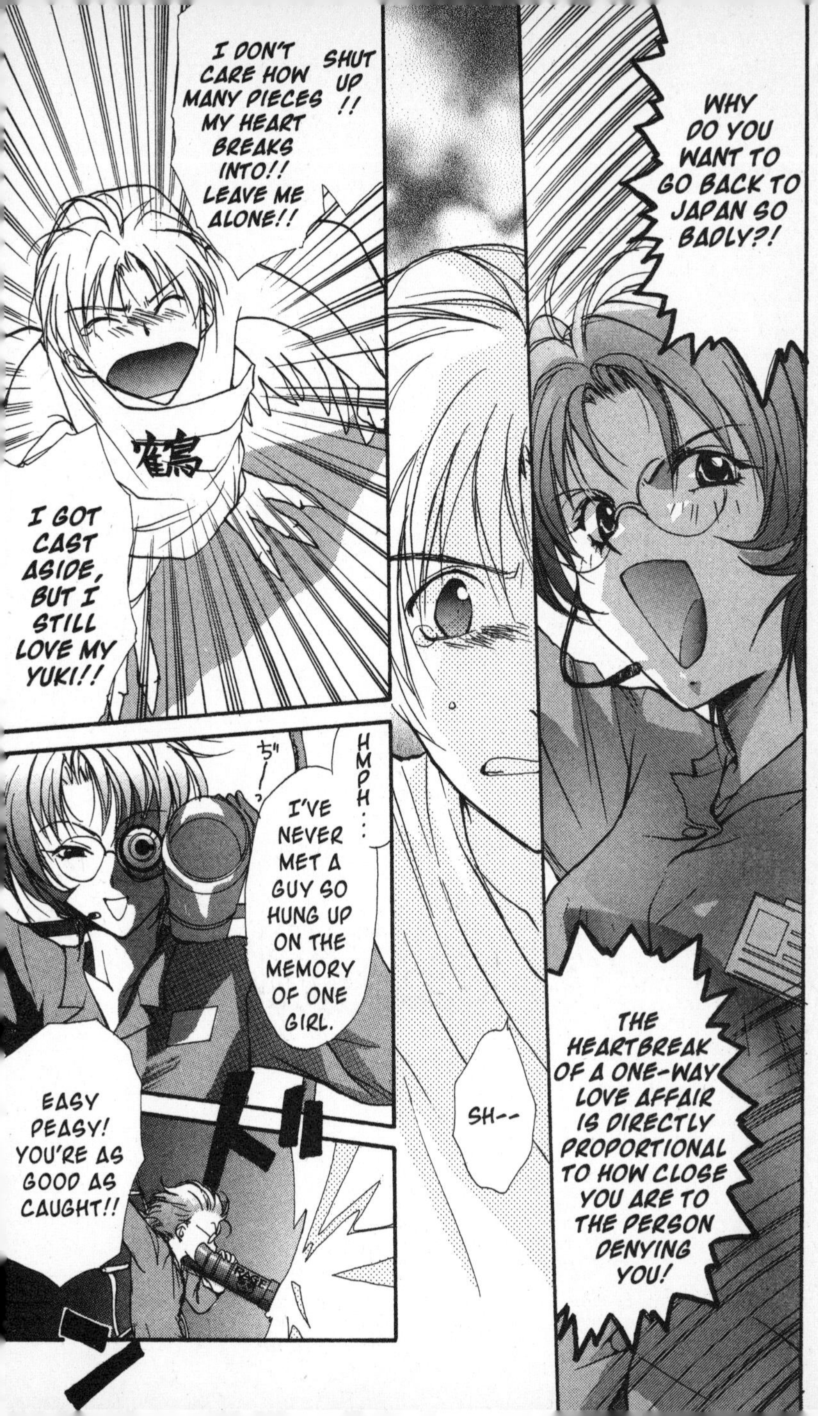

WHY DO YOU WANT TO GO BACK TO JAPAN SO BADLY?!
THE HEARTBREAK OF A ONE-WAY LOVE AFFAIR IS DIRECTLY PROPORTIONAL TO HOW CLOSE YOU ARE TO THE PERSON DENYING YOU!
SH--
SHUT UP!!
I DON'T CARE HOW MANY PIECES MY HEART BREAKS INTO!! LEAVE ME ALONE!!
I GOT CAST ASIDE, BUT I STILL LOVE MY YUKI!!
HMPH...
I'VE NEVER MET A GUY SO HUNG UP ON THE MEMORY OF ONE GIRL.
ぢー
EASY PEASY! YOU'RE AS GOOD AS CAUGHT!!

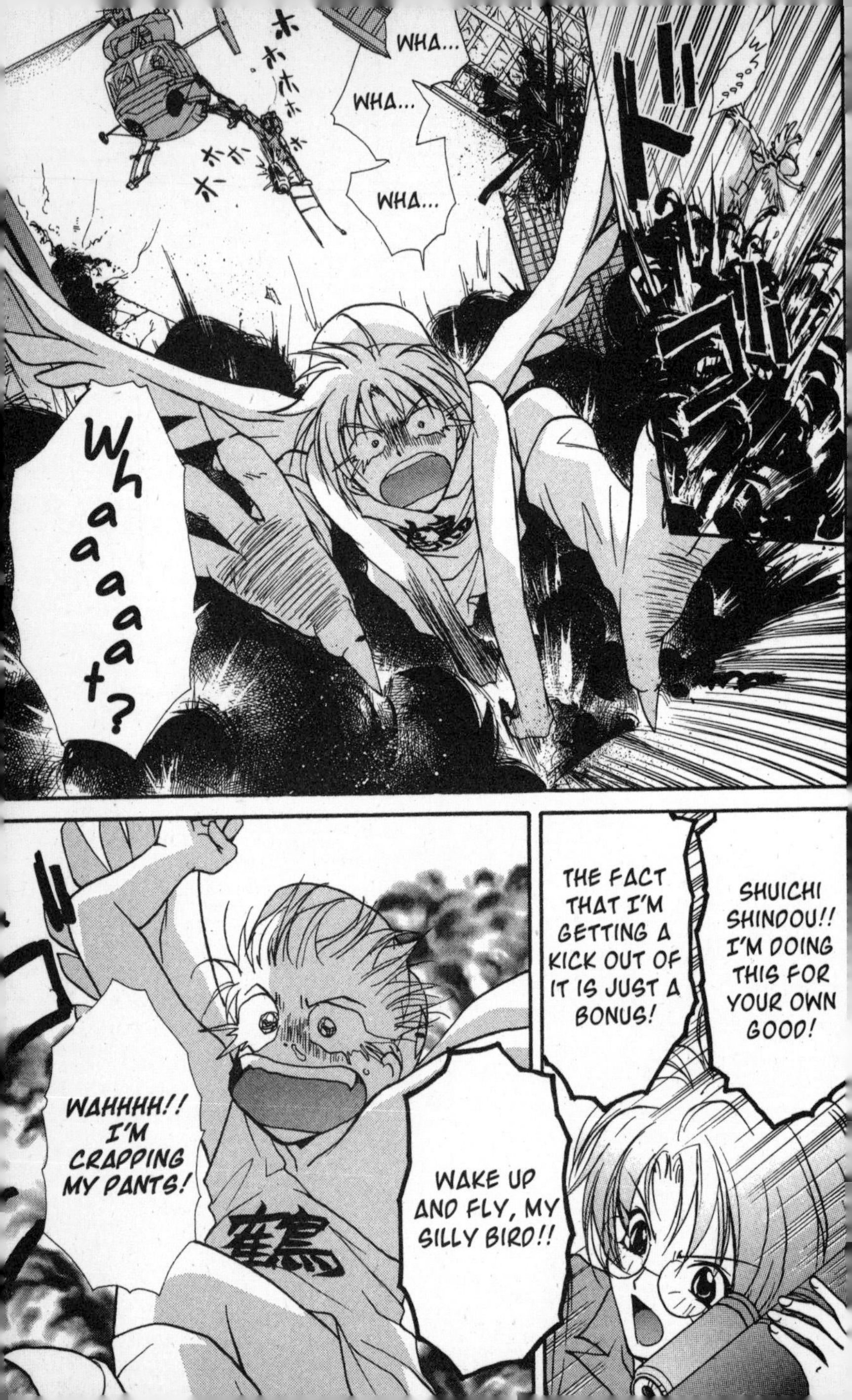

WHA...
WHA...
WHA...
Whaaaaaaat?
SHUICHI SHINDOU!! I'M DOING THIS FOR YOUR OWN GOOD!
THE FACT THAT I'M GETTING A KICK OUT OF IT IS JUST A BONUS!
WAKE UP AND FLY, MY SILLY BIRD!!
WAHHHH!! I'M CRAPPING MY PANTS!

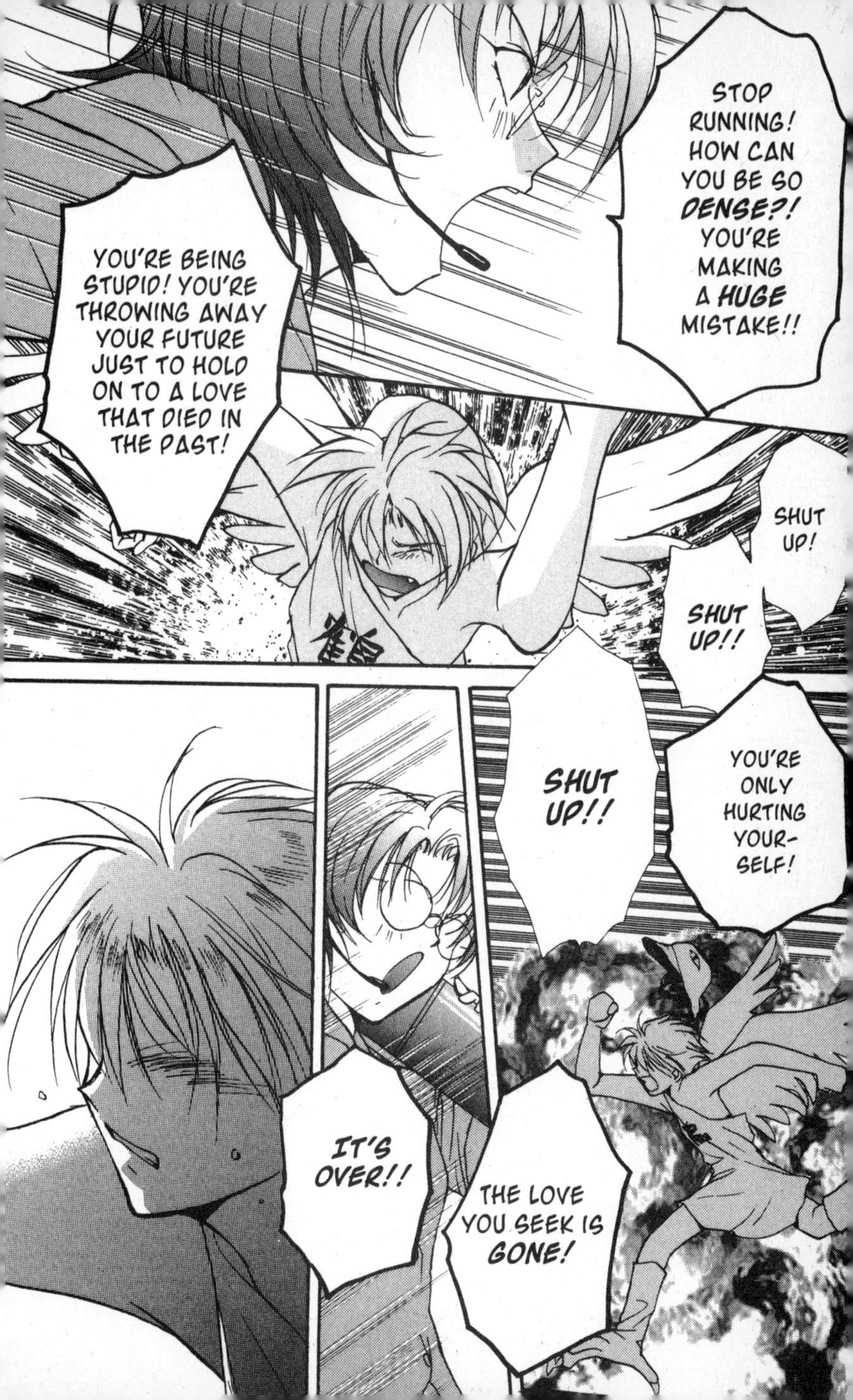
STOP RUNNING! HOW CAN YOU BE SO DENSE?! YOU'RE MAKING A HUGE MISTAKE!!
YOU'RE BEING STUPID! YOU'RE THROWING AWAY YOUR FUTURE JUST TO HOLD ON TO A LOVE THAT DIED IN THE PAST!
SHUT UP!
SHUT UP!!
YOU'RE ONLY HURTING YOUR-SELF!
SHUT UP!!
IT'S OVER!!
THE LOVE YOU SEEK IS GONE!

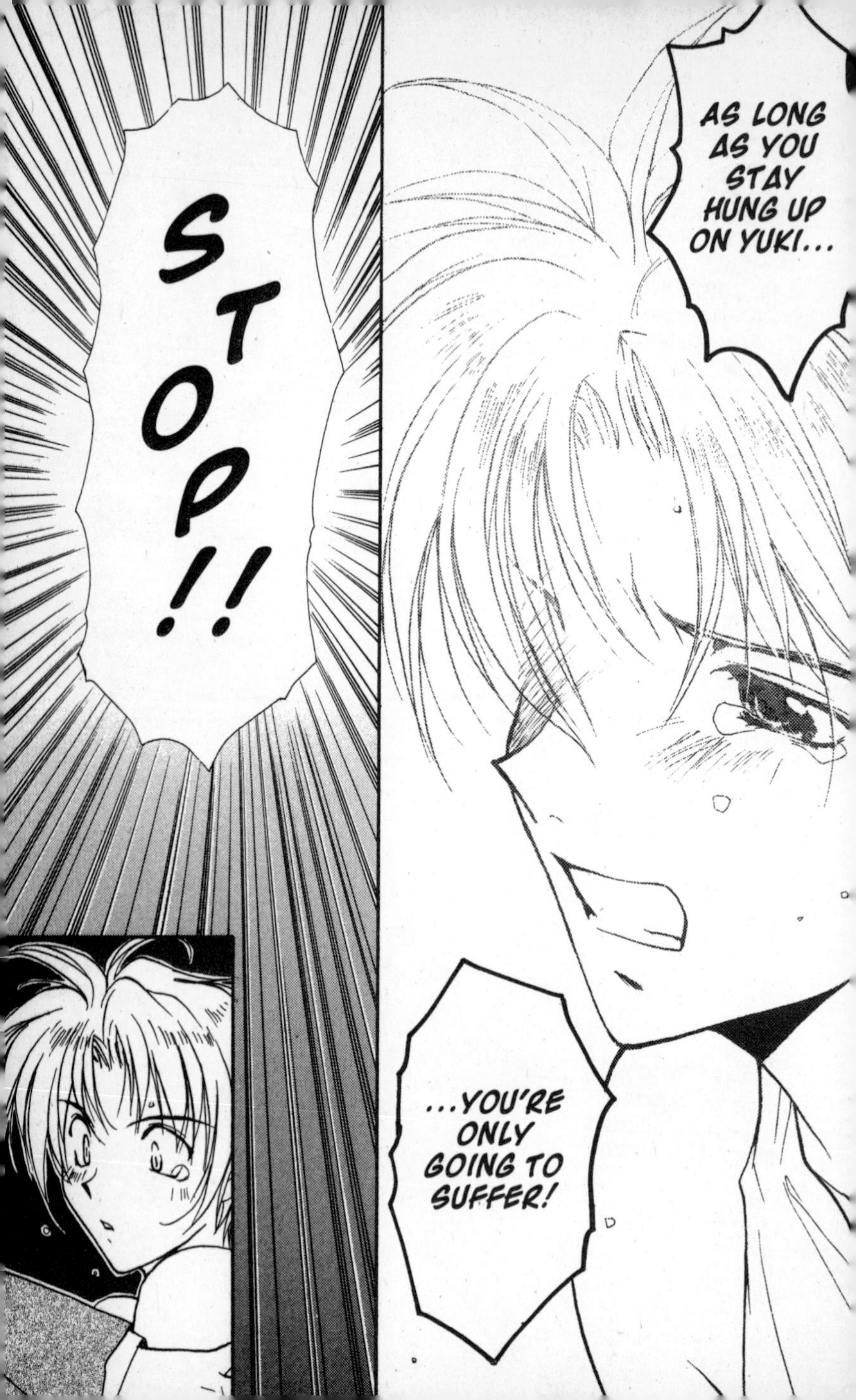
AS LONG AS YOU STAY HUNG UP ON YUKI...
...YOU'RE ONLY GOING TO SUFFER!
STOP!!

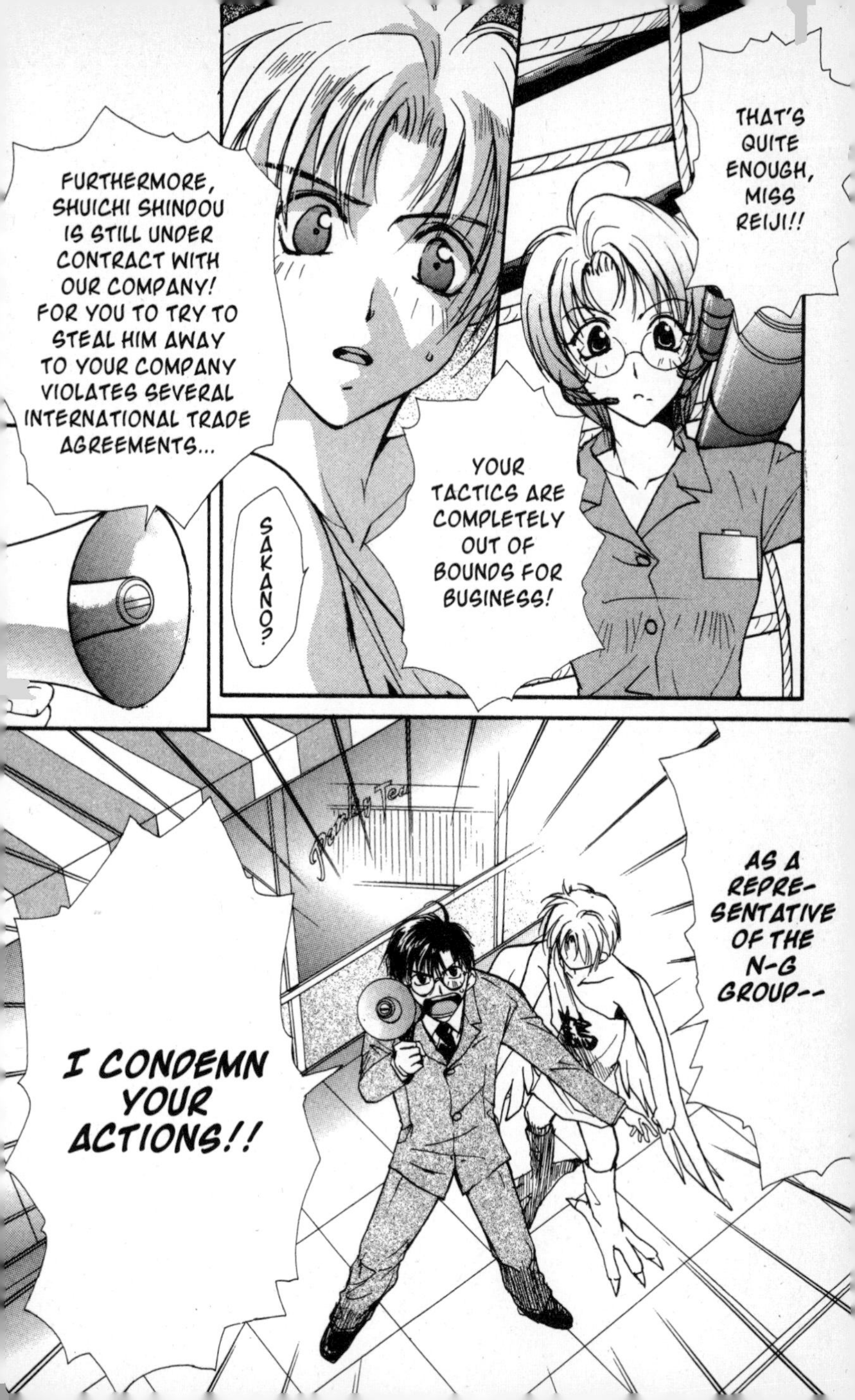
THAT'S QUITE ENOUGH, MISS REIJI!!
YOUR TACTICS ARE COMPLETELY OUT OF BOUNDS FOR BUSINESS!
SAKANO?
FURTHERMORE, SHUICHI SHINDOU IS STILL UNDER CONTRACT WITH OUR COMPANY! FOR YOU TO TRY TO STEAL HIM AWAY TO YOUR COMPANY VIOLATES SEVERAL INTERNATIONAL TRADE AGREEMENTS...
AS A REPRE-SENTATIVE OF THE N-G GROUP--
I CONDEMN YOUR ACTIONS!!

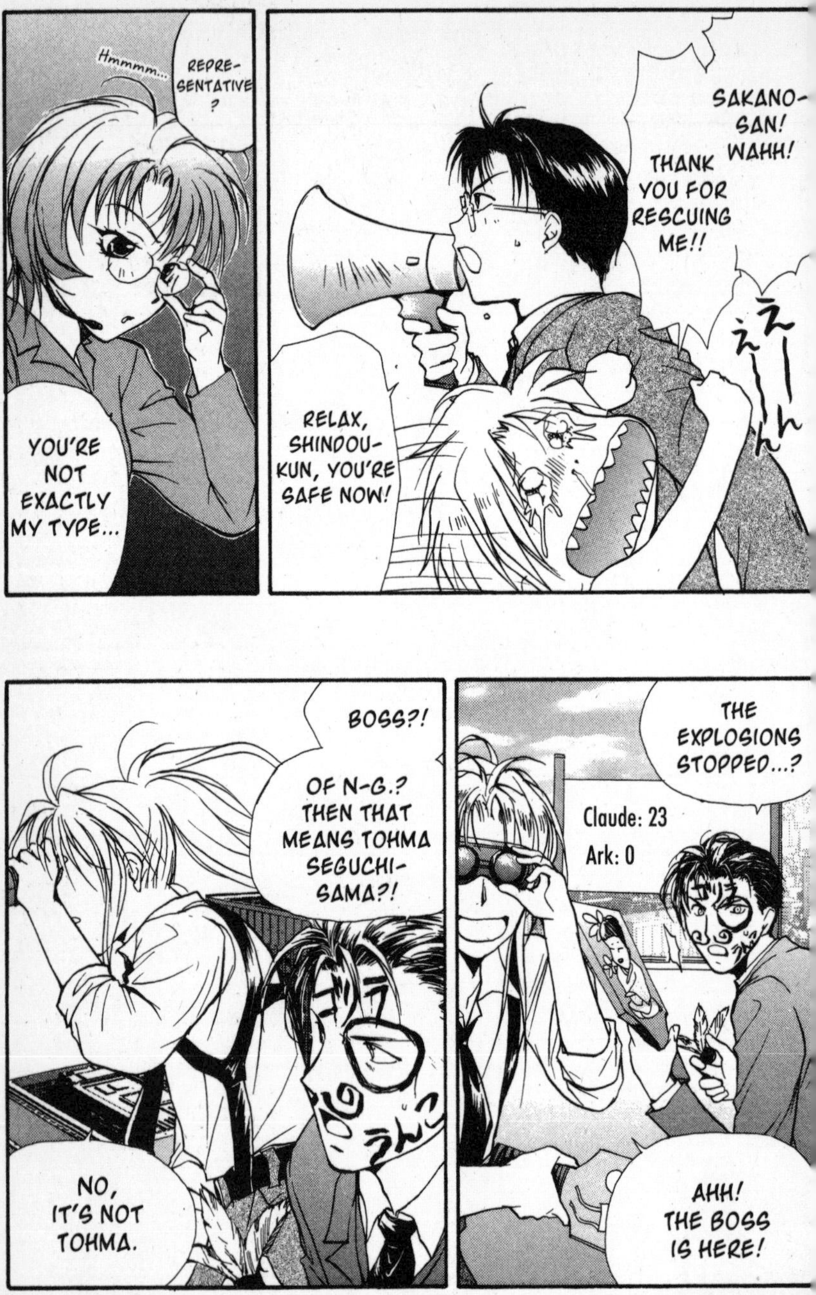
SAKANO-SAN! WAHH!
THANK YOU FOR RESCUING ME!!
えーーん
RELAX, SHINDOU-KUN, YOU'RE SAFE NOW!
REPRE-SENTATIVE?
Hmmmm...
YOU'RE NOT EXACTLY MY TYPE...
THE EXPLOSIONS STOPPED...?
Claude: 23
Ark: 0
AHH! THE BOSS IS HERE!
BOSS?!
OF N-G.? THEN THAT MEANS TOHMA SEGUCHI-SAMA?!
NO, IT'S NOT TOHMA.

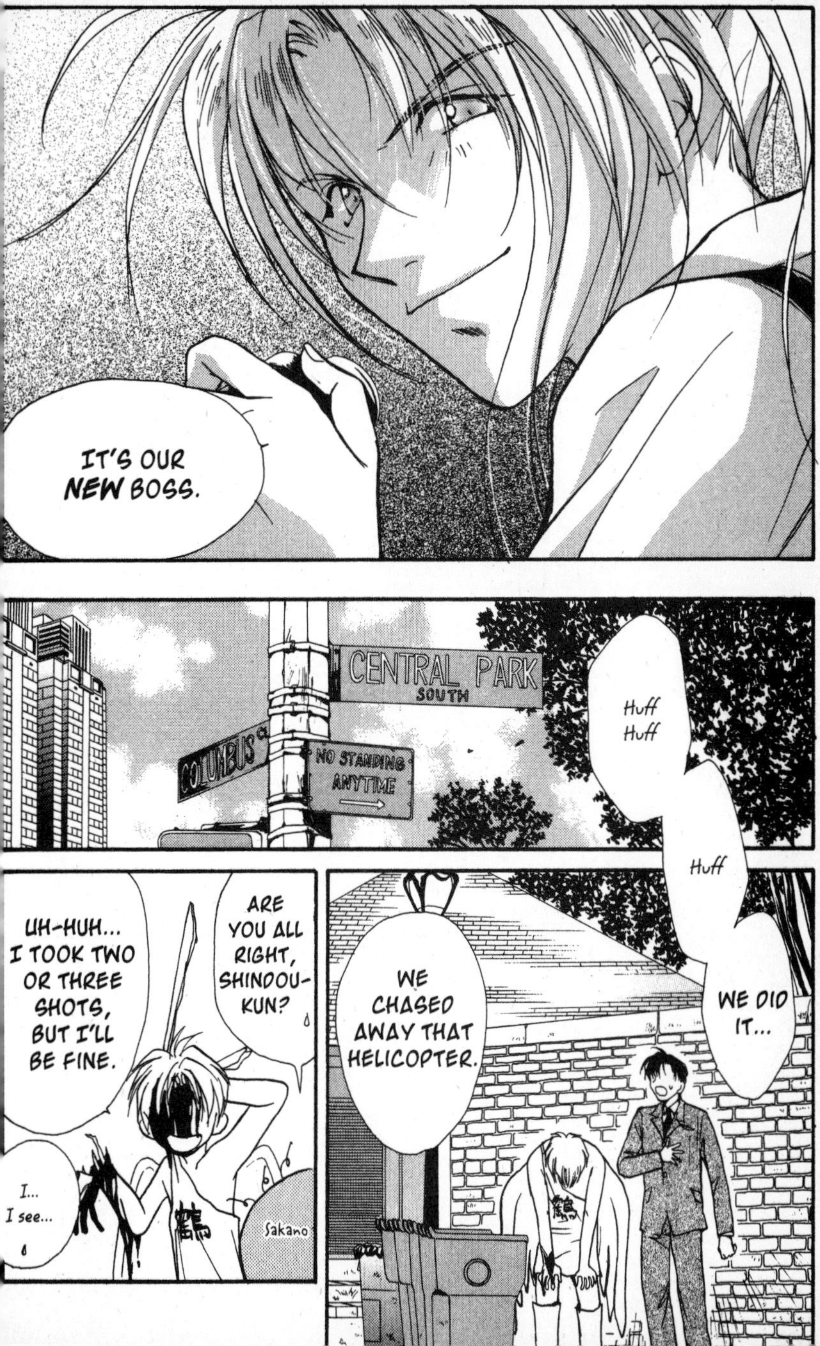
IT'S OUR NEW BOSS.
Huff Huff
CENTRAL PARK SOUTH
COLUMBUS Cl
NO STANDING ANYTIME
Huff
WE DID IT...
WE CHASED AWAY THAT HELICOPTER.
ARE YOU ALL RIGHT, SHINDOU-KUN?
UH-HUH... I TOOK TWO OR THREE SHOTS, BUT I'LL BE FINE.
Sakano
I... I see...

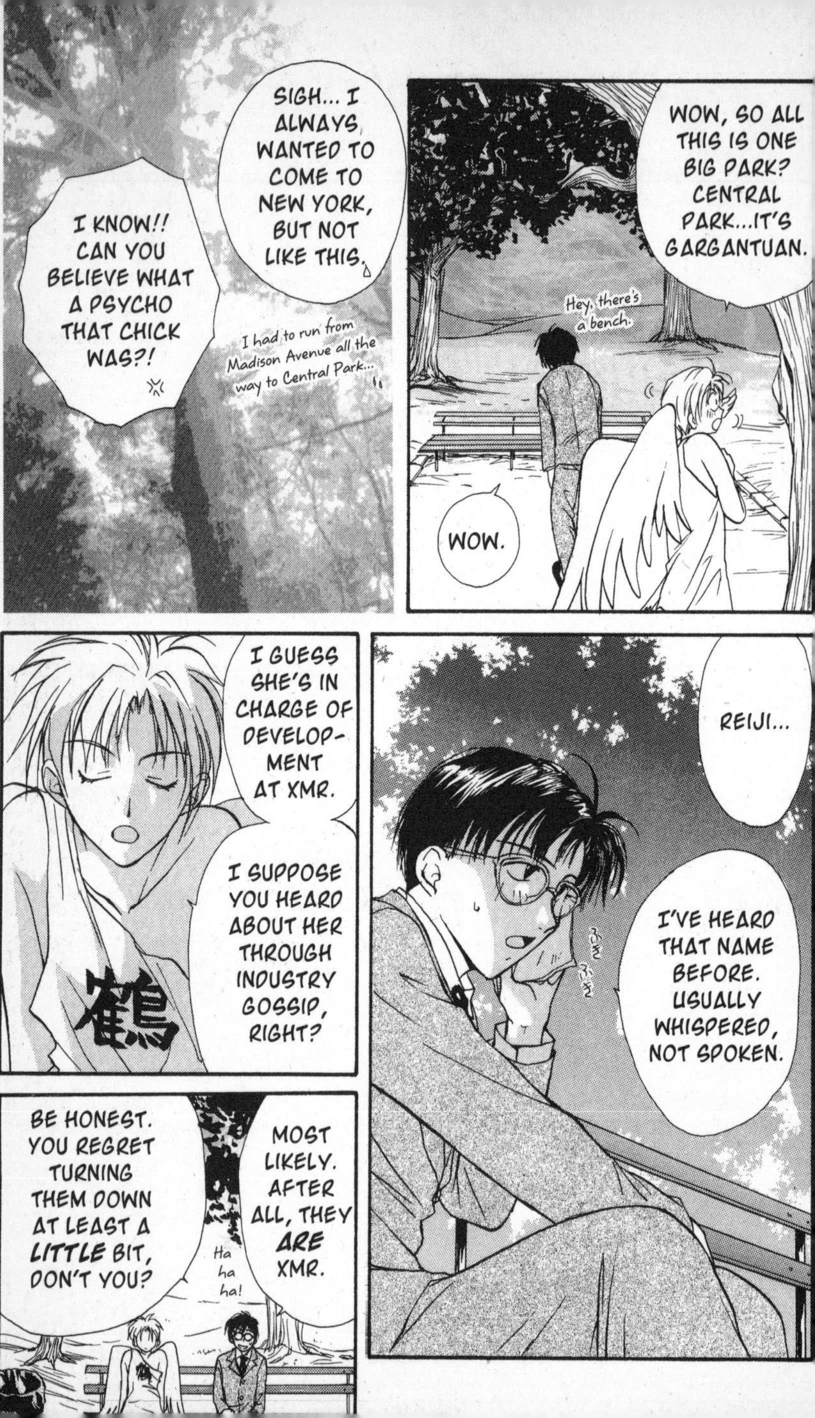
WOW, SO ALL THIS IS ONE BIG PARK? CENTRAL PARK...IT'S GARGANTUAN.
Hey, there's a bench.
WOW.
SIGH... I ALWAYS WANTED TO COME TO NEW YORK, BUT NOT LIKE THIS.
I KNOW!! CAN YOU BELIEVE WHAT A PSYCHO THAT CHICK WAS?!
I had to run from Madison Avenue all the way to Central Park...
REIJI...
I'VE HEARD THAT NAME BEFORE. USUALLY WHISPERED, NOT SPOKEN.
I GUESS SHE'S IN CHARGE OF DEVELOPMENT AT XMR.
I SUPPOSE YOU HEARD ABOUT HER THROUGH INDUSTRY GOSSIP, RIGHT?
MOST LIKELY. AFTER ALL, THEY *ARE* XMR.
BE HONEST. YOU REGRET TURNING THEM DOWN AT LEAST A *LITTLE* BIT, DON'T YOU?
Ha ha ha!

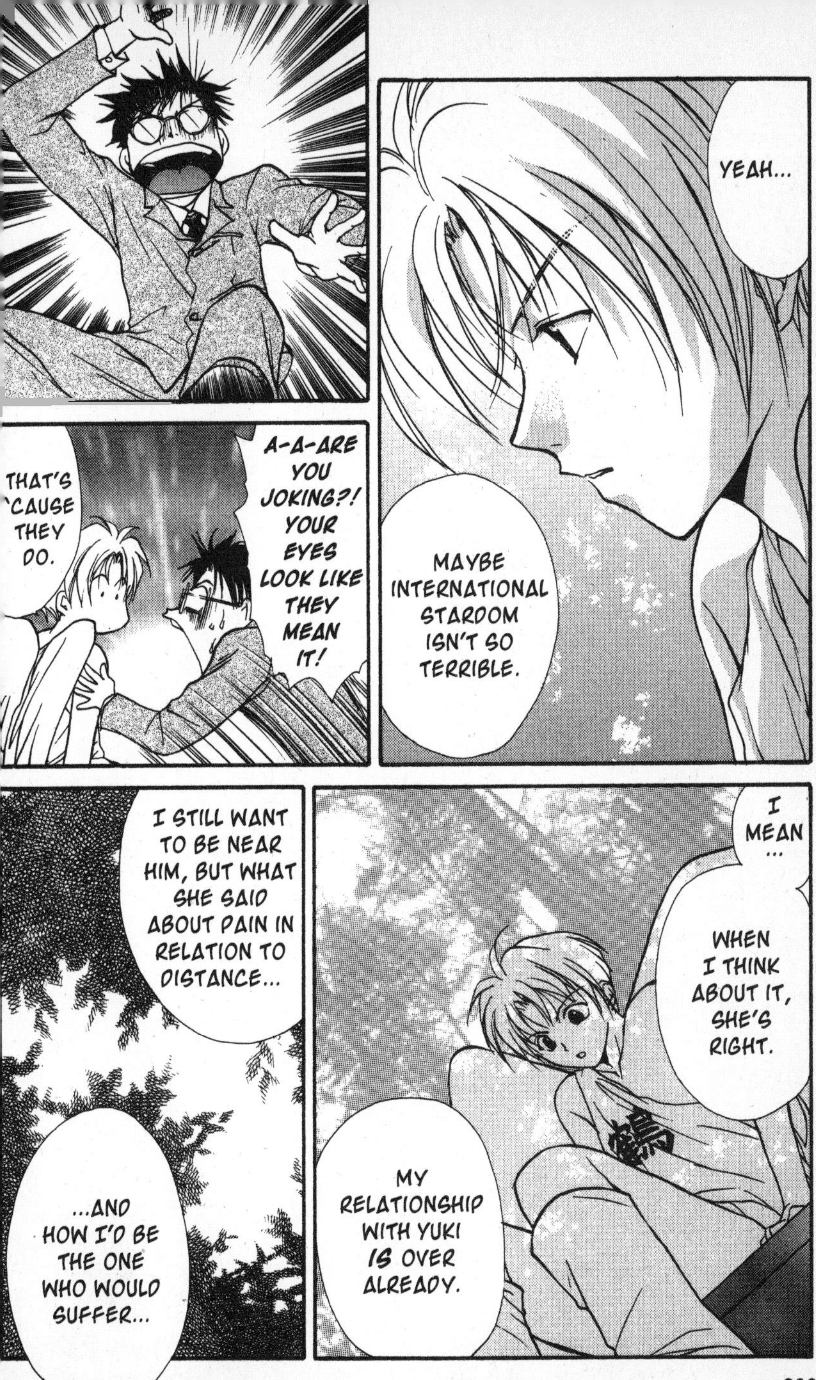
YEAH...
MAYBE INTERNATIONAL STARDOM ISN'T SO TERRIBLE.
A-A-ARE YOU JOKING?! YOUR EYES LOOK LIKE THEY MEAN IT!
THAT'S 'CAUSE THEY DO.
I MEAN...
WHEN I THINK ABOUT IT, SHE'S RIGHT.
MY RELATIONSHIP WITH YUKI *IS* OVER ALREADY.
I STILL WANT TO BE NEAR HIM, BUT WHAT SHE SAID ABOUT PAIN IN RELATION TO DISTANCE...
...AND HOW I'D BE THE ONE WHO WOULD SUFFER...

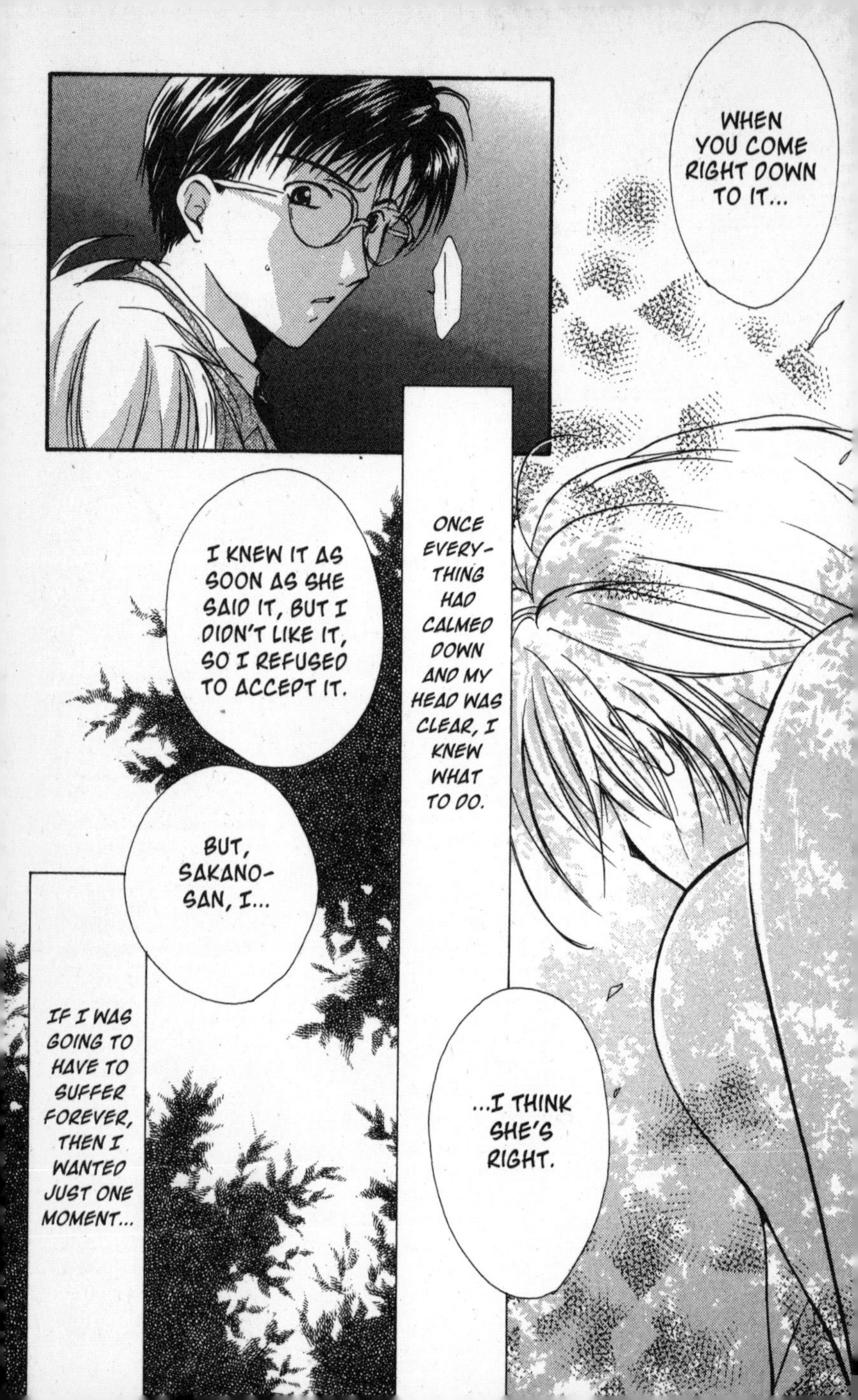
WHEN YOU COME RIGHT DOWN TO IT...
...I THINK SHE'S RIGHT.
!
ONCE EVERY-THING HAD CALMED DOWN AND MY HEAD WAS CLEAR, I KNEW WHAT TO DO.
I KNEW IT AS SOON AS SHE SAID IT, BUT I DIDN'T LIKE IT, SO I REFUSED TO ACCEPT IT.
BUT, SAKANO-SAN, I...
IF I WAS GOING TO HAVE TO SUFFER FOREVER, THEN I WANTED JUST ONE MOMENT...

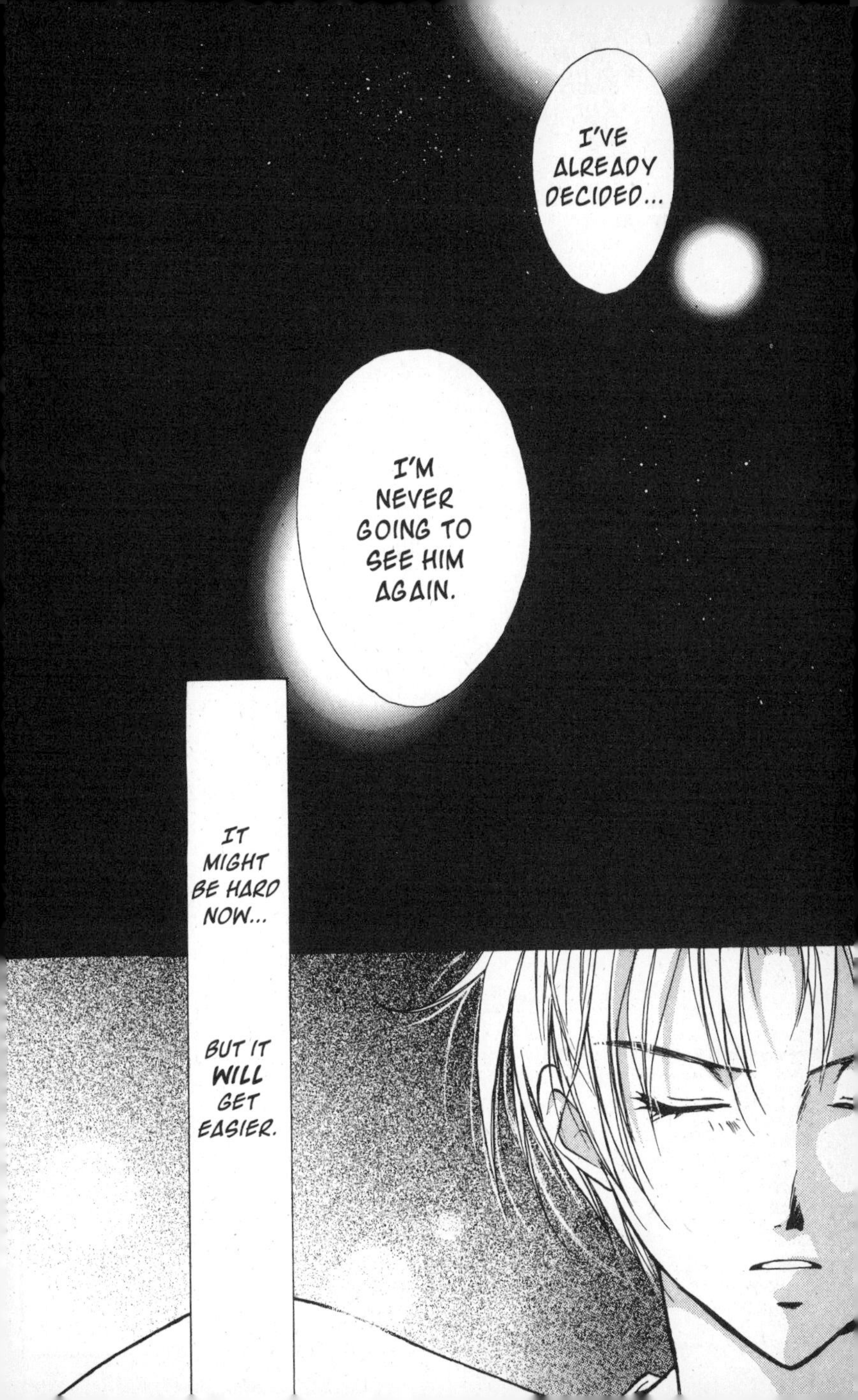
I'VE ALREADY DECIDED...
I'M NEVER GOING TO SEE HIM AGAIN.
IT MIGHT BE HARD NOW...
BUT IT **WILL** GET EASIER.

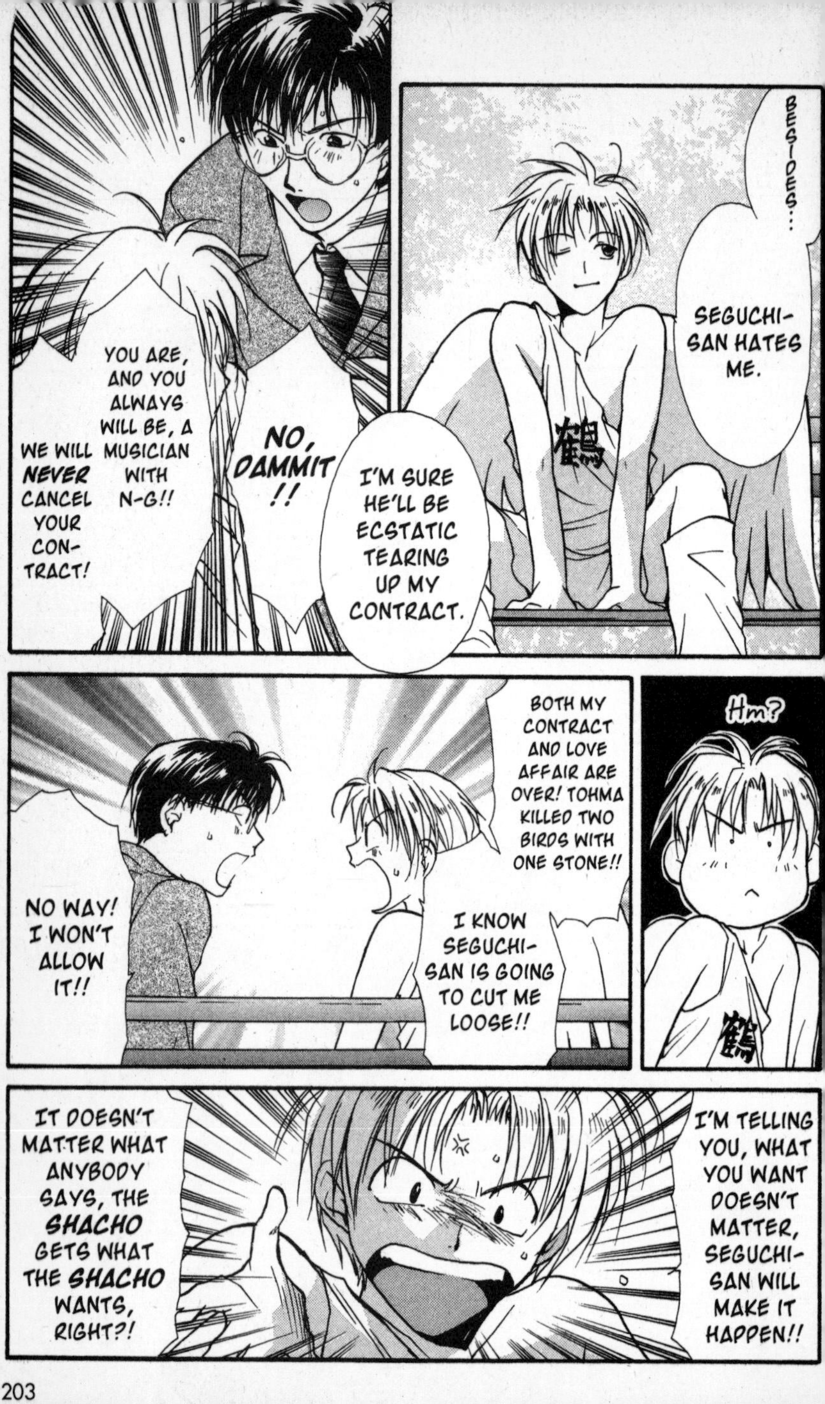
BESIDES...
SEGUCHI-SAN HATES ME.
I'M SURE HE'LL BE ECSTATIC TEARING UP MY CONTRACT.
NO, DAMMIT!!
YOU ARE, AND YOU ALWAYS WILL BE, A MUSICIAN WITH N-G!!
WE WILL NEVER CANCEL YOUR CON-TRACT!
Hm?
BOTH MY CONTRACT AND LOVE AFFAIR ARE OVER! TOHMA KILLED TWO BIRDS WITH ONE STONE!!
I KNOW SEGUCHI-SAN IS GOING TO CUT ME LOOSE!!
NO WAY! I WON'T ALLOW IT!!
I'M TELLING YOU, WHAT YOU WANT DOESN'T MATTER, SEGUCHI-SAN WILL MAKE IT HAPPEN!!
IT DOESN'T MATTER WHAT ANYBODY SAYS, THE SHACHO GETS WHAT THE SHACHO WANTS, RIGHT?!

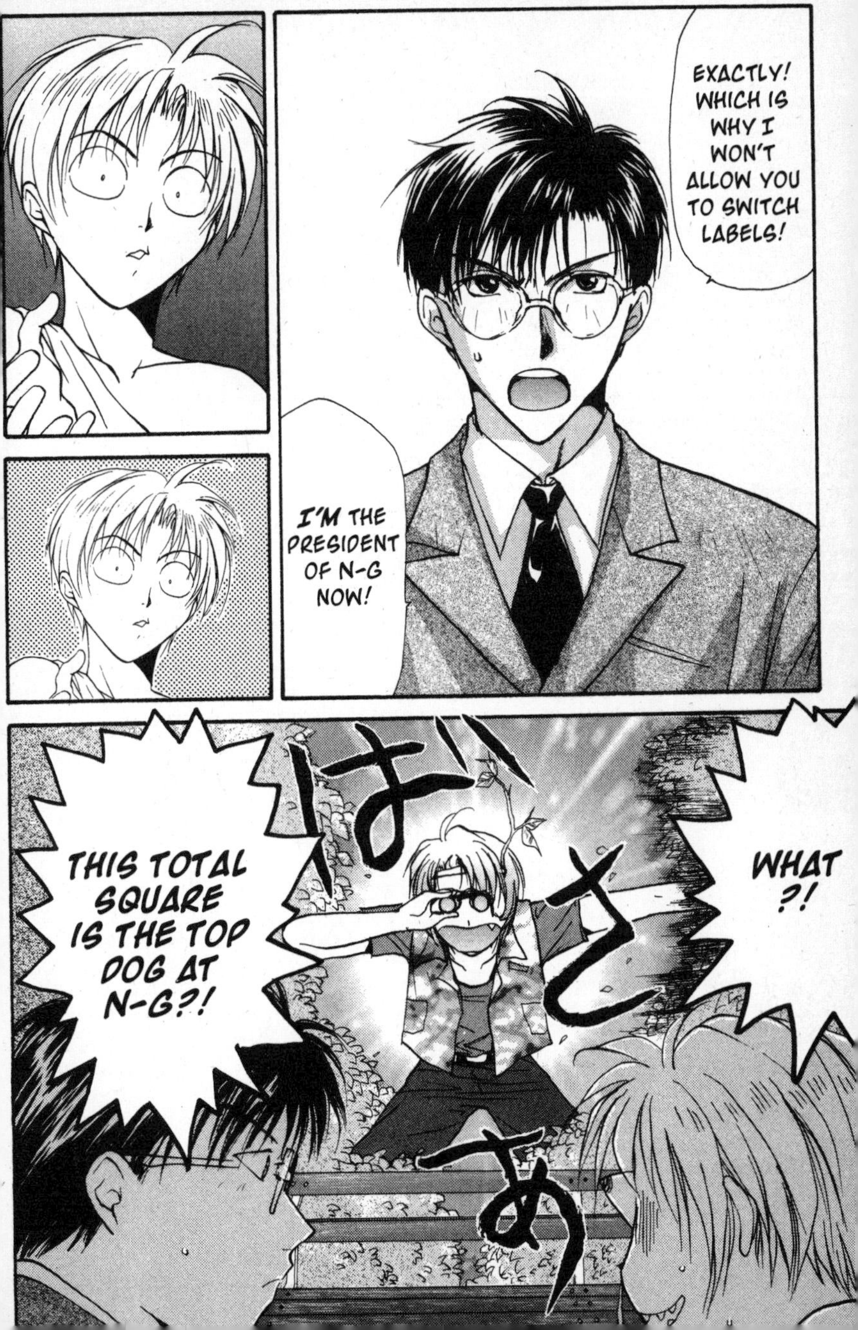
EXACTLY! WHICH IS WHY I WON'T ALLOW YOU TO SWITCH LABELS!
I'M THE PRESIDENT OF N-G NOW!
WHAT ?!
THIS TOTAL SQUARE IS THE TOP DOG AT N-G?!

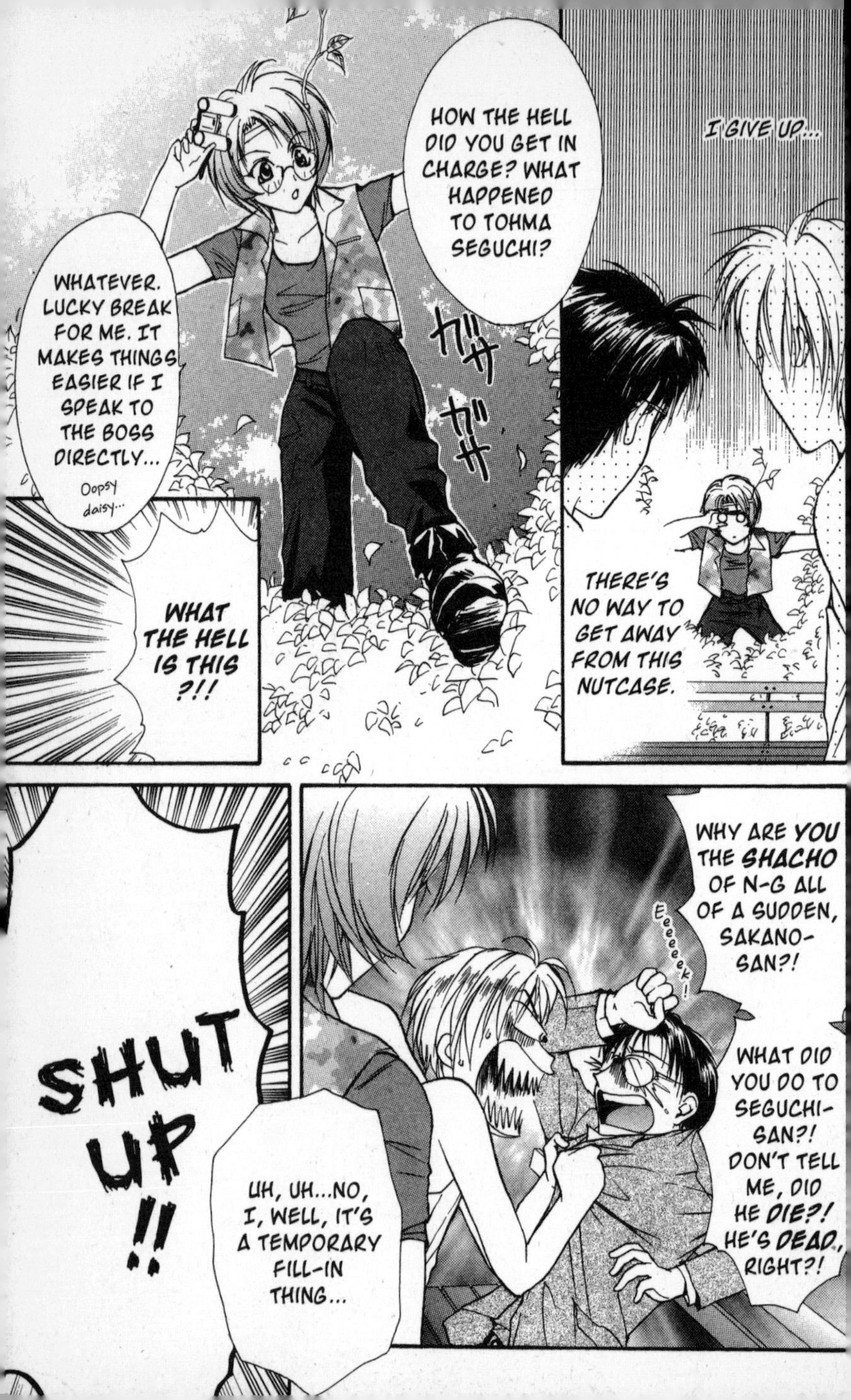
I GIVE UP...
THERE'S NO WAY TO GET AWAY FROM THIS NUTCASE.
HOW THE HELL DID YOU GET IN CHARGE? WHAT HAPPENED TO TOHMA SEGUCHI?
ガサ ガサ
WHATEVER. LUCKY BREAK FOR ME. IT MAKES THINGS EASIER IF I SPEAK TO THE BOSS DIRECTLY...
Oopsy daisy...
WHAT THE HELL IS THIS ?!!
WHY ARE YOU THE SHACHO OF N-G ALL OF A SUDDEN, SAKANO-SAN?!
Eeeeeek!
WHAT DID YOU DO TO SEGUCHI-SAN?! DON'T TELL ME, DID HE DIE?! HE'S DEAD, RIGHT?!
UH, UH...NO, I, WELL, IT'S A TEMPORARY FILL-IN THING...
SHUT UP !!

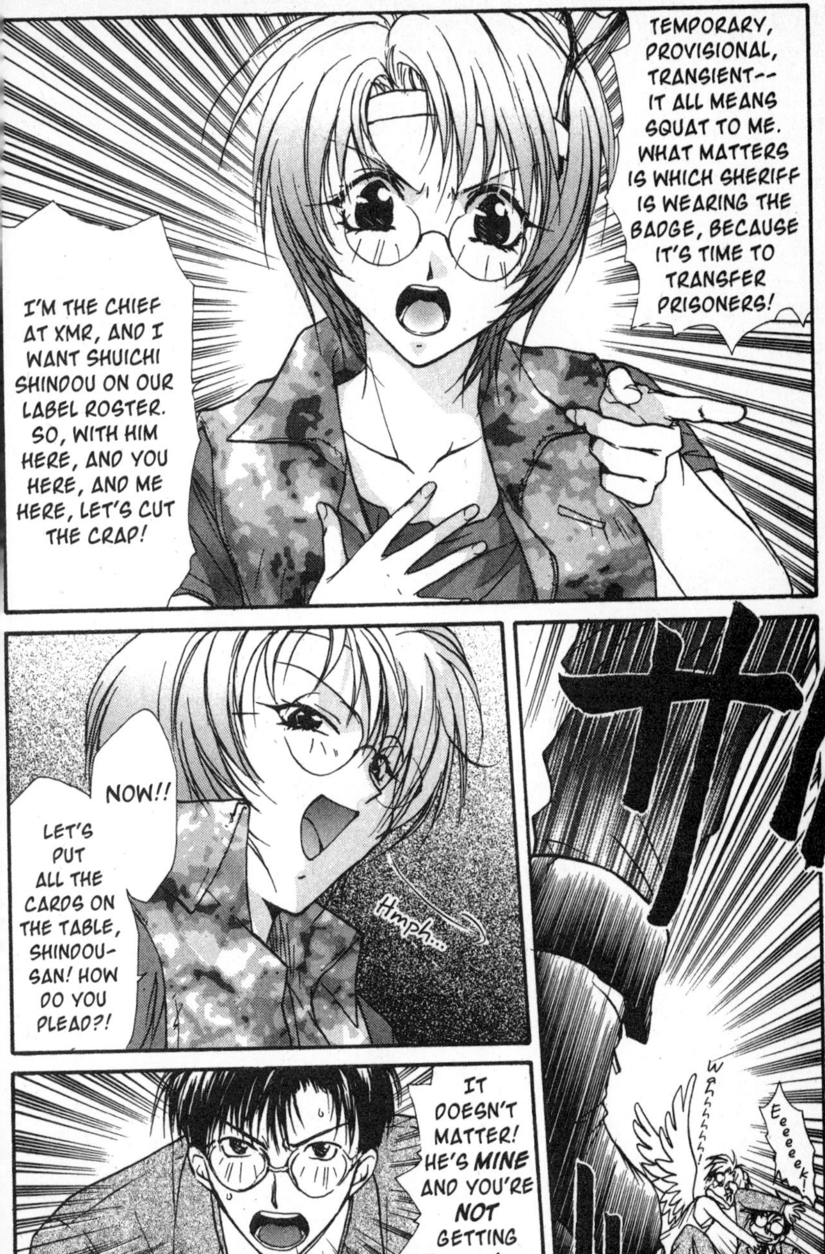
TEMPORARY, PROVISIONAL, TRANSIENT-- IT ALL MEANS SQUAT TO ME. WHAT MATTERS IS WHICH SHERIFF IS WEARING THE BADGE, BECAUSE IT'S TIME TO TRANSFER PRISONERS!
I'M THE CHIEF AT XMR, AND I WANT SHUICHI SHINDOU ON OUR LABEL ROSTER. SO, WITH HIM HERE, AND YOU HERE, AND ME HERE, LET'S CUT THE CRAP!
Eeeeeek!
Wahhhhhhh!
NOW!!
LET'S PUT ALL THE CARDS ON THE TABLE, SHINDOU-SAN! HOW DO YOU PLEAD?!
Hmph...
IT DOESN'T MATTER! HE'S MINE AND YOU'RE NOT GETTING HIM!

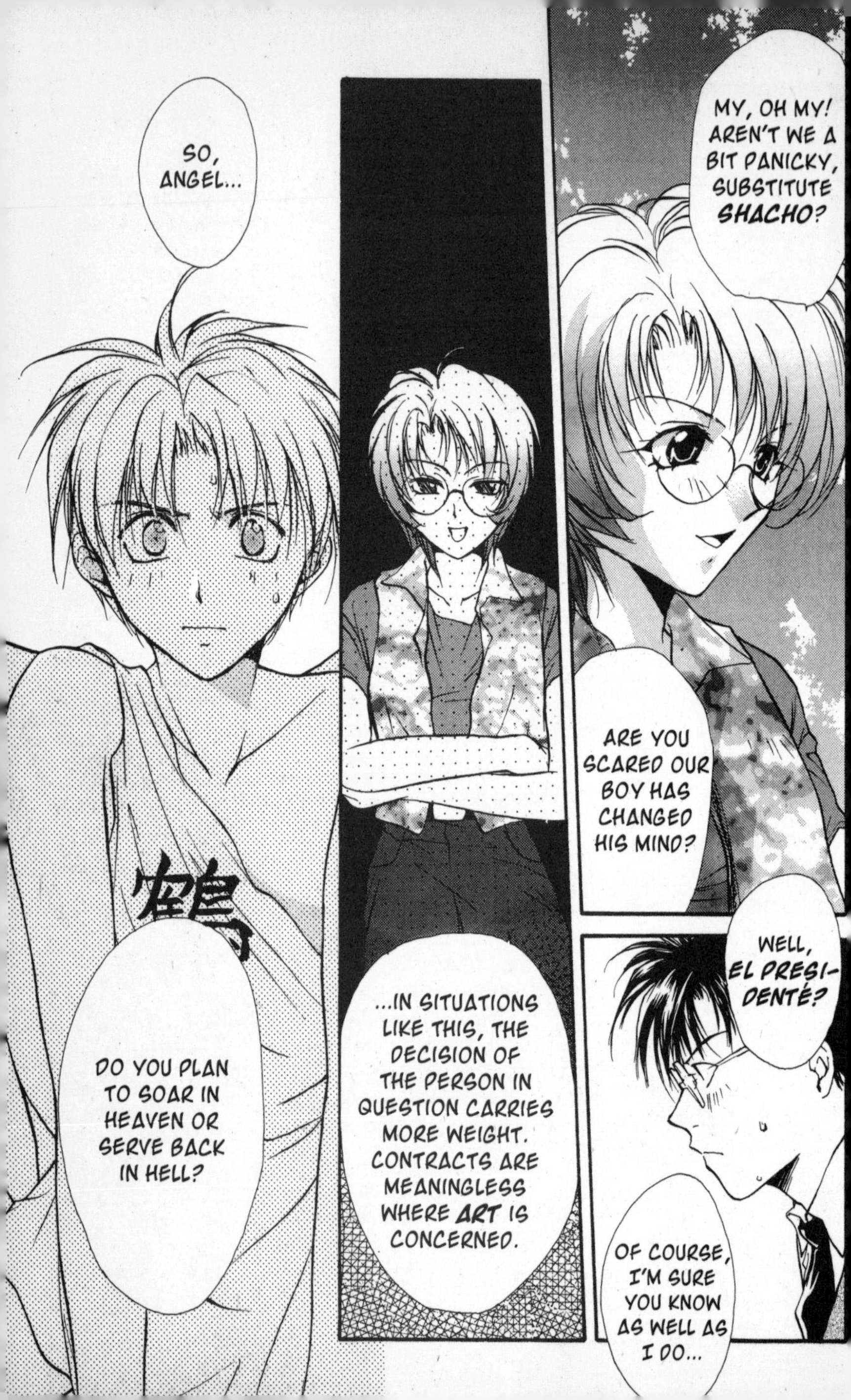
MY, OH MY! AREN'T WE A BIT PANICKY, SUBSTITUTE ***SHACHO***?
ARE YOU SCARED OUR BOY HAS CHANGED HIS MIND?
WELL, ***EL PRESIDENTÉ***?
OF COURSE, I'M SURE YOU KNOW AS WELL AS I DO...
...IN SITUATIONS LIKE THIS, THE DECISION OF THE PERSON IN QUESTION CARRIES MORE WEIGHT. CONTRACTS ARE MEANINGLESS WHERE ***ART*** IS CONCERNED.
SO, ANGEL...
鶴
DO YOU PLAN TO SOAR IN HEAVEN OR SERVE BACK IN HELL?

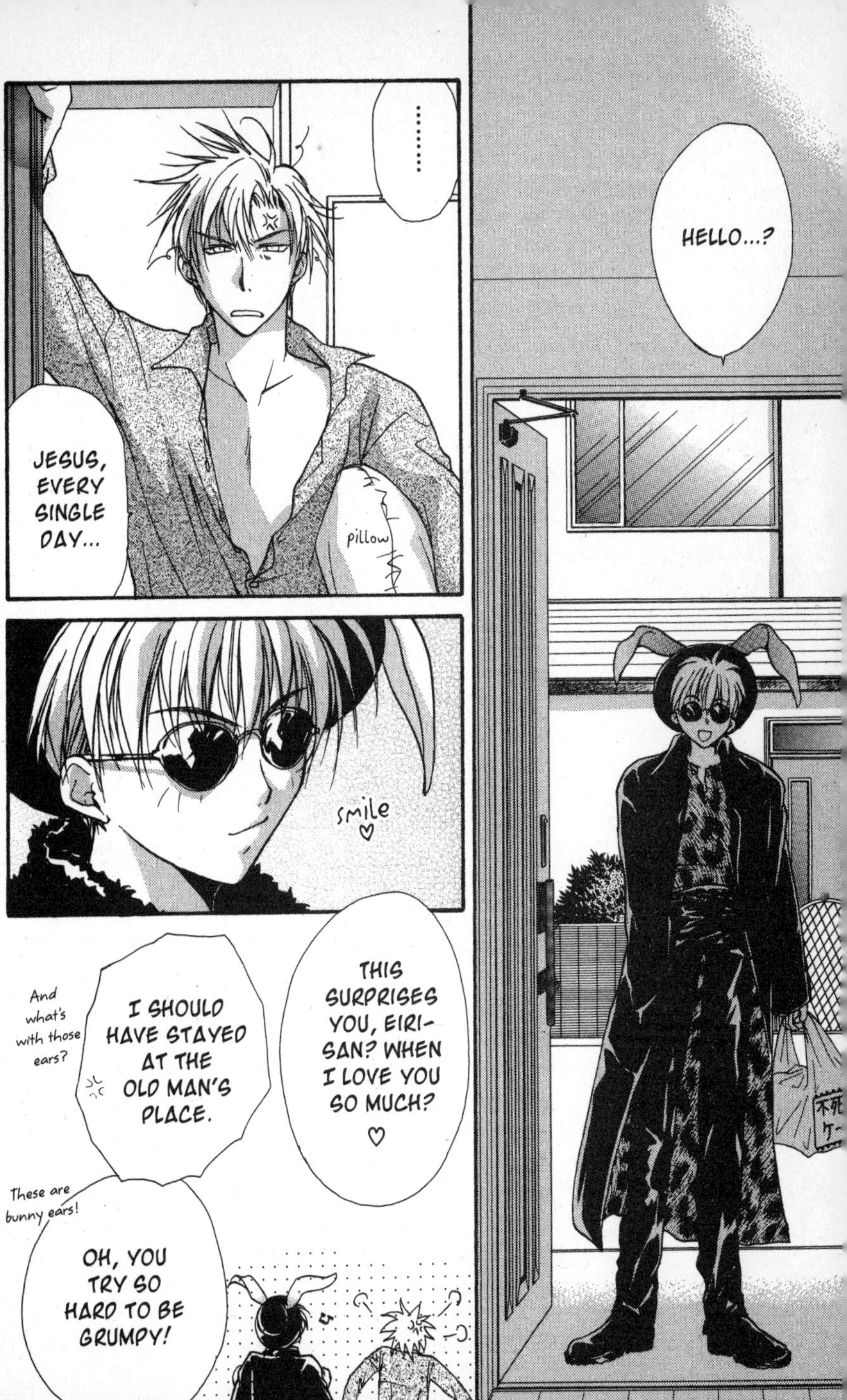
HELLO...?
......
JESUS, EVERY SINGLE DAY...
pillow
smile ♡
THIS SURPRISES YOU, EIRI-SAN? WHEN I LOVE YOU SO MUCH? ♡
I SHOULD HAVE STAYED AT THE OLD MAN'S PLACE.
And what's with those ears?
These are bunny ears!
OH, YOU TRY SO HARD TO BE GRUMPY!

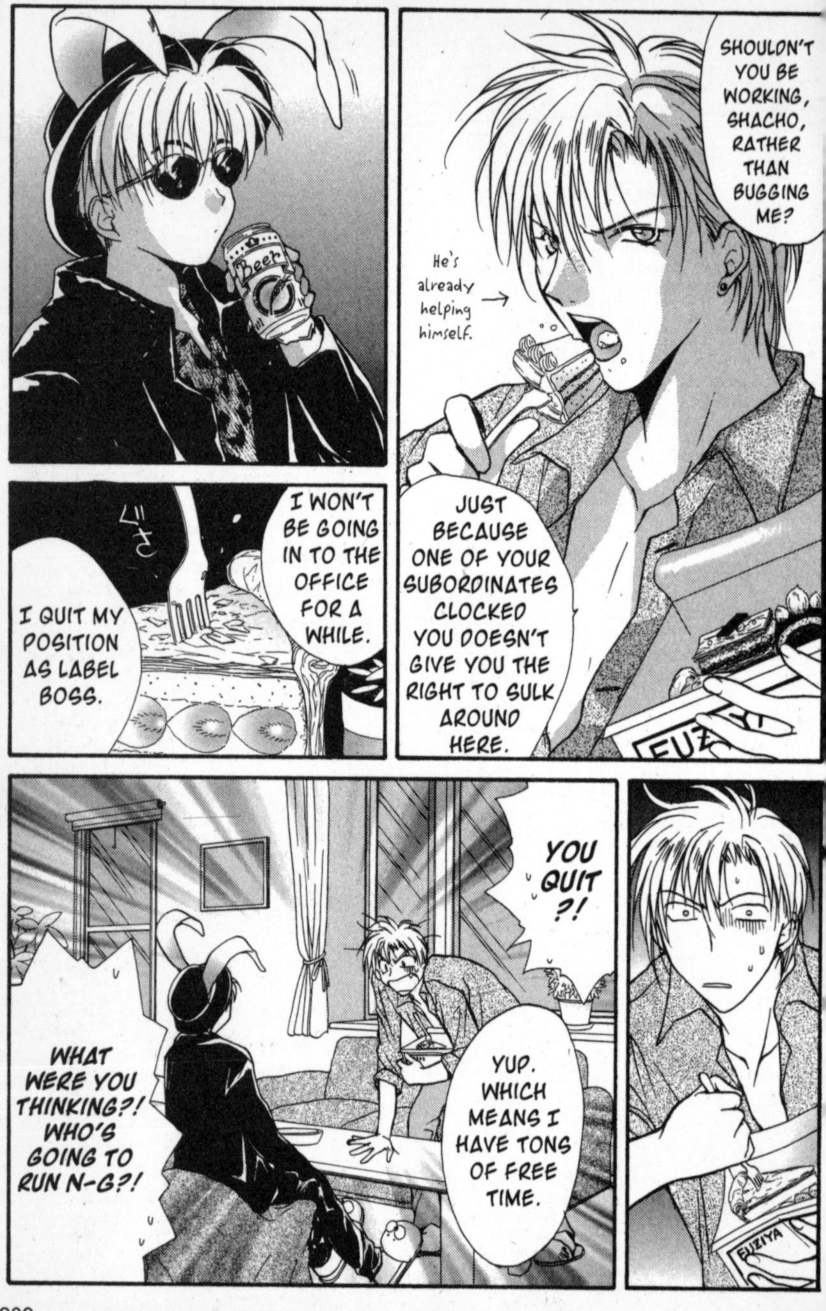
SHOULDN'T YOU BE WORKING, SHACHO, RATHER THAN BUGGING ME?
He's already helping himself.
JUST BECAUSE ONE OF YOUR SUBORDINATES CLOCKED YOU DOESN'T GIVE YOU THE RIGHT TO SULK AROUND HERE.
I WON'T BE GOING IN TO THE OFFICE FOR A WHILE.
I QUIT MY POSITION AS LABEL BOSS.
YOU QUIT?!
YUP. WHICH MEANS I HAVE TONS OF FREE TIME.
WHAT WERE YOU THINKING?! WHO'S GOING TO RUN N-G?!

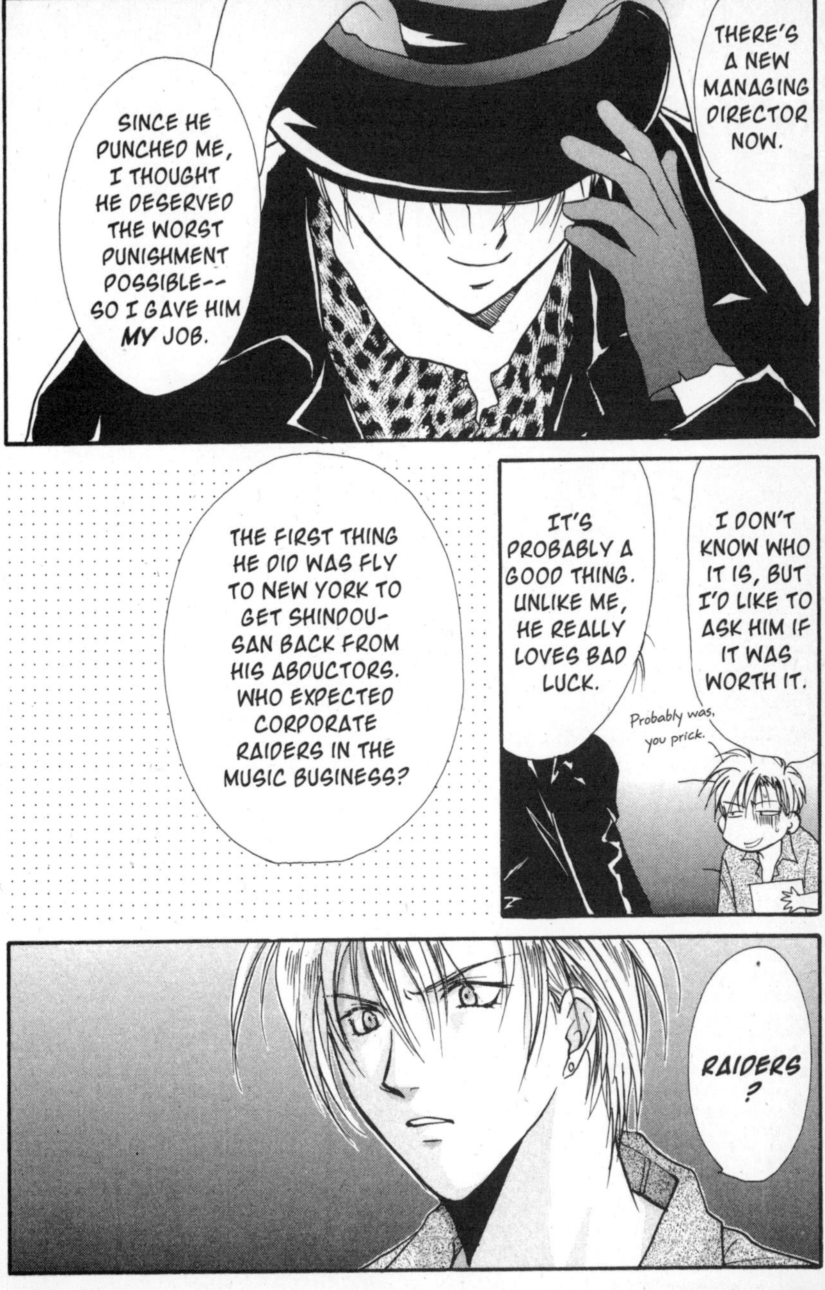
THERE'S A NEW MANAGING DIRECTOR NOW.
SINCE HE PUNCHED ME, I THOUGHT HE DESERVED THE WORST PUNISHMENT POSSIBLE-- SO I GAVE HIM *MY* JOB.
I DON'T KNOW WHO IT IS, BUT I'D LIKE TO ASK HIM IF IT WAS WORTH IT.
Probably was, you prick.
IT'S PROBABLY A GOOD THING. UNLIKE ME, HE REALLY LOVES BAD LUCK.
THE FIRST THING HE DID WAS FLY TO NEW YORK TO GET SHINDOU-SAN BACK FROM HIS ABDUCTORS. WHO EXPECTED CORPORATE RAIDERS IN THE MUSIC BUSINESS?
RAIDERS?

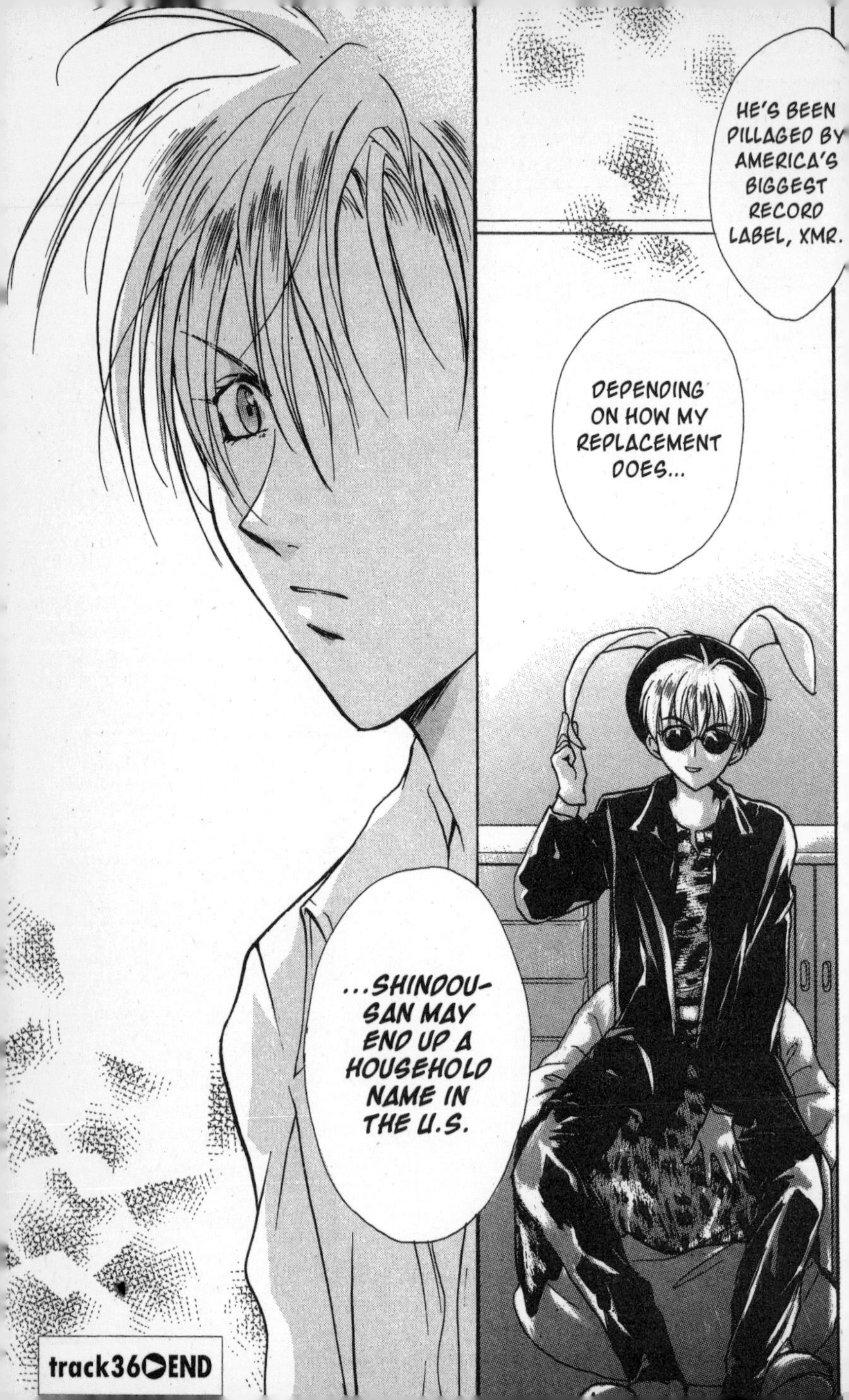
HE'S BEEN PILLAGED BY AMERICA'S BIGGEST RECORD LABEL, XMR.
DEPENDING ON HOW MY REPLACEMENT DOES...
...SHINDOU-SAN MAY END UP A HOUSEHOLD NAME IN THE U.S.
track36▶END

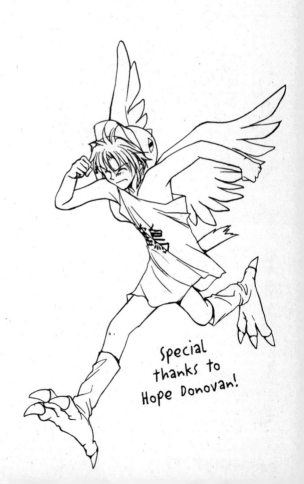

Special
thanks to
Hope Donovan!

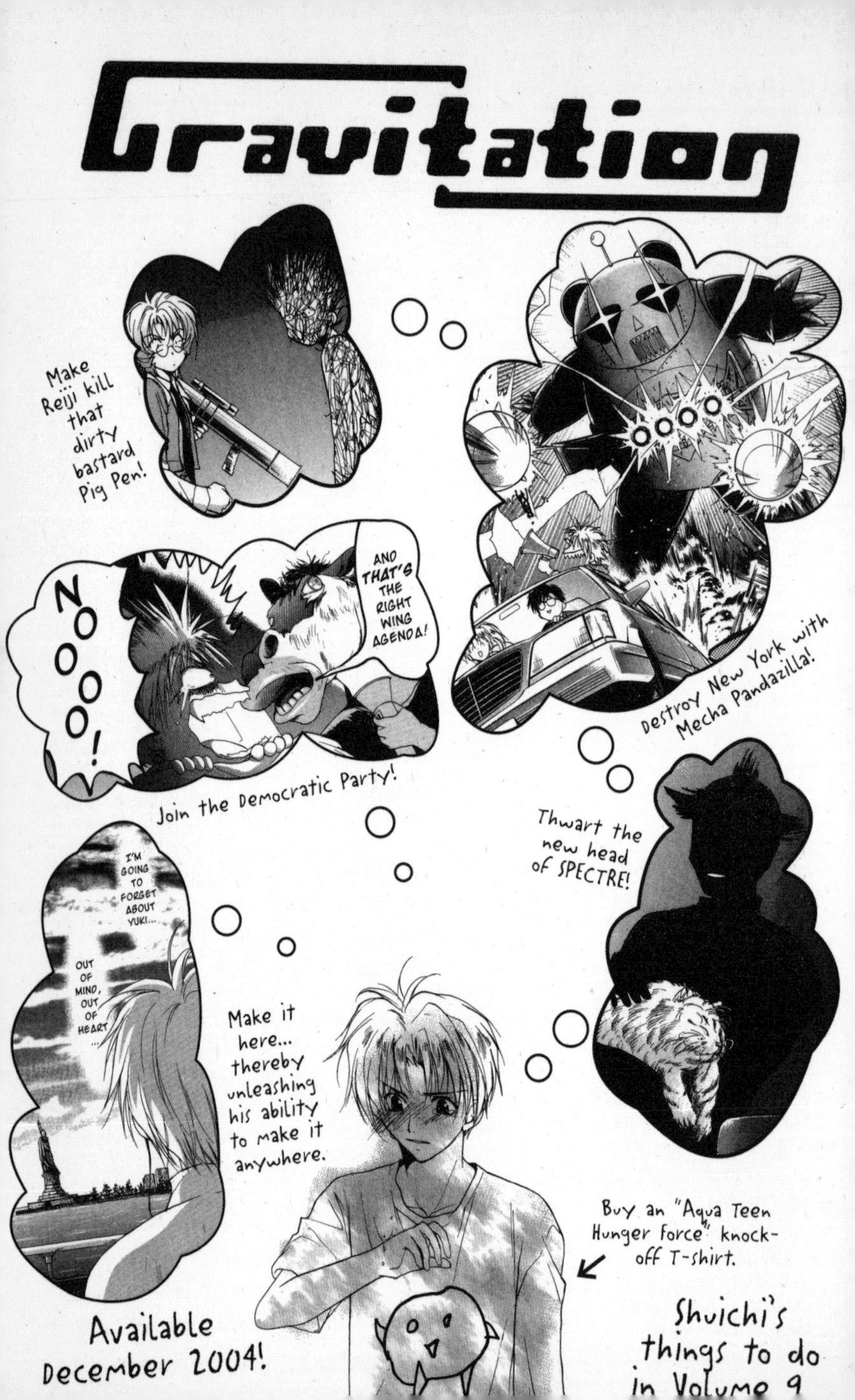
Gravitation
Make Reiji kill that dirty bastard Pig Pen!
Destroy New York with Mecha Pandazilla!
AND THAT'S THE RIGHT WING AGENDA!
NOOOO!
Join the Democratic Party!
Thwart the new head of SPECTRE!
I'M GOING TO FORGET ABOUT YUKI...
OUT OF MIND, OUT OF HEART...
Make it here... thereby unleashing his ability to make it anywhere.
Buy an "Aqua Teen Hunger Force" knock-off T-shirt.
Available December 2004!
Shuichi's things to do in Volume 9

ALSO AVAILABLE FROM TOKYOPOP®

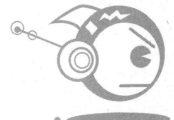

ALSO AVAILABLE FROM 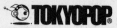 TOKYOPOP®

MANGA

07.15.04T

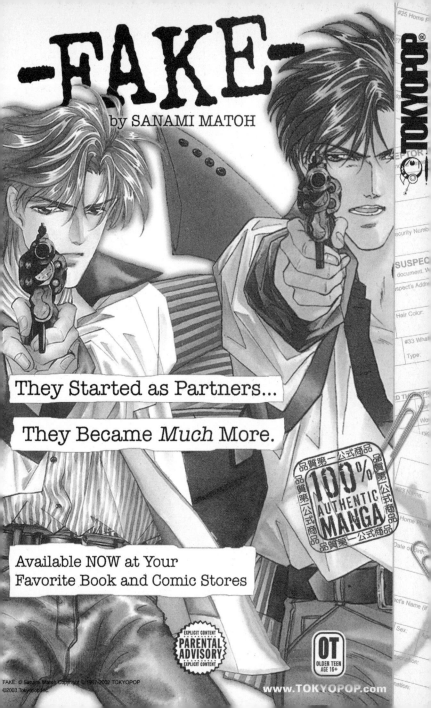

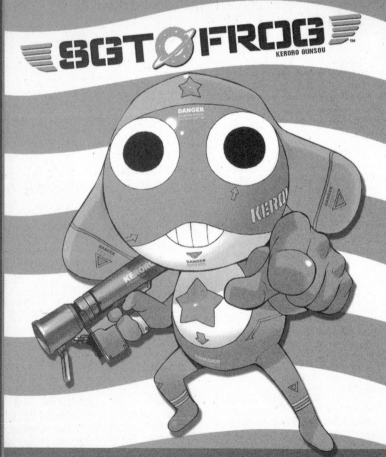

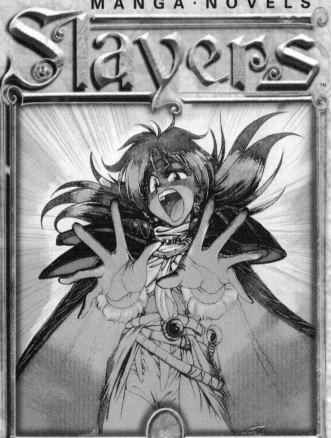

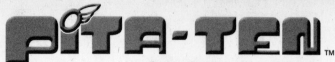

By Koge-Donbo · Creator of Digicharat

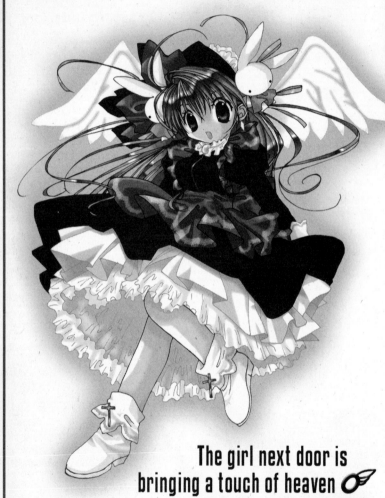

The girl next door is
bringing a touch of heaven
to the neighborhood.

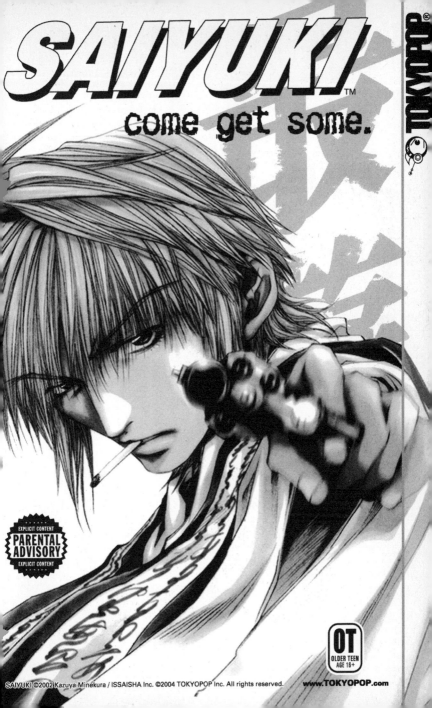

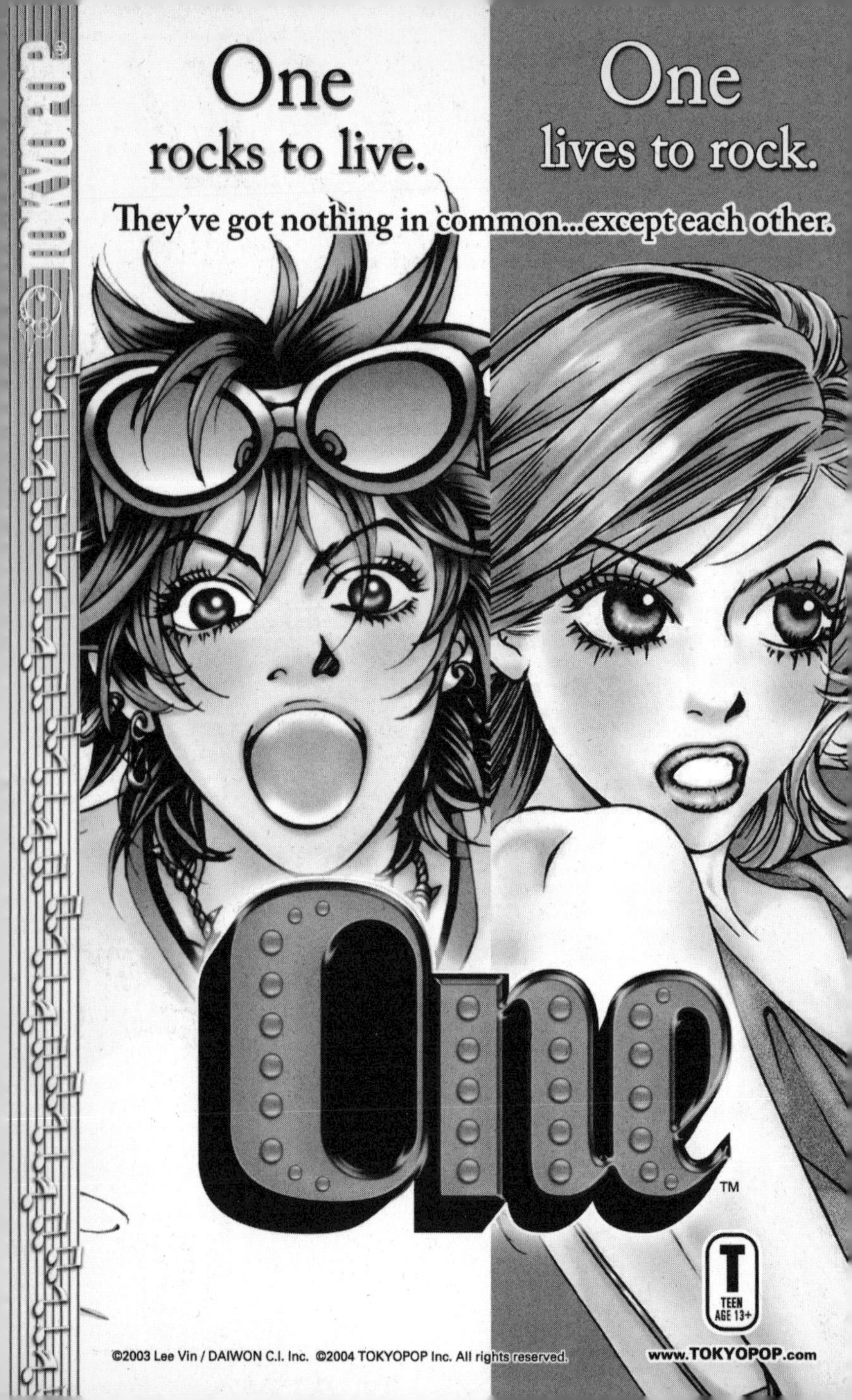
TOKYOPOP®
One
rocks to live.
One
lives to rock.
They've got nothing in common...except each other.
One™
T
TEEN
AGE 13+
©2003 Lee Vin / DAIWON C.I. Inc. ©2004 TOKYOPOP Inc. All rights reserved.
www.TOKYOPOP.com

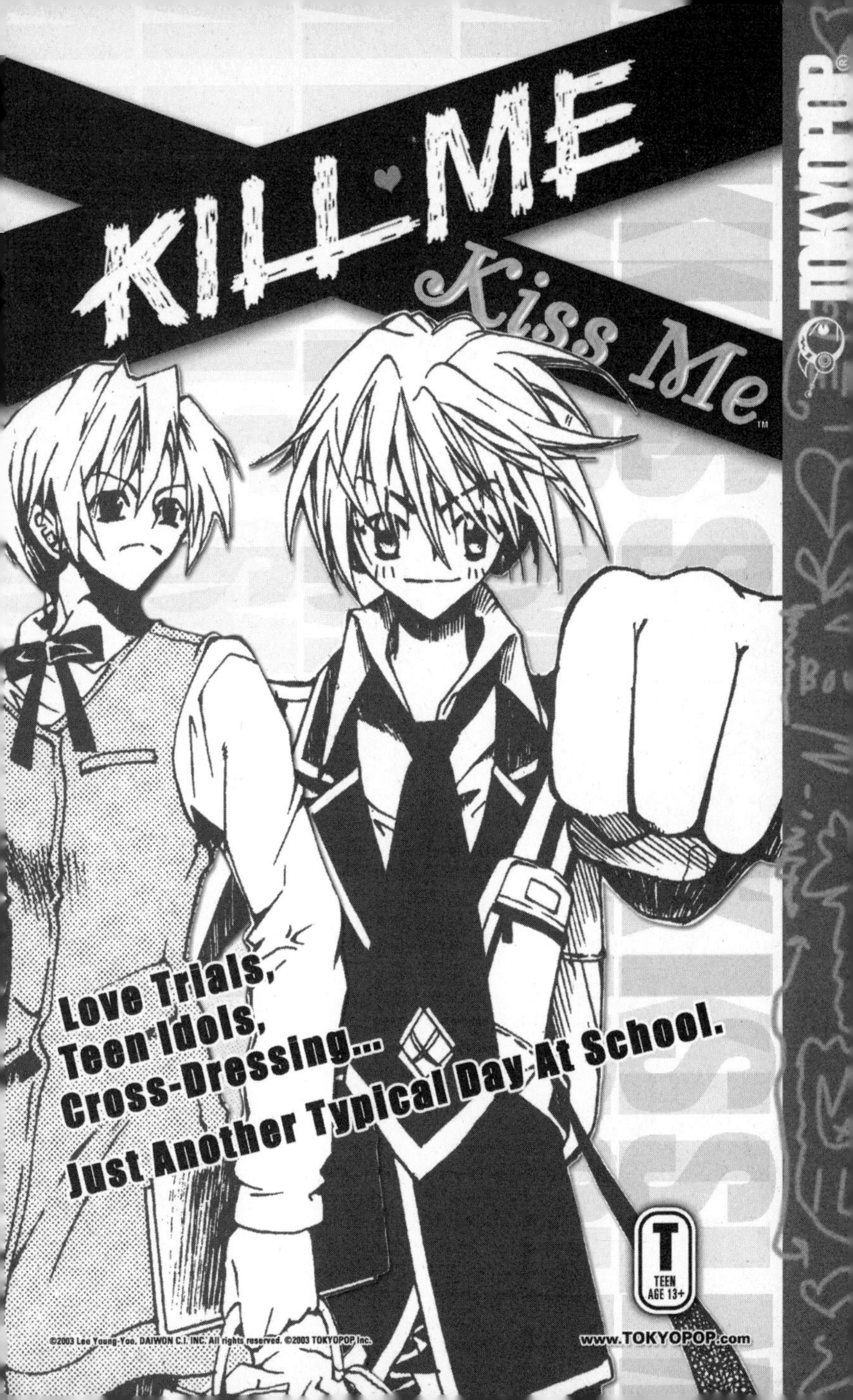
KILL ME
Kiss Me™
TOKYOPOP®
Love Trials,
Teen Idols,
Cross-Dressing...
Just Another Typical Day At School.
T
TEEN
AGE 13+
©2003 Lee Young-Yoo, DAIWON C.I. INC. All rights reserved. ©2003 TOKYOPOP Inc.
www.TOKYOPOP.com

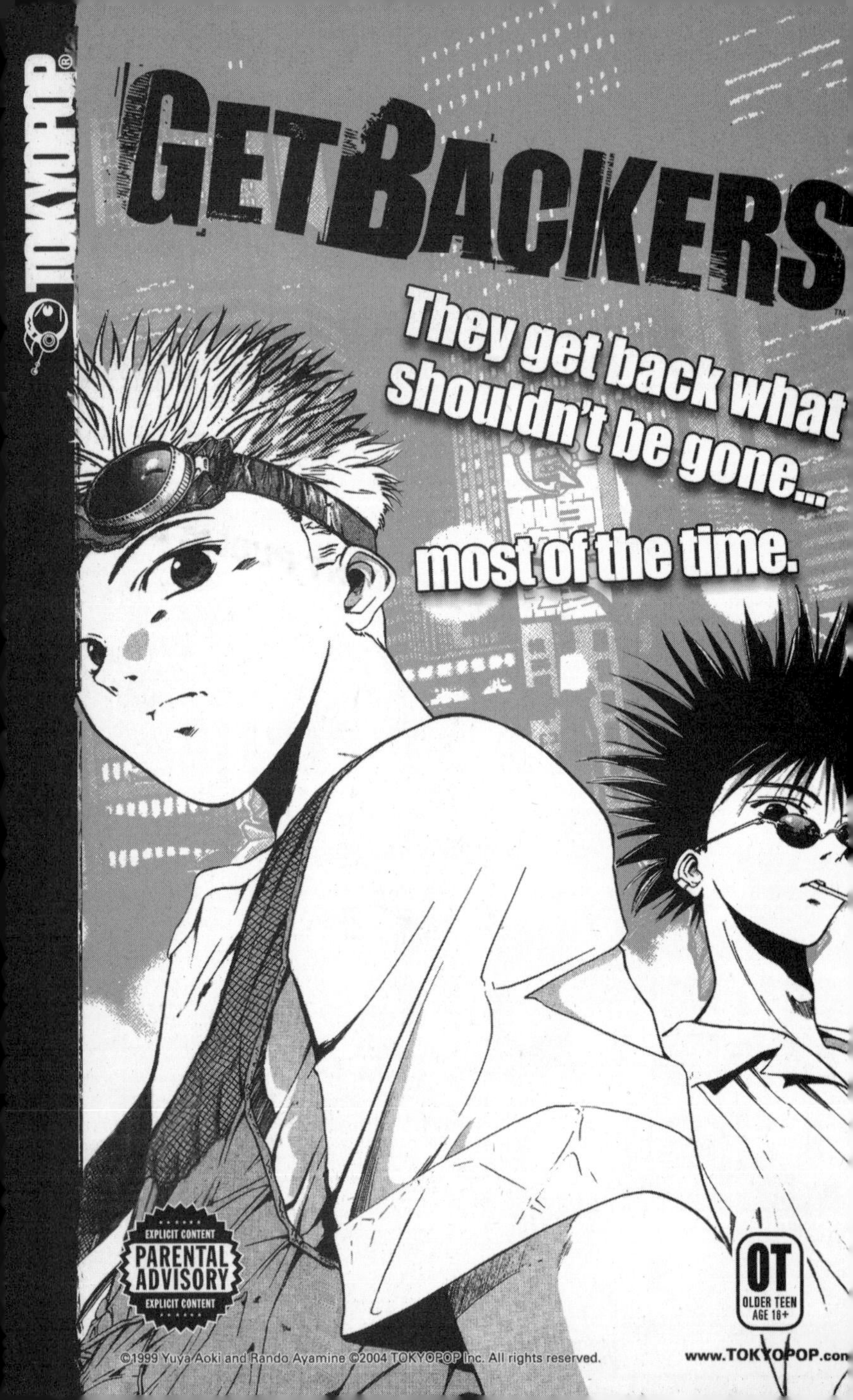
TOKYOPOP®
GETBACKERS™
They get back what shouldn't be gone...
most of the time.
EXPLICIT CONTENT
PARENTAL ADVISORY
EXPLICIT CONTENT
OT
OLDER TEEN AGE 16+
©1999 Yuya Aoki and Rando Ayamine ©2004 TOKYOPOP Inc. All rights reserved.
www.TOKYOPOP.com

STOP!

This is the back of the book.
You wouldn't want to spoil a great ending!

DEC 06

JAN 09

This book is printed "manga-style," in the authentic Japanese right-to-left format. Since none of the artwork has been flipped or altered, readers get to experience the story just as the creator intended. You've been asking for it, so TOKYOPOP® delivered: authentic, hot-off-the-press, and far more fun!

DIRECTIONS

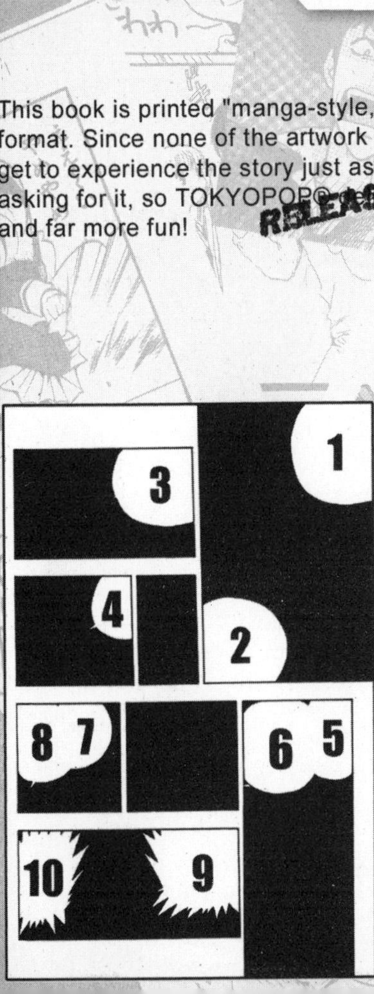

If this is your first time reading manga-style, here's a quick guide to help you understand how it works.

It's easy... just start in the top right panel and follow the numbers. Have fun, and look for more 100% authentic manga from TOKYOPOP®!

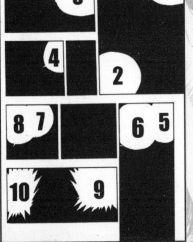

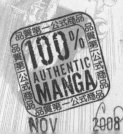

NOV 2008